SENECA SPEAKS

PART II
CAPITAL IDEA

C. Wade Spencer

SP&M

SPENCER PUBLISHING & MEDIA

Published by Spencer Publishing & Media, a Praxis Nexus, Inc. D.B.A.
7500 West 151st, 22312
Overland Park, Kansas 66223, USA

Printed in the United States of America

CONTENTS

SENECA SPEAKS

PART II
CAPITAL IDEA

Sovereignty and governance rely upon a conveyance of trust and worth.
Law, commerce and every civil discourse requires them. Forsaking an ample investiture spawns the death of a nation.

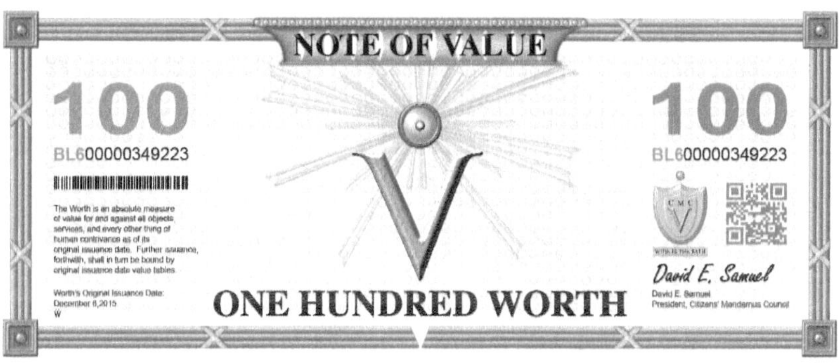

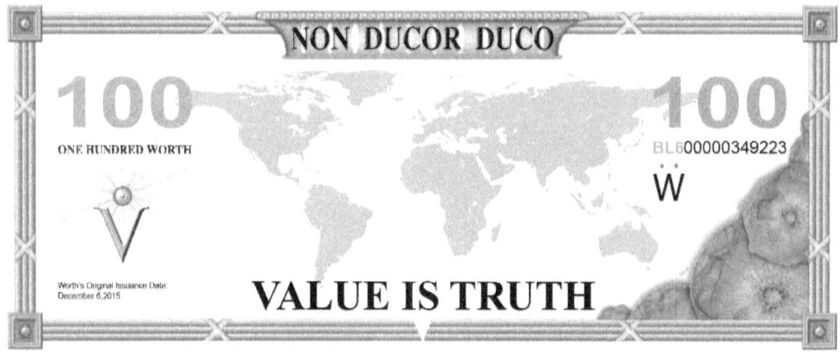

Introduction

A dark knight forces its way into the minds of those wielding influence; souls lost in the struggle to understand and control power. Visions of fire and ruination haunt the protagonists with a nightmare that cannot remain in their waking minds. Its message is grotesque. Its dominion demands acknowledgment.

"Many in Congress still go along, willing to follow anyone demanding their allegiance. Steeped in the importance of their position, legislators only know a hunger that must be fed. They'll keep their office at any cost; paying with constituency blood for the prize.

"As the second part of this story unfolds, entangled lives become mired by an undeniable force of self-destruction. The only readily civilized leverage to force a corrupt government to its knees is brought to bear. Fallout is painful for America's citizens—the cure appearing worse than the disease.

"Corruption is spoken to here; and corruption violently responds as it has throughout history. The inverted power paradigm remains as a beacon to light our way through the darkness. Humans need more power to direct their own lives, not less. Society requires greater responsibility to grow, evolve, and improve, not less. By owning the self, 'my brother's keeping' is only required when he stumbles; rather than taking up permanent residence in the head and heart—pickpocketing the right to think or feel what one wishes.

"These words suggest hope and provide a solution. Excellence is what's required of us. Past generations spilled blood and spent treasure to deliver humanity here to this point. But we can't stay; we must move forward. Now is our time. Wide is the path!" *Seneca*

Frank Lambert steps in as TTN's presidential appointee; permanently filling Sondra's vacant position. Id and ego joust over control, as Abigail chafes at his lack of creative and effective leadership. enough. Frank's tenure, for Abigail, cannot be short enough.

A sadistic torturer, Luciano Rossi provides a cunning, intelligent, malevolent soul for Ethan to contend with. As their interaction comes to a close, Luciano shows us the purity of a purpose in obeying one's master without question. There is no right or wrong, just duty; and the sadistic elation granted in the performance of that function. His life's only pleasure is savored as the bringer of pain.

Dean Walden takes on the challenge of serving in the US Senate; soon finding that even after a departure of stalwart insiders, corruption lingers—planting new seeds to one day flower destruction. Optimism chokes amidst a thorny reality.

CHAPTER

I

THE TANGLED WEB OF DECEIT

A charcoal-figured man loomed over Hubert; sharp-edged yet blurred of detail. Blackened blood covered what appeared to be an armor-clad potent. In one hand a scepter of the cheapest gold and the other a broad-bladed battle axe, dripping entrails and bone. The ground below Hubert's feet crumbled with scorched grass; sulfur billowing death's wretched odor upward.

It was the world—Hubert somehow knew it; though not the world he lived in. *Where am I?* As far as he could see, fired ash piled and spun in the wind; no plants, no buildings, no people; nothing but dim light and burnt horizon. The sky cracked with lightning, and ominous low-rolling clouds held down the oppressive humidity and heat without hope of relieving rains.

The figure caught Hubert's eye and immediately roared, "Pira anot haiy!"

Its scepter's spiked end speared the ground, shaking the surrounding terrain, disturbing cinder and soil. Hubert couldn't understand; he strained to ask who and what, but was unable to speak. His mind raced. *What does he want with me?*

The stranger then lurched at Hubert, seizing his neck; steel-encrusted fingers tearing across a naked throat.

"I—!" Hubert managed to get out before his air was cut off.

"Pira anot haiy!" the thing repeated, and then it effortlessly tossed Hubert to the ground where embers burnt his back.

While scurrying to get up, a broad circular swing brought the axe down onto Hubert's legs, taking off both limbs and his privates. The blade buried itself into the ground as the dark knight laughed aloud. His delight speaking over Hubert's anguished howls.

Hubert continued wailing as the creature delighted in discarding his dismembered appendages into a nearby brush fire; the unnamed thing carried on an unintelligible diatribe with itself, seemingly ignoring Hubert now. It disappeared into the shadows and then reappeared with steel-plated prosthetic legs largely resembling its own; bloodied, dirty, war-worn, and tipped with long spikes where they joined the hip.

As Hubert's suffering continued, the armor-clad man stood over him, stepping onto his torso, and thrust a spiked left leg into the stump where once Hubert's own had existed. Hubert straightened in agony—unable to create sound to release his pain. The creature laughed again and then drove home the replacement for the right side. A shrill escaped Hubert as he neared unconsciousness. The steel-suited tormentor then kicked him in the head and all turned black.

John had rambled on, unaware of Hubert's experience, and then broke the cadence of mindless drivel by blurting out, "We should've killed him! Regardless of Ethan Scott's popularity, the CMC would fall without David Samuel."

Still confused, Hubert felt his disturbing mental imagery slipping away. A moment later, having regained his sensibility and lost all that had filled his mind, Hubert warmed, "That ruthlessness is coming along nicely, John. At one point, wiping out the competition was not within you. In this matter I must disagree, though the sentiment's condoned. David's too well known. That kind of attention would never go away. No, it's either smear or promote."

As John watched homeless people mill about Brooklyn's unforgiving walkways outside the car window, he prodded, "So you intend to hire Samuel?"

"Not Samuel; that Ethan Scott fellow. He's the new flavor, and the one we need."

"Ethan was only recently appointed chief of their little tribe. What can we offer that he doesn't already have? You know the altruist types. Money's not their thing," John whined.

"Just secure the opportunity. I'll pitch it. Actually, you have until we get there to ensure a legitimate offer."

"Me? What am I supposed to get?"

"You spoke with Governor Franklin in Albany a few days ago."

"So?"

"Then you know what to do."

"Senator Ethan Scott; you're kidding, right? He's all wrong, and would likely operate outside our control."

"For now…maybe. But once trapped, getting out will keep him occupied—plus, I need a new mule to replace one recently-departed Senator Murphy. At the same time, Samuel will appear to be losing momentum—his prized stallion having departed for greener pastures. The media will be more interested in what Ethan does as a politician."

"Alright, I'll make the call," John relented. "Whatever's promised to Franklin you'll need to make good on."

"I've got it. Just don't go too heavy on the token."

"Geez," John grumbled while fingering his phone. "Sheridan. Yes, it is. Where're you at with the vacancy? None. I do. It's the CMC's new chief. That's the one. No, he isn't. He's had some success in media. He's got a place in Manhattan. I can't talk about it on the phone. I think you'll be happy. You will! No, he doesn't know yet. Today—can I count on this? We'll be there after lunch. Let's talk details tonight over drinks. No, I'll come to you. Good," John finished.

John looked to Hubert and relayed, "He'll do it. How do you intend to lure young Ethan?"

"Let me handle that."

An hour later, their limousine parked across from the CMC's home office. Hubert poked his smartphone. "I was wondering if David and Ethan were in. David's gone but Ethan's available, you say?" He ended the call.

"We're going," Hubert instructed.

"In there?"

"Come on."

Dashing across a trafficked street, Hubert felt the cruel anticipation of a killing shot. His skin tingled as if the dogs had treed their prey.

A disregard for the animal's desire to live pulsed. For a moment's wisp, Hubert felt the axe blade passing through flesh and bone. Shaking off the mental image as trivial, he painted on a smile as he entered the office. Approaching the front desk, Hubert said, "Sasha."

"Yes."

"Sasha, you're such a lovely woman. We spoke by phone a few moments ago and were disconnected. I was about to ask, would Mr. Scott have a bit of time to spare?"

"Who may I say is calling?" she asked—having forgotten his previous visit with David.

"Senator Hubert Riley."

Sasha smiled as she dialed the phone. "Ethan, a Senator Riley and guest are here. They wish to have a few moments of your time. No, he's not on the schedule. Yes, I can."

"And guest," John murmured under his breath.

"Senator, he has fifteen minutes. Will you and your guest accompany me?" she asked.

They followed Sasha down the corridor to Ethan's office; John attempting to pace ahead of Hubert but ultimately being funneled to the back as they reached the entrance. Ethan rose from behind his desk as the door opened. Hubert entered first.

Ethan moved to greet him. As he glanced at John to be courteous, Ethan recognized the target of so many investigations.

He frowned in response to John's presence—certain Hubert must be trouble. Cognizant of his facial expression, Ethan changed up to play the gracious host. It was evident to everyone that something interesting and not necessarily good was about to happen.

Sasha announced, "Ethan, I would like to present Senator Hubert Riley and—"

"And Senator John Stanton," Ethan interrupted.

"Oh, Senator Stanton, I am sorry. I didn't recognize you," Sasha apologized.

"That's quite alright, my dear," John offered, patting her on the shoulder.

"May I get anyone a beverage?" Sasha hesitantly asked.

Ethan rejected the courteous gesture with a "That'll be all, Sasha." The door closed behind her and they all sat stiffly upright, palms down atop laps.

"Senator Stanton, I must say I'm surprised to see you, given our past relationship," Ethan opened.

"My boy, I didn't realize we had one. However, I'll take that at face value," John blithely riposted while picking a tiny lint ball from his suit lapel.

"No. Really, this is quite a shock. Of all the people I would ever expect to come through my door, you would be last."

"Surely, you've written articles in your newspaper days about people who graced your office."

"That's true. However, the CMC's role is a bit more proactive than a local paper."

"Is it?" John pressed. "I think no more of the CMC than I do the news. You watch, much like a newspaperman. You tell the courts like you told the story. And the greatest similarity lies in the fact that the position of the Citizens' Mandamus Council, like the media, is on the sidelines and not in the game."

"John, be polite." Using John's childish argument to his advantage, Hubert added, "We actually came here to discuss that very issue."

"You want to talk about my newspaper? I no longer own the *Banner*? Perhaps you hadn't heard," Ethan patronized.

"Oh, I heard—read about the wicked splatter you made on the pavement," Hubert hit back, failing to resist the urge to step on Ethan's neck. Recovering his façade, he added. "We didn't come to talk about the failed news business. We're here to discuss action."

"What action?"

"Yours."

"Mine? What have I done to you?" Ethan defensively postured.

"Not to worry. This isn't about what's been done, but what you could do."

"Why do you care about my future, other than its possible demise?" Hubert and John gazed at each other with amused innocence. John shook his head. Hubert chuckled.

"Ethan, I know this is hard to believe, but we respect your accomplishments," Hubert cajoled.

"Forgive my dubious expression."

"Truly," John lavished.

"Our lives appear incompatible. However, we need men of action in our ranks. Governing others is not unlike running the CMC, or a well-respected news organization. It takes vision. Are you not such a man? Yet, your hands are tied," Hubert explained; sounding a mentor's concern.

"The CMC is making a great difference. There must be some perceived threat. You wouldn't be here otherwise."

"Ethan, we're not threatened and that's my point. So you can file for a writ of mandamus. What difference does it make? It's still just a response to action. Can you argue the contrary?" Hubert asked.

"We serve a meaningful public duty."

"A wonderful point you could make to a community
college freshman. But what good are you doing? It's merely an academic exercise in ethics. Don't you want to make a real impact?"

"I am," Ethan replied with calm conviction.

"Still, you can't fully act. You know it's true. We know it's true. Your move to acquire greater power was rejected outright; was it not?"

"That's correct. Be assured, we're not finished," Ethan stated.

"You'll have no more luck with further efforts. We're the government, we hold the real power, and we're not turning it over to a bunch of crybabies!" John interjected.

"So this is why you graced our office—to tell me you'll derail any other steps to add more action to our charter?"

Hubert cackled, "No! Though with no uncertainty, it's a fact. I'm here to offer you a chance to do something. Question is, will you take it?"

"What is this? What are you offering?" Ethan posed.

"You know of Senator Murphy's death."

"Of course."

"We need a successor. New York's looking for the right replacement.

America needs your help," Hubert said.

"You're offering me the post?" Ethan ventured suspiciously.

"That's correct," John broke in. "The Governor specifically mentioned your name. I told him that, although we have many times been on opposite sides, I respect the commitment to public good. Your rise in the CMC has demonstrated remarkable qualities. Those qualities are called for in Senator Murphy's successor. Will you choose to serve more greatly the American public?"

"Will you accept this honor?" Hubert solemnly issued.

"That's humorous, coming from you. What do you know of honor? Senator Riley, I'm unfamiliar with you. But I am well acquainted with Senator Stanton. Your association doesn't reflect well," Ethan cautioned.

"I'll try not to take that personally," John postured.

"Honor? I don't want your honor. What I need is the ability to arrest people like you when boundaries are crossed!" Ethan shouted, slapping a palm to the desk.

Beaming, Hubert knew he had Ethan. Closing his smile, he stared into Ethan's eyes. Ethan looked back, knowing he could do no more. Ethan understood their claims were true, though he wouldn't admit it—distrusting what they represented. However, his growing dissatisfaction with the CMC's ineffectual efforts to change the country for the better persisted. *If I possessed their influence, I could do so much more.*

Hubert turned towards John, then back to Ethan and to nail down the deal. "Good. I'm glad you're not suffering from the illusion that you'll find virtue in any of this. It was a good sales pitch, on John's behalf, but only half-witted voters ever take a bite."

"So, if nominated, will you accept?"

It was clear that both intended to manipulate him. Certain he could handle them, Ethan donned a cordial face, reached for Hubert's hand and shook it. "I accept your offer."

"Wonderful!" Hubert expressed, as they all rose to their feet.

"Governor Franklin will call on you later today to formally offer the appointment," John noted.

Hubert recognized Ethan's attempt at fooling them—that he would not align himself with their kind. This was Hubert's game. Ethan was about to be educated in the American political pyramid of power.

"There's one thing. I need a few days to explain this to David. Can I count on your discretion until then?"

"Absolutely, Ethan; take it to the bank," John assured—shaking Ethan's hand as he might a constituent while campaigning for office.

"George, this is Senator Stanton." John sounded jubilant. "What is it, John?" George was standing at his office window, feeling a little pestered by the phone call. Though needed for his purposes, he despised John's set all the same. In some ways, Congress was less desirable than the general public. With a private citizen, George could lay waste and dispense without consideration. A congressman had to be bought.

"Of all people, I know what a busy man you are, George," John continued. "I was hoping to prevail upon your good nature for a favor."

"I don't have a good nature."

"Yes, yes, well, I was wondering if there might be a willingness to persuade your operative to push our agenda in the Senate."

"And what agenda would that be?"

"Advise our new man to join my committee."

"Who's the new man?"

"Why, yours, of course; your newly appointed senator to replace Murphy. It's the CMC's rising star: Ethan Scott." "Who thought up that lousy idea? He can't make anything happen. What a waste of time."

"George, it wasn't my idea. Senator Riley felt he could be of use to us," John explained—recoiling from his position. "Use how?… Fine. You didn't seek my counsel. Live with it. What is it you want Anne to do, exactly? And don't waste my time with one of your contrived schemes to bilk me for more money."

"Absolutely not; I'm surprised you would say that. I am a United States senator with a long history of…"

"Enough! What do you want?"

"Not much, really. I've already told you what I need from Miss Preston. She simply needs to convince Senator Scott to accept my committee invitation."

"She is persuasive. I'll grant you that. But why would a former CMC executive listen to her in the first place? They outright rejected a donation from Coral Oil. What makes things different now?" George demanded.

John laughed—understanding for the moment that he knew something important George did not. He paused to savor the feeling. "Oh, then you don't know? Anne Preston and Ethan Scott have been somewhat of an item for a while. It's not common knowledge. However, I was certain you knew—it was why I called on you. This must be embarrassing, but I'm sure Anne had good reasons for keeping this to herself. I only recently found out from Senator Riley. You know how secretive he can be; even amongst friends. So you will have her do this for us, then?"

George, reeling with anger, remained outwardly calm. He said nothing. The thought that someone so close could have slipped this past him boiled his blood. It had never happened before.

George cleared his throat and announced, "It's done—anything else?"

"No. Thank you for your assistance, George."

George set down his phone with care—mulling what this implied. Anne had been a part of nearly every political maneuver he had deployed over the last decade. She was one of the few who could hurt him.

After a few moments of pondering motive, George stopped speculating. He calmed himself and then keyed numbers into the phone. "You need to be at my office as soon as possible. Something's come up."

"I'll be there shortly," came Anne's sprightly reply.

She arrived an hour later. It was obvious to George that something new occupied her time—apparent in the way she entered the office; as though she didn't need George for anything.

"George, you're looking rather stoic today. What're you up to?"

"I have a new assignment for you. It's up close and dangerous."

"Sounds naughty; I like it already. Tell me."

June entered the office and said, "Mr. Weatherby, I have the article you requested."

June laid a digital pad on George's desk and departed. He traced a note on the touchscreen and shoved it across the desk to rest in front of Anne. On the news website displayed was a picture of Ethan shaking David's hand with a headline that read, "Incoming Chief Says Goodbye To Samuel." Above the photograph, George had drawn a heart and initials that read, "A. P. loves E. S." Anne read it twice and then looked up to meet George's enraged eyes.

"What's this?" George barked.

"It's not what you think," Anne nervously replied.

"What do I think this is?"

"I've been seeing Ethan for a few months. That's all."

"That's all! That's all! When were you planning to let me in?"

"Never—I didn't think it would get this far."

"You never thought the relationship would; or that I might hear about it from Stanton."

"Both. I'm gonna open the closet on him!"

"Leave the putz be for now. Ethan Scott's the enemy; and you choose to ride 'em like a breeding-season steed. Where the hell does this leave us?"

"The same place we've always been, George."

"I'm not so sure. You've got one chance to get this right. Botch it and you won't need to worry about your next job."

"Understood; what do you want me to do?" Anne asked—now feeling a little more secure.

"I won't ask how you got involved—don't care. Convince him to join Stanton's committee. That's it. Don't," George ordered; not because he cared what John needed but that Anne demonstrate fidelity.

"Wait. What are you talking about? Is he a special liaison between the CMC and Senate? What is this?"

"Our brilliant governor appointed Ethan Scott as replacement for Senator Murphy."

"And he went along? When did this happen?"

"Today."

Incapable of accepting this scenario at face value, Anne searched for hidden angles. *Did they have something on him?* "When?"

"The appointment will take place over the next few days. Your job is to ensure he accepts the nomination to Stanton's committee. Can you get this done without your heart going pitter patter?" George posed sarcastically.

"Yes, I can. Why is this so important to Stanton?"

"Beats me—wasn't my move—let 'em live with it. Now, get out! Don't come back until he's in."

Anne stood and retreated from George's office. She knew better than to say anything more—concerned for her career, life and limb.

That evening, Ethan ate dinner across the table from Anne at his apartment. No words had yet been spoken. Anne was tottered by the loss of normalcy. A conflict in their separate selves battled between them in silence.

Anne watched Ethan chew his food, wondering, *What is love? Is this it? Why am I with him?*

Ethan's eyes followed the curve of Anne's shoulder—contemplating what ifs. *It's going to be difficult when she hears the news. Do I even care, or is this just infatuation? Is she enlightened or corrupt?*

Ethan finally broke their silence. "I have an announcement that'll be as shocking for you as it is to me."

"What is it?" Anne asked, as if oblivious.

"I'm leaving the Citizens' Mandamus Council."

"Oh. Fired you because of plummeting donations, did they?" Anne joked.

"I've been asked to assume the late Senator Murphy's position in the Senate representing New York," Ethan explained with contrived excitement.

Anne first thought to pun but then decided on truth. "I heard this afternoon."

"This afternoon…How did you find out? I was only asked this afternoon. I finished talking with Governor Franklin about the appointment two hours ago. It was not to be made public for days. Who talked?" Ethan probed.

"Don't worry. The press is always the last to know. It won't be public until you want it to be. This could be a great opportunity."

"I feel I'm betraying David and should apologize for accepting. I enjoyed working with him. Yet, I need to make more of a difference than the CMC has provision for. Does that make me selfish?"

"No. It makes you smart. You know what you want. You understand that, to get anything done, action must be taken. All the writs in the world won't make the kind of meaningful change you crave. Admit it. You expect great things out of life. The CMC is just not big enough."

"Anne, it's not like that. I don't need to be aligned with a powerful political group to feel good about myself. I just want to do something tangible. Why do I feel guilty?"

"Because of friendship—you feel you're abandoning them. The opportunity presented itself and you took it. You've done nothing wrong."

"I'll tell David before the public announcement."

"Just as a good boy would."

Ethan warmed to Anne. Somehow he felt better hearing her stated belief of his goodness.

"This leaves us in no better shape than before. At least then we were at opposite ends of the political landscape. Now, I'll be an instrument of the people and you'll be my influence peddler."

"You say the sweetest things, Ethan."

"Seriously, we need to set some boundaries."

"Boundaries; did a fence ever stop a child from swimming in the neighbor's pool? Are you going to draw a chalk line in the bedroom?" Anne poked. She then changed her tone, conveying genuine concern. "Ethan. You've been a rising star since we first met. I believe in you. Now that you're in the game, there's no more room for human sentiment. When fortune presents itself from this point onward, take it without consideration for anything or anyone. You'll need all the friends and power you can muster to survive this new path you're walking. Promise me you'll do it; and not for me but for yourself."

"Okay, I promise."

"One more thing…and this is business, Senator," Anne added in a serious voice.

"I'm not a senator yet," Ethan snapped back.

"You are. The only thing left is the formality of public theatre. Now shut up and listen. Senator, after you're confirmed in the Senate, a nomination for you to join the Energy and Natural Resources Committee will be made. Accept it without hesitation. Don't lone-wolf it out of high principles. You'll need to align yourself with a strong coalition right away to keep what you've got."

"How do you know this?"

"Ethan, stop asking questions I'm not going to answer. Let me finish. This is no different than being given a lengthy prison sentence; once put into the general population, if you haven't joined a gang for protection, you're dead meat. Understand? Don't try to control the situation with wit and fortitude. It's not enough. Promise you'll accept the nomination."

"Alright, I promise. You know Stanton heads that committee?"

"Yes. Why do you think it's available? He's a fool. Once you're in the game, fight with every ounce of viciousness you possess. Don't let him get control of you. You'll need him in the beginning until you've established a position. At that point, it'll be evident when to break away from John B. Stanton. Just do what I ask."

"I will. I've never seen you so concerned for my welfare. If I weren't mistaken, then it would appear someone's in love," Ethan said with a smirk.

"Stop it. Or I'll leave you to rot in the Senate."

Later that night, as Anne slept, Ethan stared at her in the dark and began to wonder. *Who is she? Is there a deeper woman needing my care or am I a plaything?*

Ethan considered for the first time that Anne might have true feelings for him. While remaining impressed with her self-empowerment, this softer side was also attractive.

The next day, Ethan received a text message. *Meet the governor and me at the Capitol Building. We're going a day earlier than agreed. John.*

As early morning sun beams cut across the Ethan's living room couch, Ethan tapped out John's phone number. "Senator Stanton, this can't happen until I've explained myself to David. I owe him that much. Delay this until Monday. It's just a few more days."

Not expecting an immediate call, John replied, "There's only today in politics, Ethan. Forty-eight hours is a lifetime. It's happening now and can't be stopped."

"But you extended your word that I would have time to discuss this with David. I can't simply walk away. I've left messages, but haven't yet heard back."

"Yes, I gave my word. Nonetheless, you have until noon today. The governor's private jet will be departing for Albany at that time. Ethan, accept that this is bigger than all of us. I'm one senator. There's a country to lead. Every day we're short a senator the Congress suffers. The governor has an agenda of his own. I have no influence over him. I'm only helping out the process. I've done what I could do to keep my promise. However, the real power behind this is our political body. It has a will of its own. When it decides to move, I must move with it; just as you're now learning. Do what you can do for your old boss. But as of twelve o'clock, the Citizens' Mandamus Council is in the past for you."

"I'll be there," Ethan assured, regretfully, realizing he was already crumbling. He knew that if leveraging led to more substantial outcomes, he could live with it.

Ethan anticipated David's phone call as he worked on an impromptu speech with Anne. He felt confident in the short message. Anne was particularly giddy at his decision to enter politics.

"You're gonna kill 'em," she assured him.

"If you were any other person, I'd assume you meant that metaphorically," Ethan teased.

"I would've preferred you follow in my footsteps. We could've made a great team. Obviously other plans played out. Still, we get to hike the same hill now; a vast improvement over the current molehill."

"Don't be upset if I force you to play by the rules."

"Like always, can't promise anything. Washington's a large playground—lots of bullies out there."

"That a confession?"

"A reality; to survive you'll need to toughen up."

"Seems you're not the only one that feels I'm too soft for the likes of DC."

"How do you mean?"

"Senator Stanton also contends I must adjust expectations to get along."

"That man couldn't sell snake oil to a serpent. I'm begging for the day."

"What day?" Ethan asked.

"Mum. John will fully understand when he sees me at your news conference this afternoon."

"I have no idea what you're planning. But don't spoil the party," Ethan insisted.

"Wouldn't dream of it. It's ten o'clock. You should change so we can leave for the airport."

Ethan looked pained for a moment and then said, "Alright."

"Why the gloomy face?"

"It'll be unfortunate if I don't talk with David before it becomes public. I wanted to explain in person. If I fail to tell him before the news conference, he'll be deeply hurt."

Anne grabbed Ethan by both arms and exclaimed, "You're joking, right? You need to be changed in fifteen minutes and you're worried about David's feelings? He's a big boy. David was running the CMC before he met you; and will be after you leave. Get over it!"

"It's not about feelings. It is simply a measure of respect. Enemy combatants show this courtesy on the battlefield before destroying their adversary. It's the least I can do for a friend."

"That's noble, Ethan. But you need to go. Worry about your precious honor later."

Ethan stepped towards his bedroom to change, ruminating over Anne's words. It bothered him that she dismissed integrity out of expediency. His warm sentiments for Anne were once again called into question. *Have I been right all along?* Soon after, he emerged from the bedroom in a black designer woolen suit and a blood-red tie.

"There that's better; quite regal. Senator, shall we?"

"Of course."

Airport bound, Ethan didn't speak, but cast a smile outward to the street—remaining fixated in his mind on Anne's character. Upon arrival they quickstepped onto a privately gated plane.

The governor's assistant greeted them at the door. "Senator Scott. It's a pleasure to have you aboard. The governor eagerly awaits your arrival. Allow me to provide your assistant with today's itinerary. If you'll quickly take your seats, refreshments will be served."

Without the courtesy of eye contact, an activities list was shoved Anne's way. She accepted it, rolling her eyes. The plane came to life as they sat down.

As the engines roared through their startup, Ethan went over in his mind what was to be said. Anne couldn't stand the quiet contemplation, and interrupted with, "How many senators does it take to get a bill passed? Three: one to bribe the other 48 senators, one to dig the hole, and one to kill the co-conspirators."

Ethan ignored her and focused on his address. The thirty-minute commute to Albany passed without much notice. As the tires touched down at the airport, Ethan was shaken back to reality—suddenly wondering if the right choice had been made. It was a constant source of frustration that he could do no more than investigate and file paperwork. Ethan was a whistleblower with a public venue to voice frustrations. The CMC could accomplish no more. Notwithstanding those ever-present issues, he still felt good working with the staff. They were all so driven in their belief in something better. It was this, more than anything else, he would miss. *How could such a wonderfully hard-working organization accomplish so little?*

He was leaving a council's positive purpose behind to embrace the scourge; who effectively take action—moving ideas from concept to reality. This was his curse; the power to make things happen but not without the accompanied corrupted actors. Their course was set upon personal gain with no consideration for anything ostensibly good. Ethan was torn between ideals and thirst for something tangible.

The plane rolled to a stop alongside a secluded gate. A black car waited nearby. As Ethan descended the steps to the runway, all questions ceased and his mind quieted. The time for pondering issues was finished. Like so many past moments, the new role was upon him; and life would change. As they traversed from plane to car, Ethan's stomach churned.

They arrived at the Capitol Building a short time later. The building's Romanesque and Renaissance revival styles harkened to dynasties past. White granite covered the exterior. Undulating lines of white and gray granite surfaced the courtyard's entrance; disrupting the sheer vertical lines of a many storied structure. Its ornate virtues captured the eye at each level.

Ethan stepped out of the car and was immediately greeted by a local news reporter. Shoving a microphone in his face, the young and eager woman asked, "Senator Scott, how do you feel about serving our state in the Senate? What issues will you take up?"

The governor's aide rushed around the car to interfere filming with an outstretched hand. She retorted, "The governor requested no interviews until the announcement has been formally delivered. Thank you."

Ethan and Anne were ushered into the building and through a press pool to a chamber off the main foyer. As they entered, the governor and John Stanton rose from their chairs. Having interrupted a private conversation, both attempted to conceal the subject under discussion with an abrupt silence.

"Governor, it's a pleasure to meet you," Ethan said, extending his hand to shake Sheridan Franklin's.

Surprised to see Anne trailing Ethan, John's posture stiffened. John had never relinquished the fantasy that one day Anne would be his.

"John, you do show up in the strangest places. I spoke with George yesterday. He made mention that recently you two had time to talk—wasn't that nice? You and I also have some catching up to do," Anne suggested.

John knew he had been mistaken telling George about Ethan. Though concerned with what Anne might do, he felt the candor with George would win his protection.

The others, bewildered by Anne's cryptic words, knew they would not be privileged to their meaning—so pretended nothing had been said. The governor's assistant fetched and served drinks. After she departed, the five were left alone.

"Let's have this out now. Ethan, I've seen a great deal of you in the news over the last few months. I don't really know your politics or honestly care. Hell, I don't even know what party you belong to. Some in the room here may feel that easing you into the game is preferable. I would not be one of them. So let's talk plainly," Sheridan insisted.

"That's the way I like it," Ethan fired back.

"Good. From our brief conversation yesterday, I gather you are an idealist. It's your funeral. Two things need to be understood before I go out there and announce to the press that you're my choice for the open seat.

"First, you owe me something. That something I'll collect at a time of my choosing. I'm not interested in your response. Just be ready when called on. There's no free lunch, son. Second, I don't care what causes you take up for the state of New York. Don't side with those who oppose my position. An egg timer can clock the political life of anyone that goes it alone in the Bone Yard."

"Have you heard truer words, John?" Anne added.

"Blue Coats," Ethan interjected.

"What?" Sheridan asked.

"I'm a registered member of the Blue Coats Party. However, I typically vote based on issues independent of party affiliation. I put my time where it makes the most sense," Ethan explained.

"My boy, I assume that only means good things for us both. Well, are we ready to nominate a senator?" Sheridan rhetorically asked as he got to his feet.

They all rose in kind; following the governor to fall in behind a microphone-encrusted podium. The lieutenant governor joined them, waited for the crowd to quiet, and then began to speak. "Ladies, gentlemen and members of the press, please rise to honor Governor Sheridan Franklin."

The crowd stood and clapped as normative pageantry collaborators. Applause ended a moment later as everyone retook their seats.

"Thank you for coming. It is a day of sadness and of rejoicing. New York is healing from a great loss and preparing for the future. I will be making a very brief announcement followed by comments from Mr. Ethan Scott. Senator Thomas Murphy's recent passing was a shock to us all. His death will be felt in the Senate and here at home. Tom will truly be missed. He was a man of diligence and of the people. Now, I would like to introduce to you our new man of the people for the state of New York. You know him from so many recent interviews. His work with the Citizens' Mandamus Council did not go unnoticed in my office. He is Ethan Scott, the CMC's recent presidential appointee and my choice as nominee for the senatorial seat for the great state of New York. Please stand to welcome Ethan," Sheridan instructed—clapping his hands and backing away from the microphones.

Ethan stepped up and said, "Thank you, Governor Franklin, for that warm introduction. Like Sheridan, my words will be brief. There is a great deal of work to be done, and I am eager to get to it. I'm accustomed to speaking for an hour or more, so if what I have to say seems simple, it's not meant to diminish the breadth of issues there are to address. I am a newspaperman by trade. I started my paper because of an apparent need. I filled it. That's really it, isn't it? Isn't that why we're here as politicians: to serve a useful purpose? That's why I'm here.

"After being forced out of the newspaper business, a rest seemed appealing. Soon, however, I found myself at a low point. For the first time I ceased to matter. I had no newspaper to run, and no employees to lead or provide jobs for. There were no emergency deadlines to meet and certainly no need to fill. I had simply become a consumer, and ceased to contribute.

"I joined the Citizens' Mandamus Council because I wanted to matter. In my short time with the council, I became a participant in life again; and felt good about it. I didn't want for anything; except that I desired to make an impact in your lives. When Governor Franklin called to offer this opportunity, I felt there was no choice but to accept and take the chance to make an even greater difference. It is my fervent hope that I will prevail in Washington for the people of New York. Thank you for your time this afternoon."

The crowd began to clap. Reporters then shouted questions. Ethan held up his arms to quiet the attendees so that he could speak.

Behind him, Sheridan leaned over to John and asked, "Can you control him?"

"Anne will be instrumental in this. He'll fall in line," John assured.

"John, I must say you've never taken so many liberties. If I didn't know better, I'd say you have something on me," Anne whispered to John.

"You just can't tell, can you?" John replied to Anne with confidence and force for the first time.

Ethan then said, "I'd like to hold off any questions until having had the opportunity to speak in person with my friend, David Samuel. You see, this nomination was unexpectedly presented. I attempted to talk with David about it before this press conference. However, he was unavailable and time marched on. I'll be tendering a formal resignation to the Citizens' Mandamus Council this evening upon my return to Manhattan. Thank you for your time and attention."

Ethan stepped away from the podium as cameras flashed and hands clapped. The five behind the podium returned to the room they had started from, led by Ethan. There they waited until the press and audience had departed the Capitol Building before leaving for the airport.

The return flight was turbulent. A storm front that had blown in during Ethan's announcement provided strong headwinds. Lightning flashed, filling the cabin with white light followed by thunderous howls.

Ethan and Anne arrived in Manhattan just after six that evening. Anne went on ahead to Ethan's apartment. Ethan took a taxi to the office.

Engorged droplets of rain hurried to the pavement. The cab door opened and Ethan stepped out into the deluge. He sprinted—not having a coat or umbrella, and by the time he reached the entrance, he was soaked to the skin. His suit clung to him. Water rolled off the fabric and onto the floor.

Sasha was not at the front desk. Ethan knew where he was going. He saw David's door propped open as he approached. David was staring at a wood-framed photograph of himself in front of the Manhattan office shaking the mayor's hand. It had been taken on the CMC's opening day. Fierce dedication and youthful enthusiasm was apparent on his face.

"David, I want to say how sorry I am not to have explained in person this development," Ethan offered as he sat down in front of David's desk.

David raised his hand to wave off the gesture as an insignificant matter. He didn't turn to face Ethan. Nor did he look away from the photo he was admiring.

"I can imagine how bad this must feel. You held a door open from the very beginning. You turned over the council's leadership. I understand you're angry. But, to be clear, every attempt was made to reach you before the public announcement. You weren't returning my calls."

"I know," David replied. Taking a moment, he then explained, "I was called away. My father's sick. I turned my phone off on the plane ride home and forgot to turn it back on."

"How is your father?"

"He's fine. It was just a little pneumonia. He'll get through it. We'll all get through it," David replied in a bitter tone.

"David, I tried to hold them off, but the nomination was made before it could be stopped. I did my best to make contact. In the end, I had a decision to make. The circumstances were not easy. I made the choice that was right for me."

"You certainly made a choice," David barked—turning to finally make eye contact with Ethan. He went on, "Was it that important to have your way—to cut me—to side with the enemy of what we stand for?"

"I've betrayed no one!" Ethan shouted.

"You're being led by the nose, Ethan. Don't you see? If the decision were that important, then why did they insist you quickly make it?"

"I'm not being led. The seat was empty and needed to be filled."

"But why you? There must be hundreds of others more qualified or willing to sell out. Why? Can you answer that?" David demanded.

"I can't explain why me. It was an opportunity to make a difference: a real difference."

"Oh, I see. We don't make a difference now. You accepted the position of CMC president and didn't feel it counted."

"You knew my mind then. It hasn't changed. David, what good is rattling a saber if you never use it? For all the CMC's benefit, it still falls short in the end because it cannot act."

"It does act!" David shouted.

"It doesn't! It observes and reports. That is its function. That's all it does. You built it to be that way," Ethan returned—drawing face to face distance between them.

"So the likes of the CMC are no longer good enough for you…now that you've been nominated senator."

"That's not the reason; you know better. You're making this harder. Why can't you simply wish me well?"

"Because it is hard," David replied. "Ethan, if this is what you truly want, then I do wish you well. Isn't it obvious by now that they're going to manipulate you; or worse, that you'll become one of them?"

"That won't happen. They make the laws and now I'll be a part of it. I can make a difference. Things can change for the better. Has so much faith been lost that you no longer believe one man can still make it better? This cannot stand. If we let them take everything else, we must not allow the thieves to steal our belief in the possibility of something greater. Don't believe in them. Believe in me," Ethan pleaded.

He recognized the hurt and anger in David's eyes. David could see and understand Ethan's dismay with the inability to take action as president. Both knew their short-lived time together had come to a pass.

They both got to their feet; standing tall and calm. The silence served as a salute and farewell.

Ethan extended his hand. David shook it. Ethan smiled and stepped towards the door.

"We'll be watching you," David cautioned; both with humor and in all seriousness.

Ethan stopped as he passed into the hallway, turned back and said, "I would expect nothing less from the CMC."

CHAPTER

II

POWER OF PERSUASION

Like good little soldiers, rank-and-file state senators fell in line with their vote to accept Ethan; dismissing the five-year residency requirement as an emergency measure. He was sworn in the Monday following confirmation.

Ethan found an apartment near his friend Jonathan's Washington home. Similar to the CMC transition from a few months before, getting settled into public life was a short-lived experience. He parked his suitcase and left for the office.

Murphy's staff was scheduled to stay late to brief Ethan on senatorial protocol and recent business. His predecessor had been dedicated, but lacked any discernable method. Columns of papers, books and folders were heaped along the walls.

By midnight everyone but his secretary. Jane, had departed. Senator Murphy's projects lay categorized into four groups: completed, not possible, possible, and current. The completed projects represented the largest pile.

Ethan surveyed the stacks and sais, "Jane, I can't even imagine why you do this."

"I want to be a part of something great. Working for Senator Murphy was a dream come true," she replied.

"You're so young to be in politics. What are you? Twenty-two, twenty-three?"

"I know. Government work didn't turn out to be what was sold when they recruited me in college. Still, it's exciting to be here. And, I had to do something with a business and art history degree."

"I'll up the ante as a philosophy major."

"Oh my, Senator...I'm not sure if I feel more sorry for you or myself."

They laughed at the mutually misplaced idealism. A moment of understanding was forged; giving way to their assumed roles.

The next morning, Ethan returned at six o'clock. The staff had yet to arrive. He hovered over a steaming coffee cup—staring across the desk and out the window; collecting his thoughts and mustering energy for the day. *I can do this.*

Sooner than he would have liked, staffers began to filter in. Phones started ringing with well-wishers and those wanting an audience.

The door cracked open. "Senator, another delegate is waiting in the foyer to see you," Jane once again interrupted.

"Jane, I'm giving you control of my schedule." Frustrated that he had accomplished nothing useful after opening for business," Ethan instructed her. I need not to be disturbed for the next hour. Can you do that?"

"Yes, Senator Scott," Jane replied.

Finally, I can breathe, Ethan thought—assured he would get to the imperative needs assembled the night before.

A minute later, the office door swung open. Jane marched in, followed by John.

"Senator Scott, I'm sorry to interrupt. Senator Stanton insisted he be admitted, and that you would understand."

"That's fine, Jane."

John's eyes traveled her contours from head to heel. As she departed, Ethan noticed this repeated behavior. While understanding John's preoccupation, it seemed mere force of habit.

"John, it's good to see you."

"And you," he replied as the door shut. "Ethan, you have the look of a headlight-kissing deer. Relax, my boy. If this job is taken too seriously, you won't be long with us."

"I'm just attempting to get a handle on it."

"Well, in the spirit of insanity, I'd like to throw another wrench in the works."

"Why am I worried what you're going to say?" Ethan asked.

"Humor's a good sign. You may survive after all. I want you to join my committee. What say you?"

Here we go. "John, I'm honored. But I've already received six committee invitations this morning. I haven't had time to review the proposals or even consider what special needs I'd be interested in serving."

"Ethan, I'm offering to take you under my wing. You don't know DC well enough to be out there alone. They'll eat you alive. I'm not insisting. However, I did play an integral part in your arrival. Surely you wouldn't mind returning the favor? We could use a man who knows how to get things done."

"I'll accept, with the caveat that when it no longer works, I may gracefully exit without ill feelings. Can you promise this?"

Releasing a disturbing guffaw, John replied, "Ethan, when a shoe no longer fits, do we not discard it? Of course I accept your proposal. We'll be meeting this Friday. The other members have already agreed to my nomination; so you're officially a member of the Energy and Natural Resources Committee. Welcome aboard!"

John stood to shake Ethan's hand and then left without another word. What felt most odd was Anne's foreknowledge. How bizarre that Washington clichés were true. Moreover, everyone accepted it; believing nothing could change the status quo.

Ethan then realized it was already noon; and that he was late for a lunch meeting. He grabbed his jacket and departed. Jane caught up with him in the hallway and said, "Senator, I need to confirm your interview with TTN later today."

Ethan stopped walking. "We haven't discussed any scheduled interviews."

"I'm sorry, Senator Scott. I should have assumed the networks would do anything to gain a few moments. I'll tell Miss Sanders that she'll need to get in line with the rest of the press corps."

Smiling as he listened, Ethan offered, "Maybe we shouldn't be so truculent with the networks. I like their spunk. Go ahead and give them an hour. But tell Miss Sanders that she'll need to be here at four."

"Right away."

"Thanks, Jane. I'll be back after lunch."

Ethan strutted to his car—grinning that Abigail Sanders would have to reshuffle her day to accommodate the appointment. She'd make him pay for it and that was fine.

As tradition would have it, Ethan was meeting Anne at Don Giordano's Bistro. A cab jaunt across town deposited Ethan at the entrance. While approaching the door, a homeless man turned towards him—cloaked in a tattered, dark blue pinstriped suit. His right shoe tip pulled sideways, catching the sidewalk between strides.

Ethan reached into his pocket to retrieve a twenty-dollar bill, handing it to the indigent. He smiled at Ethan and said, "God bless you. God bless you." He reeked of bad breath and body odor, like a field goat.

"God bless you," Ethan replied—the phrase feeling peculiar. Raised Methodist, he had not attended worship services since high school.

A scar above the vagrant's left eye twitched as if he was holding back a tear. He asked, "What puts such a genuine smile on your face? It's out of place for the Bone Yard."

"Recent events…I was just appointed senator to represent New York."

"Is that so?" the man asked in an understanding tone. "Go with care on the Hill. The Senate is no place for the pure of heart."

Charmed by the concern, Ethan began to ask, "What's your…?"

But the poor man had turned and walked away, mumbling to himself. In a pinch of time, the kind fellow had blended into the other pedestrians moving along the sidewalk.

Remembering lunch, Ethan reached for the door handle. Andre, the maitre d', standing at the ready said, "Monsieur Scott, we have been expecting you. Congratulations on such a prestigious appointment! Mademoiselle Preston is seated and awaiting your arrival; if you will follow me, please."

Passing Corinthian columns and cornices, Ethan recognized many notable politicians he had only seen on television until now. Anne's formal black dress caught Ethan's attention as he approached.

"Scotch, single malt," Ethan ordered.

Anne was already sipping vodka. Without a word, her approving eyes transmitted possessive dominion.

"You look lovely," he told her. "I hope you didn't gussy up just for me."

"No. I have another duty to perform that demands an equal measure of auspicious attention."

"What is it?"

"Sorry, Ethan...work. I will say that, of all my responsibilities, this one brings the greatest pleasure; settling an inequity. If you'd only joined my side—I could've shared all the gory details," Anne relayed in a darkened tone.

"Better I don't know."

"It is. Thank you for the compliment."

"You're more yourself today."

"How?"

"At your CMC office visit with David, you seemed determined to demonstrate we were an item; appearing injured and needing attention. It was shocking. If it'd been anyone else, the behavior might've made sense."

"Last week a client reminded me who I was and what needed to be done. I'm better now."

"Glad to hear it," Ethan replied. "This is quite a building, isn't it?"

"I suppose. To you it's a wonderful structure. To me it's a killing field. I've given men power and stripped others of it. On that score, I am jealous, Ethan. You look upon this place with fresh eyes. It would be pleasant to see its beauty again."

Ethan goaded, "Regret...at last!"

"Careful there; go slow and don't forget who we are. You may possess a sculptured posterior and a heartwarming sensibility. But that won't help if I must destroy you."

Why am I with this woman? What happens if we're no longer friends?

They had their drink and made smalltalk; as if a duty were performed.

"Why don't we skip lunch?" Anne suggested.

Ethan looked at his watch. "Yeah, time did get away from us. Before parting for what might be a while, tell me something. How'd you know John would offer the committee position? And how did you know I would accept?"

Anne snickered. "You are so very precious—but not far enough into the game to accept what I'd say."

"Why?"

"Because, darling, every aspiration hasn't yet been crushed and served up to your enemies. What you've volunteered for is incomprehensible."

"If what you're saying is true, then why did you encourage the decision?"

Heartily laughing, but trying not to offend, Anne replied, "Please stop, before this dress splits. Oh my goodness, my dear sweet saint; to grow, Ethan. You have great power already. What you sorely lack is an understanding of how to shape a world. What's coming will mold who you'll next become."

Ethan thought on her words for the remainder of the afternoon as he worked at his desk; Jane darting in and out of the office every few minutes. He wondered what would be next. He was certain of three things: he was busy, it mattered, and action would be taken.

Four o'clock came without notice of the day's passing. Jane barged in as she had a moment before. Assuming another task was being lumped onto the next day's list, Ethan did not raise his head.

"Senator Scott, may I present Miss Sanders?" Jane announced.

Ethan rose to meet Abigail's pleasant face with genuine welcome. They shook hands. A sudden nervousness existed and then was dispelled.

"Senator Scott. It does have a nice ring to it," Abigail charmed him.

"Jane, that'll be all. Thanks," Ethan hurried her out of the room.

After Jane had closed the door, Ethan and Abigail hugged, smiled, and hugged again. They sat down next to windows overlooking a path and trees below. Minutes later, Jane returned with coffee before departing once more.

"You have a busy little bee assisting here. She seems quite efficient, if not attractive."

"Shut up. How are you? I saw your Afghanistan piece. You're fortunate to be alive. What was your producer thinking, sending you on an assignment like that?"

"Ethan, I'm in the news business; and that's where it is. Though, an unexpected management change didn't help matters. I can't imagine the cretin currently in charge will keep the position."

"This cretin isn't going to send you on any other dangerous assignments, is he?"

"Hard to say. I was a field reporter before riding an anchor desk—it wasn't my first time in the mud. Stop treating me like a child."

"Whew! Yep…Still have all my fingers. I'm just concerned. It would've been sad if you'd lost your life. The death of those reporters was tragic."

"I'm still numb. It was lucky timing—I can't think about it anymore. Let's change the subject. How about this career hop of yours? I never knew you had political ambitions."

"I didn't then and still don't; just want to be in the middle of things. By the way, when was it that we set up this interview? I've only been here two days. It could have easily slipped my mind in that time," Ethan jibed.

"Fine, I didn't have an appointment. I assumed you'd give me one. And I knew you'd want me to be the first to interview the newly appointed senator for New York."

"You knew all that, did you? I wasn't sure—had my eye on that fetching anchorwoman from your competition. What's her name?"

"Sky," Abigail exaggerated its pronunciation; attempting to imply a lack of intelligence.

"Yes, that's it; Sky. She seems to be going places."

"I'm sure. So what would you like to be called now…Your Highness, maybe? Or can I still call you Ethan?"

"Senator Ethan Scott if you please," Ethan replied haughtily, pointing his nose upward.

Abigail laughed at the farcical display. "So what are the ground rules?" she asked, changing to a more serious tone.

"What do you mean?"

"Ethan, your friend Stanton and his lot are easy targets. They ask to be exposed by the media every chance we get. But, in general, the network frowns on roasting politicians. To tell the truth, I was astonished when I was first hired on with TTN that this is the way things are. A few years back I produced a piece on a stiff with solid evidence and witnesses. It wasn't run. I was taken aside and told that if a congressman were pursued again without network authorization, then I'd be shown the door."

"I'm stunned, Abbey. The networks obviously favor their own parties. To answer your question, you may ask whatever you wish."

"Let's do it then. I'll have my crew set up here. We'll be ready in ten minutes. I'll have my makeup girl get started."

"That's fine. Truthfully, I think you like watching your staff put makeup on a grown man."

"Ethan, stop pretending you don't like it. How many interviews have we done this year? I lost count. I think you get more excited about the primping each time."

"Mr. Weatherby, Adolphe Dubois of Gillet is on the phone."

"Put him through, June," George replied.

"Monsieur Weatherby. What a great pleasure to speak to you today. How is the temperature there this time of year?"

"It's hot. Adolphe, did you call to discuss the weather or is there something else of importance?"

"Straight to the subject at hand…I like you, George. You never waste time. I'm afraid I have some bad news. The fifty million you spent with us has been exhausted. We're going to need more to keep your operation alive."

"How could it be gone so soon?" George demanded.

Adolphe was tickled. "How, you ask? With a big boom! That is how. Actually, there have been many booms from the mortars, bullets and landmines you purchased. You have an army that is beginning to run low on food and a means to fight. What do you want to do?"

"I want them to do the job I'm paying them to do. That's what!"

"George, George, George, you really must calm down. This kind of stress cannot be good for your health. To be clear, you are no longer paying anyone. You have paid, of course; and we thank you for your business. However, if you want to keep Operation Sequel alive we are going to need more; a lot more."

"Why did I know this was coming?"

"George, you misunderstand me. I am not taking you for a ride. War costs money. Fifty million bought you a start…and a good one. But we're not wiping out defenseless civilians or some poorly armed tribal community. This is the United States Army. Your people are well-trained. They don't leave until ordered to.

What is more, we cannot hold the high ground to the northeast if you do not rearm your insurgency soon. We could also use a few more soldiers to replace the ones that have been killed. The Americans are penetrating farther out from their bases now. The element of surprise is over. They are hardening under constant bombardment. It will only get worse, and quickly, if you do not act within a week."

"A week! What is it that I am to do within a week? You told me this would cost fifty million; I gave you fifty million."

"Yes, George, you did…as I said, it was a good beginning. But that is all it is."

"Why didn't you say so from the outset?"

"George, tactics are not my strength; or frankly my job. You hired us to perform a service. It was rendered conscientiously and professionally. What more could you ask for?"

"Time, Adolphe."

"Time…for what?"

"Time for our efforts to work: I paid for results."

"But it is working. It needs more. That is all."

"For someone who is not a tactician, you played this one well. Tell me what this is going to cost," George pressed bitter breath.

"We need an additional one hundred and fifty million dollars to continue."

George became strangely calm. "Why do you think an additional sum of that magnitude is required?"

"The math is quite simple. Your insurgency will have exhausted its funding by month's end. We project that it will take the better part of three months to rout out the Americans from the smaller bases in the southwest. After that, we would not feel comfortable offering any suggestions.

Until your government makes its next military move, we can only project short-term outcomes. The extended plans must come from you. Frankly, George, we assumed you would have prepared that far ahead. Whatever your exit design is, I hope you are ready. Unless you can outspend the American government, I think this is going to be a short-lived insurgency."

"I'm not the only one involved in this, Adolphe. I can't promise anything in a week."

"Maybe I am not making myself clear, George. You have a week to come up with the money."

"Sounds like a threat."

"George, I also have people to answer to. They have risked much to bring your war. For them, it will not be easy to pull out of this so soon. What would you suggest I tell them? Let me also explain that the Moborak are not civilized. They will not show you the same courtesy I provide."

"As you said, Adolphe, you're not the tactician. How can you know what will be needed in the next three months, or what could happen over a longer span of time?"

"What are you saying, George?"

"I'm saying that I can promise nothing."

"So that is what you have to say…fine. I also have something to say. Those people I mentioned a moment ago; the less civilized ones. Well, I will be calling them next. They want their next payment and are expecting me to tell you have agreed to the additional sum. When I explain your sentiments, there are no guarantees what will happen. Do you understand what I am saying?

"Yes."

"Good. George, I do hate these kinds of conversations. They are so unpleasant and cloud the day with horrid feelings. I will call on you then in a week. Goodbye, George."

After the phone line clicked, George began to think about other people who might be willing to assist. There were only a few in the world that would put up their own resources for a move like this. George already knew their positions. It could only be one person. As the phone rang, he anticipated flippancy.

"George, what is it now?" Darby asked upon answering the call.

"Nice to speak to you too. I wanted to provide an update on how the money has been spent."

"I don't need to know and don't care. You have the dough. So manage it—don't want to hear the details."

"I was thinking you may want to take a trip to New York. Stop in and see me while you're here."

"What's going on? Look, George, I have too much work to waste time on a visit. If you've got something to say then say it."

"I'd rather talk about it in person."

"I don't have time for this. I'm coming to New York in a couple months. We can talk then."

"Can't wait that long."

"You know where I am."

A day after Ethan's resignation from the CMC, the executive board requested David's presence to discuss the situation. He arrived before the scheduled meeting in an attempt to leverage home-field advantage. Anticipating his ploy, the board had assembled an hour early to await him.

When David entered the room all eyes were fixed on him. Emily Watson rose and looked around the table. No one spoke.

"David, why don't you have a seat?" she offered.

"I'd rather stand."

"As the executive vice president, a difficult task lies before me. Just a few days ago the CMC possessed a known quantity that wasn't the case a year ago. Within the short time Ethan worked here, a new public awareness and support has revitalized our purpose and mission. Donations have never been so plentiful.

It's dangerous to lump unchecked power onto the shoulders of a single man; and still his performance was undeniable. What can we say that would do his work justice? Nothing comes to mind.

Rumors have circulated. Why did he leave? Was it something we did or something that was done? Where does the council go from here? I for one have posed these same questions myself. The same concerns continue to flood my office.

"David, he left because it was time. Ethan's reasons were his own. But what do we do now? Words considered countless times throughout the ages." After a pause, she continued, "David, it is the executive board's deliberation that you be reappointed to the position of president while maintaining your post as chief executive officer."

To David's astonishment, the members applauded. He had entered the room certain blame would be issued; of which he'd be apportioned a lion's share.

David smiled wryly at Emily. "That was the most I ever heard you say at one time."

"I had to practice in the mirror."

David opened, "Thank you for honoring me this way. It's been a struggle to forgive what I felt was a mistake. And yet, Ethan's gift to us was the passion to act. He obviously needed something more. I hope my friend doesn't lose himself. Would you all applaud for our former president, who has offered up his life to acting in ways we cannot?"

The board clapped and cheered. David sat at the head of the table and continued putting his hands together. Nodding to the others, a tear rolled down his cheek. He felt pulled into his seat. The applause seemed to go on and on.

Over the next few days, David's lamentation turned into anger. *Why was the CMC not sufficient to keep him? So what if we don't possess police powers? Let them incarcerate the criminals!*

Shaking his head in retreat of a questionable faith, David dialed his desk phone. "Daphne Cook, how are you today?"

"Fine, sir. What can I do for you?"

"I'm going to begin a new speaking tour on the West Coast and need you to assemble the standard remote office support. Also, have Ted Stevenson look into the resubmitted Stanton Bill. It's supposed to include funding to support the upcoming Afghan military response. I want to know what the bill is really after. If John Stanton's involved, it can't be good."

"I'll get started right away on tour preparations and speak with Ted after lunch. Will that be all?"

"One other thing, Daphne, call me David. A little informality is fine. You're the vice president of Operations now. I won't bite."

"I'll do that…David."

CHAPTER

III

SHARP TONGUES AND DULL WITS

Abigail pored over Ethan's interview; hoping to complete the segment in time to run that evening. If she didn't finish soon, it would need to wait until Monday's broadcast.

TTN was different since Sandra Buchanan's departure. Broadcast delays and lower advertising revenue had become common. Daniel had not shown his face all day—hiding and stressing over a lack of solutions to deal with network operations. The idea made her smile. More than these distractions, her clouded thoughts were not in the editing process. The work failed to elicit a response or uncover anything newsworthy; other than a freshman senator taking his post. Ethan was under her skin. She suffered; not wanting to analyze what he had to say.

At the beginning of their pristine dialogue, she caught herself laughing at his subtle jokes. Abigail warmed towards Ethan and hoped, not just for him but also the public, that he achieved his ends. It was delightful to watch someone take such joy from what they did.

Time and again, Abigail hammered out a story that played more like a campaign advertisement. She would begin from the same raw footage with the intent to produce something useful and hard-hitting. Each attempt ended the same frustrating way.

"Fine, you like him," she admitted to herself.

Angered and relieved now that her forbidden thoughts were entertained, she could edit with a critical eye. Settling in, Abigail found a rhythm, cutting and assembling unpolished work in a new direction. The story was certain now to make the evening deadline.

However, a knock and an open door ushered in yet another delay. Looking up at the runner with frustration,

Abigail asked, "What is it?"

"The board's waiting on you upstairs, Miss Sanders."

"I wasn't told about a meeting."

The woman shrugged.

"Tell them I'll be there in a moment."

This has got to change, she thought. Abigail marched to the elevator—shaking her head that it was likely a problem Daniel invented. As she ascended, a myriad of ridiculous potential issues thrown at the executive board came to mind. Daniel's interim presidential status would not be short enough for her.

The doors opened. After stepping out into the foyer leading to the conference room, Abigail was met by a perky and attractive pubescent-esque—an assistant to someone on the board. Her only purpose was to greet; and remain pleasing to her employer.

"If you'll follow me, Miss Sanders," the girl invited brightly.

"I know the way," Abigail shot back. She stalked past, offended by the debutante's choice of professions.

Irritatingly, the girl did not seem to notice her hostility. "Let me get the door, Miss Sanders."

The board was seated around the table's far end; Daniel at the other. Daniel wore the face of fear. Abigail hoped for a gigantic Daniel-blunder.

"Abigail, glad you could make it. Why don't you take a seat next to me?" Xavier Cohen offered.

"Certainly!" Abigail chirped.

"Before we discuss the matter at hand, I want to congratulate you on the Afghanistan coverage. Looks like you went through hell in Kandahar."

"Thank you, Mr. Cohen. Though if we're going to lump accolades, then there are a few others I'd like to make mention of."

"Who?"

Daniel sat up straight; thinking Abigail would laud his leadership choice in sending her.

"First and foremost was my cameraman, Jake Noland. He kept shooting every step of the way. Without him, I wouldn't have a story to tell. Also, there was a young sergeant named Teddy Middleton. He provided security and led us through the mortar barrage. We would not have survived without him."

"I'll see to it that they are properly recognized and rewarded. Gracious of you to mention them, and spoken like a true leader!" Xavier proclaimed. His expression turned from pride to disgust as he rounded on Daniel. Daniel's shoulders sank and his eyes widened.

The remainder of the board ceased rustling now, ready for the main event, and Xavier cleared his throat. He snarled, "Why did you send an anchorwoman into a war zone? Did you think she needed more field experience? What if she'd stayed put with the others to swallow exploding ordinance? Would that have made a big enough story for you?

"Daniel, you're my brother's son. He's an idiot. The apple clearly didn't fall far from the tree. I just can't get my mind around how you thought shipping off our greatest talent to a meat grinder was a good idea.

"We have a staff of squeaky eager reporters that would eat dirt if I asked them. The newbies have so little experience that if they didn't survive it wouldn't matter; as long as the camera kept recording. Do you have any idea how many years this network has invested into Abigail's development and brand name?"

Abigail broke in, "Xavier, I hate to interrupt, but I'd like to think there was quite a bit of natural talent to work with before TTN set its hooks into me."

"Not now, Sanders!" Xavier snapped.

"Got it, boss."

"You hear that, Dan?"

"Hear? What do you mean? Hear what?" Daniel asked.

"Boss…She called me boss!" Xavier barked, as he gestured to Abigail with his thumb.

"Yes, I did."

"She understands something you seem to have missed when you begged me to give you a job any monkey could do. She recognized me as the man in charge with the final word. I might add that there was even a hint of understanding in the tone with which she said it; denoting a sense of servitude. Yes, I believe Miss Sanders demonstrated a keen understanding of who signs her inflated check each month; and that a certain measure of courtesy, respect and intelligence in the way she does her job is expected. So tell me, Daniel. What were you thinking, sending Abigail Sanders into a war zone?"

"I don't know. It seemed like a good idea at the time. I think that demographics show—"

"Shut that pie hole! You're fired! I do believe you had a shorter executive tenure than that Scott character Abigail just interviewed. Wasn't he the CMC chief for five or six weeks?"

"Four," Abigail corrected.

"Yeah, four weeks—you're demoted back to the news desk; junior anchor. Say another word and you'll be out on the street." Silence suddenly split the room wide open. "Good! Now that our half-baked issues are resolved, I'd like to turn our attention to more exciting news," Xavier announced, looking towards Abigail.

"What are you planning to give me, a raise?" Abigail quipped.

"Sort of—we want you to take over Sandra's duties."

"Xavier…I'm honored. But what about Sandra; surely she'll be back?"

"She won't. Your loyalty's admirable, but misplaced. Her break was a long time coming. The executive board isn't certain she's dependable anymore. Business moves on."

"She's your daughter. Surely you'd want a family member at the helm?"

Xavier's face deadpanned. "What does family have to do with anything? Do you think family counts a bit here? Look at the mess my idiot nephew's made in a handful of days. I would've taken a year or more to find a suitable replacement. However, that timeline's been shortened—given your handling of a crisis under real fire. You know the business and deliver under the worst possible circumstances. That's what we need. You're the person for the job. The position's yours if you want it."

"Thank you, again, for your confidence. With respect, I must reject the offer at this time. I like the news desk and chasing down stories for your network. However, when I'm ready to walk away from the camera, I hope the option is still available. I'm holding out that Sandra will recover soon enough to rejoin us."

"Sure about this?"

"I am."

"Can't say I'm happy about it; but you've earned the right to say no. Alright, you can keep the desk. You're promoted to senior news anchor. Sorry, you're stuck with Daniel. If he gets out of line, then handle it. Not sure I could endure it."

"Xavier, I have a favor to ask."

"Name it."

"Not now. When the time comes for me to run this network, I'll let you know."

"Fair enough."

"I don't mean to leave you in the lurch."

"Don't worry, there're plenty of suits lined up to take over where Sandra left off."

"Good. Hey, make sure the john isn't too stiff under the collar," Abigail joked.

"I hear you," Xavier replied with a grin.

The conversation switched to lighter topics about the city's goings-on. Daniel slipped out of the boardroom without notice, sulking his way to the elevator.

Abigail left a few minutes after Daniel's silent departure. He was still waiting for the elevator as Abigail arrived. The doors opened and both stepped in. A bell sounded and it began moving.

As they tried not to make eye contact, Daniel said, "I'm sure you enjoyed every moment."

Abigail frowned. Daniel went on, "Go ahead and have a good laugh. It's what you wanted all along. Make note, I'm not going to let you take it from me. You're not even family."

"Daniel, I really don't care about your bruised feelings; not even to an insignificant degree. Please understand these words. You don't matter to me at all…One last thing, are you listening?"

"Yes," he petulantly replied.

"When I'm finished with the senior anchor job, or it's finished with me, then I'll be network president. The position's mine. It was never yours. You were simply a doorstop. I like that. It's fitting. You're my little doorstop."

"We'll see. I'm not going to be your junior forever."

"Daniel, we can only hope."

"Mr. Weatherby, what a pleasant surprise! I don't think Mr. Adams is expecting you. He's on a conference call at the moment. I'll let him know you're here," Stanley explained. "You do that."

Stanley hurried off while George waited. Tapping his fingers atop the reception desk announced his displeasure with waiting. Moments later, Stanley returned.

"Mr. Weatherby, Mr. Adams is nearly finished and ready to receive you. He did ask me to explain that he could only grant fifteen minutes. It's a very busy day."

"Let's get moving then."

"Right this way."

As they approached, Darby's shouts escaped behind closed doors. "That's wonderful, Brad! Tell 'em if production output has not resumed in twenty-four hours, then I'm pulling the contract and building my own refinery. One more thing, if they try handling me again, I'll waste ungodly sums digging the hole they'll be buried in!"

Stanley opened the door and announced, "Mr. Adams, Mr. Weatherby is here to see you."

"That'll be all, Stanley," Darby grumbled.

George sat down and rejoiced in Darby's obvious issues. Where there was anger and leveraging, George always found comfort.

"Well, George, you surprise me yet again. It must be bad news to get you on a plane here. Don't bother with the song and dance. Just get to it."

"What happened to first names with the staff?"

"I'm Mr. Adams today."

"I heard. Sounds like the old 'refinery at half capacity' excuse; and will take at least four months to repair. That right?"

"Down forty percent; they're going to cost Fountain over two billion dollars."

"Is that Brad Tincher over at Brunson Energy?"

"Yep."

"They tried that with me too. Brad's just building up fat cash reserves for the winter months. I threatened them with an EPA contact—something about their emissions standards. He went away. I'll give them a call on my way back to New York this afternoon."

"Greeks bearing gifts, George—what do you want?"

"To update you on our progress; I thought—"

"George…enough already—I told you on the phone, I'm not interested in particulars. You wanted the money. I gave it. Manage the problem and leave me out of it."

"Okay. I just need to let you know about the—"

"Stop! I don't have time for this. It must be pretty bad. What's the deal?"

"They need another hundred and fifty million."

"They—the people from France, is this the 'they' you're talking about?"

"They're the ones."

"I've never known a larger bunch of dualistic backstabbing elitists. The French claim to be a people of freedom and independence. Their actions diametrically oppose it."

"Darby, we do it too."

"No, George, we don't. You do it."

"Get off your high horse. I knew you when you were half as big. Tell me, Darby, while you're moralizing…how many companies have you decimated? How many lives were destroyed in the pursuit of more?"

"That's yesterday. Why do you insist on keeping the past alive?"

"Because it's who you really are. I'm tired of watching you waste time on this feeble beneficence. Things work better between us when I can count on your barbarity."

"Ha. That's it, isn't it? What's the matter, George; afraid to be alone in the grand palace?"

"And you, denying your nature by allowing staff to use given names? What makes you any different?"

"I am and you know it. Your absolution is unnecessary. My path is clear…different than it once was."

"Whatever. Darby, the insurgency needs money. I'm ready to put down seventy-five. I'm looking to you for the rest."

"Look all you want. This is the end of the line."

"These people don't take no for an answer."

"So, blackmail is it? The world's filled with no-talent sloths—living off the sweat of others. How many piranha do you intend to feed, George?"

"They're leaving us no choice, Darby."

"No choice. What's money if not choice? You and I are drowning in a sea of limitless options. How can you keep a straight face, suggesting we're against the wall? So, you feel backed into a corner? Fine, allow me to offer an alternative to this seventy-five million dollar bounty. Invest in my alternative energy solution. That much money would purchase a large block of Fountain stock.

If buying into my company is incomprehensible, then build your own. Do something before the future replaces you."

George jumped up, grabbed Darby by the shoulders, pulled him close, and shouted, "Damn fool! Didn't you hear me? They're expecting payment within the week. Stop sermonizing about rainbows and just give me the money!"

Pushing George's hands away was Darby's first move; and then a solid right cross—sending George to the floor. Without missing the rhythm, Darby kneeled atop his chest and let his fists fly.

Again and again he hammered George's head. Methodically and savagely Darby barked between blows, "I thought—you would have known—better by now—than to lay a hand—on me! The next time you visit with an unwelcome touch, I'll beat you like I own you. Tell me, George, is this what you miss so much? Here it is—why don't you have some more!"

Darby ceased the attack and hovered over George to survey the damage: blood flowed from George's nose, his eyes were swollen shut and his mouth cocked open, jaw disjointed from the socket.

As fury waned, shock and disgust flooded Darby's mind—he was still capable of this? George began to move; hands shaking as they covered his face. With eyes still closed he mumbled something inaudible.

"Why George…why do you want this? Why can you not let me be? Why do you prefer brutality over humanity? Why!"

In a low and pain-filled voice, George answered, "Because it is what we are."

John handed Hubert an open envelope bearing the handwritten word, "Farewell." The letter inside read: *"Dearest, as is true of all things, your time in the Senate has come to an end. You were once steeped in power, but now that's gone. It's time to move on.*

"This is not deception. You accepted five hundred thousand dollars, coerced the committee you chair, and ignored expert findings that clearly demonstrate the financial and systemic flaws inherent in Bill S.4021. We have lovingly come to know it as the Stanton Bill.

"Take your payoff and go away. If you disregard this directive, then the world will be informed.

"No further warning shall be tendered. Farewell. A"

Chuckling at the finish, Hubert crumpled the paper and handed it back.

"It came this morning," John lamented.

"You're really in it this time, aren't you?" Hubert asked between giggles. "Do you have any idea who this 'A' character is?"

"Not for certain. But, I have a suspicion."

"A suspicion; you better have more than that if you hope to save yourself. Who is it? More importantly, is it true? Not that it needs to be. But, I'd like to know where you stand before I stick my neck out."

"As I said, I'm not sure. It may be Anne Preston with Coral Oil. I stress that it *may* be true."

"Anne Preston," Hubert repeated. "She's Weatherby's hired gun—he sure can pick 'em. You see, John, that's your problem; women. Every time a pretty tail walks by, focus is completely lost. It's been great entertainment. I always knew a peach would bring you down. It was assumed you would've at least bedded an office girl. But this one: Wow! I bet she got the better end of the bargain. You probably didn't even lay a hand on her either…Schmuck."

"It's not like that, Hubert."

"Like I said, probably didn't touch her. I'll assume you took the money—don't care what you did with it. You accepted and she knows. The bitch sounds committed. She's got nothing to lose; and obviously getting something from you leaving the Senate. Your choice seems pretty straightforward, Johnny boy; time to go. Sorry to be the one to tell you. Strike that. I'm not sorry about anything."

"Hubert, you've gotta help me. This isn't right. How can they do this? I'm a United States senator with years of—"

"Really, this hurts my ears. You're a grown man. Don't start crying. It's over. I can't…won't help you. You're going through this, like it or not. Look. Take your money and quietly leave. I'll keep the DOJ off your back; but only if you disappear. Whoever they are, 'A' means business.

I'm not falling on anything for you. Hell, even if you were innocent I wouldn't help. This is politics. I'm not your friend. I used you and you, well…you've tried to use me; unsuccessfully, I might add. The delusion you're suffering from that we're united against whoever this is is making it worse.

Just do what I tell you. Don't do a press conference or some ill-conceived fare-thee-well shindig. No one will miss you any more than they'll miss me. Trust me on this. You can spend the remainder of your days in jail or on a golf course. Today's choice determines whether you'll wear prison stripes or those goofy plaid pants—the ones you like to strut around in. That's all I've got for you, pal. Liam, pull over. I'm going to drop you here, John. I've got a meeting. The Senate Office Building is only a few blocks away."

"Sure," John stammered—stunned that it was over. "Thanks, Hubert," he managed as he exited the car. But he immediately turned to reenter the car. "This can't be it. Help me!"

Hubert cocked his leg and kicked John in the stomach, sending him outward and onto the pavement. John got off his back and attempted to force his way back in. Liam grabbed John's torso and shoved him to the sidewalk. Hubert tossed the wadded letter at John and shook his head as the car door shut.

John picked up the paper ball, stood up, and straightened his suit. He had always envisioned leaving public life in a grand gesture at a time of his choosing. As he moved along the sidewalk, the concrete went missing; feeling neither ground nor forward motion. He was numb; power that once defined him had vanished.

John entered his office via the rear door. He sat at his desk and quietly looked about the room. He realized these would be his last moments as a United States senator.

He noticed the delicate floral carving details along the ceiling molding for the first time. The ornate window woodwork was quite impressive. *How could I have overlooked something so beautiful— representing hours of painstaking effort by the craftsmen who built this office? How did I miss so much?*

The office phone rang while John reeled—oblivious to it, and his assistant calling over the speaker. *How could this have happened? Why would Anne do this? Haven't I always worked with her? I'm a United States senator! How dare she threaten me? Does she have any idea who I am? How does she think she can get away with this? Maybe it was her oil buddies. Don't they know how important I am to the Senate? A man like me doesn't come along every day. Who do they think they'll find to replace me? I have critical talents and skills. This is absurd!*

Cassandra, his assistant, stuck her head through the doorway and informed, "Senator, you have four calls on hold and a page in the waiting room who needs to deliver a package to you personally. Is there something wrong? You look upset…Senator."

"Um—yes, Cassandra—no, I'm fine. I'm going to step out for a moment. Just take care of my calls for me, will you?" "What about the package?"

"Yes, the package. Just take delivery and put it on my desk. If they won't turn it over to you, then tell them to come back later. I'm going out the back way."

The office quieted after her departure. His stomach gnawed as if being eaten from the inside. The silence was excruciating savagery, demanding, *Off with his head.* Slouching forward, nauseous and hollow, John scratched out on official stationery, *"It is with great regret that I relinquish my position as a United States senator. Recent family matters have called me away. It has been a privilege and honor to serve. Sincerely, John Stanton, US Senator."*

A tear dropped to the page while signing the document. His hands shook as he folded and stuffed it into an envelope. John scanned the room one last time—ill prepared for the emptiness. He then slipped out the rear entrance, leaving the door ajar.

"Apologies for not arriving earlier—I was only notified thirty minutes ago of the emergency meeting. Sounds like it's kicked off in fine Washington fashion. What've I missed so far? Who's being roasted at the spit?" Ethan asked.

"Not much. We've been speculating about the possibilities of such an abrupt exit. None of us have heard from him. Stanton's secretary was quite upset when she called to report the resignation letter left behind," Senator Peck explained.

Senator Beatrice Peck had been the committee's secretary for over two years. Her polite mannerisms served to soften John's overbearing personality.

"What's the committee's consensus about our absent leader's abrupt departure?" Ethan probed, as he settled into his chair.

"We hate to speculate. There could be so many reasons for such a hasty move," Beatrice replied.

Ethan smiled and panned his gaze round the conference table. "We don't hate to speculate. It's in our nature to gossip. I would venture that there've been more than a few far-fetched stories tossed about. Don't worry, boys and girls; I'm new to the committee, but not to people. My lips are sealed. All joking aside, what's on our agenda today?"

"The first order of business is to nominate a new committee chairman; the Senate will ratify later on. We should also discuss John's pet projects. We tended to follow his lead on the most pressing issues," Beatrice replied.

"Yes, we did. I for one would like to see a change in that policy," Senator Sidel blurted out.

Dean Sidel was the kind of man that wanted just enough power to hold office, but not so much that he would be visible or held accountable. He often opposed John just to exercise some authority. After making a stand, Dean would sign on with the prevailing consensus so that the responsibility was not his.

"Senator Sidel, I wanted to talk with you about the last meeting. You voiced some concern over an issue with the revised Stanton Bill. Could you shed some light on it for me?" Ethan asked.

"Senator Scott, maybe there would be a better time to discuss my personal views. We should get on with the committee's priorities," Dean suggested.

"Isn't that a priority? As I'm sure all of you remember, I worked for the Citizens' Mandamus Council. We purposely attacked the methods used to achieve this legislation's end. Now that I'm a member of this body, I still have reservations about the Stanton Bill. As a senator, I must submit that it may not be in the best interests of the American people. We might better serve our constituency by readdressing its problems, and possibly pulling it from further consideration. Are there any among this body who have similar concerns?" Ethan probed with an earnest heart, as he looked round the assembly.

They were silent—each senator turning to the others for support and direction. Senator Clark finally piped up, "I didn't wholeheartedly agree with how we pushed through the expert testimony; especially financial feasibility. I think we could look more closely at findings rejected under Stanton's leadership. There were clear indicators that solar and other electrical sources would be viable sooner than John would accept."

Hanover Clark was a legacy appointee who used a reputation from two previous generations to get elected—his father and grandfather had both been senators. Hanover's seat was held by familial ties and company deals. A mouse of a man, he followed ancestral tradition; though never wishing to serve in government. He always wanted to teach history, but lacked the courage to resist his father's will.

The remainder of the committee mirrored Hanover's sentiment. Then, the previously unmoved became alive with suggestions.

Hanover offered, "I've heard of a group in San Francisco that can produce a gigawatt of power from twenty pounds of seaweed."

Beatrice added, "What about Solartron's new mirrored solar panels? I read that in ten years a cell the size of a tablet will power a home."

"Wave generators seem to have promise as well," another committee member chimed.

Dean asked, "Has anyone heard about quantum hydro-converters? They're supposed to extract hydrogen from water, generating electricity and recapturing ninety-five percent of the mechanical energy produced."

"This is a committee that I think can make some great legislation possible. Look at all the wonderful ideas you've brought forth just now. I'd like to make a motion that we rescind the Stanton Bill submission to the floor for consideration. Will anyone second my motion?" Ethan asked.

Enthralled with imaginative solutions a moment before, now their assembly skidded to a halt. Ethan's call to action required commitment and competence; attributes in question within their minds.

The rest knew what Ethan did not; each of them had taken the money. They would not have supported John's bill otherwise—in secret wishing the legislation would go away.

Senator Jefferson Duncan spouted, "I think Ethan's on the right track and has shown the endless possibilities we missed under Senator Stanton's rule. However, why not take this one step at a time? We should readdress its core values and measure them against expert findings from the beginning; allowing our decision to fall in line with fact."

"Second," Beatrice said eagerly.

"All in favor," Senator Duncan moved.

A unanimous show of hands testified. Everyone appeared happy with the decision. Ethan was pleased that, for the first time since taking office, his wishes and will were shaping and taking action. It felt like a well-worn tool in the hand of an artisan.

Senator Duncan went on, "It's obvious that a leader has risen among us. He's shown that enthusiasm and direction can galvanize this committee into a force for change. I would therefore make a motion that the newly appointed senator from New York be nominated as our new chairman. Will anyone second?"

"I will," Senator Clark confirmed.

"Are there any other nominees?"

"I would like to nominate myself," Senator Sidel submitted.

"I'll also second this," added Senator Clark.

"Any other nominees? Then let's put it to a vote. All in favor of Senator Scott, please raise your hand. All in favor of Senator Sidel, please raise your hand. Congratulations, Senator Scott. You have the vote; nine in favor to one opposed. I'll submit our committee's choice up the chain. If ratified by your party's leadership, will you accept this position?"

"Count on it," Ethan cracked.

As the remainder of the committee clapped and nodded, relief was shared at having passed on committee chairing responsibilities. They hoped momentum would carry Ethan away.

The next morning, footsteps approached from behind as Ethan exited his car. He turned to find the vagrant encountered outside Don Giordano's. "What a surprise to see you here," Ethan lightheartedly offered.

"I get around. When you've been in Washington as long as I have, you know where all the good spots are. I wanted to thank you again and repay the generosity."

"I can't accept your money."

"Oh, no, young man, I'm unable to pay you back in script; but maybe with something of greater value."

"What's that?"

"Information…that is, if you have lasting plans."

His claim delighted Ethan. It seemed that even a homeless stranger had advice for his survival. Humoring the man, he replied, "Alright, how can you help me?"

They started strolling together towards the parking garage elevators. The man opened, "If I'm not mistaken, you know Senator Riley."

"Vaguely."

"How far into him are you? What I mean is, how much do you owe him? Has he done you any favors?"

"I don't owe Senator Riley anything."

"That's good. Don't go into debt with a man like that. He's the kind of—"

Hubert emerged from his car as they passed between parking stalls. The vagabond locked eyes with Hubert and let out a frightful scream, "Eeegh!" After wincing, head bowed and shoulders sunk, he turned away and began to leave.

"Good morning, Senator Scott," said Hubert. "You get into the office early too, I see."

"It's an old habit."

As Hubert and Ethan faced his erstwhile walking companion, the vagrant shuffled off towards the exit ramp. Ethan noted, "That's odd. He was quite sociable a moment ago." He remembered the man mumbling to himself the first time they met and assumed it was mental illness.

"Old Seneca...he's a character. Seneca's tolerated in places off limits to the general public—a permanent fixture to the joint. He's harmless," Hubert assured.

"I see," Ethan replied, attempting to accept Hubert's explanation.

"Congratulations! I understand you now head up the Energy and Natural Resources Committee?"

"News travels fast."

"Now that you're in Washington, do you find yourself missing the CMC's exploits? I'm sure you've ruffled more feathers in this town than most would care to admit. Of course, that's old news. It's good to see Congress will be putting your talents to use."

"Hubert, my good fortune is humbling. A month ago I would never have suspected this is where I'd be."

"Ethan, we both know there's no such thing as luck. Fortune, my friend, favors those prepared for it. When it comes, snatch it without regard. We are objects. It's the irresistible force. Take your recent senatorial appointment. It was no accident. Or, even more curious, being asked to run the committee you were nominated to. Can you honestly say it was an accident that they asked you to lead?"

"No. They needed someone to team-build and direct group assets. I simply made a few suggestions that made sense."

"Poppycock—I heard about the meeting. From my understanding, the moment you sat down strength poured out. More importantly, they perceived that you were meant for the role; and every senator fell in line. Best of all, you didn't lift a finger to achieve it. That's power—and it is always in short supply!"

"I will say, Hubert, you do a fine job of building up the bench. Tell me what you're selling—I can't promise to buy. But if you're straight, then at least I'll listen."

"Ethan, I'm going to like you. I can tell already. Let's get to the point. The Senate Majority Leader is intending to retire sometime this fall. Want the job?"

"You're joking. I just got here a month ago. What good could I do?"
"You may have just arrived, but you're already well-known. Business experience makes a prime candidate for almost anything in Washington. I might also add that you have the President's ear."
"Hubert, I don't yank on a single presidential appendage." "Really? That's not what I understand. You had lunch at the White House with him last winter. Isn't that so?"
"It wasn't a private gathering. There was a room full of people. I ate with the President that day."
"Ethan, don't be coy. You sat next to Anderson. He thanked you for an article you wrote about him. Did I miss anything?"
"No, that's about right."
"While most would find your unpretentious response endearing, I think it's repugnant. I'm not a maladjusted, emotionally stunted, underachieving, misanthropic, midlife crisis, forty-year-old constituent of yours. You're a man of power. Stop apologizing for it with that detestable Midwest Protestant work-ethic performance a mayoral candidate would use to get elected in Minersville, Missouri. This is Washington. Demand everything and don't apologize."
"Well, Hubert, this has been quite a conversation; and all before my first cup of coffee. Still, I should be moving on. There's a long day ahead."
"Ethan, it was a pleasure chatting. Think about what I said. Standing still quickly becomes a backward slide. Don't be surprised if that appointment is offered."

CHAPTER
IV
A SINGLE PAIR

Darby's encounter with George was a hot skewer poking his mind. More than a fight between old rivals; a nerve had been touched. He was driven by rage to destroy George, and would have continued were it not for future plans.

What coursed through Darby was deeper anger than George could touch. It was self-hatred and a wish to remove what once was. Neglect had gnawed at Darby's heart until he could no longer ignore it.

Darby picked up the desk phone a number of times; struggling to initiate a conversation with George. The event and what followed it incessantly replayed in his mind. After the EMTs had collected George from Darby's office, George exclaimed, "Hospital! Not a chance. Take me to my jet—keep your southern degenerate physicians to yourselves."

Resigned that there was no easy way to go about it, Darby called George's private line. It rang. George picked up with, "I can only imagine how you're going to top our last conversation."

Feeling a little let off the hook, Darby asked, "What did you expect, George? You can't grab a man like that and assume he won't fight back. You were in my office telling me what to do. Honestly, I should have knocked you on your ass sooner."

"There. You got it out. Feel better now?"

"You know, George, I really do. Thanks."

"Can I infer then from your much improved disposition that you've come to your senses and are ready to settle the seventy-five million?"

"Infer all you like. You'd be incorrect. I called because there are important things to discuss."

"If you're not going to pony up, then I have nothing to say. Darby,

I'll remind you that this is the Moborak we're talking about. They're believers, and don't like 'no' any better than I do. They'll kill for an ideal."

"Sounds awful familiar to me—though you wouldn't kill for an ideal; just power and money. Why did you hire them to begin with? They're crazy. This really was a bad call."

"Look who's talking, Darby."

"What?"

"All of it. You're just like them. Only you continue this philanthropic charade to cover every ugly thing done for the prize."

"I didn't call to argue. I'm not that man anymore."

"What about yesterday?"

"You had it coming—I would've done the same thing to our janitor. That's your problem, George. You treat everyone as if they live for your pleasure."

"Again, old pal, same thing."

"In what way?"

"São Paolo, dear chum. Brazil is calling."

"That's different, and it doesn't matter anymore. I'll make it right."

"How do you propose to do that, short of raising the dead?"

"George, stop. Just stop talking so I can get to the reason for my call."

"I'm all ears."

"It's time, George, for us to move forward on these technologies we're sitting on."

"You're the only one sitting on an alternative energy that actually works well. And you aren't doing anything with it."

"I'm going to release the technology."

"You sound certain. Who's to say you're right?"

"How much more money do you need, George? What are you holding on to?"

"It's not about the money, Darby. It's power. I'm not giving it away."

"Who's suggesting otherwise? I'm talking about setting the human race free. You have enough to last a hundred lifetimes. I've got more. Why are you so averse to seeing the rest enjoy what you take for granted?"

"Because they'll squander it—tell me the average American idiot understands the nature of true power, or that they'd know what to do with it. I'll tell you what'll happen; they'll squander it buying unneeded things to fill the void in their puny little hearts. People have no idea who they are or what they're capable of. The rabble knows one thing: how to waste resources when they're abundantly available."

"That may be true for some or even many. But they have the right to find out. How much more can we squeeze them before they get fed up? We're not needed! God help you if the public ever wakes up to that truth."

"God help us, you mean."

"It's time, George. We've reached a point in history where the wealthy can no longer shake down the poor because we have the power to do so—like how starving some people is more lucrative and maintains market pricing, or how pharmaceutical companies stopped curing disease fifty years ago because it's outrageously profitable to treat a patient for life instead. Humanity's ready to move on. With innovation's advancing speed, how much time is left before we're obsolete? Do you intend to wait that long? George, the future's almost here. Don't you think it's time to do something about it?"

"What are you saying, Darby…in plain English?"

"Our hold over energy is coming to an end. I see a window of opportunity and it's that engine of mine. I'm going to sell it like a refrigerator or washing machine. It'll take two billion just to start up production. Invest in it. We'll be at the forefront of a new age."

They both fell silent. Darby held his breath, hoping for sway.

Then George burst out, "Never! If you release the contraption, I'll tell the world how it was acquired."

"Good afternoon, George."

"Wait a minute! We haven't finished. What about your share?"

"My share? George, I never agreed to pay more. As it is, sounds like my money was wasted. I have no intention of throwing more away."

"Don't make this more difficult."

"No, George."

"This problem isn't going away. They want the money within a week."

"They want the money. They want my money. Mine! Let 'em come and try to take it. It's bad enough that we buy our own politicians to get anything accomplished. This is beyond toleration. I am finished being back-doored. Finished!"

"Truer words, Darby."

Xavier had yet to replace Daniel—allowing Abigail to pursue her own stories with the understanding that she would assume most of the operational roles until a suitable candidate could be hired.

Arriving in Washington, she drove straight to Senator Stanton's office from the airport. Abigail expected John would be working to pack away a large mess of papers and plaques strewn about the office. In her mind, handshakes and hugs were being exchanged—so many memories and events had shaped their lives. Instead, she found Cassandra sitting at her desk and no one else in sight—everything still in its place.

"May I help you?" Cassandra asked.

"Yes, you may. I'd like to speak with Senator Stanton,"

Abigail carried on, as if she had an appointment.

"The Senator resigned last week."

"Of course—he'll always retain the title. I was merely being polite. May I see him?"

"I'm afraid he's not in."

"When do you expect his return?"

"Never...I've not heard from him since finding the resignation letter."

"Will he come back for his private property?"

"I haven't the slightest idea," Cassandra replied—then she burst into tears.

"What's this all about, Miss…?"

"Cassandra Kennedy. I'm sorry. I don't know what's happening here. I don't know when he's returning for his things. I don't know if I even have a job anymore. No one's told me anything. I keep coming to work, hoping not to lose my position. I just know I'll be replaced by someone younger and more attractive." She began to sob again.

"I'm sure you're very good at what you do. Whoever fills Senator Stanton's position in the Senate will want to retain you. Who else could be as helpful with getting up to speed in the senatorial game as you?"

"I hope you're right."

Drawing closer to Cassandra's desk, Abigail suggested, "Maybe you can still help me."

"How?"

"You know the Senator better than anyone."

"Of course."

"Where would he go under the circumstances? Who would he confide in? Are there any establishments he frequents?" "I've tried calling. He's not answering his home or mobile phone. I can't begin to tell you who he's closest to in the Senate. Over the years, I've seen nearly every senator walk through these doors. Though of late, Senator Riley has been here more than any of the others.

"You know Senator Stanton chaired the Energy and Natural Resources Committee? They gave it to the senator from New York. Can you believe it? He's in office a week and already heading a major committee."

"Senator Scott is the Energy and Natural Resources Committee Chairman?"

"Yes."

"You don't say. Who's behind his nomination?"

"Got me."

"It's an absolute certainty that someone's hands were washed."

"Nothing's more inevitable about this place. You can't get a parking spot within ten miles of the Capitol without owing, buying or leveraging someone."

Entertained by Cassandra's candor, Abigail noted, "Senator Riley, you say. That's helpful. Where does he like to dine?" "Don Giordano's. It's where they all go."

"If I wanted to meet the senator there, how could I get in touch with him?"

"I don't know. As I said, he's not returned my calls."

"Maybe he'd return mine. Would you write down his mobile number for me?"

"Miss…ugh, I'm sorry, I didn't get your name."

"Abigail Sanders."

"Oh my, Miss Sanders, of course—I don't know why I didn't recognize you. I can't give out the senator's contact information. Under normal circumstances, it could be remedied by scheduling an appointment. But things are not normal round here."

"As you said Cassandra, he's not a senator any longer."

"I know. But, you're asking me to betray a trust. I have no idea what you plan to do with his number."

"I just want to talk with him about the decision to leave office. There're a lot of people that would like to hear what became of such a longstanding United States senator. Don't you think people need to know?"

"I don't really know what people need. I'm too worried whether I'll be able to make rent to stew over what the public wants to learn about John Stanton's retirement status."

"That's right! You do have your career and financial stability to consider—doesn't seem to have crossed Senator Stanton's mind. Did he leave you with a severance to get by on until another position could be secured?"

"He didn't."

"Okay, well, at least he had the common decency to tell you why he left in such a hurry. After all, you're his most trusted assistant. He would've rendered that professional courtesy."

"You'd think so, wouldn't you?" Cassandra added bitterly. She blushed red, wrote down John's mobile phone number and handed it to Abigail. Out loud, she reminded her, "As I said, Miss Sanders, it would be inappropriate to give out Senator Stanton's private information. Is there anything else I can do?"

"No, thank you. Good luck. I hope the incoming senator will see your talents and make use of what is clearly an irreplaceable public servant. Good day."

The moment Abigail exited the building, John's number was dialed. She intended to leave a message when the line picked up, and was caught off guard when he actually answered. "John!" she exclaimed, preparing to probe him for information.

"Yes." John's tired voice drifted out of the phone. After a moment he asked, "Anne, is that you?"

Abigail wanted to see where the conversation could go, so she said nothing. "I knew you'd get in touch. Why did you turn against me? Haven't I always done what you asked? I don't deserve this."

Abigail cleared her throat. "Senator Stanton, my name is Abigail Sanders of TTN. I was hoping to get a few words regarding your precipitous retirement from public office. Would you be willing to tell me your side?"

"My side of what? How did you get this number? Who put you up to this? No, I won't talk with you. Go away. Don't call this number again!"

"Senator, who's Anne; and how was she connected to your career?"

An abrupt click reported the phone call's conclusion.

After pecking a familiar number into the keypad, she said, "Senator Scott, you're a busy man. Rumors are circulating about you. I need a favor and was hoping you had time to meet today."

"Wish I could. It'd be nice to catch up. But my itinerary is full until nine tonight. Doing a story on anyone I know?"

"Maybe."

"You fit in well here. No one ever gives a straight answer. If the building was on fire and I asked how to escape, it'd take someone ten minutes to point out the exit sign."

"How about tomorrow?"

"I can meet you at the end of the day, around six. Will that work?"

"See you then."

Hubert and Jack traveled in a black government limousine. A uniformed police officer gawked at them with suspicion—not grasping why a sitting senator would help serve a cease-and-desist order.

Dismayed, Jack thought, *Why is this senator using the DOJ to stick the CMC?* He could've made a speech. What threat does the Citizens' Mandamus Council pose this guy? The more he tried to understand the propriety of this legal function, the more he disliked the senator and his part in it.

Hubert peered across the car at Jack without any regard, or acknowledgement that he was someone he owed professional courtesy. If their seats hadn't faced, Hubert would not have even turned Jack's way.

Hubert relished the moment. He could do almost anything in the name of national security; and he loved it.

As the car passed in front of David's building, Hubert demanded, "Driver, stop here! Don't bother looking for a parking spot. This is government business."

From the front seat, the officer looked back at Hubert with subdued disdain. It was an unmarked car. Traffic would bottleneck in no time. The three left their car for the office. Blinking brake lights demonstrated that no one else on the street mattered.

Charity, the receptionist at the Washington CMC office, greeted them as they entered. "Welcome to the Citizens' Mandamus Council. How may I assist you?"

"Ted Stevenson," Hubert tersely posited.

Jack interjected, "Is Mr. Stevenson in? We have an important matter to discuss."

"Yes, he is. Let me see if Ted's available."

"Thank you," Jack replied.

After Charity had disappeared down the corridor, Hubert, angry and condescending, asked, "What are you doing? We're not having a cup of coffee with the guy. You're here to serve a writ and court order. Act like you work for the Justice Department and not some lousy not-for-profit legal-aid office. You represent the United States government in matters of law."

"Thank you, Senator, I wasn't certain of my duties until you explained them," Jack returned.

"Watch it, counselor. That's not a tone I'm accustomed to hearing from one of Donald Ruiz's flunkies."

"Senator, what are you doing here? No, hold that thought for a moment. What am I doing here? You seem to know something I don't. Why does a staff attorney need to accompany a police officer to serve a standard court order?"

The officer quietly watched as Jack and Hubert sized each other up. He understood his role as a functionary. Not knowing why something so trivial needed two powerful men, there was a good chance that trouble would become a part of this action, making it less than trivial.

"Just do your job—stop asking questions," Hubert snapped.

"Yes, sir—Masser."

Charity returned and announced, "This way, gentlemen."

As they entered Ted's office, Jack asked, "Are you Ted Stevenson?"

"Yes," Ted answered, rising to his feet from behind the desk with worry etched on his face.

"My name is Jack Miller with the United States Department of Justice. This is Officer Malloy of the Washington DC Police Department. To my right is Senator Hubert—"

"Riley. Yes, I know Senator Riley. The CMC has investigated him before."

"Investigated me? That's hot!"

"You obviously have some duty to perform. So, proceed."

Jack read from the court order. "The Federal Court for the District of Columbia hereby orders the Citizens' Mandamus Council, its board, employees and contractors to cease all surveillance, investigation, fundraising and all other normal daily business activities. This writ of mandamus accompanying the court order requires the Citizens' Mandamus Council to be dissolved, as its only legal function has been halted by said court order. Copies of this federal writ and court order shall also be filed with the secretary of state of the state of New York; home of the Citizens' Mandamus Council's corporate registration."

Jack handed Ted the paperwork. Ted sat down.

Hubert beamed a smile. "There now…We've performed our circus act for the sake of the justice. Gentlemen, I'd like a few private words with Mr. Stevenson."

The police officer hoofed it out of the office—now even less certain why he had been required to attend. *Not good,* Jack thought, shaking his head as he, too, departed. Hubert sat down and quietly waited for the door to close.

"My only regret is that we didn't do this sooner. Why we allowed crackpots to carry on this charade for so long is beyond comprehension. I must be slipping in my old age," Hubert posited, as though he were thinking out loud.

"This won't stand. You know it; it's why you gloat. The people won't allow it," Ted defiantly claimed.

"What do the people have to do with this?"

"How do you do it?"

"What?"

"Forget those who put you in office?"

"They didn't put me in office. I did. I simply let them believe they elected me. Please don't tell me you believe we're living in a republic. You work in Washington and should know better."

"A poor republic, to be sure; if that weren't so, the CMC wouldn't be needed. You can still be voted out of office."

Smiling, Hubert suggested, "But who would want that?"

"We're going to catch you one day. Count on it."

"My friend, there's no more 'we'. The CMC is finished. That piece of paper is my license to lock you and David Samuel up for as long as I can buy a judge to do so if you violate its terms."

"Senator, no amount of money or influence will save you from what's coming next."

"I like your spirit, but there's nothing to the threat. It's hollow and empty, like the Citizens' Mandamus Council," Hubert stated as he rose to his feet. He turned to walk out but then stopped. Without turning to face Ted, he said, "You know, I thought there'd be more pleasure in ending you than this. I feel cheated. After all the headaches you've given me, I was certain elation would overflow. But there isn't any at all. I really couldn't care less." He then looked to Ted and said, "Maybe that's what I've learned from this. Your sort are meaningless to those in power. No matter what we do to you, there will be no satisfaction. Still, at least you'll be gone—that's something."

Hubert lifted his head with relief as he left the office. Shoe heel strikes echoed as he strode down the hallway—an ominous rhythm resembling drums for the dead.

Grim-faced, Ted tapped out David's mobile phone number. He couldn't believe what was happening.

"Hello."

"David, it's Ted."

"I assume you received notification."

"How's you know?"

"Every office has been served the same writ and court order."

"Every office…I can't believe it. Who served you?"

"What do you mean?"

"Senator Riley was present, along with a DOJ attorney and a DC cop. He had a few unsavory words for the CMC."

"Riley must really want to make a point."

"What point? Bone Yard corruption is piled so high that elected officials no longer need to hide their degenerate affiliations," Ted offered bitterly.

"You may be more right than you know."

"What are we going to do?"

"Exactly what the court has ordered."

"What! How can you say that?" Ted exclaimed angrily.

"I just wanted to see if you were alive. Ted, this is only the first round.

They picked a fight with a legal cohort. Think about the firepower at our fingertips. We have over sixty attorneys under the CMC's umbrella; all dedicated to the concept of holding the government accountable. The writ is a slap in the face—so what! Everyone takes a hit in a schoolyard scrape. The court order is the meat and potatoes. We are to cease surveillance, investigation, fundraising and all other normal daily business activities. Tell me, Ted, what've we really lost?"

"Everything—this is what we do."

"Sure, but so does most every other person on the planet. Cease surveillance; it can't be enforced unless they plan to surgically remove our eyes. Cease investigation; when was the last time the CMC sued for private information? It was eight years ago—we've only done it five times. All the data we collect is public information granted to every citizen of this country by the Freedom of Information Act. It can't be enforced. What does normal business activities mean? It's too vague and cannot stand.

"Fundraising may be a problem. Our endowment can't indefinitely sustain operations. Without donations we'll eventually dry up. This is our first lawful salvo to be fired: the appeals process—and must begin immediately."

Ted was champing at the bit with enthusiasm. "What do you need to me to do next?"

"Arrange a companywide conference call for later today."

"Why wait?"

"I'm not waiting. More information is needed. Why was Senator Riley involved? Who else is with him? There's more to this."

At five o'clock, David dialed into the conference call. "Could I ask everyone to mute their phones?" Voices and conversations ceased. He then said, "Thank you. It's the first time our family has come together for such a call.

"As I'm sure you're aware, the Department of Justice has taken up a position against the Citizens' Mandamus Council. Outwardly, there appears to be large support from the United States Senate on this move; given Senator Riley's prominence and presence at the DC office.

"My first response to this crisis was the same sensation experienced years ago when our first office opened. What a journey it's been opening a branch in each state. The CMC has brought countless ruthless tyrants to their knees in submission to the rule of law.

"When first reading the court order items, little of it concerned me. After all, as I explained to Ted Stevenson earlier today, most of what we do is legitimate for any citizen in the United States to do. This was my thinking when conceiving this organization: hold those in power accountable within the confines of our legal framework.

"As a young attorney, I would advise any lawyer facing legal action to seek impartial advice. Working in the company of attorneys, this humorously left me to call on a law professor from my schooldays. As was discussed on more than one occasion in class, he would caution that law is a fine and noble pursuit, but don't look for justice in the courts. Then and now I struggle with that truth, which continues ignorant of its own impotence.

"Conversations with those in the land's highest court proved surprisingly disappointing. It's the opinion of four United States Supreme Court Associate Justices that the Citizens' Mandamus Council is an unnecessary organization—creating confusion and cowboy legalism in a system already congested with too much bureaucracy. Our services, in their opinion, neither serve the public good nor stop corruption of power.

"Though this is not an official legal opinion, it's one personally held by those associate justices. Any appeal reaching their court would likely be denied by at least those four judges. With eight Associates and one Chief Justice sitting on the Supreme Court, it's likely we would lose. Knowing that success is unlikely makes a wise man pause.

"The remaining question is: Should prudence prevail? Earlier today, I was certain most of the court order could not be upheld. Now that my counsel has advised that the alternative is so, I'm forced to consider breaking the law for the first time in my professional career.

"The Citizens' Mandamus Council has always abided by our country's laws. Should I advocate breaking them now that their taste does not suit me? I'm not a moral relativist and this leaves me in conflict. I'm at war with my conviction to work within the confines of a legal system, which no longer serves the common good; favoring only the privileged.

"What must we do? All who have taken a journey of great risk have asked this. I don't have an answer for you right now. I'm not advocating capitulation. The Citizens' Mandamus Council must not surrender its birthright in human history.

"As of the close of business today, I am instructing all of you to report to work each day. Please keep the home office informed of your current caseload. But, cease any further activities. We will be seeking further advice before the executive board determines the best course of action.

"You'll be informed of our decision and direction in the coming days. Thank you for your continued hard work and dedication to such a worthy cause. I'll be addressing you again soon."

David ended the call and leaned back in his chair. The silence of the office pounded his head. He imagined every office was experiencing the same terrible void. His mind's eye saw fear on the faces of his employees.

CHAPTER

V

TOP TO BOTTOM

The savory aroma from Ethan's cup invocated the day as he studied the newspaper headline, which read, "The CMC's Last Writ." He leaned forward in shock; surveying the article. It discussed the Attorney General's thoughts on the matter and recounted the CMC's most important accomplishments.

He felt worse about his own choices; being away from the CMC when it needed him most. Ethan reached for the phone and then stayed his hand—deciding not to call David just yet. *If I can't help, then who can? I've yet to force anyone's hand in Washington. Some sort of emergency meeting would get things moving. Who would I convene? Anne could help…maybe. Corruption always begins with a favor. Not a good idea. What do I do? Who's trustworthy?*

As he scoured his mind, Hubert knocked and then cracked open the office door.

"Are you available, Senator?" Hubert asked.

Ethan emerged from his stupor, not really aware of who was talking, and replied, "Yes. Please come in."

"Senator Scott, you're in the office early…again. The news just wouldn't let you sleep?"

"I get most of my own work done in the early morning.

After opening for business, nothing concrete is achieved."

Laughing and nodding, Hubert said, "But this is reality. Nothing's supposed to be completed. The system is built on inefficiencies. The quickest way to accomplishing nothing in Washington is by doing your job."

"I can't accept this axiom. Much is realized in the wee hours."

"For now, maybe—it won't last. You might just as soon move a mountain as change the self-preserving nature of politics. No one here lives long without friends. Friends come with a price. Any friend that doesn't cost something is a fraud. But this conversation is way too serious for the morning. I only dropped by to check on you. How are you getting along?"

"Quid pro, Senator Riley—what's this concern costing me?"

"Right now…absolutely nothing. I'm following up on a bet."

"A bet?"

"Of sorts—I'm certain this is not where you'll end up; it's only the beginning. Like I said last week, your future's bright. Have you put any thought into my suggestion?"

"None."

"That's too bad—no rush, though. I'm simply keeping the idea alive. You'll know what to do when the time comes. Off topic…you must have a few thoughts about what's happened to your old friend."

As Hubert asked, resentment bubbled in Ethan's mind. The question's tone denoted a satisfaction in the council's demise.

"This is rubbish. They'll be back in business within the week," Ethan replied, staring into Hubert's eyes.

Hubert laughed. "Ethan, you do possess a certain charm. Loyalty is a splendid characteristic and highly valued. However, I differ with you on this point. The Citizens' Mandamus Council is down, and is going to stay down; even if it doesn't know yet."

"You say that with such confidence, Hubert."

"No less than you advocate the alternative."

"But I speak from experience—knowing the man you denigrate. David will not relent."

"I too am in the know. The desire for the CMC's cessation is near unanimous. Without support, it must come to an end."

"It's got support. I've delivered speeches to crowds numbering in the thousands; as has David. People love and subscribe to what he's doing."

"What does that have to do with this discussion?"

"Everything—we're talking about the people's support."

"No, we're talking about support. That's a different animal. America's a lie. This republic exists as a shallow reflection of democratic idealism. Without the blessing of those holding true power, one cannot exist here."

Ethan smiled—feeling superior to Hubert's position. "You're talking about power-brokering? This is what won't last—it flickers, burns bright, and then disappears, leaving its holder cold in the dark."

"Is there a philosopher in the room? You orate with such assuredness. Do please educate this old man on politics and power," Hubert ribbed.

"Not intimately knowing you, I would hate to offend with generalizations."

"So your pet theory lacks the specificity needed to be grounded in reality."

"I just don't wish to hurl a brickbat."

"Ethan, you can't. I am a senator. Nothing you say or do will ever hurt."

"Fine. The power you're talking about has some grounding; but only on the surface and only for the moment. What you claim the Senate wields over our people is not power—merely unchecked corruption."

"Sounds compelling. What are you proposing will check and balance—staving off evil corruption?"

"Accountability."

"Accountability…really? You think so—of whom and by whom?"

"Just average everyday people."

"Here we go again with your high-minded notion. Power is not with the people. They, as a whole, influence nothing."

"That's because, as a whole, they largely choose not to. Most every citizen of this and every other country simply wish to live life—having as little to do with government workings as possible. They just want to do their job, make their living, raise their family, live their lives and go home at the end of the day."

"That's a fairly broad assumption…and a lot of theirs there," Hubert joked.

Ignoring the humor, Ethan continued, "No, it's not. It's self-evident, or more people would run for public office."

"I'd agree the average Joe wants it given to them on a silver platter. What of it?" Hubert poked.

"This…Just because the everyman wants nothing to do with politics doesn't mean they lack power. They merely want to live in peace. You assume that if one had power, then they would put it to use like so many you've referenced from the Bone Yard."

"Ethan, this is getting off the point."

"No, Hubert, it's actually on target. What you've failed to demonstrate is that you grasp the nature of power. You have only admitted that there are corruptors who would use it for their own gain."

"Tell me then, since you appear so certain of your superior position. What's the nature of power?" Hubert asked.

"Power is neither good nor evil. It's the force behind the lever, which moves the world. It's a means. It is; whether humans exist or not. Would the sun still shine if humans never existed? That's the proverbial falling tree in the forest. What good would the sun do a human if he didn't exist: Nothing, right? But, the sun would still shine."

"Alright, we can agree that the sun shines regardless of human presence. This is not the same as human power," Hubert stated.

"Human power: What's that? Are you saying there are different kinds of power?"

"Obviously."

"Hubert, I think we are getting somewhere."

"It's good you're catching on."

"I'm catching your misconception. You claim there are many kinds of powers. I would offer that there is one power, utilized a multitude of different ways."

"This conversation's getting a little strange."

"Stay with me for a moment. I want to nail this down."

"Fine, convince me that electricity coming from a wall socket feeding your desk lamp is the same power I wield in the Senate," Hubert demanded, crossing his arms.

"Easy enough—tell me, Hubert, would my desk lamp illuminate without electricity?"

"No."

"In the United States of America can a bill be passed into law without the Senate?"

"As our laws stand today: no."

"Good. Tell me what makes the lamp produce light and what makes a bill become law."

"You pay your bill. The local utility company provides electricity. Power passes through the lines in your office and into the lamp, providing a lightbulb the required juice to illuminate."

"Perfect. Now the law; tell me how it's made," Ethan pushed on.

"Rudimentarily speaking, a bill is proposed by the Senate or House of Representatives for consideration. It's sent to the proper committee for study and consideration. After a lot of wrangling, the legislation is okayed and put on the calendar. It's then debated and put to a vote. In the end, if it raises enough congressional and presidential support, the bill passes. If not, it fails."

"There you have it."

"What do you mean? I've done nothing other than provide a description of two completely different things," Hubert huffed.

"Not true. In both narratives power was needed to complete the task at hand."

"Yes, but the kind of power was different."

"How?"

"The lamp needs electrical power and the bill uses political power."

"Ostensibly, you'd be correct, Senator Riley. Let's tease out the nature of these supposedly different power types. Electrical power—is it the light that makes this room bright so early before the sun has risen? I would say that it's the bulb, which produces the light with electricity's help. Would you agree?

"Yes."

"Excellent. So does this make it the leverage, which forces the light to come forth?"

"I would have to agree," Hubert capitulated, annoyed.

"Again, on the surface you appear to be correct. However, in reality you're not. A lever is simply a long rod, which forces a heavy object upward with the application of enough downward force on the opposite end. I would say that the lever is the filament inside the lightbulb, which emits light when enough electrical current flows through it. The electricity is the force applied to the lever. The object forced up or outward is light. Can we agree on this?" Ethan asked.

"It seems to make sense," Hubert agreed—becoming intrigued by the conversation's abstract turn.

"Good. Let's move onto a bill's passage then. I think it's obvious the bill is the object lifted. Would you agree?"

"Yes."

"Wonderful. Let's identify the other pertinent particulars. What might the lever be, which forces the bill into existence, Hubert?"

"Senators write the bill, push it through the system and finally put it to a vote."

"That's correct. Now, tell me what force exerts downward upon this lever?"

"The will or desire of the Senate, House of Representatives and the White House to push through the legislation,"
Hubert said.

"Perfect. I could not have said it better myself. So, by your own words, the power needed for these two examples to exist is electricity and a will or desire. Is this correct?"

"Yes."

"On the face of it, you're once again correct. At this juncture clarity will not prove you wrong, but merely elucidate that they are the same in reference to power."

"Prove it."

"Are not both of these things a force?"

"Yes."

"One is a force of will and the other a force of nature."

"But here's where you're flawed, Ethan: one is will and the other is nature."

"Maybe or maybe not—allow me to pose you a very simple question. Is the force a particular of will and nature, or is the will and nature a characteristic to describe force?"

"You're employing a rhetorical shell game to influence the argument's outcome."

"No, I'm not. I'll ask you an even simpler question. It was mentioned a few moments ago that the sun has not yet risen. Was this not uttered?"

"Yes."

"When the sun rises, light will strike the earth in many different colors. Do you agree this will happen," Ethan asked.

"Of course."

"Tell me: are the colors a characteristic of light or is light a characteristic of color?"

"Colors are characteristic of light."

"Without light, colors cannot exist. Do you agree?" Ethan probed.

"Yes."

"Would you agree that one must accept visible light as primary to a color's existence for human eyes?"

"Yes."

"Good, then let me charge you once again. Can will exist without force?"

"No."

"Can force exist without will?"

"Yes, but in other things."

"That's fine. But it's your contention then that will is subordinate to force."

"I guess so."

"What about electricity's force of nature? Using the same line of questioning, what is subordinate? Can this naturally occurring and manmade event exist without force?"

"No, it cannot."

"Then, you would agree that electricity's nature is also subordinate to force?"

"I would say so."

"As you agreed earlier, power is really a reference made to the force applied to a lever which moves an object."

"Yes, I did."

"Now that we agree upon the definition of power, would you also agree that it exists in its true nature outside human beings?"

"Meaning what?"

"Meaning that just like the sunlight example, it exists whether humans do or not. Can you agree with this?"

"I suppose I would need to."

"With that agreement then, the human use of power, whether it would be electrical, political or any other is also a measure of choice. Would you agree that one must choose to use electrical power in one's home or exercise political will to push through a piece of legislation?"

"Yes."

"Then it would follow that just because a person doesn't choose to use electrical or political power does not mean they cannot when they choose to."

"I suppose so; even though everyday practice of political power seems to point the other way."

"Then you agree with me that what you said was a true exercise in power by our senatorial kinfolk is merely a corruption or misuse of the power granted them by its citizenry—the misused trust of the public's abdication to be wisely ruled. The people's failure remains not in the lack of power, but their mistake in not holding accountable those appointed to office. Would you agree to this?"

"No, Ethan, I don't. One has nothing to do with the other. You may have rightly described the fundamental nature of power, but haven't proven its application in the example of senatorial power verses that of the people."

Frustrated by the lack of gained understanding and realizing the day was once again beginning to get away, Ethan suggested, "Hubert, let's save that conversation for another time. I have so much to do. Maybe the next time you stop by we can debate the issue further."

"Another time then—though it's unlikely you'll convince me otherwise. Ethan, there is one thing I came here to discuss with you. More to the point, I wanted to help. It's about your friend. You should do everything you can to stay out of it. It's for your own good. We allowed the CMC to exist for as long as it was convenient and stayed out of the way. That time has passed. Their continued disruption of our business matters has to come to an end. Do yourself a favor and don't get involved. That's all I needed to say. Have a good day in the Senate," Hubert offered—as if granting Ethan partiality. He then walked out, leaving the door open.

A smart chirp announced a text in Ethan's inbox. Ethan felt a sharp disgust for his professional constituency. He shook his head, smiled, and tapped the phone's screen. A text message opened. *Ethan, your entire committee is in it; same as Stanton. Do something about it.* Ethan pushed his chair back from the desk; stunned and angry. Not recognizing the phone number, he pecked out the reply, *Who is this?* His confused mind raced as he awaited a response. *There's no way these people are all guilty.* And then the minutes and seconds of his committee interactions made sense; *hesitancy to address questions; the nervous nature of their responses—they always seemed skittish.* Excited that he had solved a problem with his Hubert dialectic, the dread of another step backwards following forward movement churned his stomach. *I'm not running their race anymore—got to do something worthwhile. There's no way to know that this message is authentic. Until someone lays evidence at my feet I'm presuming nothing. If this is selling out, so be it. I've got to keep moving; CMC or no CMC.*

As Hubert made his way towards the elevators he thought about Ethan's discourse. Though exalted in its notion, Hubert, felt convinced of his power over others. As the door opened, he entered, mulling the question: *Is this power or drunken corruption?* After the doors closed, Hubert tired of the deeper implications. *Doesn't matter.*

Suddenly, like a lightning strike, Hubert fell to his knees, feeling the axe blade cutting through his legs. The dark prince laughed in the unseen distance. Hubert wailed in agony as coal embers burned his shins. Then it was gone from his mind; and Hubert couldn't remember why he was kneeling, dripping sweat. He immediately got to his feet and shook his head as if waking from a daydream.

Ethan's busy routine had set in. Wasteful meetings and discussions filled every spare moment. At the end of the day, after his last meeting had ended, he remembered Abigail would soon pay a visit—rousing him from a monotonous lockstep.

Jane opened the office door and said, "Senator Scott, a Miss Sanders is here to see you."

"Thank you, Jane. Show Miss Sanders—"

"Hello, Ethan," Abigail said as she passed through the doorway.

His face flushed red. Jane pretended not to notice, closing the door behind as she departed. Ethan rose from behind his desk to shake her hand, but Abigail embraced him with a warm hug instead.

"It's good to see you. No interviews, right?"

"None, unless you've got inside information about the Senate you'd like to share."

"Nothing yet—I'll get back to you when there's something good. So whose heels are you nipping this week? I know you didn't come for the museums."

"I'm doing a story on Stanton. No one seems to know his whereabouts. I reached him by phone, but he wouldn't say anything. I was hoping you could help—any idea where I might find him; or know someone who does?"

"You're asking me? I just got here—seems like nothing moves in the cemetery. Honestly, if I ran my newspaper like our government, then I would've been out of business. That's off the record," Ethan injected with a grin.

"Don't worry, Ethan, I won't out you. It's not exactly a secret."

"I was just speaking with a senator this morning close to Stanton. I can see what he knows and get back with you."

"Thanks. Your world's been an interesting place the last few weeks. I heard about the Citizens' Mandamus Council—you must be infuriated."

"I'm not. I was surprised. But David's a fighter. This is not the end."

"Know something?"

"You're always working an angle. No, I don't have anything."

"You getting involved?"

"Don't think I can. Whatever could be done would fill a few lines of news; but that's the extent of it. This is a legal slug match and will be won in the courts. I'm just a senator. My job's to make laws and represent people; not act out of personal gratification."

"You're the right man for the job, Ethan. I hope you weather this choice well. Washington's not a place for likes of you."

"That's dark."

Smiling she went on, "It's fine. I deliver good and bad news every day. But…I don't know…in recent years corruption has metastasized. There isn't a day that goes by when I don't report someone or some organization dedicated to doing good was put down—all for money, fame or influence. Your friend David's a perfect example. What could he have done to deserve this?"

Ethan agreed, "It's a real loss. But, I can't believe it'll hold. The CMC's too important. Who's left to hold these greenback-jockeys accountable? Every other regulatory and watchdog agency has sold out. I don't know what the solution is. But David will find it."

"How about you—has it all turned out like you thought? Are you making a difference?"

"So far: No. I can't seem to break away from the day-to-day minutiae to actually work on projects that would benefit anyone. This'll change. It must. If I need to stop seeing everyone who comes through my office door, then that is what it may come to."

"Does that include visits and the occasional interview from me?"

"Exceptions could be made."

Abigail's lips indicated that she was pleased. "It's nice, you know."

"What's that?"

"To see someone invested in something they're passionate about— wanting to make a difference and willing to do what it takes to achieve their goals. On the altar of progress, work and invention have been sacrificed—replaced by efficient production models and bureaucrats that no longer build or offer anything useful; other than justification for their existence."

"You give me too much credit, Abbey. I'd agree that a large measure of my day is spent paying homage to the system of government and not governing at all."

A pause found its way into their conversation. It was a brief moment—perceived by both to span onward for a while.

"You're seeing someone, aren't you?" Abigail asked.

Ethan reluctantly replied, "I am seeing someone. You?"

"I'm happily wed to my job. He can be tedious at times, but quite the faithful fellow. It's that woman I saw you with in Dallas, isn't it?"

"Yes."

"You're cagey when it comes to romance, Senator."

"It's a part of the business," Ethan shot back—hoping to divert any more questions about Anne.

"Well?"

"Well what?"

"Tell me about her. Who is she? What does she do? How did you meet?"

Smiling, Ethan stalled, "You're awful nosy."

"Part of the business—now quit evading or I'll do a series on the Washington dating scene and profile you."

"Alright, her name is Anne Preston. She's a lobbyist for Coral Oil. I met her on a plane last winter."

"Oh my…you're in trouble aren't you? A sitting senator seeing a lobbyist: I can't think up gossip this good."

"Abbey, you promised."

"I promised nothing…Alright, my lips are sealed. Tell me more. Is it serious?"

"I don't know."

"Just when I thought you were the only man on the planet grown up enough to talk about his emotions without feeling emasculated, you flip the chicken switch."

"It's not like that. I can't tell you because I honestly don't know."

"You're seeing her. You must feel something for the woman. She's beautiful, by the way."

"She is attractive, and very independent I might add: both features that are attractive to me. I don't know, though. The relationship vacillates so much. At times I think I know her and believe that a future is possible. Other times her actions make me question my thinking."

"Are you making it more complicated than it needs to be, Ethan?"

"My relationships have always been challenging; especially when I was younger. This time it's not my doing. I think our dynamic is just that: complicated and undefined."

"But should it be that hard?"

"I've often asked myself that same question. Guess the most immediate response is it shouldn't. Still, human beings have a way of making it so."

"What about us?" Abigail asked.

Not expecting that question, Ethan stumbled to ask, "What do you mean?"

"I think we're friends. I've never asked for friendship. Nor have you. Yet, I feel very close and want good things for you. I felt all that without the need for definition. Shouldn't relationships be that simple?"

"They should, but aren't."

"Why?"

"I would say that honesty is the culprit; and the character to be honest. When deception finds its way into any dynamic, confusion flourishes."

"Do you believe Anne is dishonest?"

"No. But there are times when I'm not sure I know her. Maybe that's my real hesitation. I don't truly understand Anne. Like you, I believe that this should be the easiest of things. Maybe it's hard because this relationship is wrong. I'm still watching how it all unfolds."

"Sounds ominous."

"Maybe; or maybe it's better than I interpret."

"How long will you wait to make a decision?" Abigail asked— realizing it was important to her.

Ethan understood the meaning behind her question. Though he

wasn't going to make a decision today, discussing Anne pushed her into the forefront of his mind. He liked Abbey much more than he had taken time to acknowledge.

Ethan replied, "There are times for action. Actually, it's almost always a good time to act. However, I'm going to let this relationship reveal itself."

Shaking off the mood, Abigail found her mind's way back to Stanton. Clearing her throat, she said, "So you'll call me if Stanton's whereabouts are uncovered?"

"Count on it."

"Word is you were bumped up to his old position as committee chairman."

Ethan smiled—attempting to appear humble. "I was. It's no big deal. I'm really just the fall guy if something goes wrong. That's all it means to be in charge."

"Ha! Ethan, don't campaign for me. Yes, leadership is being willing to assume responsibility for those subordinate to you. But it's much more and you know it. Don't placate. You'll ruin my respect for you."

"Just trying to be gracious."

"A regal quality, albeit unnecessary; you already have me. I mean I already think of you as a friend," Abigail quickly clarified to cover exposed feelings.

Mindful of the context, Ethan provided an exit. "I'm sure you've got plans tonight. I still have a few more hours of work before cutting out."

David perched in his cave, waiting for the office to empty. Sasha had left for home on foot moments before. Heat still radiated from the concrete sprawl like midday. Sweat fell with each step. Ominous shadows stretching from bowels to building tops striped her face as she weaved through pedestrians.

After the last stragglers had cleared out of the office, David locked the entrance door and returned to his desk in a pondering solitude. *I'm not lying down. There's got to be a way to fight them, but they'll counter every legal angle I know.*

Feeling closed in, David got up and trudged to the conference room. Leaning against the window, he watched the city slowly grow dark—taking in the silence as a dreary cityscape spilled in through the windows.

He then noticed the twelve empty chairs surrounding the conference table. His thoughts were not thoughts at all; but an attempt to order overwhelming feelings. The Citizens' Mandamus Council was more than a workplace. It was home. His identity and all that was held close enmeshed this thing. It appeared for the first time since the Council's birth that its end might be near.

David's mind then shifted. *Two decades—might as well have been five—so much sacrificed for the CMC's sake. Countless holidays, family, friends left behind in the pursuit of perfection. After all that's been accomplished for justice, so little remains to demonstrate I ever existed. 1996…my God—life's flown by. Look what's become of me.*

In an explosive rage, he grabbed the closest chair and threw it at a window, breaking the inner pane. Shards flew in every direction after the crash sounded; the chair falling to the floor and resting on its side.

David drilled the ceiling with his eyes, raised arms and yelled, "Why! Wasn't I good enough? Haven't I sacrificed enough? Why would you do this to me?"

He clawed for answers, knowing they would not be forthcoming—David was on his own. Done in with life and himself, he eased into another chair. Then he slammed fists upon the table, attempting to release his anger.

With fury, he ranted aloud as if addressing another person, "How stupid could I be to think I would change the nature of humanity… even a little? We're lost! It would seem that I'm the last to acknowledge the fact. I am a complete and utter imbecile! What kind of fool spends his life looking out for a population that won't help themselves? What am I, a herdsman? Should I have donned a proper cloak and cane to guide the mindless twits I ridiculously believe will hear my words…and act on them?

"My words…why did I believe my words had any value or were worth hearing? I spoke the truth and what was in my heart. When did this ever do anyone a bit of good? How many martyrs have lost their lives this way, while the cowardly hordes stand by—watching a human with a backbone slaughtered for shaking up corruption's monotony?

"I must be completely raving mad! Decades swept under a rug as if they were never spent. My work has mattered not one iota to these people. Twenty years! I haven't been away from the Council in all that time. My youth is gone! My youth never existed! When I was young, there was romance; but not for me. No, sir…not for David. The CMC was his lover. What was I thinking? How could I believe the best of circumstances would prevail? This only had one ending and I am living it. You idiot; you Godforsaken lunatic; you deserve every bit of this. I hope you rot in a dark lonely sewer."

David cradled his head in his hands and wailed; deep and sorrowful howls at the loss of his identity and what should have been. His cries echoed again and again until his throat grew hoarse. Silence then fell on the conference room.

What a waste. There were so many other paths. This was the one I chose; the one with the greatest possibility of failure.

Like waves returning to the shore, the flotsam and jetsam, his life was a debris field of good intentions scattered amongst the detritus. He could not regain lost time, the beauty and strength readily granted to the young. His life had become the wager that did not pay.

David rested his head on the table. The ache of exhaustion pulsed through his muscles. Emotional disparity transmitted a phantom physical injury, as if an arm had been torn from his shoulder.

David sat up, hair in disarray, eyes swollen and cheeks reddened by forceful tears. Calming from hysterics, the only question left unanswered had yet to be posed. *Why did I do it? Why did I create the Citizens' Mandamus Council to begin with?*

As the reasons and rationalizations moved through his mind, David once again bellowed. "Where are all the people I've helped? Surely some of them feel they owe me something? Where are they? I stopped countless government officials over the years from doing their worst to an unsuspecting public—and this is the thanks I get? Where's my help? Why is no one standing up for me?

"How can they call themselves Americans when all they've ever done is take; take from programs, charitable organizations, or anyone with a bleeding heart? These people who've always been in great need of saving will always need saving. When are they going to step forward and risk for someone other than themselves?

"I can't stand this! This can't be what and who I've suffered for. 'Please, Mr. Samuel. You must help us. They're taking our program dollars and using them for their selfish wants. You must stop them for us. We don't stand a chance without you.'

"Countless; I cannot calculate the number of people I've fought for. From those many, not even one will sacrifice for the sake of the CMC. Not even one person has spoken out about this. I can't believe these are the people I have been fighting for! This can't be the same country I was raised in. I'm betrayed by those I've sacrificed and lost everything for. This is madness! Am I crazy to have ever accepted this responsibility?"

His head fell forward in the dark—a defeated heart bleeding slow enough not to die, but more than enough to be critical.

CHAPTER
VI

TRYING NOT TO THINK

After the last contentious directors' meeting, Shane Ashby felt the adjacent park would diffuse egos and tempers. East of the Mission Control Building, vehicles from previous NASA missions were nestled throughout a forty-acre forest.

As they entered the park from the west, Shane said, "I'm glad you all could make it. We have a lot of ground to cover."

"Would that be literally or are you chewin' the fat? The arboretum is huge," Charlie jibbed.

"Both."

"This isn't going to be one of those nature hikes where we sing around a campfire, tell personal stories and cry, is it? I've got dibs on Simon. If I'm gonna sob and slobber, money better be involved. It's the only thing worth crying over," Mark said.

"Hear, hear—I'll second that," Simon offered.

Pleased that humor was working its way through the group, Shane went along with the joke as they walked, "Sorry, Mark. Glenn's already claimed Simon. I'm putting you and Charlie together."

"Great. I was hoping to spend some time with my good friend Charlie. I've been meaning to sit down with him to start my Russian lessons," Mark joked.

"Inertial compensators," Charlie teased.

Mark's face turned red, but he then calmed down knowing Shane would lecture if anything more were said.

"Charlie, grow up, would you? Let's stop over here by the Gemini Mission capsule," Shane suggested.

"Geez…he's wearing that high-school social studies teacher look; like we're about to receive a history lesson," Simon chaffed.

Ignoring Simon, Shane said, "This is the Gemini Five space capsule;

flown by Pete Conrad and Gordon Cooper in 1965. Its mission, like ours, was an integral part of a great many things to come. Their mission's success made it possible for Neil Armstrong to set foot on the moon. Think about that for a moment. Gemini Five's mission was to test the battery fuel cells in space for the future fourteen-day flight to the moon. This first week-long mission in space completed one hundred twenty orbits. Without its success, the moon would have remained out of reach."

They clapped, as if Shane were giving a mission award acceptance speech.

"Enough. Listen, I need this team working together. Solve these problems or there won't be a mission to Mars. I brought you here because our last meeting didn't go well. We don't have any more time for nonsense. Take a look at this capsule and understand the great undertaking you're part of.

"You're building the ship that will one day be the first to shuttle a one-hundred-person crew to Mars. That's historic on a scale unknown to humankind. Every day is precious and cannot be wasted, as our launch window approaches in four and a half years.

"The men who flew these Gemini spacecraft were pioneers. We're the caravan bringing forth settlers. Let's not forget the sacrifices made before you were born; to reach towards the stars and press a human footprint into the universe.

"With that in mind, let's start this meeting with eyes focused up and minds down here on Earth. Simon, we'll begin with you. Where are we with our under-the-table Russian money?"

"I like that, Shane. Go directly to Dad for the cold hard cash before asking how his day went," Simon joked.

"I always got more out of my father by asking straightaway over slathering him with butter," Shane replied.

"I hear flattery will get you far with Charlie," Mark poked.

"Field emitters," Charlie chimed; furnishing a toothy grin for Mark to ferment.

"Did you two not hear me?" Shane charged, as if he were about to launch into a long-drawn-out teamwork lecture.

"Alright, Shane, we get it. We'll stop. Please, Simon, continue," Charlie offered.

"Yes, we have their money. It's parked in a Swedish bank. The Vice President will need to personally sign off on its release. Don't ask where it came from."

"Great. I'll call on my Russian counterpart this evening. Simon, you're a miracle worker!" Charlie exclaimed.

"Not so fast, Charlie. I'll be talking with Fulton later this afternoon. Wait til I've confirmed that we can go ahead before celebrating," Shane cautioned.

"Someone's always raining on my parade. You see, gentlemen, this is why I always advocate discretion. It's easier and always more rewarding to ask for forgiveness than permission," Charlie's well-worn euphemism instructed.

Everyone laughed and nodded at the obvious, except for Shane. He shook his head, trying not to smile. He then raised a hand to signify that they should settle down.

"Now that money is no longer a problem, can we get back on schedule? What's been done about fabrication, Charlie?" Shane asked.

"The new production model is perfected—processing has been halved. Safeguards against future power outages have been implemented. Moscow has also graciously agreed to produce alloy for the remainder of the ship's components; to assist the other producing nations if they wish," Charlie explained, as if granting Shane a personal favor.

"That's wonderful, Charlie! But wouldn't it be easier to share their innovation with the other component-producing nations—allowing everyone to enjoy increased efficiency? Fabrication innovations could buy this mission some much needed time to buffer against any further setbacks," Shane suggested.

Charlie winced and explained, "I don't think that's such a good idea. If we fall behind in other areas, or some of the other producing nations run into trouble, then they may consider it. However, as it stands they would reject the idea."

"You're joking, right? They made a mistake and lack the stones to tell their superiors. So, we arrange to pay for their bungle to the tune of one hundred million dollars and they won't share the benefit we're financing. Forgive me for seeming childish, but Charlie… really…what are you thinking?" Simon asked with incredulity.

"Charlie, I'm going to side with Simon on this. How can you justify a request like that?" Glenn politely asked.

"I'll argue with or take a cheap shot at Charlie; even for no good reason. But this is too easy. They're dead right. Who do the Russians think they are, peddling that kind of attitude?" Mark added to the outward dissent.

Shane's eyebrows arched. Charlie assumed they would object. However, he underestimated how tightly they would hold their feelings.

"Look, as I've repeatedly explained, my job is about managing influence. It's not an easy task. It would be a mistake to poke this bear in the china shop," Charlie counseled.

"Why, Charlie?" Shane queried, growing annoyed.

"Russians value strength."

"You don't say. It's a good thing the other producing nations don't care about that, or we'd be in a lot of trouble," Mark commented.

Charlie made eye contact with them all and then said, "You people have the luxury of working with equals who speak the language of your disciplines. I deal with those who garner, amass and exercise great political power. That's all they care about or understand. A Russian oligarch is extremely dangerous with diminished power. They're big risk-takers by nature. The less they have, the more they're willing to stake—often to the detriment of anyone nearby. The more they have, the more there is to lose.

"It'd be better to simply make this happen and forget about leveraging. Let them grow fat with the success of this improved process. If we need it, then it'll be made available to us; but only if we need it. It's unwise to allow them to feel that they've lost their advantage. To a Russian, having the appearance of great strength is the same as possessing it.

"Americans are the exact opposite—only interested in what we can really do. We're still a majority shareholder in this mission. More Americans will be on the flight than any other nationality. We're in a position of strength. Let's allow Russia to feel the same. It's better for us all."

"Are you a communist?" Mark childishly asked—breaking the serious tenor of Charlie's message.

"He's right. Charlie, we'll follow your lead on this. Still, wait for my call before breaking out the caviar with our Bolshevik brothers," Shane reminded.

"This probably is the right way to go, and was inevitable," Simon added.

"What makes you say that?" Glenn asked.

"Oil is way down right now. The Russians' oil supply has already peaked. With a recession pounding their economy, we can't have them falling behind—whatever the reason. Financial resources there, like here, are scarce. If we're going to meet that launch window, then all the producing nations need to be more open about their fiscal health. Money, and the lack of it, will end this project faster than a faulty bulkhead," Simon said.

"It's not just their finances that we are struggling with. The other producing nations' fabrication specialists have complained about working with their Russian counterparts. The Frogs and Brits have already requested that they take over the Russians' responsibilities," Glenn explained.

"What did you tell them?" Shane asked.

"I told them that I didn't have the authority to make the call; nor would I know how to go about asking the Russians to leave."

"Even suggesting this would be political suicide. It's not an option," Charlie stated.

"Oh, is that how this works? Charlie has all the powerful friends and he decides who can come to the party," Mark scoffed.

"You're blowing this out of proportion, Mark. That's not what I meant. You know the trouble this could cause would be much larger than whether or not any Russians flew on this mission."

"What are you saying? I'm too stupid to understand the finer nuances?"

"Mark, if this is any measure of your political acumen, then I'd tend to agree," Charlie jabbed.

"Did you hear that? Charlie doesn't think we're good enough to play his greasy chess game. Everyone, bow to the Grand Master. He has spoken," Mark exaggerated with appropriate hand gestures.

"Is it as bad as you're making this out to be with the French and British?" Shane asked, ignoring Mark's wounded ego.

"Not yet. It could get there. However, this money should plug the hole," Charlie assured.

"Sure, money fixes everything. My ex-wife felt the same way when she took it all," Mark quipped.

"With production back on schedule, they'll have nothing to complain about. Lacking any other major issues, this could be the end of our Moscow problems. Let's try to keep a little perspective—a thousand things could still go awry having nothing to do with fabrication. Instead of worrying about what could swerve off course, let's rejoice these little victories along the way. If there's one thing the Ruskies do right, it's celebrate life every chance they get," Charlie offered.

"You have a point, Charlie. But I don't have the luxury of not worrying if the project will fail for any number of reasons. I won't get a good night's sleep until that bird has left the orbital docking platform," Shane said.

"What about that fine speech you gave as we huddled round this tin can they flew in space decades ago? You rambled on about how their mission was critical to future missions."

"Sure. So?"

"That's all we can do here, Shane; one victory at a time. Each success along the way must be affirmed. We're not getting to Mars in a day. There're a number of days before us—waiting to be lived and worked through. Heck, I'm not even sure we've come close to seeing how difficult this mission could get. I bet plenty of horrible catastrophes will show themselves before this undertaking is put in the history books. There's no time like the present to crack open a bottle, as my Russian colleagues would say," Charlie said.

The early-morning sun had risen an hour before. Darby sat on the front steps of the Metropolitan Museum of Art in New York City, awaiting George's arrival. He had something to say and needed to make a point in person.

Dew coated everything. As the air warmed, steamed freshwater filled Darby's nose. Thoughts of boyhood fishing trips came to mind. Many summers had been spent casting a line in hopes that a fish would bite.

Approaching footsteps roused him from his reminiscing. George had walked over from his nearby office. Darby's handiwork was still present on his face. There was no mistaking that George had been in a fight. He wore his bruises with pride, as if a kingly virtue. Darby laughed inside.

"Quite a shiner, George."

"Thanks. An old friend gave it to me. You'll be getting the bill."

"What, no frivolous lawsuit?"

"Why? I don't mind taking your money; don't mind that at all. I just despise paying a legal weasel to get it. I retain the best law firm in town and hate the lot of them."

"See, you surprise me all the time, George. I always thought you admired sharks."

"A lawyer isn't a shark. Hell, I like sharks; like their purity. They're at the top of the food chain—imposing their will; and do so without any misguided sense of morality. They simply are the strongest and eat everything in their path. An attorney is no such animal. Lawyers are more like slugs; living off what is discarded—leaving a slimy trail wherever they've been. You can't touch one without picking up their slippery residue. Like slugs, I'd happily squash them all; flattening counselors underfoot so as not to pay a contrived toll to exist in the business world."

"That's sweet, George."

"So why am I out here this early in the morning? Don't say you came to see art. They won't be open for another three hours."

"Sure, Jojo. That's why I showed up. Let's get outta here already. There's a body of water on the other side of the museum with a walking path."

"You know how I hate that nickname."

"I know; trying to lighten the mood. We need to address some issues. It's either going to end well with us or not."

"The park reservoir; how quaint."

They moved on west towards the walkway. Runners circled the park in a rush to finish and begin the rest of their days. At times, large groups would congest, like automobiles bottlenecking at the scene of an accident.

"I hate watching other people sweat; unless I'm the cause," George complained.

"I would have never guessed that about you, George. You're the very model of compassion," Darby drawled sarcastically.

"Fine, we're rounding the pond. Spill it."

"George, I need to know where you stand. We've both made threats. It appears that commitments outside our oil concerns have been made and could lead to conflicts of interests. I meant it. The Darby you knew as a young man is not who I am anymore. There's no desire to go back. I've moved on. Either join me, or leave me unmolested."

George smiled and shook his head. "Unmolested? Listen to yourself! I'm not trying to peek under your skirt. You're making grave mistakes here. First, this engine of yours is not going to work. Second, not paying the Moborak is most certainly going to lead to trouble."

"I never promised that crazy group you hired anything."

"Nonetheless, they're expecting payment in a few days."

"So pay 'em."

"I already did."

"Great—squared up!"

"No. I settled my half. They expect the rest from you."

"And who fashioned the impression that I owed them anything?"

"I did. When I spoke to my French contact, it was made clear that by accepting seventy-five million from me, they would explain that I had fulfilled my commitment; and you had not yet decided to follow through."

"George, call your man and take care of it this morning."

"Like I said, old buddy, I covered my end. It's up to you to pay the remaining balance," George said.

Darby could feel his face turning red as he grew furious. George was elated; feeling he had gained control over Darby.

"Still think the new and improved Darby you're so proud of can best the blood of old flowing through your veins? You wanna rip my head off. I can see it in your eyes. Face it, Darby, you're a shark like me."

Darby stopped walking, grabbed George's arms and screamed, "I don't want to be a shark. Why is it so important that I keep a continuous state of brutality?"

"You're a killer…and you know it. This, of course, leads us to the next topic of discussion: your engine; well, your ill-gotten engine."

"So this is what you want, George; you want the killer in me?"

"Yes," George gushed, as they began walking again.

"Fine. Get those psychopaths off my back or I'm going to kill them; and then I'm gonna come looking for you," Darby added with cunning exactitude.

George clapped and laughed aloud. "Do you hear that? It's music—a man seizing his destiny; asking no one for permission and making no apologies. Angels are singing."

"You're crazy."

"Maybe—I'm still not paying your half."

"You've been warned, George."

"And so have you."

"My engine, George…I assume, having heard nothing from you about it, that there's no interest on your part."

"My interest is in seeing it buried."

"I'm going to do it, George. I need to know what you plan to do about it."

"But you know my plan. If that contraption is launched, then I'll be left with no choice but to destroy it and you. After all, you'll be waging war on my way of life. It's only fair that I fight for what's mine."

"It's the future."

"It's not necessarily the future. It certainly is not my future."

"On that point, George, I think you're right. It's not your future."

Having come to a path that branched in two directions they stopped walking. George looked to Darby and said, "I think this is where we separate."

"So it is."

"It doesn't need to be like this," George offered, trying to appear concerned.

"Yes, it does."

Turning away, Darby veered right taking him to the west side of Central Park. George continued on the walkway they had been taking; returning to where they entered the park. The morning air had further warmed. George was drenched in sweat by the time he reached the museum.

Darby caught a taxi to the airport, where his private jet awaited. While riding through the busy streets he began to plan what was to be done with George. In his mind, there was no choice left.

After settling into an idea, he felt relief. George was all that remained of what once was. Not an innocent, Darby still wished to live as one. He desired joy, not madness; creation instead of destruction; life and not death.

Today, I begin anew. Darby felt energized as when he was a young businessman—wanting to make profit and a meaningful improvement. Idealism, dormant some thirty years, cracked open a long-hardened heart. He was alive in his humanity once again; and it felt good.

Abigail returned to New York empty-handed—not a further peep out of John Stanton. Step by step, she walked through the away assignment in her mind, chasing answers and blame. *What went wrong?* Soon after picking up her bag at the terminal carousel, a different angle suddenly became apparent: *David's demise had been overlooked.* Instead of a return to the studio, she found herself outside the CMC's office building.

After paying the taxi driver, she tapped her phone. "Andy, it's Abbey. I need a film crew at the CMC's headquarters. No, not yet. I'll see if he's willing to talk. Just send them. Better to be ready. Thanks."

Abigail entered like she owned the place. Sasha, seated at her desk, attempted to look busy, tapping her keyboard. When she recognized Abigail she sat up—feigning composure and self-assuredness but bleeding credibility as her eyes moistened.

"Sasha Ericson, isn't it?"

"Yes, Miss Sanders."

"Your interview went well. Sandra was impressed. Did Miss Buchanan mention when she planned to bring you on board?"

"I'm afraid not. She did speak of a position she had in mind for me. That was the last I heard of it."

"You won't likely hear from her again. She's no longer with network. Call me next week if you're still interested."

"I'll do that. Thank you," Sasha replied, a look of relief on her face.

"You're welcome. Is David in? I was hoping to get a moment."

"Miss Sanders, I am sorry. David's in, but not taking meetings for the time being."

"It would only be a few minutes."

Hesitation gave way to self-preservation. "Let me see what can be done. I'll be right back."

"Thank you, Sasha."

She knocked on David's office door and announced, "David, Miss Sanders is here to see you."

David looked up from a blank stare towards the desk. "I told you, no visitors today. Please take a message. I'll call her when I can find some breathing space."

"I know you're going through a difficult stretch. We all are; not knowing what's coming next. Maybe a few words with a friend would help."

"Miss Sanders is not a friend. She's media. They're nothing more than—"

"Than what?" Abigail asked as she squeezed past Sasha.

"Miss Sanders, why don't you join me?" David offered; trying and failing to appear pleasant.

"Thank you."

Sasha slipped out without a sound, closing the door behind her.

"Came to pick over the carcass?"

"How do you mean?"

"Abigail, you can't pull off bashful. Why don't you come out and say it? You want to put me on television so the world can gawk at what has become of David Samuel—the joke of a man who dared to try and make a difference. That's why you're here, isn't it?"

"Not about the gawking part."

"What else could you want from me?"

"I came out of courtesy to a friend. I was in Washington yesterday working on another story—visited with Ethan. He spoke highly of you. In addition to getting a story, I wanted to check on you so I could tell Ethan you're fine. Direct enough?"

Too exhausted to make her leave, David took in a deep breath and let it go. Liquored stench spewed from his mouth.

"Alright, Miss Sanders, I'll grant you an interview on one condition."

"What's that?"

"Tell me how you do your job."

"My job?"

"Yes. How can you walk into a man's office, uninvited, calmly sit down, and watch without any emotion as he drowns before your eyes in a sea of corruption? How can you do that? Where's your heart? Don't you have an ambulance to chase? How can you be so good at sifting through the destruction of others' lives—and then dispassionately report as if buying a cup of coffee?"

"That's a lawyers' shtick. I just count how many suits are galloping after the hospital-bound accident victims."

Abigail's sarcasm didn't invoke the intended effect. Still, she was taken aback by his indictment of her character and the news profession as a whole. He was emotionally falling apart and for that she sympathized—compassion ended there.

"How can you do what you do? People clearly don't want you to police their politicians. How many stepped forward to help when your life's work was halted for no good reason? How can you be so good in the face of such wretched behavior?"

"Abigail, those are good questions. How can I do what I do; given those questions?" He paused for a moment and then paraphrased, "How can you do what you do? Isn't the pertinent question, why? Why do you and I do what we do?"

"Fine, why then?"

"Why indeed. Because we must."

"We must. That's it?" Abigail demanded.

"What else need there be to explain such a simple answer?"

"An explanation."

"There's a natural order to things. Wouldn't you agree?"

"David, you're losing me."

David sat up in his chair, showing signs of relief, as a wrinkled forehead relaxed. His shoulders fell and he began breathing slowly.

"How could I have done this for so many years? Why did I create the Citizens' Mandamus Council in the first place? Why have I protected the rights of citizens who have done nothing in my time of need? I do it because I must."

"Why you?"

"The answer lies in what we do here at the CMC."

"The answer lies within the lawsuit?"

"Do you really want to know or are you placating?"

"Yes, I want to know. No, I wouldn't waste time with trite emotional manipulation."

"We're not merely a gaggle of lawyers wasting time in court to justify our paychecks. Let me ask you this fundamental question: do you think the CMC does any good?"

"How do you mean?"

"Stop—you're making this unnecessarily difficult. Do you think we do any good?"

"What kind of good are you referring to? There are many kinds of good."

"Again, Abigail, you're overcomplicating this process. Just answer the question with a simple yes or no. Does the Citizens' Mandamus Council do any good?"

"Yes, it does."

"Now, tell me what good it does."

"As a whole, you seem dedicated to upholding the United States Constitution and the laws of individual states."

"Good. Simply speaking, that's what we do here…or rather what we did. But why was our existence even necessary?"

"David, there's no need to lead me about with childish questions."

"You're obviously not a child, and possess a keen intellect clearly communicated through your nightly news broadcasts. But you'd be incorrect. Simplicity is absolutely called for. Simplicity provides a clarity that even children can understand. That clarity makes terribly hard the prospect of benefit for those corrupt. Corruption only flourishes in confusion and obscurity. Our constitution is quite a simple document. Its genius lay in straightforward language. A school-aged student may read it and understand that he or she has inalienable rights in this wonderful creation we call the United States of America. So please don't misunderstand my manner of speaking as an insult to your intellect. I'm clumsily borrowing a method of men far wiser than myself. Going back to our subject of the good you claimed we were doing; I thank you for that. It was what I always intended."

"I meant it."

"Next, I'd like to pose another rudimentary question. What if I had not created the Council?"

"Then you would have done something else with your life. I'm sure of that."

"No, what I meant was, what would have happened to United States? What would have been different for the United States if I'd not built the CMC?"

"Are you asking in relation to the CMC?"

"Once again, Abigail, you are fashioning a silk purse when a sow's ear will do. You claim we do good; correct?"

"Yes."

"Did the good the CMC provide serve a particular purpose?"

"Yes."

"What's that purpose?"

"To protect the people's constitutional rights and uphold the law."

"Yes, but simpler yet."

"I don't understand what you're driving towards. That's what you do."

"Alright, let's go at it this way. If you'd never experienced sight, would you know the difference between darkness and light?"

"No."

"But they exist all the same. They're irrevocably bound together and equally oppose one another. Would you agree this is true?"

"Yes."

"So then, what's the good irreversibly bound to and in equal opposition from?"

"The bad."

"Yes!" David replied with great excitement—almost floating out of his chair, temporarily freed from a devastated existence. "So, then, to answer the question of what might have happened had I not created the Citizens' Mandamus Council that brought so much good into being, the bad we fought would have flourished."

"Agreed—a great many fraudulent politicians would have manipulated the system far longer and may have continued on even to this day."

"And the corporations too; don't forget the corporations. We haven't spent nearly as much time as I would have liked keeping them in check. This was the next step to focus on before Ethan's abrupt departure."

"I'm sure you would've done a large measure of good there as well."

"Again, thank you for the gracious compliment."

"You're welcome. Tell me something, though. Why must you do good? You said that you and I must do what we do. What if you had chosen not to do good? What if I had chosen not to pursue the news? Then what? How would this good get done? What would happen to this must?"

"That's such a fine question. It reminds me of my college days; so many idealistic debates. I miss the university environment. Nowhere else in society may minds of differing cultures and persuasions come together under enlightenment's common auspices and feed one another, without the need to take away the other's right to exist or hold a unique thought. In fact, individuality is celebrated instead of destroyed there. The must, you ask. Have you ever noticed how nature has a way of balancing all things?"

"I suppose so."

"Mankind can build a dam to last hundreds of years. However, given enough time, the laws of physics will eventually reconcile and the dam will give way; entropy and gravity."

"Okay."

"If I had not built the CMC, then someone else would have; maybe not now or maybe not with the same mandates, but something like it or someone like me would have taken up the fight. Do you agree?"

"I'd agree that history has demonstrated this from time to time—bad and good take to each other in the form of war and political change. This doesn't ensure that someone would have done it now."

"Maybe not now, but if corruption continues on unchecked, then our system of government eventually collapses…all systems of government really. Would you concede?

"Yes."

"I would too—not just because I believe it, but also because history shows this to be true time and again."

"You still haven't proven this so-called must theory of yours."

"It's not a theory, Abigail. It's nature. Maybe I should change the word I'm using. Try to think about it like this: Existence is a whole. Do you understand?"

"No."

"Existence can be thought of in that one word: Existence. Do you agree?"

"That I exist or the universe exists: is this what you mean?"

"Certainly, that example would do nicely. Let's choose something small, like you, for instance. The universe is quite a large place to consider and may lead to confusion. So you're a whole in and of your own existence, correct?"

"Yes."

"If I were to remove your arm, then would you say that you were incomplete as a whole human being that is born of two arms?"

"Yes."

"For you to be whole in this particular example, both arms would be necessary, right?"

"Absolutely."

"Tying this example into our discussion, when we agreed that bad and good were naturally connected, for you to be whole in your example you must have both arms. In existence for bad to be present, good must also have its place."

"That would seem to follow. Still, why must you be good? Why must I report the news?"

"Abigail, if you didn't do it, then someone with your integrity would eventually find themselves doing your job. If I had not built the Citizens' Mandamus Council, then someone else would have. Oh, there might've been a great many differences that group or organization would embody. However, its function would've been the same: to balance the whole of existence with its being.

"Why must you report the news? Because of your genetics, family background, life experiences, preferences and all the other factors that bear on your decisions. For your personal life to have symmetry, you must make the choices you make. For my life to have balance, I too must make the decisions that I have. The philosophical notion and need to balance human existence has been discussed since mankind could deliberate. This is not a novel idea. It's a naturally occurring truth."

"I like the idea of a naturally occurring truth."

"I thought you would—being in your line of work. Theoretically, news, like the law, is society's watchtower of the truth. The watch-keepers are people like you and Ethan."

"I think it's safe to count you in that company, David."

"Most gracious. You mentioned that the CMC has culled the political herd. That's exactly what we're discussing right now. It's homeostasis. Nature has a balance it seeks out. More clearly, the native inclination of our existence is to move towards a point of harmony. The Council's fundamental principles follow this idea. We sue politicians and corporate officers; utilizing the writ of mandamus to shunt their selfish behavior—forcing them to simply do their jobs. Absent any fiddling with public trust, there are no actions for us to take."

"David, really, don't you feel that in some ways Ethan was correct—seeking arrest powers? Wouldn't this have made your efforts more effective? You may have even saved yourself from destruction by acquiring those powers."

"Ethan was incorrect—well-intended but wrong. The CMC was rightly conceived as serving to remind the beast that its job is to pull in the direction the driver chooses; not meant as a buggy-whip feverishly striking the horse's back."

"That's quite grand, if not a little naïve?"

"It's not naïve, Abigail. It's nature. Let me ask you one last simple question: what holds power in balance and what does it look like unbalanced?"

"A gun: metaphorically speaking. When it is not balanced, it looks a lot like Washington DC does today."

"Wrong, though I appreciate the sentiment. Power in human hands, my dear, is kept balanced by the holder of that power; and is done so by means of personal responsibility and accountability. Corruption is what power looks like when unbalanced. If the CMC were to seek out unnecessary power to hold a politician accountable, then we would plummet into darkness and our own corruption. We only seek to balance power, not to have it."

Abigail leaned closer to David and said, "You're a good man, David Samuel."

Smiling back at Abigail, he said, "If that's true, then it's so only because I must."

Their discussion lifted David out of his depression. He soared in truth and glided with only well-crafted ideals to stay aloft. Sweet relief was his for a time, but it slipped away as he settled back into his chair. A cloud once again found him, cold and wet. David's shoulders crept up to swallow his neck.

Abigail observed the change of heart and knew she would have to seize the moment before its passing. She asked, "Would you be able to do that interview now? David, you've said some important things here today that people need to hear."

Weak and pathetic once again, David replied, "I'm sorry my dear, that time has come and gone. I can no longer grant your request. Now, if you'll excuse me, I have an appeal to prepare and a board meeting later today."

Abigail frowned, "I'm sorry you can't accommodate. Thank you for your time all the same. By the way, Sasha's interview went well. As soon as a position is available, we intend to present her a job offer."

"That's fine. I'll pass the news on," David replied as he picked up a document and turned away.

"David, I'm truly sorry for what they've done to you. I hope you'll remember that they really didn't hurt you; but brought great harm upon themselves. You haven't stopped being David Samuel."

CHAPTER
VII
THE POLITICAL BODY

Senator Sidel's report had carried on for thirty minutes when Ethan interrupted, "I think it's obvious that the Stanton Bill can no longer receive this committee's recommendation for submission to the floor."

"Ethan, the Energy and Natural Resources Committee is more than a group of yes-men. I can't speak for the remainder of us but I don't think you can simply sweep the matter under the rug," Senator Peck nudged back.

"Beatrice, you're a fine senator and have been the committee secretary for some time. You know as well as I do that the chairman does in fact possess the right to do just that. I might have phrased differently my last comment to address any questions or concerns this committee might have. Since you've brought it up, let's address the issue outright. Who among us opposes my suggestion that the Stanton Bill be abandoned? Especially since the bill's main sponsor quit his post," Ethan put forth.

Senator Sidel lamented, "Surely we should have a say in this? We did nominate you as chairman. You should have sought our counsel before making such a decision."

"Dean," Ethan said.

"I prefer to be regarded by my title," Dean asserted.

"Fine. Senator Sidel, I didn't make a decision—rather a suggestion. Still, have your say. Can you think of any reason, given your own report, why this committee should not reject the Stanton Bill's viability?"

"Well, that's not the point. I just felt we all should've been included."

"You were. We're all here. This is an official committee meeting."

"Yes, well…"

"So let's make it the point. Senator Peck, do you agree that we should ditch the bill?"

"I do!" she proudly stated.

Senator Clark, emboldened by Senator Peck's outspoken position, she bolstered. "I too feel it's time to put an end to this."

One by one, the remainder of the committee endorsed Ethan's position. After the last senator assented, the others exulted in their consensus. Ethan marveled at their elation that a cohesive agreement had been reached. Most interesting to him was that their joy was not derived from doing anything meaningful. Each senator seemed to find contentment in getting along with the others regardless of the reason. They simply wanted a direction to follow, which would not single them out as the one who caused this issue or that problem.

Witnessing their lethargy made Ethan ruefully smile; reminding him of repeated experiences and the kind of leaders that persist: Those who act and those who simply hold a position. Ethan discovered long ago that life is largely comprised of the latter.

"I then move to shelve the Stanton Bill. Is there a second?" Ethan orated.

"Second," Beatrice spouted.

"All in favor...all opposed...it's unanimous. This committee's recommendation to the full Senate is to reject support for the Stanton Bill."

A general relief immediately found its way to their faces. After a brief pause, Ethan doled out responsibilities for the next meeting. As they received their assignments, each senator stood up to leave; seemingly thrilled that some great event had occurred. Ethan reclined in his chair—stunned at the lack of individual character in this body of political might.

As the last, Senator Sidel, rose to depart, he stepped back from the conference table, locking eyes with Ethan. "Senator Scott, you know Heinrich Willems?"

"He's the Senate Judiciary Chair, yes?"

"He's also a cosponsor of the bill; and not likely gonna give it up."

"What can he do? We just killed it."

"He can reintroduce it; might even keep the name to spite you. Hank's too invested to just let it go."

"Look, Dean, what's it going to take?"

"You know."

"Know what? What are you talking about? What am I supposed to know?"

Smiling, hesitating, and moments later relenting, Dean said, "It all comes with a price. What are you willing to give to get?"

Ethan's head ached as his forehead tensed; his lips squeezed together as if to hold back the regretful words: Nothing will ever get done!

"What've you got?"

"Dean, none of this is mine to give!"

"Well, there's your answer," Senator Sidel replied, as he turned to leave.

Distressed with the thought of losing what had just been accomplished, Ethan caved. "Wait." Dean returned to the table— waiting in silence—a desperate moment stretching into forever. "Do we share any mutual initiatives with Judiciary?"

"Nope," Dean smartly replied.

"There are no programs where Energy and the FBI work together?"

"Loosely, yes; but it's a stretch at best."

"What about budgets? No money goes back and forth or is shared between the committees?"

"Strictly speaking, no; but surely the FBI investigates on behalf of Energy and Natural Resources, or has at some point." Dean's eyes grew wider as a smile appeared.

Ethan knew what he was implying before he said it. "Talk to him, Dean. See what it'll cost to focus on his committee's job instead of this useless piece of legislation."

Later that afternoon, Ethan arrived at the steps of the Capitol Building to address the public. With the majestic structure in the background, a podium stood at the base of the front steps, complete with microphones and a reporter pool.

Ethan looked over the crowd, hoping to catch a glimpse of Abigail. Not finding her face, he settled into his speech.

"Thank you for coming. It's been a difficult time in Washington the last two weeks. With the sudden departure of Senator Stanton, the Senate is once again left with a vacancy. I've been told that Governor Dunback of Maryland has begun the process of finding a suitable replacement.

"With Senator Stanton's leave, a leadership vacuum has halted Bill SA2002A8's movement through the legislative process; otherwise known as the Stanton Bill. He was the legislation's author and primary sponsor. Without his presence, support for it has quickly waned.

"The Stanton Bill's most prominent article was the repeal of the Alternative Energy Bill, which mandates that the United States separate itself from all outside US energy resources. For the Alternative Energy Bill to achieve its goals, many longstanding tax breaks will be repealed or allowed to expire. More than a few large corporations and government offices have lobbied against the Alternative Energy Bill by supporting the Stanton Bill. Many previously exclusive American corporations, now global companies, will find once-coveted tax umbrellas no longer shielding them from the rain of a fair tax burden—the very same water falling on rest of society's head.

"Hunting corporations was not the Alternative Energy Bill's goal. However, with each new innovation older technologies must give way. So too it is with our fossil fuel addiction. The Alternative Energy Bill uproots these toxic fuel sources. We must allow this process to continue; not only for our economy and the environment, but also to check corruption. Human progress has never been accomplished without sacrifice.

"After careful consideration, and by unanimous decision of the Energy and Natural Resource Committee, we recommend that the Stanton Bill be dropped from consideration—based upon its lack of purpose to serve the public and its ultimate goal to only support the interests of many US-based multinational corporations.

"I would like to take a few questions at this time. Yes," Ethan said, pointing to a hand up in the crowd.

"Is it true that you were appointed as Chairman of the Energy and Natural Resources Committee?" a young reporter asked.

"It's true. Next."

"Did you want the position for yourself? Was that your plan?" another young reporter probed.

"No. I didn't want the position; and had no intention of assuming that role when appointed to the committee."

"But you still took it!" the same reporter continued.

Annoyed by questions straying away from the announcement's intended purpose, Ethan asked, "What news agency do you represent?"

"Clifford Price; *DC Inside Examiner*," the reporter boasted.

"I see. Well, Clifford, you're correct. I accepted the position; but did so only because I was asked," Ethan clarified, wanting to move on. Ethan knew the publication was more interested with intrigue than facts. A piece of bloody gossip was worth more to the rag than ten dead US soldiers. Clifford held the look of a person who might attend a boxing match, eyes gorged by a vicious thirst for destruction.

"So you don't want the job then? Do you think you're too good for the likes of—" Clifford chided.

Ethan interrupted, "Next."

"Tell us, Senator, what do you intend to do with all the Americans who are going to lose their jobs because of the Alternative Energy Bill? Don't you care about the people?" an attractive and well-dressed woman asked.

The questions continued to detract from the gathering's intent. The news professionals seemed less interested in what Ethan had to say or what he wanted to accomplish than in finding something they could hang him with. These were not the same people he had spoken to at CMC rallies; people looking for hope and inspiration. They came for his hide, heart and soul if they could get it.

"People, this has diverged in the wrong direction. We should get back on track. However, so that I have answered your question, some may lose their jobs. Still, many more jobs will be created. Look at what the automobile industry did to replace the horse and buggy. And, yes, I care about people."

"Well then, Senator, what else did you come here to talk about?" a female voice belted out from the crowd.

A TTN press pass flashed at her waist as she pushed forward through the gaggle. Ethan was certain it was the friend he hoped to see. Her face was not Abigail's, but that of a youthful and aggressive reporter wanting satisfaction.

"You're with TTN. I've spent a great deal of time under your network's watchful eye."

"Yes, I am."

"To answer your question, Miss…"

"Miss Klein."

Ethan smiled, because just the thought of Abigail was enough to calm his nerves. The reporter was also respectful in her approach. It provided a sense of ease as he began to answer her question.

"Miss Klein, I'm glad you posed that question." Most of the reporters laughed, understanding the humor beneath the comment.

"I'd like to announce some of the most aggressive measures regarding the Alternative Energy Bill's efforts. To date, it would seem little has been accomplished in regards to the outright pursuit of alternative energy. There certainly have been quite a few fine speeches. Still, little else has borne fruit. After this year, many tax breaks that benefit the wealthy and multinational corporations will expire. As a new revenue stream flows, it's important that we quickly put these tax dollars to efficient use. To this end, I have tasked the ten senators of the Energy and Natural Resources Committee to aggressively take actions assigned to them.

"I am proud to announce that our committee is now taking applications from US-based companies to receive grants or government loans to develop viable alternative energy technologies. We were able to put a man on the moon in a decade. In accordance with the Alternative Energy Bill, we will be energy independent within four years. All my efforts in regard to this committee will be devoted to that end. Next question, please."

The reporters came alive in frenzied barks. Clifford said in an incriminating voice, "Senator Scott, isn't this just another lame decision to waste more of our tax dollars and line your pockets? Sounds just like the Mars Bill: ten trillion dollars."

Frustrated, Ethan squinted his eyes, hesitated, and then asked, "Young man, how old are you?"

"Okay, fogey, twenty-five," he antagonized.

Ethan smiled as he gazed over the crowd's heads for a moment before returning his eyes back to the reporter. "I remember twenty-five; seems like yesterday. You speak to me in such a rude tone. From where does your disdain come? You haven't lived long enough to carry on with the anger in your voice of someone twice your age. You haven't paid the amount of taxes it takes to speak to me as though I've squandered your life savings.

"Now that we're level, let me directly agree with you that Washington has an abhorrent reputation of wasteful spending—but not under my watch. I've only held public office a few weeks. I cannot control how the remainder of the government spends their budget.

"However, having built and managed a successful news agency, I know how to be frugal and thrifty. What I can control here is how the tax dollars raised by the Alternative Energy Bill will be spent. Rest assured these monies will be put to proper use.

"You slighted me by attacking the Mars Bill. I don't say this to be contentious, but I'd like to directly address your example. Ten trillion dollars is quite a price tag. The project in its entirety will cost a total of fifty trillion dollars. This is by far the most expensive endeavor in human history. Listen to those two words: human history. They have an awe-inspiring sound, don't they? Is space not still out there for humanity to explore?"

"But at what cost, Senator?"

"At great cost, it appears. Let me ask this, not just of you, young man, but all of you here today. When did anything great ever not come with great cost? Everything here you see came by way of sacrifice. We stand on the steps of the Capitol Building in the United States of America.

"Every footfall down through the ages in our struggle to create a more equitable society culminates in what you see here today. This building behind me is representative of those sacrifices. The freedoms you all enjoy by the simple action of questioning your representatives without fear of reprisal was purchased with human life. How many lives have been sacrificed since the time of Greece in the name of freedom? It's in the hundreds of millions.

"To those who have offered up their existence onto the altar of freedom, what would any of you have to show them as a contribution? What have you done for your humanity? What great human undertakings have you sacrificed blood for in the effort to continue our growth and progress through time?

"If you've offered nothing, then what do you have to say in life that is meaningful to the rest of us? It's a part of being human to continue reaching outward; exceeding the reach of our individual grasps. It's in the attempt that our grandeur is revealed to ourselves and our fellows.

"Space exists. It's an obstacle to permanently overcome, to master as a domain and to one day make our second home. We cannot turn away from it because of its cost or difficulty. But then, this has been said of all worthy endeavors."

For a brief moment after delivering these words, Ethan felt pride in what he was doing. Then, his chest tightened as he stared over the faceless crowd, awaiting the next useless question; no longer there but beating upon himself in a torture chamber of his making. Hating that in that critical moment earlier with Senator Dean Sidel, doing right meant doing wrong; he couldn't beat the system and couldn't reconcile his heart.

David plodded from pier to pier in silence along New York City's eastern shoreline—the morning sun having just broken the horizon. Fog billowed from the water like a simmering pot. A cold front had pushed in the night before, whispering fall's near-arrival. Reflections danced in the water—tangerine sparkles dotted his eyes.

The smell of salt and sea life infused the air. With each breath he thought of the ocean's deep and dark places. Its blackness lurked in David's imagination—he envisioned his lifeless body sinking to the bottom; finally resting face-up. Vague undulating white-capped waves crested far off atop the distant surface where the living stayed. At the pier, slip guides bobbed in the water. Ships came and went, their transience contributing to his somber mood. He had held off this moment when first served the court order to cease Council operations. After long consideration and battling for options, he had accepted that, for the moment, there was little to be done.

Self-examination was a natural ritual in such a predicament. David, in tune with his state of being, detested self-reprobation. While listening to waves gently crash against the docks, it began, rolling in and out, entrancing his mind. The ocean's sound grabbed hold of his heart and opened it to prosecution.

Twenty years, he thought. Where did they go—so many awesome and monstrous things? Did I do any good? Surely something made a difference. I can't count the number of crooks I've held to the full measure. There's been good. I have made a difference. Still it seems all of this has been for nothing. You heard them. They tolerated me long enough. Were they toying with me? Could they have done this at any time? If that's so, then have I wasted my time? Why didn't they do it sooner? Why now? Maybe they needed me doing my job. But why would they need that? How would it have benefited them? Why has this now become too burdensome? What's happening in the world that can no longer allow for accountability?

I've squandered two decades—for what? What do I have to show for my sacrifice? The CMC's endowment will be spent within a few years, and we can't raise new donations. Should I even try to hold on? What chance is there? This can't be right.

I should've spent my time differently. They were going to take it away from anyone daring to change the system. Why should I be the martyr? No one's stepped forward to be crucified with me. I should have made money instead. I deserve it! Haven't I given enough for one person? Haven't I given enough for ten people? Who'll take care of me?

I hate this place. I hate it! I hate who I am! My life has been defined by seeking out justice for the sake of others. Where's my justice? Why am I indicted for the crime of pursuing justice? If I'm the criminal, then freedom's a prison. I'm such a jackass!

What good is it to seek justice for the sake of others? The ambiguity of individual justice is clear to me now. Who am I to impose ideals on the American people? They didn't ask me to do it. Why did I fight for them? I don't even know these people. What the hell is justice, anyway? Is it to ensure everyone has had a fair chance in America? Is it an assurance that all have their personage respected as sovereignty in and of itself? Who am I to decide any of this? Why did I ever think I had the discernment to make those kinds of decisions? Look what it's brought me.

Ha! Balance, what a joke! What do I know about balance? It's a myth; a manipulative tool sold by charlatans and psychiatrists to keep the mindless clients coming back for more punishment in a never-ending inquisition of self-examination. You just need to find balance. You just need to find balance. A mindless therapist offers this for their hourly wage. What a sham! Balance can't be had. Even on the rare occasion balance visits the home of our hearts, it departs before having the chance to settle in. This was not meant to be held. One can only pursue it like a monastic minion chasing down heavenly enlightenment with chastity. It's our modern-day snake oil, offered to the masses as a cure-all for what ails them. Just seek balance and call me in the morning.

"Ugh!" David groaned out loud to an ocean that wasn't listening and would not respond. He then yelled, "What was I thinking!"

An old man interrupted David's outburst. "You young people always come down here to holler at the world; lookin' for answers. I've got news for you: no one's listenin'." He then turned to tie off his tug to a mooring. Behind his boat towered a cargo ship he had just guided into port.

"Is that so?" David asked.

"Pretty sure; in seventy-three years, shaking my fist at God has yet to earn a reply. I'm certain that yellin' out there'll get ya nowhere."

"I'll keep that in mind," David replied, attempting to be polite as he inched away; wanting to be alone.

"You seem hell-bent on punishing yourself this morning. What happened? Did one of your investments lose all its equity, or did you not get elected to some board?"

"Something like that," David responded as he moved off.

The old man began walking with David. He continued, "You know, a young man like yourself has nothin' to worry about."

"You're not going to try and save me with religion, are you?" David asked.

"Not on your life! That's a useless piece of nonsense. I've been alive long enough to know that anyone claiming to have a handle on the Almighty is sellin' somethin or trying to talk ya outta yer money. The closer I get to that moment, the more I hope there's something after. Aside from that, I don't know diddly."

"Good. Not in the mood to hear a sermon."

"Whatever's botherin' you, don't go throwin' yourself at Poseidon. I've worked down here over forty years. You wouldn't be the first I found floating face-down. Lots of things worse than what you're going through are happening all round. Try to find a way to be thankful. Our money's plummeting against countries we once dominated. There isn't a single public official you can trust anymore; though I'm not sure I ever did," the old man offered, laughing to himself.

"Thank you for your consideration. But I really would like to be by myself."

"I understand. I was young once. A man of your years is going to punish himself regardless. You'll get past it one day. Look to gratitude. It's the only light you'll need to get through the darkness. Good luck to ya. Remember what I said now. Don't go entertaining any ideas of endin' it all in the soup. You won't find any peace or answers by becomin' fish food."

"Thank you," David mumbled as he moved on ahead, leaving the elderly man standing at the dock.

He continued on his walk, returning to his ponderings. Now that I'm leading a company committed to nothing, what am I?

George's private jet followed a company cargo plane on its way to meet Adolphe. Seventy-five million dollars had been wire-transferred. Too soon to conduct another sizeable transaction under a watchful banking regulator's eyes, the remaining balance would be paid in gold bars.

A ten-man contingent of specially trained security operatives kept on his payroll guarded the shipment as it moved out over international waters. The night was clear. Warm light reflecting from the moon surrounded the lead cargo plane. George's plane trailed to the right so that he could keep an eye on it.

His plane's cabin comfortably seated twenty-four passengers with a crew of three. Seats faced in all directions, arranged to create an opulent atmosphere. Deerskin leather covered the Italian furniture. George preferred to fly alone. He did not share creature comforts. When traveling for pleasure, he required companions to fly ahead to meet him at the destination.

The flight was quiet and uneventful. Air hissed by outside the cabin. The steward emerged from the galley and approached George. She was a striking young woman with youthful sharp lines, Prussian blue eyes, and light brown hair worn up in a bun. He looked up with pleasure and then scowled at the young lady—remembering she was the help.

"Mr. Weatherby, our convoy will land in Iceland to refuel and then continue on to Charles De Gaulle Airport. We're forty-five minutes out of New York City and have reached a cruising altitude of twenty-six thousand feet. Can I get you anything?" she asked.

"A glass of water," George barked—angry for allowing this guttersnipe to please him.

"Right away," she replied, quickly turning to retrieve the drink.

The plane shuddered, knocking the attendant into George's lap. She attempted to rise to her feet but could not gain a footing propped high in his lap. Annoyed, George pushed her forward so that she could stand.

"My apologies, Mr. Weatherby."

"What was that? There shouldn't be any turbulence at this altitude."

"I'll check on it."

"My drink," George reminded.

"On its way, sir."

She darted through the galley to the front of the plane. George leaned his head against the window and gazed at the cargo carrier. Light from its cabin glowed. Indicator lights at the nearest wing's leading edges blinked. Men moved from seat to seat, sharing conversation with their comrades.

He wondered, *What are they talking about? Have they served together in battle before coming to work for me? Are they close, like brothers? What dire circumstances have they endured in black places where hope left them to die? What would it be like to trust someone like that?*

Then the cargo plane blinked out—cabin lights and exterior markers disappearing. The night sky swallowed the plane. And then the dark blue atmosphere silhouetted the large and cumbersome airplane, its nose jutting. The carrier slowed down, taking a position alongside his smaller corporate jet. Then it fell behind.

Where are they going? George thought, as he jumped to his feet. *What's going on?* As he stomped towards the galley, he shouted, "Is the captain asleep at the yoke?"

The attendant emerged from the galley with a frightened look on her face. The plane jerked violently up and down. George was launched upward, striking the ceiling with his head, and then forced back into his seat. The attendant also collided with the ceiling on her backside and then was thrust to the floor face-down. She lay prostrate and unconscious in the aisle.

Cabin lights flickered and went out. The engines wound down and then shut down into silence. The flight became smooth and level, with only a light whisper of rushing air to indicate they were aloft. George released his grip from the chair, stood and rushed to the galley. He stepped on the attendant's leg as he opened the galley door. Dishes, food, water and pans were strewn about. He waded through the mess towards the cockpit door. Faint blue light spewed in from the galley window, illuminating his way.

As he opened the door, the captain barked, "Start the checklist!"

The copilot replied, "Yes sir, no sir, negative, check."

The cockpit was devoid of any artificial light, except for the luminous coating of the dials, arms and digits. All other instrumentation was blank. The small space was filled with dull ambient atmospheric reflection and a menacing yellow hue from the full moon.

"What's going on, Captain?" George demanded.

"Sir, I need you to take your seat. We're a little busy just now."

"I'm not leaving without some answers."

"Sir, I'll send word when there is something to report. Now, take your seat."

"Look, young man, your stewardess is down. How do you plan on informing me of anything?"

"Sir, I'm going to ask you one more time to take your seat. If you refuse, my first officer will seat you."

"Son, I own this plane and pay your salary. You do what I say. Right now, I want a report."

"I don't care if you're the President of the United States. This may be your aircraft but it's my flight. Now sit down!"

George went nowhere. He silently glared at the captain. The cockpit's view of the world indicated that the plane was slowing. A dark ocean lay far below, but gradually rising in the horizon, as the captain worked to keep their plane from stalling.

To the side, George watched the cargo plane pitch upward as it lost more speed. The craft reached a pinnacle where its massive weight could no longer be held airborne. Its wings rolled right as it swung near George's jet, passing under and plunging into the darkness beyond.

"Jumbo One is going down, Captain," the first officer said.

"Can you see her?"

"No, she's passed out of visual range."

"She'll have about three minutes of glide time before ditching."

"Shouldn't we follow them in?"

"Not yet. Let's see if we can breathe some life back into our girl. Continue on with the checklist."

"All primary systems offline."

"Check."

"Secondary systems offline."

"Check."

"Air speed."

"One ninety and falling."

"Check. Watch your trim. Keep it level."

"Yes, Captain. The yoke has become unresponsive, sir," the first officer said in a fearful voice.

"Hold it together, First. We're going to work the problem. Where are we with landing sites?"

"We have some small islands 180 miles ahead off the coast of Greenland. There's nothing within reach given present conditions."

"Hold her steady, First Officer."

"Sir, I need your help here. The stick is dead. It's going to take both of us to move it."

"Alright, we're gonna ditch. Let's see if we can turn around and take her back towards Jumbo One's probable landing site. Are you with me?"

"Yes, sir."

"Mr. Weatherby, it turns out you can be of assistance. Your job is to reach the life-raft and jackets stored in the back."

George froze, oblivious to the captain's words. He was incapable of understanding the likelihood of losing his life in the next few moments. At their speed, striking the sea would be no different than striking pavement. Lacking control was a foreign notion to him. His wealth and power could not save him. Fear jailed his reason and assurance that everything was for sale. Fate was driving them into the sea and George could not bargain for better odds.

"Get back there now! We need that raft ready the moment she stops moving in the water."

The captain looked at George one last time. There was no reaching this man—his eyes were wide and glazed.

"Alright, First Officer, we're going to execute a bank to the right on a heading of 260 degrees. On my mark, execute. Ready…mark."

The plane began turning back to the right. The sensation of diminishing forward momentum and then an increase in acceleration could be felt as the maneuver was carried out. The plane's nose pitched downward as the ocean filled the entire cockpit's view, leaving the sky and the moon behind.

"Two hundred sixty degrees, sir."

"Okay. Let's level out."

"Sir, she's not responding. She won't pull out of the turn."

"Don't quit on me. Pull!" the captain yelled.

"Sir, the stick's dead."

They bled off, added, and again reduced speed too much, lacking sufficient forward momentum to maintain lift. The turn then accelerated as their craft fell from the sky. Centrifugal force sent George through the galley and passenger seating to smash against the rear storage compartment. Pinned against the door on his back, George noticed the moonlight pouring first through the windows on one side of the plane and then the other.

His heart pounded. He wanted nothing more than to live. George wanted his life—he was not ready for it to end.

As if an ancient greasy-geared machine seized, a loose tool having fallen into the mechanism's workings, all movement trudged. The plane appeared to spin slower now. His neck swelled and he could not swallow. His heart beat a fearful rhythm, attempting to explode through his sternum. A drumbeat thumped in his ears with the rhythmic cadence of a death march. Surging with greater pressure, blood pulsed through his engorged chest; vomit spewed outward along his cheek as bodily function now controlled the man.

Papers, food and dishes slowly floated in the air, bouncing about the cabin. Window-cast shadows moved across the floor, driving the dark away. The force against the fuselage growled like an animal approaching to kill and devour its cornered prey.

George's mind perceived his life as something outside himself. He considered this man about to lose his life, never having lived without dominion over another. Only now, at the end, about to perish, did he realize this control was wasted effort and didn't even exist. This man had fought, leveraged and destroyed for empty gains. He labored a lifetime over nothing.

Black, blue, then yellow streaked across the cabin; colors continued calmly passing from side to side. *What's happening*, he thought, and then remembered the plane. *This man is about to die. Yes, this is so. It seems like we've been falling forever. Maybe we won't die. Maybe this is a dream.*

Outside the cabin the grunting grew louder, pulling George's attention back into himself. The beast was closer now. His fear of not wanting to see the creature about to feast on him was overwhelmed by the need to know the truth. *Is this a dream or really happening?* Shaking in horror, he turned his bloated, bile-covered face to peer through the exit-door window. Rows of teeth separated. A mouth, hungry and dark, gaped.

The foreboding ocean was now near the horizon, as the cockpit crew still fought to level out their aircraft. The Atlantic churned about as it always had, oblivious to the lives it was about to take. A deafening boom reported into the blackness—flash, confusion, pain, cold, *can't breathe*, blank.

Darby sat with hands clasped behind his head, undisturbed by the newspaper headline on his desk, "Coral Oil Chief Lost At Sea: No Loss." It made him smile.

George really is gone, he thought. *His constant nagging's finally over. I never thought he'd stop baiting me. Still, I've known him longer than anyone. That abrasive nature—the scraping and scratching— was never going to cease.*

Stanley walked in with morning coffee, beaming a smile at Darby; always even-tempered and happy to serve. "Darby, there's a Miss Preston here to see you."

"Miss Preston?" Darby asked.

"Anne Preston. She's an associate of George Weatherby."

"She say what she wanted?"

"No. Miss Preston simply asked for a few moments of your time."

"Show her in, Stanley."

Stanley stepped out and returned. Anne followed as Stanley showed her to a chair.

Anne's black dress followed her body's curves like a fitted glove—makeup plied to perfection. If not for her infamously cunning nature, Darby would have found her company welcome.

"Miss Preston, may I get you anything?" Stanley chirped.

"No, thank you."

"That'll be all, Stanley," Darby said.

Stanley left the office, closing the door behind him.

"So he's Stanley Huffington. George told me one of theirs was working for you; seems nice enough."

"I'm the wrong person to butter up. If you want his family connection then just ask the boy," Darby suggested with a grin.

"I'll make note of that."

"So what can I do for you, Anne?"

"I wanted to offer my services."

"You don't waste any time. His body isn't even cold yet."

"Well, George has finally met his match."

"How do you mean?"

"Oh, you know…life. It gets the best of us all one day. Still, it's curious that his plane went down in a clear night sky."

"Do you suspect foul play?"

"Always; George was not widely loved."

"Two planes crashing at the same time is not unheard of. They could've bumped each other."

"Two planes: What makes you say that? The news only knows of his private jet. What do you know of the second plane?" Anne probed.

"I know all the people George knows. I was told thirty minutes after he was reported missing."

"I can get the kind of information his cronies don't know exist."

"I see…Look., I don't want your help. I have as many heavies as I'll ever need."

"I'm sure you do. Sometimes it takes something a little more delicate than a sledgehammer. There's no one more connected in Washington than I am."

"Connected," Darby interjected, half angry and half laughing. "I want to be disconnected! I've been trying to rend myself from that Beltway bunch for some time…and you want to keep me connected? You're as bad as George ever was."

"Worse."

"Of that I am sure. Your reputation precedes you."

"Thank you. I've earned it."

"I'm sure your parents are proud."

"They're dead."

"Didn't get the car you wanted after college graduation?"

"Clever. No, they were killed by a drunk driver when I was twelve."

"Sorry to hear that."

"Don't stop now. You'll disappoint my expectations. George has bored me on more than one occasion about you two in the early days. He said you stacked up quite the body count in destroyed companies on your way to building this empire. Don't let familial sentiment keep you from being authentic. They were killed. It was tragic. I adjusted and grew fiercely independent."

"Still...my sympathies."

"Ugh. Please, no more platitudes."

"Well, at least you're consistent. Your reputation as a cold-hearted dragon lady is well deserved."

"Thank you. It took years to fashion. I would hate to lose my éclat over a sentimental discussion about Mom and Dad."

"Your standing's safe here."

"Wonderful. Now, back to business. You want to separate yourself from the DC set then?"

"Yes."

"I'm your gal."

"You're not my gal. You were George's. Having you in my life is not going to help with where I'm going?"

"How do you know? Where are you going? Maybe I can be of assistance."

"Not likely. I'm done with your kind. If you really want to make a difference for me, then stand up, turn towards the doorway and walk through it."

"What about São Paolo?"

"What?" Darby asked with urgency.

"George was right. Brazil is your vulnerability. I can help you with it."

"You can help me with nothing."

Darby wondered what she knew. George generally only told people what they needed to know. It didn't make sense that George would have relayed anything specific unless he thought it necessary for insurance.

"George told me you had some trouble in South America and that would always be your Achilles heel."

"And did George say what that might be?" Darby probed.

"Maybe I shouldn't say. It wouldn't be polite."

"You're not a polite woman. You don't know anything. That's what I think."

"Is that so?"

"I also think you're a parasite and only exist for the sake of existence. You do nothing tangible to benefit any other human being but yourself. This is not your sin. A selfish person can be a positive force even if it's only for the self. You can't even make that claim. You are your own disease."

"Maybe I should shed a few tears. Would that make you feel that I am a better person?"

"No. Not even the loss of you. You're the illness that has become what power appears to be. You extort and leverage, yet have no real ability to do anything other than destroy. I want nothing of that life, you, or Washington anymore. You're a walking corpse. I'd like you to leave now."

After a brief silence, Anne rose, gently smiled and said, "I know you would…and you know that I'll always be around."

As Anne walked out, Darby rued the truth of her words.

CHAPTER

VIII

CHAINED TO FREEDOM

Reveling in his victory, Ethan departed from the front of Capitol Building. Happy with his efforts, he decided to take a walk. Hubert waited for him at the exit doors. Unaware of the full extent of Hubert's efforts to thwart his direction with the Stanton Bill, Ethan greeted Hubert with a smile.

Accepting that the first round had gone to Ethan, Hubert came prepared to move him along. Extending his hand, Hubert offered, "Congratulations, Ethan. That was quite a move—seventy-four to twenty-six. I knew you were going places."

Firmly shaking Hubert's hand, Ethan asked, "Can I assume you were pulling for me?"

"You know better than to ask what cards were played after a hand has folded. I played a strong round."

Smiling more brightly, Ethan added, "You're right. I don't care which way you went. I achieved what I set out to do."

"Ethan, walk with me for a moment, will you?"

"Certainly."

Frustrated with the Stanton Bill loss, Hubert would need another way to save expiring tax shelters. Openly battling Ethan was not the way to defeat his alternative energy movement.

"I must appear unmoved by your successful maneuver. The truth is, you've caught my attention. More than my attention—there are quite a few senators on both sides of the aisle who have taken notice of your achievement. It's clear you're a man who knows how to invigorate our body into a productive force. I'd like to do something about that."

"What've you got in mind?" Ethan asked.

"Senate Majority Leader."

"You must be kidding. Why would you want me to take over that position? A seasoned veteran would make more sense."

"But you've put your finger on our party's biggest problem. We hold a Senate majority. Yet our Majority Leader lacks a backbone—and seems to be taking orders from the Senate Minority Leader."

"I think you over-exaggerate. I've watched Senator Halstead. Brad seems competent."

"He's weak at delegating the Senate agenda. Did you catch how the Minority Leader, Senator Olivia Smoot of Kansas, kept the day's business and recognition on track to bolster your position—thereby winning your cause?"

"All in all, I thought it was good work."

"Yes. Good for you but bad for our party. The Senate Majority Leader possesses preferential treatment to be recognized on the Senate floor at any time of his choosing. Did you see what happened in there today? He made use of that privilege once. Once is utter absurdity! This is Washington. Halstead should've dominated the floor so much that the news would have reported it as a filibuster."

"Isn't that an abuse of power?"

"Ethan, I can't believe you asked. Did you not hear me? This is DC! If you're looking for someone to hold your hand, then pack your bags and get out. You'll do no good for our party here."

"I think I can do a lot of good with or without the party. My committee, in conjunction with a few House members, approves applicants for grants and low-interest loans mandated by the Alternative Energy Bill. Now that any current roadblocks are gone, I'm eager to begin accepting applications."

"Careful there, hotshot. You've had some preliminary success. Don't let it go to your head. And especially don't start thinking you'll be the first politician to go it alone. Not going to happen."

"Is that a threat?"

"Hold up. I'm only looking out for you. We've steered off course. I only wanted to tell you what a fine job you're doing and offer an opportunity to do more."

"What about my other committee chairing responsibilities?"

"It's not as difficult as you'd imagine. You work with the Senate Minority Leader to schedule Senate business. There could be a few instances where you may be asked to lend a hand to the House of Representatives. It's more procedural than anything. However, given the right circumstances, you could have a large influence over the Speaker of the House of Representatives. Are you following me, Ethan? The party needs a young and energetic senator like you to give the other side a healthy push when they're not willing to cooperate."

"That's all good and well, but I'm busy. Let me think about it."

"Ethan, what's there to think about? It can be done tomorrow if you'd agree to it."

"You seem certain about that. Don't you suppose Senator Halstead will have something to say about it?"

"What can he say? After what just happened, I wouldn't be surprised if half our party wasn't in his office trying to hang him from the nearest attic vent. The party is meeting tomorrow. This matter of business will be brought up at that time. I think you're the man for the job and I'll nominate you."

"Hubert, really…thank you for your faith but I'm not certain it's right for me at this time. I'll put thought into it. I can't promise anything."

"Think carefully. I know what kind of man you are. The only way you'll ever be happy in Washington is to possess the unlimited power it would take to do the job your way. This is an integral step in that direction."

"I'll think about it. Tomorrow, then," Ethan said as he walked away. Hubert and Ethan separated at the entrance, not having moved since beginning their conversation. Hubert reentered Congress and Ethan descended the steps, wanting again to simply enjoy the day's win. When he reached the bottom, he followed the walkway to the sidewalk adjacent First Street. He cleared his mind and began walking north.

After having moved just a few yards, Ethan came across Seneca begging a well-dressed man for money. It stirred in Ethan a paternal instinct to help. Seneca too recognized Ethan and ceased talking to the stranger in mid-sentence. The man seized the chance to escape Seneca's panhandling, striding away before Seneca could plead anymore.

"Seneca, how are you doing today?"

"I'm just fine there, Senator Scott. You can't ask for better weather," Seneca returned while reaching to shake Ethan's hand.

"Call me, Ethan, and take this. I want you to put this hard-earned money to good use—don't buy candy with it," Ethan kidded as he handed Seneca what bills he had in his pocket. They both laughed.

"Can you walk with me, Seneca? I was hoping for a short stroll before returning to the office."

"Sure."

They moved along the sidewalk just enjoying the quiet. Seneca sensed that Ethan wanted peace. He was happy to share it with Ethan.

"Tell me something, Seneca. How will you fare this winter on the streets of Washington?"

"I think Washington picked up the pseudonym Bone Yard on account of the bone-chilling winters and the breeze off the Potomac River. But I'll be alright. If I can finish at the top of my law-school class and hold down the position of Law Review editor, then DC winters should always be a walk in the park."

"So, do you miss the law?" Ethan asked in a patronizing tone, not meaning to be rude.

Seneca ignored it, knowing why Ethan might question his claim. He replied, "You know Ethan, I think the greatest problem with the law today is that there's too much of it. Really, think about that for a moment. Haven't we, as a society, legislated ourselves into a corner—so that no matter which direction a person turns they've broken the law?"

"I suppose you could be right."

"Think about it in terms of the Western United States in the nineteenth century, before the westward expansion was completed; aside from small towns and settlements. Largely there was very little law except for the US Constitution to serve as a guide for those on the open prairie. Many towns may have had a lone peacemaker and those that widely interpreted the law. For the most part there was harmony. People made it work just fine. They had to rely on common sense to guide their daily decisions. Though a little rough at the edges, it served the common good."

"Wouldn't you say that the expanded laws we have today provide for greater fairness than in the untamed West?"

Seneca stopped walking and asked, "Do you really believe that? What fairness is afforded anyone in the United States today that doesn't involve politics, banking or multinational corporations?"

"You're right, Seneca. I can't believe I actually said that out loud. I was caught up in wanting our country to be more than it is for the sake of argument."

"That's okay. I loved a good debate once upon a time. Besides, if the laws don't get you the courts surely will. It never stops amazing me the people that sit on the bench in this city—mmm hmm."

"While I'm enjoying our conversation, I should turn around and walk towards the office. I have a desk full of work waiting. Take care, alright?" Ethan implored. He shook hands with Seneca and began moving towards his office building.

As Ethan made his way, Seneca bellowed in Latin, "De minimis non curat lex."

Ethan turned back towards Seneca and replied, "The law does not concern…"

They finished the phrase together, "…itself with trivia."

"Yes, you see," Seneca added with a broad smile. "Now I think you understand a little better. Don't worry, you'll get it. You go on now," he said comfortingly, as he turned away and moved off.

Ethan was baffled by Seneca's words; unsure if he was telling the truth about law school. He thought, *If it's true, then why is he homeless and on the streets? It doesn't make sense. His Latin was perfect.* As Ethan returned to the walkway, he felt unsettled—out of place in a rational world.

The following morning the Blue Coats Party convened at their Washington office. Blue Coats formed before the US Constitution was signed. Many Constitutional Convention attendees were party members.

Controlled by members of the wealthy elite, they believed in small government, large military presence and fostered economic dominance. The membership tended to attract philosophical and religiously conservative politicians—in truth only interested in the appearance of those qualities.

Ethan arrived before the grand speeches commenced. As with most political discussions of any magnitude, the tradition of congratulating party leadership was observed. Ethan ignored the formalities while reading through the syllabus.

After the last politician conveyed his gratitude, Senator Brad Halstead stood up. "My fellow party members, I won't bore you with the details of what I'm about to say. Please trust that I have your best interests at heart. It is my greatest regret that I must step down as Senate Majority Leader for family reasons. Please accept my thanks for your support. I know you will appoint the right person for the job. Thank you."

The audience of senators grumbled, but applauded nonetheless. Senator Halstead sat down—outwardly angry—raising and lowering his hand to acknowledge the attention.

He leaned over to Hubert and whispered, "There, I did it. We're square. If you ever mention my affair, I'll eviscerate you."

Hubert snapped, "Brad, we're even."

"He's so green. How can you think this is a good idea?"

"Brad, you're making a scene. Trust me. It's for the good of the party."

"You mean it's good for you. What are you getting out of this?"

"The same thing you are. Now clap and be silent, you hack."

After the applause ceased, Brad rose again. "As customary I possess the authority, albeit an obscure charge, to name a replacement; or pass the duty onto our membership to be put to a vote. Given the nature of this party, it's only prudent to choose a successor. Getting a consensus out of you is like pulling teeth. It gets the job done but hurts like the devil and leaves a hole in your head."

The audience applauded, laughed and cheered at his candor and the pathetic truth. Brad continued, "Again, feeling charitable today, I'll spare you another long speech. I therefore name Senator Ethan Scott to take the position of Senate Majority Leader."

Surprise seized the audience's faces. That position would typically have been given to a senior senator. Something was happening they were not privy to. The clapping that ensued was respectful but subdued.

"Senator Scott, please rise," Senator Halstead enjoined.

Ethan rose, baffled that Hubert had actually arranged it. Though Ethan had thought it over the evening before, he didn't believe it would ever come to pass.

"Senator Scott, do you accept this nomination to the position of Senate Majority Leader?"

Ethan, still surprised, replied, "Absolutely!"

The other senators laughed.

"Then step forward and be recognized." As Ethan stood before the crowd, Brad said, "My fellow senators, it is my pleasure to present your new Senate Majority Leader, Senator Ethan Scott. Congratulations, Senator Scott. Please say a few words," Brad finished as he took his seat.

Hubert said, "Thank you, Brad."

"Go to hell," Brad bit back as he smiled and turned to hear Ethan's words—fuming that he had been coerced into giving up a position that took years to get.

"Fellow Blue Coats, I must say this is quite a surprise. It was only yesterday that the opportunity to serve the Senate in this manner was brought to my attention. I'm excited to make a difference in the lives of those who serve this country. Thank you," Ethan offered as he sat down.

The next day was one unlike any other for Ethan; even more challenging than his first day in the Senate. Phone calls and special requests swarmed his office from open to close. The remainder of the week was no different. Much had been discussed in those first few days; and yet less was accomplished than before.

The following Monday, Ethan turned off the phones and assembled his office of now ten, including an assistant, two secretaries, two runners and five law-school student volunteers. "I hope you had a relaxing weekend. It'll be your last for a while. Jane has issued your individual assignments. I want to explain why. The how is up to you. "You're all incredibly talented. You've committed to something important. This office is not simply a title held. It stands as one of mankind's highest aspirations: to achieve and maintain civil society. We've been at it for thousands of years. You're now a part of it. When you find yourself tired or frustrated, don't forget that our toil is one of dignity not unlike the kings of old. And, like those elevated historical figures, we will prevail through diligence and strength of character.

"These lofty words seem more appropriate to describe endeavors like discovering a new world. Washington is stinking with the detritus of walking corpses calling themselves Senator, Representative and so on. Our capital has become a home for those who accomplish nothing by wielding impotent power. We can do better. Last week's performance will not be repeated. I want you to delegate. You're no longer an assistant, secretary or intern. You're an extension of me. I don't have time to waste. You, then, do not have time to waste. If someone calls with a demand, issue, or problem then task them to provide the choice of solutions. We're in the position of making decisions. That's our task. The Washington gaggle-shimmy will not exist inside this office. Don't hesitate. Don't fail our people. Now, get started," Ethan sermonized, motioning upward with his hands for the staff to stand and depart.

"Senator Scott, I forgot to mention, Miss Preston is waiting for you in the foyer," Jane updated him. She had been enthralled by his words and was the last to leave.

"Please show her in, Jane."

Ethan remained standing, waiting for Anne to enter. His enthusiasm with getting a handle on his new responsibilities filled him with positive energy. He beamed as Anne sauntered in. Jane departed, closing the door behind her.

"You're wearing quite the grimace today," Ethan noted.

"And look at you so chipper this morning. It sounds like I missed rush week."

"Just getting a handle on the new workload."

"I heard; Senate Majority Leader. If I didn't know better, then I'd say you were my type of guy. How did that come about?"

"It was all a matter of happenstance. I explained that I was already too busy. They nominated me anyway."

"You don't really believe that, Ethan. There're no accidents in DC."

"I didn't say it was an accident. Senator Riley somehow arranged it."

"Say no more. I know all about it now. Ethan, you have no idea who Riley really is."

"I've had a few conversations with him. Can't say we share the same political goals or even a common understanding of true power, but he seems okay."

"Of course, that's what he wants you to see. He's the Homeland Security and Government Affairs Chairman."

"I know."

"You know bupkis. That man has a hand in every pot. He makes Byron Anderson nervous."

"No, he doesn't. I've met the President. He's not a pushover."

"Ethan, every man breaks. It only takes the right weakness to exploit."

"You're a bit darker than normal."

"Ethan, I could bring you to your knees. With all your integrity, it would take one phone call to change the world as you know it. You have no idea how dark I can get."

"Where did that come from?"

"Like I said back in New York, you can no longer entertain a schoolboy sensibility if you intend to survive the Bone Yard."

"That's fine out there. But in this office, I'll have my refuge."

"You will not! It's nowhere to be found. Didn't you hear me? This is the Bone Yard. What happens in a Bone Yard? Your bones are walked on and crushed. I don't want to see that happen to you. So if you don't keep your head and act right, I'll just as soon destroy you myself—save watching the rest of them having a turn at you."

"What's going on? Is this about your boss's plane going down? You're lost—so you came here to take a few swings at me, work out your anger; or hurt because your cruel benefactor has gone missing and is not likely to return? He may still turn up somewhere in a life-raft or stranded on an island."

"Ethan, you're charming," Anne replied. "Spare the shrink yammer. I'm just on my way back to New York from the South. Thought I'd stop in for a visit. I can see now that it was a mistake. I truly feel worse now than while waiting for you to wrap up your rally with the troops."

"Look, maybe you should go. I've got work to do and you clearly don't need me to feel better. I'm not your punching bag and I do hit back. So holster the attitude and get moving. Call me when you can talk in a pleasant and civil tone."

Anne got up with a look of exhilaration and viciousness. She said, "I'll visit the next time I'm in town."

"Come with a nicer disposition, will you?"

"Can't promise anything," Anne replied with a disturbing smile, and left the office.

Anne was shaken; outwardly manipulative instead of her typical guile. She walked past Jane—ignoring her gestures but feeling no joy in the act. She felt an emptiness not known since childhood—an era marked by neglectful parents consumed with their own pursuits.

Later in the day, Jane entered Ethan's office. "Senator, your two o'clock is here."

"My two o'clock?"

"You said to delegate. It's Miss Sanders. I assumed you wouldn't mind. She was hoping for fifteen minutes."

"With Abigail, it's never fifteen minutes," Ethan happily noted.

"True, but only because you won't stop talking," Abigail interjected as she walked in.

"That's all, Jane. Thank you."

As they sat, Abigail said, "You're singlehandedly making my career. Life would be a great deal easier if you could move the senatorial office to New York so I could cut down on air travel—easier to get face-time, you know."

"I'll get right on that; though I think the President would need to sign off."

"I'm your constituency. You have to do what I want," Abigail joked.

"If I had a vote for every time that's been said since taking office, then reelection should be a cinch. So you want to do this again? Don't your viewers get tired of seeing me?"

"I don't know about them, but…" she smiled cheekily, before turning serious. "I'd like a few comments regarding your latest appointment. But that's not the entire reason for my visit."

"Okay."

"I spoke with David last week. He's a shell of the man I interviewed last spring. I've covered plenty of defeated politicians, business leaders and natural disaster survivors. I know when someone's permanently going down. David's paddling his last strokes. I normally don't emotionally attach to interviewees. I'm not sure what it is with you two, but I can't simply report this story. I need to get involved. Ethan, you need to get involved."

"What can I do? I'm a senator now and he's the president of a corporation duly served a court order to cease all operations. I know he's in a fight for his company. However, it's inappropriate for me to intervene; no matter how much I care for him, or the CMC for that matter."

"Why? You're the Senate Majority Leader. Are you saying there's nothing you can do with that authority?"

"Precisely that—Washington is what it is today because this kind of systemic manipulation is acceptable. It may be a good cause, but it's improper to coerce due process. As much as I hate what's happening to David, he must take it to the courts and win his day there. Anything else is an oligarchy." Ethan's stomach turned, knowing he could do more, corrupt more, but he couldn't accept what he was becoming and didn't want to lose Abigail's respect.

"Is there anything in your oath of office which precludes you from talking to a friend? Ethan, he needs help finding his way again. Can't you take a day trip to New York—drop by his office just to show you care? I've seen men die terrible deaths before. The ones that had friends nearby passed in peace. I don't have a crystal ball. I hope he finds a way to turn around the CMC. However, if saving it isn't possible, then he shouldn't have to endure it alone."

"You're right, Abbey. I'll go," Ethan relented, almost ashamed of his earlier words.

Relieved that Ethan had agreed, Abigail changed the subject. "Do you mind if we keep this short? I'll shoot the standard questions."

"Wow! So that's how to get a pass from Abigail Sanders; you've gotta slip her a favor." His good humor moderated as he made eye contact with her. "I don't know why I was given this position. It's not par. Why would an appointed senator with so little experience or connections be nominated to Senate Majority Leader?"

"Maybe they just thought you were the right man for the job," Abigail replied, attempting to be supportive and surprised by the question.

"Don't misunderstand my meaning. I can manage the responsibilities. That's not a concern. Why me? It doesn't make any sense."

"Which part makes no sense to you, Ethan?"

"All of it. What I know of Washington, I already knew before arriving. Heck, everybody knows that nothing gets done in this city without owing or being owned. How am I holding such a coveted senior position? It's quite the puzzle. Something's at work—but to what end?"

"Your ascendancy has been swift—definitely not unheard of, though."

"There are always exceptions. However, if I'm not mistaken, those people were assassinated."

"There've been a few in the last two centuries. I understand your thinking, but are you sure this isn't paranoia?"

"It may be that—hard to say. You know what I like about business, Abbey?"

"What's that?"

"What typically happens makes sense."

"How do you mean?"

"You buy a cup of coffee and a pack of chewing gum. It costs a few dollars. You pay the vendor. They give you the coffee and gum. If all goes well, you come back the next day and on it continues."

"And what does this have to do with what you're experiencing?"

"It makes sense. The vendor pays his coffee supplier, the concession company and pockets the remainder as profit. This idea is fundamentally how all businesses work.

"In a town like Washington, where it's common knowledge that nothing gets done without coercion or favors of some kind, why would I be given such an accolade for having only been here a month—all the while owing no one? I don't buy it, Abbey. Something's wrong about all this. I'll do as much good as I can while here. I'm just not sure why I'm here."

"If what you're saying is true, then whatever is wanted from you would certainly be made evident sometime. Wouldn't you think?"

"Yes. I'm normally a patient man. However, I've never been surrounded by so many who do nothing more than vie for as much power as possible. It's like watching an orgy feast where nobody succumbs to a burst stomach, but simply lies waiting for the servant to bring another plate of food to devour. Meanwhile, countless numbers starve just outside the chamber walls. I don't like the feeling that at any time, someone's going to sneak up behind me."

"This is Morgan Brasher with KNTU 950 Talk Radio Houston on this sunny August day. With us this morning is none other than Darby Adams, CEO of Houston's own Fountain Oil. Darby has joined us this morning to discuss what he describes as the future in alternative energy. Darby, I'd like to welcome you to the show. Good morning," Morgan briskly announced, pointing his finger at Darby in the next sound booth to indicate that the microphone was live and ready for him to speak. Morgan was famous for his obesity; he used it as an advantage by maintaining the jolly caricature of a man that laughed at his own grotesque appearance and encouraged others to join in the laughter.

Seated at the control console, Morgan reclined. Food fell from his mustache. He chuckled while wiping away the debris. Rubbing his hands together over the trashcan completed his hygiene routine as the interview began.

"Good morning, Morgan. Thank you for having me on your show."

"So tell us something. That's some claim you've made; especially coming from such a powerful name in petroleum."

"It's true that Fountain Oil has enjoyed success. But this has more to do with the future of alternative energy than oil. In fact, it has nothing to do with Fountain Oil. This is a technology owned by Fountain Alternative Energy."

"Wow. You do keep busy, don't you?"

"You're the busy one. I understand this is one of eight media shows you work on or produce. Is that right?"

"That's right. But this isn't about me, Darby. Tell us why you decided to make your grand announcement on radio medium."

"Speaking plainly, the major news and cable networks are no longer interested in the news. Ratings and revenues seem to be their only concern. Your show is important because it's available to the public unvarnished. I want to talk about this technology without network influence.

"This is not our only marketing effort. There are events, official television, social media and internet releases following this show today. Radio is live and broadcast instantaneously over the airwaves, satellites and internet. Those who would oppose its release would interfere with the information we intend to share. This way, they can only report it."

"I want to hear about the future in alternative energies."

"It's an electric engine. Fountain Alternative Energy has been working on this project for years. We're now ready to begin production of the first units."

"What does it run on: solar, wind, or some other source?"

"Nothing," Darby stated with a thrill he had not experienced in a long time. Not only was he embarking on a new journey which could take the remainder of his life to walk. But someone other than himself would benefit from it.

"Nothing…that's physically impossible. What do you mean?"

"I mean nothing. It's self-perpetuating…well, nearly."

"Again, sir, I put it to you that this claim of yours is not consistent with high-school physics. Forgive my ignorance. I studied journalism in college. However, if I'm not mistaken, energy cannot be derived from nothing. Something must go into this engine of yours to get power out."

"That's correct, Morgan. A further explanation would be in order."

"I'll say. Now, you said this engine of yours takes nothing to run. You're contradicting yourself."

"No, I'm not. It's all in what that something is that makes it nothing."

"Your responses are rather esoteric. Can you provide our listeners with more detail?"

"Certainly…it's fundamentally no different than your average everyday AC electric motor. A coil moves from pole to pole collecting voltage; ergo, we have electricity."

"Seems simple to me—but what's turning the screw?"

"That's the billion-dollar question, isn't it?"

"More like trillion."

"Maybe…what I can tell you is that the motor's dynamic but also static."

"So it moves and doesn't? Am I missing something? So it has no moving parts?"

"No, no, Morgan, you misunderstand. It works like an ocean-wave generator; rising and falling with the incoming surf, but without the ocean."

"Sounds awful technical—how is this up and down motion generated? What did you say…like an ocean-wave generator?"

"Close enough, anyway. That engine component is nearing completion of the patent process. Needless to say, its secret drives the collector."

"Amazing!"

"We're quite proud of it."

"My next question is why. Why do any of this? If I were in your shoes, I'm not sure I would choose to create a technology that would undo my own company. Wouldn't creating this perpetual motor destroy your oil company?"

"First thing is that I'm not hurting my oil company. It'll take another two hundred years to discontinue fossil-fuel use and replace it with electricity for transportation and heating. A large portion of the world has yet to maintain a stable economy and political structure. Several generations will need to join the global community as equals before adoption is standard.

"Our petroleum output will continue at current levels. What's not publicly known is that Fountain Oil will never increase production beyond current numbers. Growth will come from technology, alternative energy and systems of the future.

"Another important point to make is that this engine we're about to begin production on is by no means a complete power-production solution. The segment we intend to serve makes up the average American household. Within the innovation resides its limitation. It must be fixed to a stable platform. So it can't be used in transportation. Additionally, there's a drop-off in voltage, which limits its capacity to the output of an average American home and maybe two electric cars on any given day.

"As I alluded to before, this is one solution among many. It's a good one, though, and destined for use. It's also built on a fundamental resource readily abundant to our planet. I have no doubts that one day it'll be replaced by a more ingenious and effective technology. Most important is that we begin cutting the tether of oil dependency. It's frightening—change always is. But with the coming innovations are newer frontiers and freedoms for mankind."

"So why now?" Morgan asked sincerely.

"What have all the great ones said: The time is now? Right? Now is the time: not only because it can be done. All of the known oilfields are depleted or have reached their midpoint stores, except for protected territories and lands—and they'll be tapped eventually. It's all downhill from here.

"It should also be done because the pollution the industry creates is destroying the only planet in our solar system that currently sustains life. Does it make sense to continue poking holes in the life-raft keeping humanity afloat?

"Finally, a problem that's very close to my heart is the issue of power; or more clearly corruption of power. I've been fortunate to live a life; historically, known only to a few. I can do anything or have anything I want. I'm not alone in this position.

"A great number of others also control the world's oil supply and power production. They're not interested in human posterity, what they're doing to this planet, or the inhumane corruption they swim in. They only care about money and power. Everything and everyone is second to that. Don't for a second doubt a syllable of what I just said."

Morgan was silent, allowing suspense to build, understanding the profound nature of the moment. He then solemnly asked, "If all that you've said is true, and you're a part of that group, then why would you want to help the rest of us?"

"Morgan, I'm tired down to the bones. I am fifty-nine years old. I feel ninety-nine. I've spent my life accumulating wealth and garnering perceived power to force my will onto someone or something. A few years ago, I realized that I simply couldn't do it anymore.

"I've enjoyed the life of a wealthy man. And yet I feel as though I haven't lived. That life is now a part of the past. I simply want to produce something useful for humanity. I wish to build instead of compete. I want to live richly in my heart and give away foolishly. This engine is my new beginning."

"Darby, that really is something. When will this technology be ready for purchase and what will it cost?"

"The company is in the process of assembling the production line. We have four facilities in different states. It should take about two years to roll out our first units. Its cost will likely be around the price of an average home heating unit. An ancillary benefit is the engine's portability; it can be taken with a family if they move."

"I'm truly astonished, Darby. I was certain this would be another ploy to push the cost of gas up. I haven't been caught off guard this much since my wife left me for our mechanic," Morgan mused, laughing at his own misfortune. "I can't imagine you'll be very popular amongst your buddies with all the greenbacks. What're you going to do about them? Don't you suppose they might try thwart your plans?"

"They might just do something about it. I can't say for sure how they'll react."

"Your old friend, George Weatherby of Coral Oil, would certainly not approve," Morgan suggested to steer the show's tone in another direction.

Caught off guard by Morgan's question, Darby's face turned red. "You're right about that. George and I have spoken at great length about these very issues. He couldn't let go of his market position and was not ready to embrace the industry changes emerging before his eyes. I suspect it's always been this way with newer technologies pushing older ones aside. George will be missed," Darby added, attempting to sound respectful.

"He will at that. This is Morgan Brasher with KNTU 950 Talk Radio Houston wishing you a good Saturday. The news is coming up next after a few messages from our advertisers."

Darby stood up—still disturbed by Morgan's final question. He felt claustrophobic in the sound booth, as he pulled off his headphones. Darby slipped out of his own booth and abruptly shook Morgan's hand.

"Listen, when that engine of yours is ready, give me a call. I would very much like to have you on my show again."

CHAPTER
IX

TRUE TO ONE'S SELF

Abigail tapped her heel as she hitched an elevator ride to network headquarters. Being called back to New York was a slap in the face. On Stanton's trail, in a few instances, she missed seeing John in person by mere moments. He made a habit of only staying in any public place for no more than thirty minutes. She was getting closer with each movement in her investigation.

The doors opened to Joseph waiting with a cup of coffee; Abigail's new college intern was eager to prove his worth. Handing Abigail her beverage as she stepped out, he said, "Miss Sanders, Mr. Lambert has been asking of your whereabouts for the last hour. He's held up the staff in the conference room for your arrival."

"The meeting wasn't scheduled to begin for another hour."

"He changed the time this morning. I tried reaching your mobile phone but you didn't answer. Three messages were also left with your service."

"I was in an airplane flying back for this ridiculous meeting. Alright, tell me. What do you think of the new chief?"

"Ma'am, I think that he is…" Joseph stumbled, reluctant to finish his sentence—not wanting to sound incompetent or judgmental.

Abigail stopped short of the conference room, looked Joseph in the eyes and asked, "Is it Joseph or Joe?"

"Joseph."

"Joseph, you're not going to keep your job another day if you ever call me 'Ma'am' again. Next, I need the people I count on to be straightforward. Can you do that?"

"Yes, Miss Sanders."

"Good. If you work hard and smart I'll keep you. No amount of political correctness will save your hide if you can't provide those things. Now, take this bag to my office. Meet me there after this useless gathering is over; hopefully sooner than later."

Joseph ran off as instructed. Abigail entered the conference room. The remainder of the staff were already assembled and quietly seated at the table. Frank Lambert stood at the head of the conference table. Dressed in a dark blue pinstriped suit, he appeared pompous in appearance and posture—looking the part of a fatted bureaucrat. His pointed nose sat upon a face of contemptuous judgment.

As he spoke, his double chin shook. "Ah, Miss Sanders, it is good of you to join us; albeit late. Do please take a seat so that we may begin."

"I'm not late. I'm actually early. You can't reschedule a staff meeting the same day and expect those on assignment to make it. The news doesn't happen on a schedule."

"This is true. But, perhaps you have heard of mobile phone technology. It's been prevalent for going on twenty years. You might try using one. You'll find the constant changes in itinerary much easier to accommodate," he sarcastically replied.

Frank cleared his throat to address the room. "Thank you all for coming to this staff meeting on time. My name is Frank Lambert. As many of you know, I am the newly appointed president of TTN. I was invited aboard to take over the running of this network. You may have noticed that I carry myself with a certain formality. I find it creates a professional environment in which one can count on nothing but exemplary performance and attitude held by all. I expect you, the network staff, to uphold this as an example for the remainder of the network, and our affiliates in other cities throughout the United States.

"My predecessors, Miss Sandra Buchanan and Mr. Daniel Walters, with us here today, ran the operation in a fashion they felt worked best for them. You will quickly find that my leadership is dissimilar." He halted his monologue and offered, "Mr. Walters, this is not meant as an insult to your leadership." He then returned to addressing the group as if Daniel did not exist.

Frank had been privately educated from childhood through graduate school. What he knew most was how everything should fit together. He lacked the imagination to think outside the confines of what he had been taught to believe.

"I expect precision and a certain economical use of time. Your time is now my time. I do not care to have my time wasted. Please see that you make this so and we will all get along swimmingly.

"I have taken the liberty of reassigning a few departmental directors. Please see to it that you familiarize yourselves with the newly designated leadership. I know you will do a fine job for them.

"Now, if there are no other questions, then please return to your duties. Thank you for your attention. May I ask the reporting and anchor staff stay on for a few additional announcements?"

After the support staff had departed, Frank panned around the room at the remaining silent faces; ensuring each person made eye contact with him. He then said, "I want to express to you, the personalities on our daily broadcasts, that I think you are all fine people. Because you are in a position of celebrity, an additional responsibility befalls you regarding the remaining staff.

"They look up to you. If you are dedicated and committed, then so too will they fall in line; and we'll all have a happy and efficiently run ship here at TTN. However, if you find yourselves taking shortcuts in performance or not considering the rest of the network while at the news desk or on location, then they too will follow your example. I would simply ask that you be cognizant of your actions. They will be watching. So too will I.

"The only other change for you at this time regards content. I will be assigning all stories from now on. I know many of you were provided more freedom under Miss Buchanan's reign. I, however, run a different newsroom. I like to know where my greatest assets are at all times.

"Be sure to check with me before taking on any assignments. I would also ask that you be more frugal with company time. Time and our employees make up our greatest holdings. Waste is no longer acceptable. That is all. Thank you for your additional patience. Now, go find us our stories to tell," Frank announced—miserably failing light-hearted inspiration.

Everyone stood and let out of the conference room. Not a single happy face survived. Daniel bumped into Abigail as they exited.

Daniel puttered as they walked down the main corridor, "How does it feel to no longer be the office darling? Sandra hated me. Growing up, she was even mean to me at Christmas parties. But with this new guy…watch out. He sure has your number."

"Daniel, you've never mattered to me. With Sandra gone, there's even less to care about."

"How's that?"

"She constantly reminded me how worthless a man you are. With Frank at the wheel, I'll ponder you even less. If what you're saying is true, I'll be granted a favor. Now, is there anything else you want to stammer on about or are we done here?"

"It's evident that this'll never go anywhere—a shame too. I would have enjoyed you," Daniel snubbed as if retracting an offered courtesy.

Disgusted by Daniel's remark, Abigail smiled. "What a loss. Maybe I'm wrong. I know. Why don't we all sit down and talk about it— you, me and your wife? Maybe she could explain the catastrophic injury I'd experience not having a go at you. What do you say—up for a cup of tea with the little missus?"

Daniel's face turned white as all expression withered away. He skipped off ahead, ducked into his office, and slammed the door.

Frank made his way through the group. "Miss Sanders, I was hoping to get a private word."

"Call me Abigail."

"Thank you, but I think Miss Sanders will do. As I mentioned a few moments ago, I prefer a bit of formality in my business dealings."

"Fine…then what can I do for you?"

"I wanted to discuss your work habits."

"Certainly. Why don't you join me in my office? I just got back from the Bone Yard. We can talk while I get settled in."

"I should think my office would be more appropriate. Don't you?"

"Whatever you wish is fine."

Abigail closed her office door and followed Frank. As they entered, she noticed Sandra's decorations had been replaced by two walls of leather-bound books and a model ship collection.

"Why don't you have a seat? Can I get you anything to drink?"

"No, thanks."

"Good. Then let's get right to it. You, far above your colleagues, travel the most on assignment. It is my assessment that this kind of work is better suited for field personnel. You're an anchor for this network, with a rightful place behind the news desk. Yours is a face that people trust. The more they see it, the higher our ratings will be. You understand, don't you?"

"I understand my years in this business garner a measure of credibility. That's why having that face out there for the really important stories lends credence to our coverage. I saw the ratings from my time in a combat zone. They overshadowed all of the other networks that week. A news person goes where the news is."

Shaking his head, Frank said, "Miss Sanders, inasmuch as I understand your thinking, let's save ourselves a drawn-out debate over journalistic philosophies. I have been charged with running this network to the best of my abilities. To that end, all my efforts are focused. May I assume we have an understanding?"

"Mr. Lambert, I completely understand you," Abigail cryptically responded.

"Good. It is all settled. That will be all then. Good day to you. I'll be watching this evening with great interest."

Abigail rose and nodded to Frank before turning to walk out. Returning to her office, Abigail felt Frank had been somehow diverted from his true calling as a factory manager manufacturing rubber ducks for children.

Ethan stood before the Energy and Natural Resources Committee. A body once only known for pushing political agenda was implementing policy and building the foundations of future energy sources.

"It seems that we've finished this week's tasks in short order. Please stay on track with our projected weekly output. All of you are exceeding my expectations. Let's continue this trend.

"I've looked over the applications for grant monies. There are some intriguing ideas. Those of you on the approval committee, please ensure the untried technologies submitted for consideration are verified by an independent third-party research firm. We have an ample budget here. But I don't want a single cent of it being wasted. That's your mandate.

"Now that business has been attended to, I'd like to talk about a personal issue. As you know, I was elected Senate Majority Leader—an unexpected advancement, to be sure. Acceptance accompanied the caveat that I not lose control of this committee. I'm dedicated to the Senate and my constituency. This committee means a great deal more to me than heading up the Senate. I think both are possible, but can't be done alone.

"I have an idea that'll seem strange to some of you. Hear me out first before making up your minds. Everyone here belongs to a political party. I'm a member of the Blue Coats. We're known for our conservative nature. Some of you are from the Britches Party, given to more liberal ideologies. We even have two on the committee from the independent-thinking Liberty Party.

"What I'm proposing is in contravention to your doctrinal affiliations. Yet, when considering what we've jointly accomplished in a short amount of time, I'm convinced this idea can work; so long as we agree to remain focused on the goal and not partisan politics.

"I would like to delegate my Senate Majority Leadership duties to all of you, much like how this committee functions. We can do this. It will anger quite a few people; especially those belonging to the Britches and Liberty Parties—since you currently exist as a minority influence in the Senate. My own party will be unsettled by the decision. However, if I am to maintain committee control and these appointment's duties, assistance is requisite. You're all capable, possessing talents which could be harnessed to that end.

If we work together, imagine what can be done! Just look at what's been nailed down in a month. This alone should inspire you to visualize what could be over the long haul. In the process you'll be a part of something monumental. Greatness comes to so very few. Fewer yet recognize when the opportunity is presented. I ask you to seize this chance. Together, we all will do great things."

A single clap sounded and ceased. All eyes fell upon Senator Dean Sidel. He sarcastically declared, "What a wonderful gesture you're making. We do your work and you get the glory. What's in it for us?"

"Senator Sidel, you ask a fine question. The answer will be served up in two shakes. Let me finish here first. Thanks."

Ethan nodded and smiled towards Senator Sidel with appreciation for his patience. He then burst out, "Senator Clark!"

"Yes," Senator Clark replied in surprise—not expecting to be called upon. His response was that of a drowsy student nodding off to sleep in class and jolted awake by the teacher's voice.

"You could help me out and not need to do very much in the process."

"I'm your man."

"I thought you might say that. You're a third-generation senator, are you not?"

"Yes, I am."

"With your family's political influence you could leverage the Senate's business in line with our party's overall agenda by flexing a little bit of that legislative muscle you carry about. Would you terribly mind doing this for me if called upon?"

"I wouldn't mind at all," replied Clark—relieved that he hadn't been asked to exert any more effort than he already put into his job.

"Excellent. Thank you. Senator Peck, you're needed for a special assignment. Upon you the weightiest responsibilities will be conveyed. I need you to schedule the Senate's daily, weekly and monthly business according to my party's agenda. You have shown extraordinary capacity as secretary of this committee. With your ability to manage large and small tasks equally well, nothing will get left behind. Will you do it?"

"Ethan, call me Beatrice. I appreciate such a lovely compliment.

You know I'm a member of the Britches Party. As much as I want to help, I'm not sure the Senate Minority Leader will approve my directly working on behalf of your party's position."

"Beatrice, if I could help you sell the idea, would you do it?"

"Absolutely," she exclaimed.

"Alright then, this is what you tell Senator Smoot. Tell her that by assisting my needs, you will be in a position to influence the Senate Majority Leader. She'll accept this. I know Olivia. I even voted for her once."

"I'll convey what you said word for word."

"That's all I ask, Beatrice. Thank you. Now, a lion's share of the Senate Majority Leader's responsibility is to be on the Senate floor or somewhere near it. Beatrice, your job will be to keep the day-to-day business minimized. It's not that we should short the American public our best efforts. However, posturing for the sake of politics must be culled. Beatrice, you will be on the front lines of this effort. Senator Sidel, this is the best place to reap rewards for yourself and the Britches Party you belong to."

"Yes, I'm listening," Senator Sidel chimed in, sitting up with interest.

"I've noticed that you're normally a man of few words who prefers to work efficiently at all times," Ethan lauded with a straight face. The words that secretly came to his mind were: blow-hard, peddler, and sloth. "I could use you most here. Keeping control over the goings-on of the Senate each day is large in scope. I need someone to maintain a watchful eye over the general senatorial temperament: what the outliers are thinking; who might be making a surprise move; pitfalls I should be watching out for. What you can take back to Senator Smoot is that you will be advising the Senate Majority Leader on a regular basis. This will make Olivia beholden to you. You may use that political currency she provides any way you see fit."

"I like it. You can count on me, Ethan."

"Wow, Dean! Does this mean we can be friends?" Ethan joked, attempting to elicit a smile from Senator Sidel.

"I suppose so."

"This is wonderful. Okay, there's one other thing to accomplish. Senator Duncan, this is where you come in. I need you to organize and mobilize the remaining senators of this committee. When Beatrice calls for help to keep Senate business on track, you and your team will quickly complete any task she assigns. Will you accept this request I'm making?"

Senator Duncan nodded. The remaining senators also acknowledged with a smile their willingness to participate. Senator Duncan especially beamed. He had nearly lost his last election and hoped for an opportunity to distinguish himself in the Senate before facing the ballot box a third time. A short and stout man of forty-six years, he had turned completely gray after squeaking by—a person of conviction attempting to recover from the broken promises that got him elected to a first term: routing out corruption in the lawmaking process.

Late Wednesday afternoon, before the Labor Day weekend, Hubert lingered in the Senate Office Building lobby. He knew Ethan would leave his office soon. He patiently thumbed the newspaper—waiting for Ethan to emerge from the elevator. The front page article read, "Afghanistan is a bust! Insurgents have halted aggressions. American military leadership dumbfounded."

"Jeez," Hubert exclaimed out loud.

In a related article, President Anderson cited his key role in the current outcome. "It's American exceptionalism which forced cessation of aggression. While we will not back down, our ultimate goal is peace. I wish to extend this olive branch to the Moborak. Take it while you can. War is not desired, but necessary at times. I also wish to thank the American service members in harms way. You are our beloved warriors."

Hubert couldn't stomach any more propaganda and so moved on to the next story. "Great Scott, a discovery is made! Senator Scott's meteoric rise astounds us all. Without missing a beat, Scott has seamlessly assumed his duties as if he'd performed them all along. The young senator's methods have changed old Senate habits in short order—with little problem arising from the decisions. If the remainder of the United States government carried on in like fashion, it would quickly eliminate billions of dollars in inefficiencies long plaguing Washington. There's a new sense of teamwork in the Senate. It bodes well for us all." The author finished by citing recent accords made between the Senate majority and minority parties.

If I don't get Ethan under control then we'll never reintroduce the Stanton Bill. Looks like I'm going to have to bury the little turd.

Engrossed in thought, Hubert missed the elevator doors opening. He looked up as Ethan's shoes struck the granite tile, crumpled the newspaper and tossed it into the garbage.

Ethan's head turned towards the sound to see Hubert stand up. He stopped and asked, "Hubert, what are you doing for the holiday?"

"An old friend on the House side is taking me sailing off of Cape Cod; should be relaxing. How about you? What does DC's newest wonder boy have planned for the weekend?"

"Not much, really; staying in Washington. I'm meeting an old Army buddy with the FBI on Saturday for lunch. Aside from that, I've got work to catch up on."

"Work...yes, well, that's what I wanted to discuss."

"Have I made some sort of misstep? It doesn't seem like any time passes in this city before something drastic requires a complete redefinition of priorities."

"No, Ethan, that's just you. Washington never changes. You're continuing to astound people here. The way you assumed the role of Senate Majority Leader without shirking your other responsibilities surprised even me. You were clearly undervalued."

"That's too kind; and an exaggeration. I simply married talent to the task."

"As did I...and don't be genial. You're the right man for the job. I knew it when recommending you. Want another challenge?"

"Oh, Hubert...thank you. But, no, thanks. I don't think I can manage any more."

"Nonsense! Look at what you accomplished in two weeks—forged alliances with parties diametrically opposed for decades. I could go on, but that's leadership and you know it," Hubert proclaimed with heart—almost convincing himself. "And that budget thing you finagled with Justice Committee; that was a piece of work," Hubert whispered suddenly.

Ethan smiled, trying to be polite, and wanting a quick subject change. He then asked, assuming it would be some small favor, "What do you have in mind?"

"President pro tem—you interested?"

"What?"

"You heard me. Senator Barrymore told me the other day that he was taking early retirement. He's done his bit for king and country. To tell you the truth, I can't blame him. He is an old battle-axe with more than a few scuffs in his career to talk about."

"That's the number three seat in line of succession to the President; behind the Vice President and the Speaker of the House. Hubert, I'm honored, but not ready for that kind of responsibility."

"Shut it. I know better. So do you."

"A committee chairman or even Senate Majority Leader is one thing. President pro tempore is another type of responsibility altogether."

"You're the man for the job!"

"Alright, I don't want the job."

"Better, direct, but I'm not taking no for an answer."

"Senator Riley, I'm not exaggerating when I say that this is not what I wanted when accepting the nomination to this office."

"You know, Ethan, great opportunity often presents itself when least expected or easily accommodated."

"Hubert, this is much more than I can take on. I have so many other responsibilities. There's no way I can run the Senate's business, my committee, and be pro tem. Is that even legal?"

"You'll handle it all just fine. And to answer your question, it's not illegal."

"How do you even know that I would be granted this furtherance? This is just a conversation."

"That's how it starts. Actually, the appointment process is pretty simple. It just takes a vote from the Senate to appoint you."

"How am I to do my job; any of it?"

"The responsibilities of the pro tem are insignificant. You can keep your position as chair with Energy and Natural Resources. There're only a few additional duties. You appoint a select number of congressional officers, commissions, a few advisory boards and some interesting committees. By your own hand, you've experienced how to rally power.

"As pro tem you're the appointed legal recipient of all Senate reports. This includes the War Power Act reports—with that authority you and the House Speaker may direct the President to call Congress back into session. It's not the button. But you can push the button of the person who pushes the button."

"Thank you, but no; and the rest of the Senate would not stand for it. No one's putting that much power in the hands of one man," Ethan replied, gleaming a polite grin to demonstrate resolve.

"It's yours, Ethan. I'm going to toss your name in the hat today. Barrymore will be announcing his retirement at the conclusion of business this afternoon. Don't be surprised if it's put to a vote first thing tomorrow morning."

Ethan stepped closer and urged, "You have the wrong man. I won't accept."

"Ethan, I hate to spout patriotic nonsense. But, your country needs you. We're spinning out of control. Think about it."

Ethan shook Hubert's hand and then walked away—wondering what just happened. *Why me—and for that matter, why would the others go along with something so outrageous?*

The next morning, every senator was present in chambers. Senator Barrymore's career plans had stirred the hornets—in normal times, a body of secrets only to the unelected or outside public service. Few present knew what was happening or why. Senator Barrymore roosted behind the podium to address the Senate. Applause sounded as Barrymore smiled and waved. From his chair, the Vice President motioned for silence. Applause quieted as everyone took their seats. Senator Theodor Barrymore profiled the ideal politician: coifed full head of silver hair, standing six foot one, piercing hazel eyes, and trim body. A white carnation adorned his charcoal suit lapel. As Theodor droned a generic farewell speech, Ethan stirred the hope that Hubert had heard him; he would refuse the nomination if offered. Ethan's recent conversation with Abigail came to mind. None of this made sense—no one had stepped forward to claim their due from Ethan.

Theodor's speech was brief. He closed by offering, "Once again, I'd like to thank the supporters and numerous spirited political contestants who took up against me during my twenty-four years as a senator." Applause rang out.

Vice President Fulton replaced him behind the podium and said, "As President of the Senate I must bring to your attention the next item on this morning's agenda. A new president pro tempore must be elected from a member of this body. Thus far two senators have been nominated: Senator Niles Campbell of New Mexico and Senator Ethan Scott of New York. Are there any other nominees to this auspicious post?"

Senators murmured after Ethan was named. A brief pause later, Vice President Fulton said, "I, then, would begin the roll call vote for Senator Barrymore's replacement. Please rise when called upon and answer Yea for your candidate of choice."

The first senator rose and followed the edict. One by one the ritual slowly worked its way through the assembly. Ethan sat stupefied— hoping Senator Campbell would win. Ethan was a child the last time he felt this much anxiety about a decision.

Hubert got up in turn and said, "I cast a vote of Nay for Senator Campbell and Yea for Senator Scott."

Ethan tallied as senators cast their votes. It became obvious that Senator Campbell's early lead was eroding. Numbers were even with a little less than half the senators to still vote.

Ethan's turn came. He stood up and announced with resolve, "I fervently cast a vote of Yea for Senator Campbell and Nay for Senator Scott." He felt his face flush. After his vote was cast, a small number of senators laughed. A few even applauded his wish not to assume the post.

Fulton banged his gavel. "Order, so that we may proceed."

It continued on until the last vote was cast. By then, the winner was obvious. Ethan had received nearly all Yea votes after Hubert's turn. Ethan stared forward in shock. *I will not accept the nomination.*

"Order…We have a final count. Senators Campbell and Scott, please rise. Senator Campbell received thirty-three Yea votes. Senator Scott received sixty-six Yea votes. Senator Scott, do you accept the position of president pro tempore; with all the rights, privileges, and responsibilities thereto?" Fulton asked formally.

There was a silence. Ethan could feel the eyes of ninety-eight senators upon him. *It's not what I want—and I won't be bullied into the position.* Feeling steady and sure, Ethan slowly opened his mouth. "I accept the position of president pro tempore."

Stunned by his own response, Ethan froze as his fellow senators applauded. He panned a gaze around the Senate—taking in the mixed expressions of admiration, suspicion, contempt, hatred, and mockery. Ethan felt a terrible mistake had been made; one of the worst.

This'll be the end of me. I'm losing control. Confused by the decision, Ethan felt his life and actions were being orchestrated. Yet, in his heart's dungeon he still yearned to do greater things and make use of the opportunity—thrill and self-loathing swirled through him.

As the clapping continued, Vice President Fulton said, "Order! Senator Campbell, please take your seat. Senator Scott, please join me to take the oath of office."

Ethan made his way to the podium and faced Senator Barrymore. They nodded to each other. Fulton stood between them and read from a leather-bound book. The only words Ethan heard after being instructed to raise his right hand was to pledge, "I will".

Like an automaton, Ethan yammered "I will" each time he was instructed. He couldn't think. He felt nauseous. None of this made sense. It wasn't right.

When it was done, Fulton recited, "Oh Lord, sanctify the United States of America; we pray your whole spirit descend upon us, bestow your grace and grant us peace. May god bless this republic."

Still gawking at Senator Barrymore, Ethan reached out to shake his hand. The audience rose and applauded now that the proceedings were concluded.

As their hands clasped, Senator Barrymore asked, "You have no idea what you're getting into, do you?"

"What?" Ethan whispered, still entranced by his decision.

"Thought so—I'm finished with Washington. I can't do anything here—not sure I ever did. If you're smart, kid, you'll take a vacation…and do it sooner rather than later."

Without reply, Ethan kept shaking hands; his palm numb. Ethan then turned his attention to the crowd; zeroing on Hubert grinning— grinning and nodding as though he had provided Ethan a favor. Others simply clapped and blankly stared ahead like someone waiting at a subway station, dead to the world and only worried about their own destination.

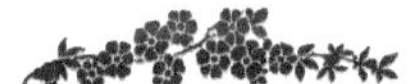

David stepped off the elevator onto the ninetieth floor of Horton Hotels' headquarters. It was early Tuesday after the Labor Day holiday. David had flown to Dallas that morning on an audacious whim.

As he approached Douglas's office, Horton's assistant, Susan, looked up from her desk and said, "Why, Mr. Samuel, what a surprise. How can I help you?"

Feigning calm, David replied, "Susan, I was hoping to visit with Douglas this morning."

"As you know, Mr. Samuel, Mr. Horton is fully scheduled six months in advance. Today is an especially busy day. Why don't you sit down and I will ask Mr. Horton if he could spare a few moments."

"Thank you, Susan."

David sat, quiet and composed. He focused his thoughts—not on the CMC's dire straits, but on his old friend, Douglas Horton. *I'm sure he'll help; after all the Washington favors and money I've spent on Horton Hotels. David sighed. I should've called Douglas weeks ago.*

Susan returned. "Mr. Samuel, Mr. Horton can see you."

Susan led David into Douglas's office. Douglas was already standing when David entered the room. Susan left, closing the office doors.

"David, what a delightful surprise! I'm so glad to see you. Please sit down."

Douglas sat in front of his desk next to David. "Now, David, tell me all about what is happening to you. I've heard so many stories about the Citizens' Mandamus Council. Is it true? Have they shut you down?"

"For the moment, Douglas, we are standing fast. There are legal angles we're working. Still, if we're to keep our integrity, then the CMC must yield to the court order; however misguided the bench may be."

"I am so very sorry for what you are going through. Is there anything I can do to help?"

"Actually, Douglas, that's why I'm here. I need your help. You are one of my dearest friends. If anyone can help it would be you. I need your influence with those who lobby for Horton Hotels in Washington. They know the right politicians that can get this ridiculous motion rescinded."

"David, how can you show up uninvited under the banner of friendship and ask me to do such a thing?" Douglas exhorted.

"Wait…"

"No, David, you wait one moment. How dare you bear the emblem of honesty on your chest and then ask me to shill some contrived backdoor deal to save your precious organization? You have waved a self-righteous flag of moral superiority for years. Now, in a moment of need, you're willing to ignore all of the things you claim to hold dear because it's hard. What kind of man do you take me for?"

"Douglas, please stop. You've misunderstood my request."

"Well then, why don't you enlighten me?" Douglas dryly requested. "It wasn't easy for me to ask this of you. I've risen on my own efforts—I never imagined it could come to this."

"Your own efforts, you say! So that ten million dollars I pledged over three years was not earned by Horton Hotels? How much did we actually give you this year—three million, three hundred thirty-three thousand dollars, wasn't it? I suppose you earned that money all by yourself and allowed me to give it back. Is that how you see it?"

"No, Douglas…that is not what I meant. I—"

"I suspect this is exactly what you meant. Little peasants thinking they will change the world are a laughing stock. Don't you know that people are mocking you? You have become a cautionary tale. Come one, come all and see the ridiculous man in his impossible attempt to change the nature of man. That's right, ladies and gentlemen, he is the genuine article. It's the greatest show on Planet Earth. He'll dazzle you with words, he'll fill your heart with hope, and he'll take your money," Douglas theatrically recited, intending to make David feel embarrassed and small.

"Douglas, I didn't set out to change the nature of man—only to demonstrate that the nature of power was not limited but infinite. I spoke to people about the balance of accountability and those who hold public office. Most importantly, I championed that it was within each person's ability to self-empower; merely requiring an assumption of a few universal truths. I'm guilty of this—a single person at a time. It's how the world is changed for the better."

"Rhetorical rubbish," Douglas defiantly charged.

After explaining himself, David gained an emotional footing. David was certainly surprised by Douglas's initial attack. Now that he had laid down a defense, he felt sure of himself; and certain he didn't want help from a man like this.

"Douglas, I must admit you had me. I've been under the impression that you were a man of impeccable taste and high moral character. I can see I was wrong…about the character." David smiled for a moment and went on, "You do have fine taste; that I cannot impugn…well, maybe."

Douglas laughed heartily. "That's it. Finally, David, you have grown a backbone. I like it. You would have gotten further today had you just approached me like a man. Ethan called me Doug the first day we met. Oh, don't be so surprised. You don't think I haven't noticed what lengths you have gone to accommodate my fussy nature. It took you seven years to speak up to me. Take due notice, I'm not likely to ever lift a finger to help you. Also, you may rest assured that I will not be fulfilling my pledge for the remaining six million dollars; not that there will be a Citizens' Mandamus Council by then."

"Since we're expressing ourselves so openly, let me say that I've never cared for your hotels. They are predictable and boorish. Every major city in the United States has a Horton Hotel, and each is identical—lacking imagination and originality. Your fees are sorely out of line with the quality of service rendered. And those uniforms— did you design them yourself? What were you thinking?"

"Ungrateful little son of a street whore! You sorely lack class, attempting to drag me into this mess you've created for yourself. The Citizens' Mandamus Council never did any good for anyone—it was good for nothing and that's the truth. It's what you are: nothing. David, you're a bad actor. Society is much better off this way. You do nothing but live off the great works of others. It's no wonder Ethan left you for the Senate. Did you hear? They made him Senate Majority Leader. He was right and smart to leave behind the hellhole that is your organization."

"I must say, Douglas, this was not the direction I thought our discussion would go."

"It had to happen sometime, David. You were getting too big for your own good. Trying to tell those with money what do was always a foolish venture that could not last forever. It was only a matter of time before those with real power got rid of you."

"Hmm…didn't I tell you, Doug, I haven't been fighting with those who wield power? I've been holding accountability against those who are corrupt. I'm not trying to take away anyone's power. I am simply showing those who will listen that they have all they would ever need to deal with you and your kind."

"So we are done then, yes? I don't need to worry that you will be begging for your meal outside my door again?" Douglas jabbed with a vicious smile.

"Didn't you get the memo, Doug? You were our last corporate donor. We decided last spring that taking sizeable donations from large corporations was not in our best interest or consistent with addressing our responsibilities fairly. Any donations we may be able to collect in the future can only come from people. So you can keep your puny monies. The donations we've seen from our speaking engagements well overshadow your little table tip."

"Get out!" Douglas barked.

David slowly rose, smiled and drawled laconically, "Sure, Dougie… whatever you say." He turned his back and walked out of the office, leaving the door wide open and ignoring Susan's 'good morning'.

CHAPTER
X

PRESIDING OVER NOTHING

Ethan passed through the White House security checkpoint—repeating the authorization process he had experienced in the spring. The guards even asked the same questions.

Like before, the Marines outside the entrance door snapped to attention. One formally reached to open the door. Again, the President's aide, Cynthia, greeted Ethan as he entered. The repetitive nature of it all made Ethan laugh to himself—security, protocol, and ostentation testified to the mindless nature of public life.

"Senator Scott, it's a pleasure and honor to receive you this evening. Good to have you back, sir," she greeted him.

"You remembered. I was certain you would've forgotten me."

"That's my job, Senator. In case of war, I also ensure the President presses the right button."

Ethan nodded in amusement as they walked. "You have a sense of humor. I didn't know that was allowed at this level of government."

"I'm glad you recognize comedy. Yes, there is a preponderance of decorum surrounding the Secret Service. I assure you, it doesn't end at the Oval Office door. President Anderson is quite the joker. You need to keep on your toes around him."

"Glad to hear it. I was expecting another awards ceremony that dragged on for hours."

"Your expectations are astute. This is likely to be a long and tedious night," Cynthia added bluntly.

"Wonderful! So fill me in. What's on the agenda?"

"Right on cue, Senator—we're nearing the ballroom so I'll give the quick version. The other guests have arrived. The first hour will comprise handshakes, cocktails and an inordinate number of polite yet vacuous conversations. I would suggest a stiff belt. Dinner will then be served. You, of course, will be seated at the President's table; along with Vice President Fulton, the Speaker of the House, Congresswoman Talbot and other committee members. An hour later, the awards ceremony begins. The President will say a few words, and then you'll give a stirring speech. You do have a stirring speech, don't you?"

"I thought I'd wing it. Do you have an opening joke I could borrow?" He winked as they reached the ballroom entryway.

"I'll have one for you by speech time. Good luck in there," Cynthia offered, winking back as she opened the door.

The room was filled with Washington society elite and those wielding the highest governmental influence. Cynthia guided Ethan through the crowd. Emerging through a large group he suddenly stood before President Anderson.

"I'll leave you then in the President's capable hands," Cynthia announced.

"She's great, isn't she? I couldn't do my job without her," Byron said.

"Yes—she explained that if it weren't for her, you might push the wrong button," Ethan quipped.

"Ha! I love that one. Cindy's a gem. It's hard to find someone who can be serious only when it's absolutely necessary. She's kept me out of trouble more than once with visiting heads of state."

"So do we have her to credit for the recent cessation of hostility in Afghanistan?"

Laughing heartily, Byron replied, "No, that was a convergence of need versus want. The Moborak had no choice but to cease their attacks. They ran out of beans and bullets. We could hunt 'em down, but there's no political payoff. We're still baffled by their motivations. Prior to their attacks, we were unaware of their distaste for America. Still, it happened and was dealt with. Changing the subject…am I mistaken that six months ago it was stated in this very room that you had no political aspirations?"

"I still don't want anything to do with it."

"And yet here you are. Not only here, but leading the pack like I thought you could. I find it humorous that you fight it so much. You're a natural."

"Thank you, Mr. President. But I don't consider myself a politician. I just want to make a difference."

"I'd say you're doing just that."

"Not yet."

"How's that?"

"I haven't really done anything yet."

"Well, whatever it is you think you haven't done seems appealing to many in Washington. I don't think I've ever seen another senator rise through the ranks so quickly who didn't campaign for it. Honestly, Ethan, you must've done something to make the right people happy. Normally, I'd already have the skinny. But, this time I must admit to being stumped. From what I can tell, Hubert Riley and his set have taken a liking to you."

"That too has baffled me. I know very little of Hubert, other than a few conversations. I'm tucked under his wing for unknown reasons. The hows and whys are sure to present themselves in due course, though."

"What makes you so sure?" Byron prodded.

"Because, Mr. President, nothing's free. Free, like freedom, comes with a price. Someone feels I owe them something. Why else was all this opportunity lumped on me in such a short amount of time?"

"Let me know when you find out. I'm sure it'll be something that wiggles your toes," Byron humored with a slight chuckle to his voice. "Excuse my rude behavior. Ethan, you of course know Vice President Richard Fulton and the Speaker of the House, Delilah Talbot."

"Senator," Richard said.

"Mr. Vice President," Ethan replied.

"Congratulations on your appointment—quite impressive," Delilah complimented.

"Thank you. It would seem that I'm your second," Ethan humored.

"It's true. Now all we need to do is get rid of these two," Delilah suggested with a devilish smile while curling her arm around

Ethan's back, then giving him the once-over.

"You see, Richard, they're already conspiring against us," Byron belted out, slapping Richard on the back.

As they all laughed at the President's remark, Hubert made his way over to them. The four turned to Hubert as he joined the group. Looking dapper in his tails, he smiled as if he had heard and understood the context of their discussion.

"Good evening to you, Mr. President, Mr. Vice President, Madam Speaker, and of course Mr. President Pro Tem. That was quite the roll call. How do you feel now, Ethan? You've become the man of the hour here in Washington," Hubert said.

"Thank you, Hubert, though I'm still waiting for an explanation," Ethan returned, stone-faced.

"For what?" Hubert asked, depicting innocence.

"This, all this—it made no sense before; and now I'm still twiddling my thumbs in wonder."

"Ethan, what are you getting at? You're the right man for the job. I don't know what else to say that'll—"

Byron interrupted, "Ethan, don't go looking a gift horse in the mouth."

"One of these days, a little understanding might prove helpful. I see that many of my committee members are standing off to the side alone. Since I'm outnumbered here, I think I'll join them," Ethan said.

As Ethan departed to join his committee, Byron removed the smile from his face. "Would you two mind if I had a private word with Hubert? Thank you both."

Richard and Delilah walked away and began another conversation. As they leaned towards each other, it was obvious they were speculating what Byron wanted to discuss with Hubert. Byron turned away from the crowd, guiding Hubert to a quiet corner of the ballroom. A black-suited Secret Service agent nodded to the President as he repositioned himself nearby to protect their privacy. "Hal, the kid's right. What do you have on him? Or should I ask what you're trying to get on Senator Scott?"

"Byron, you have this all wrong. Senator Barrymore was on his way out. Ethan did such a good job as Majority Leader that he was a shoo-in as Barrymore's replacement."

"I know Theodor Barrymore. I'm also sure he wasn't planning to leave until after the Presidential Inauguration in January. He's been one of my biggest backers during this campaign cycle. He pledged to support me right up to the end. You're trying to tell me that he would commit political suicide months before his career finished on a high note? Campaign contributors already promised him a cushy job and salary after retirement. What's the angle?"

"Look, Byron, you've got the wrong man. You might want to talk with some of the folks on the other side of the aisle. I'm in your party. Why would I scuttle your reelection bid?"

"Why indeed! Before we get to that, since it's damn near impossible for you to offer a reasonable explanation, answer this for me: Why did you nominate him for Senate Majority Leader in the first place? He'd only been in the job a few weeks. He's not a career man. What possible favors could he provide you?"

"It's not what it appears to be. You know as well as I do that Senator Halstead wasn't doing his job of controlling the Senate. He was a Majority Leader that allowed the Britches Party to push their agenda on the floor. What did you expect me to do about it: nothing?"

Byron stared straight ahead—annoyed by the distortion. He then returned his eyes to Hubert and said, "The Stanton Bill never had a chance. I liked the good ole days as much as you. But they're over. Oil is unwinding. The only reason it gained traction over electricity was rout—oil barons a century ago bought off the House and Senate. Like eight-track tapes, it's had its time and is now finished. You'd be smart to accept this."

"Maybe it has and maybe it hasn't. I can find experts who'll refute every new-age scientist claiming alternative energy is the way of the future. I can do the same for the global warming cult. I say oil still has a ways to go," Hubert claimed in defiance.

"Say so all you want, but the American public believes differently. Oh, and those so-called experts you're waving around are only the best scientists money can buy," Byron joked with a smile.

"We'll see how much influence Street-Corner Joe has on the future of energy."

"Let's not get into a sociological discussion about American voters. It's wasted breath. Just understand, I had my suspicions that you were behind this. Now I know why. There are two things you need not forget, Hal; and don't drag your feet. It could be the end of you, if you get my meaning. One, don't sell Ethan Scott short. He started from nothing and in ten years became extremely successful without any outside help from anyone, let alone Senator Hubert Riley. He may surprise you in doing his job too well.

"Second, you better increase support of my campaign to make up for the lost points because Barrymore's gone. If I lose this race with my current lead, then I'm going to come looking for you. I've been in the game a lot longer than you. I'll make it stick."

"I think it's time for dinner. Why don't we take our seats," Ethan was suggesting to his committee across the room.

The Energy and Natural Resources Committee place cards perched upright at the same table. The President's card was pitched next to Ethan's. Within a few minutes everyone was seated.

The ballroom became alive with tuxedoed waiters refreshing drinks and accommodating special requests, as the servers introduced the appetizer course. A string quartet trifled; conversations increased in volume to meet the music level. The seemingly successful cocktail hour finished to welcome dinner with agreeable guests. Awestruck at the President having joined their table, Ethan's committee hushed.

"Ethan, are you ready to astound us?" Byron grandly exaggerated.

"Don't put too much hope in that. I'm a novice speaker at best."

"I've been made to understand you know how to prod the herd."

"I can spin a yarn or two. That's the extent of my talent."

"So humble pie is on the menu tonight? I've been told that you've addressed crowds in the thousands—folks teetering on the edge of their seats the entire time. Furthermore, I've heard people donate millions to hear you stump. There're only a handful of people in this room with the political stones and ability to do it.”

“The CMC was different. I was different. The crowd was different. I could inspire them. This isn’t the right venue for high-minded rhetoric.”

“I don’t know if I buy that, Ethan. Look at all these baby-kissers—they’re here to see you. That’s inspiring given the short time you’ve been in Washington.”

“You’re right—I haven’t been here long. But these congressionals and their dole-boys didn’t come to be moved by lofty sentiment. They’re here out of self-preservation and the urge to power-monger. They either want my support or to leverage me if it can be devised.”

“That may be true. But you are here, and, if I may add, haven’t fallen into the typical Bone Yard traps yet. You’ve been knocked down… hard—and know how to get up on your own. You could be one the like of whom DC hasn’t seen in a while. You may actually make a dent in the work to be done. Most of them will never get to it—too busy positioning themselves for more favors.”

“So how could I ever inspire people of this ilk?”

Smiling at Ethan, Byron responded, “Good question.” He paused to think and then scanned the table of senators. “Senator Clark.”

“Yes, Mr. President,” Hanover Clark yelped—startled that he had been called upon.

“I knew your father. He was a towering politician. Your grandfather too made his mark here in Washington years ago. Now you’re here following in their footsteps. Would you agree that everything Ethan said is true?”

“I’d say that, by and large, he’s correct; though there are a number of exceptions to that generalization.”

“What about you?”

“How do you mean, Mr. President?”

“I mean, are you inspired by our young hero here?”

“Inspired is such a strong word. I’m not sure if—”

Byron interrupted, “Fine. What would you say about Ethan, then? He seems to have mobilized you. Meaning no offense, Senator, but I haven’t seen a church mouse as quiet as you. You’ve lived off your father's and grandfather's name since you were elected to office. You haven't been fired up about anything until now. You wouldn't say that is inspiration?"

"You are right, of course, Mr. President. Let me add that I meant no disrespect to your opinion. Senator Scott's caliber is a rare thing in this town."

"Ethan, you've moved those who would not be moved. You're a much stronger politician than you realize or will openly admit."

"But, I am not a politician," Ethan protested, without thinking. He then realized Byron's words were true. He had unwittingly become one.

Byron chuckled loud enough that the surrounding tables grew silent; attempting to eavesdrop on the conversation. He went on, "Ethan, I'm willing to wager that you can move even this crowd. I'm so sure this is so that I'm willing to pledge more open support of your alternative energy efforts. Don't misunderstand that my saying this shows any bias for the fossil-fuel lobby. However, they're still around, and just because the Alternative Energy Bill passed doesn't mean those with influence aren't trying to undo what's been done."

Ethan grew excited by Byron's challenge, given the dark revelation of what he had become. "I would need to do it my way."

"Do it any way you like. I want to witness the miracle."

"If roaring applause from the audience fails to manifest, then what will I owe you?"

"Nothing…for now." The President showcased his best Cheshire Cat.

The main course had arrived. Ethan looked about the room to ensure everyone had been served—it appeared that everyone was satisfied with their meal. Ethan dropped his napkin on his plate and surprised Byron by abruptly rising.

Ethan walked to the podium and tapped the microphone. A pop rang out. He grabbed the microphone and moved amongst the seated guests.

"Ladies and gentlemen, may I have your attention? The President just laid a wager at my feet involving all of you. I'd like to meet that challenge. Please do not stop enjoying your dinner. This isn't the proper protocol for giving a White House speech. However, I think it might be the best way to overcome the obstacle before me. President Anderson bet that I could inspire all of you. At first I disagreed. But then, true to my nature, I had to try.

"A moment ago, I surveyed the room and wondered if moving you was even possible. To find the answer, an important question needed to be posed. The question was this: Cumulatively speaking, how many speeches has every politician in the room endured throughout their career? It must be in the thousands.

"There are over three hundred people here this evening. I thought to myself, if I'm going to invigorate those who couldn't possibly want to suffer another sermon, then it would need to be something pretty different. Don't you think?" Ethan asked, mugging into the crowd— receiving nods, grins, and near-silent laughter in return.

"I'm not going to give a speech at all. Instead I'll shoot you a break—a free pass to enjoy this expensive dinner. All you need to do is eat."

As Ethan moved through the seated dignitaries, nodding at them all, a small measure of applause rippled around. As Ethan joined in, the remainder of the crowd accompanied him.

The clapping died down quickly. He then said, "I'm almost finished. Since you've received this news so well, I thought we might also skip the President's parlance as well. You've heard the good ones already. This is an election year, for crying out loud. How much more bellyaching can you squeeze in before election night, Mr. President?"

Ethan nodded, clapped, and smiled. The crowd gleefully clapped and whooped louder than before. As Ethan passed his table, the President wagged a playful finger at Ethan, and Ethan guffawed along with the audience. As the room silenced, all eyes returned to him—anticipating the next humorous jab.

Ethan thoughtfully panned over the attendees and said, "I don't know why I am being honored. A year ago I was an out-of-work private citizen in my forties struggling to rediscover the American dream. I no longer made a difference.

"I set out in New York to change this, and life took me to Washington. So here I am, trying to matter. I don't know most of you. Until a few months ago, most of you hadn't heard of me. I'm not indebted to anyone here. No one here owes me. I think it's a good place to start making a difference. Don't you think so, too?"

Ethan let silence fill the ballroom, took a solemn bow, and then put down the microphone. A single clap exploded into roaring applause as they stood to honor him. He made his way through the room to the exit. It took all he had to slowly swallow the saliva that had backed up in his throat; hoping no one would notice he was fervently attempting to cover the overwhelming emotion because he had lied so openly about his political indebtedness. Everyone remained standing as he left the ballroom.

Cynthia approached the entrance door as Ethan emerged. "Senator Scott, I have that opening for you." She handed Ethan a written card.

"Thank you, Cynthia, but I won't need it after all. I think the President might."

Cynthia looked puzzled.

"He'll know what I mean."

"Are you leaving before the awards ceremony?"

"Most definitely."

"I hope you felt honored this evening. It's much deserved."

"It was something," Ethan replied as he turned to walk away.

Ethan suddenly realized that he had taken another step towards utter corruption. Had the wager gone afoul, he would have owed Byron Anderson a favor—ceasing to be a public servant; instead a lever.

Before politics, Ethan had never allowed himself to be compromised. He didn't like it; feeling enslaved, unable to do enough good to undo selling out. Whether he belonged in Washington bothered him throughout the remainder of the evening. In the quiet of that question, the answer was one he could not accept.

As President Anderson addressed the gathering, Hubert's mind drifted to another place. Like an automaton, he laughed and clapped; cued by the peripheral awareness of the other attendees' responses.

Staring off into the distance of a burnt-out land, a familiar sensation filled his consciousness; like a waking dream. He suddenly remembered this place—this dark potent—and the ballroom faded away.

Darkened clouds hung low; joining land and sky to a saddened horizon. Embers popped at Hubert's feet. As he looked to his mechanical legs, attached at the hip, pain from the spikes piercing his flesh reminded him of what this dark prince had done to him. It was agony—he now thought he would lose bowel control. Hubert reached with his hands to grasp the prosthetic thighs, and immediately recoiled, shrieking from his palms' branding. The smell of cooked flesh displaced a sulfuric stench—his hands feeling ablaze with nothing to soothe the injury.

A stinging slap and the grating of steel-clad gloves crossed his face. Hubert looked up to face the ominous figure as he swung through the slap. The dark prince then screamed, "LHal!" and pointed off in the distance at a large mansion set ablaze.

"Am I to go there? Are you saying I did that? What do you want?" Hubert shouted, and began to vomit from blood loss. The world disappeared in a blink as the ballroom and applause came back into focus. Hubert felt his branded hands clapping. He stopped the rise of bile in his throat by swallowing.

I was there. I remember…I think. What was that? My hips ache. What's going on? Suddenly it was gone, except for the certainty that he had just been somewhere else. His mind returned to the clarity that he was Senator Hubert Riley; but also the lingering dread of something else controlling him.

The next morning, Ethan woke unsettled. A thorny fact pricked his mind—removing it would hurt.

Sitting up, he reached for his phone. After the line clicked, he said, "Jane, it's me. I know it is early. I want my appointments cancelled for the morning. Do it when you get there. Book me on any New

York City flight leaving in the next two hours. Thanks. No, it's a personal matter. I'm not sure. I'll likely be back by mid-afternoon. I will."

Ethan quickly dressed and left his apartment. A taxi waited for him at the curb. The cool morning air announced summer's passing. Damp fog drifted and engorged empty spaces, as it always did this time of year—hazing the cab's windows as it sped away to the airport. Ethan swiftly made his way through security; given preferential treatment as a United States senator.

Seated in first class, he gazed forward as business and coach class passengers boarded. The engines sounded as Ethan reminisced about the flight where he first met Anne. He smiled at the naïve faith in his ability to discern a person's qualities. Anne was what she appeared to be. Yet, with hindsight, Ethan would have made the same decision.

The flight seemed to end as soon as it began. Ethan's ride into the steely city brought back thoughts of newspaper days. *That life defined me. For all this busy Senate business, I still lack a distinct purpose.*

After crossing the Brooklyn Bridge into Manhattan, the buildings began to close on his small cab. They swallowed his taxi, like a beast in a fabled children's story. Monstrously long glass panes and metal bit down on his life, chewing it into ever smaller pieces the farther in Ethan went.

The taxi rolled to a stop in front of the CMC's office—its sign turned off. As Ethan reached for the door handle to pull, he paused, wondering if this was the right thing to do. After making eye contact with Sasha through the glass, she beamed a smile; encouraging him to smile in return.

Sasha jumped up from behind her desk and hurried to the door as Ethan entered. She hugged him as he laughed. "What are you doing here, Ethan…I mean, Senator Scott?" she asked, pulling back to see his face.

"Good to see you, Sasha. It's still just Ethan, please. I was hoping to visit with David for a few minutes. Is he in?"

David emerged from the storage room, witnessed their embrace, and approached. After painting on a smile, David attempted to sound gracious. "No, I think Senator Scott suits you better."

Ethan turned towards David's voice and offered, "It's good to see you. You've been on my mind for some time. I wanted to come sooner, but duties have kept me buried."

"I imagine they have," David cryptically poked.

Ethan first thought to hug David; but offered his hand instead following David's cold response. David begrudgingly shook it.

"Why don't you join me in my office? I have as much time as you need. We're not too busy around here," David lamented as he turned away.

Ethan traipsed off, looking to Sasha with bewilderment. Sasha appeared concerned—fearful the discussion would likely destroy what remained of their friendship. Ethan closed the door and sat down in front of David's desk. The halogen light flickered as they made eye contact. Ethan adjusted in his seat and the chair squeaked, shattering the silence. Ethan wished he had not come.

As both stared across the desk, the chilled air choked out unspoken words. Bitterness pooled in David's eyes. Ethan seethed in discontent. Both wore the exhausted face of their choices.

"What happened, David? The last time we spoke you wished me well. Have I said or done anything to you after that discussion to earn such a reception?"

"You sided with the government; a body continuing to bloat on our citizens' blood and itself. Look at you. Look at what you've become. What did you promise to amass this much power so quickly? I hope you demanded it all," David lodged with disgust.

"You knew when I came to work for the CMC; it's not about money. It's about impact. I didn't sell out to anyone. Your accusation would be offensive if it weren't so absurd."

"Absurd! How's it that you've only been in the Senate a few weeks and now are third in line of succession to the President of the United States? Explain this away, please."

"Honestly, I can't. Every time I ask, a litany of vacuous

rationalizations are offered. It doesn't make sense to me either. What's more, Washington is far more broken than I could've ever imagined. Few politicians aspire to anything other than lining their own pockets or gaining more influence. It's a miracle this government functions at all. The one thing I now know for certain is that elected representatives are not in charge. Corporations, through intermediary lobbyists, are running things. It's pervasive the world over."

"Do you remember our discussions about the inverted power paradigm?"

"Of course; it's what attracted me to the Citizens' Mandamus Council."

"It's still the only way. Until people accept that we're already empowered, and that the preoccupation with heaping a measure more is a waste of time, we'll relive the same mistake millennia after millennia—build up and then self-destruct…again and again. The cycle could end today.

"Mankind has all the power it could want. Accountability… that's what's sorely lacking. The inverted power paradigm clearly demonstrates that the higher we go, the more people there should be. This idea exemplifies abundance, expansion and growth. It is a belief in life.

"All one must do to enjoy the promise this philosophy purports is to accept responsibility for one's own actions. It's so simple that it should come naturally. It requires no politician, no shaman or spiritual leader; no one need be their brother's keeper if they would simply keep themselves. It's the pattern of our universe and a fundamental definition of balance. It speaks for itself without saying a word," David sermonized with a tone of light-hearted hope.

Inspired by David, as he had always been, Ethan recited, "Wide is the path."

"Yes, Ethan, wide is the path."

For the first time in weeks, David felt at peace. His own words had lifted him out of a self-imposed darkness. He needed to speak of hope and a future filled with wondrous possibilities.

"David, you're still correct. There's no other way."

Now fiery, David bawled, "We're bogged down until people embrace personal responsibility for their own growth."

"But how do you encourage a population that doesn't care anymore; or worse, doesn't believe anything better is possible? I know it happens one person at a time. However, DC has already shot the messenger."

"Ethan, it starts by unseating those who the people misperceive to have power. At that point, you show them that power over their own lives always resided in themselves and teach them about true accountability. Those of authority who have abandoned any semblance of duty to the electorate must be removed. This can only be done by bankrupting the currency legitimizing their position. Without a viable means of exchange, the military cannot be paid. A will lacking the force to impose it is nothingness.

"That is the function of the state: to provide for the common welfare of the body politic—and that's accomplished with a standing army. Without it, their political power disappears."

A silence once again filled the space between them. David and Ethan smiled at each other—they were fighting for the same cause on separate sides.

Relieved that they had secured a fragile friendship once more, Ethan extended his hand to David and said, "I trust you won't be jumping off any bridges. There are quite a few to choose from here."

Smiling with a grateful spirit, David said, "I don't think so. My way was lost for a time. It's a difficult thing when life changes—resistance creates pain. I didn't accept the pain or the change. That was my mistake."

"Sounds like resignation—you're not giving up are you? The world still needs the CMC."

"No—simply adapting. Thanks for reminding me why I chose this occupation."

"It's good to see the David I know with a purpose. Besides, how can anyone with an endowment like the CMC is sitting on have cause for anything but celebration?"

"We could've existed for years without any fresh donations doing business as usual. However, I have something new to think about."

Since Frank's takeover, Abigail found herself more distracted than usual. Being relegated to the news desk was not a chore required of her in the past. When Sandra had been in charge, only the story mattered; and not making mistakes getting it.

Though Abigail proficiently performed her duties, she no longer enjoyed them. Each night she entered the studio earlier than necessary to sit at the news desk, as the production staff prepared the set for the evening's broadcast. She missed being out there—telling the story where the news happened. A short temper was not something her support staff was accustomed to—catching many off guard. By week's end the entire production department kept their distance.

She read the prompter over and over again to occupy time long before going live. Abigail carried out her mind-numbing drudgery with perfection. Beneath the buzz of thoughtless activity resided a notion: escape. It wasn't freedom that soothed her soul, though. It was a person. He was special and secret to her heart; complex, primitive, and forsaken.

CHAPTER

XI

SETTING OUR SHIPS ABLAZE

The doors opened to Fountain Oil's floor. Hubert was blinded by the ambient sunlight reflected throughout the office's open, modern, glass design. As he approached the front desk, Stanley rushed up to greet him.

"Good morning. You must be Senator Riley," Stanley said obsequiously.

"I am. I have an appointment with Darby," Hubert growled—annoyed that Stanley addressed him as if Hubert were a roadshow groupie.

"As I explained to your assistant, Darby's booked solid for the next two weeks. I can try to squeeze you in between appointments. If you'll have a seat in the waiting area, then I can find you if something comes open."

Hubert looked over at the waiting area, crowded by reporters and scientists waiting to talk with Darby about this new engine.

"No, thank you. I'll stand."

"Whatever makes you comfortable," Stanley offered, turning away to announce, "Mr. Brown, Darby will see you now."

A short, stocky, balding man in a cheap gray suit stood, and with briefcase in hand walked past Hubert as he followed Stanley to Darby's office. Further annoying Hubert was the view of the man's backside. His shoe heels were worn at the outside edges; clearly not a man of means and therefore nobody to Hubert. He hated having to wait on this loser's account. A minute later, the portly fellow hurriedly exited the office, passing Hubert at pace. Stanley expressed concern, not knowing why Mr. Brown had let out as soon as he sat down.

"Senator, it would seem that fortune has favored the bold. Darby may see you now," Stanley said.

As Hubert trailed Stanley, he turned back and said, "Senator, my parents have always been supporters of your candidacy."

"Really?" Hubert's tone changed. With a new measure of respect, he asked, "And who might your parents be?"

"Palmer and Jane Huffington," Stanley politely replied, looking Hubert in the eyes.

Hubert concocted a smile and patted Stanley on the back. "Well, why didn't you say so? Yes, your parents have raised quite a large sum of campaign contributions for me over the years. How are they?"

"They're fine," Stanley replied, maintaining eye contact. He opened the door for Hubert and said, "Darby, Senator Riley is here to see you."

"Be sure to tell your parents I asked about them the next time you talk."

"I'll do that, Senator," Stanley assured, grinning as he departed.

"That's some kid you have working for you," Hubert said.

"Yes, Stanley's a hard worker. Please have a seat. What can I do for you, Senator?"

"Please, call me Hubert."

"Alright, Hubert, what can I do for you?"

"I'm here to find out if your claim is true."

"Hubert, I didn't realize you served on the Alternative Energy Committee."

"I don't."

"Then I don't understand."

"I'm the Homeland Security and Government Affairs Committee Chairman. Just curious if you're telling the truth or if this is some market ploy to affect crude pricing."

Before responding, Darby tried to remember if he had any connection to Hubert. After a moments' consideration Darby was certain there were no prior dealings.

"Tell me, Senator, what do my business ventures have to do with you?"

"The same thing all matters of power in Washington have to do with me: influence; the balance of who does what to whom; who receives how much and why; where it's all going; and who possesses the most control. I want to know if you're capable of stripping the cart of its apples."

"You mean corruption, Senator. You wanna to know how many sellouts will still do what you tell them to do. Does that about sum it up?"

"Yep," Hubert gleamed.

"It's hard to say, really. Washington's thick. What happens to one of you typically infects the lot."

"You're fencing, Darby. I'm simply curious if you can produce this technology."

"I said I could, didn't I?"

"Are you sure you're not a politician? You responded with a question."

"Sorry, Senator, I work for a living. I know it's an old joke—never stops being funny though."

"Darby…"

"Yes, I can produce the technology. I already have. There's a working prototype running right now."

"Can I see it?"

"Absolutely not!"

"I just want to look at this modern marvel you've created for the benefit of mankind."

"I'm sorry, but it's not ready for public viewing."

"I could make it a national security issue."

"You may be able to make an issue of it; of that I'm sure. But, it has nothing to do with our nation's security."

"What about our enemies?

"My only enemy is sitting in front of me."

"There's certainly no need for hostility."

"Hubert, this isn't hostile. This is truth. Hostile might look like me reaching across this desk, clutching your throat, and squeezing you for the blood money you and yours have extorted from me over the years."

"Extortion, taxes, fees, it's all the same. You shoulder a greater responsibility than is obviously understood. You've amassed so much more than the average citizen. That's something! You can't believe all that wealth can be kept to yourself. Humankind won't have it. You must share with those who can manage it best for the welfare of all Americans."

"You make a stickup sound so noble."

"Darby, this bickering is useless. I want to know when I can see it."

"You'll see the unit when everybody else does."

"That won't do. We must protect the public, Darby. If this technology fell into the wrong hands, then imagine what they could do to America."

"Yeah, our enemies could provide us free zero-emission electricity. You sure know how to scare a guy," Darby patronized.

Ignoring the sarcasm, Hubert said, "You know, Darby, we're going to need to form a congressional panel for this device. You can't just create, produce, and bring a new device to the American marketplace without someone looking into its feasibility. This could take a little more time than you think. If this contraption is everything you claim, then we're going to need an impact study too."

"Why waste your time? I'll tell you what'll happen: Oil prices will plummet for the first thirty days around the world; gasoline production costs will likely trim off any profits whatsoever.

"Next, one of the countries we buy cheap goods from will likely steal the technology and ignore patent rights in an attempt to flood the market. I'll fight back at great personal cost; but will hold 'em.

"Finally, after about two years, the world will relax and embrace it as merely a part of the next generation's power supply. Those who aren't ready to switch will wait and watch early adopters to ensure it's safe. After a decade of debate, the question of whether alternative energy can really supplant oil will be answered. Within a hundred years, eighty percent of all energy output will be other than fossil fuel. There's your impact study."

"You're wrong, Darby. That technology, if it works at all, will only be utilized by a few. What it'll do is drag on the dollar. Some of our toughest global competitors will greatly benefit from decoupling the dollar as the world's default currency. The long-term effects could be catastrophic to America."

"Catastrophic…to whom? Would that weigh down the average laborer who doesn't need to pay for electricity anymore? If that same worker retires his home mortgage and any form of transportation fueled by electricity, then I can't say this would be all that hard on him.

"So what if the bank note in his pocket looks a lot more like forty cents? At least he wouldn't be your slave. He may make less money. But he'd need fewer resources. The only calamity would befall your far-reaching influence. You might actually need to sweat for a change in the Senate."

Heartily laughing, Hubert exclaimed, "My, my, you are self-righteous, aren't you?"

"I'm simply telling the truth."

"Please, let's not have a philosophical debate. Not three weeks ago a junior senator engaged me in such a discussion—made me nauseous."

"Imagine that: a thoughtful senator," Darby said wryly.

"Let's get to the point. You're deluded if you feel superior to me. Look at you. You're big oil. How many spills has your company caused? How much carbon monoxide has your gasoline put into our atmosphere? How many degrees' increase to our global environment can we attribute to Fountain Oil? Really, tell how you can sit there with that smug look and condescend to me?"

"Hubert, George Weatherby and I chewed that fat not so long ago. I told him then like I am telling you now: It's not like that anymore. I may've once chased crude with abandon; but no more—I gave it up. Oil operations are no longer a primary focus. Alternative energies and its benefits are where all future bets are being placed."

Hubert injected, "George Weatherby…an unfortunate accident. The Navy recovered his jet's main fuselage. The wings were ripped off on impact. He and the crew were found bloated inside."

"George was always bloated."

"Sounds uncaring, coming from an old friend."

"I've known George since we were pups in the field. He was a complete ass of a man. Any friendship we shared died off a long time ago. We had business dealings together—nothing more."

"Tragic and suspicious how he died; wouldn't you agree?"

"How do you mean?"

"His and the lead cargo plane ditching at the same time on a calm flight: What are the chances?"

"What are they?"

"It certainly raises a lot of questions," Hubert suggested with a tiny smirk.

"Are you implying something?"

"Not at all; George was the CEO of one our country's largest oil companies. If a state enemy had him killed, then my senatorial committee would want to look into it. There are of course his many international dealings. But then you know all about those, too."

"I don't know anything about George's business."

"Don't you? I'm certain you both made contributions to the same organizations in the past," Hubert opined with a pious frown.

"Listen, Senator, the conversation's been fun. But I do have a full schedule; you saw my waiting room. So, this visit must come to an end. Have I answered your questions?"

"Quite. You'll think about what I've said, won't you?"

"How could I forget?"

Hubert jumped to his feet, while Darby remained seated. He extended his hand and smartly shook Darby's, and quietly turned to leave the office.

"Darby, are you ready for your next appointment?" Stanley asked, leaning his head through the doorway.

"Give me five minutes, will you?"

"I'll do that," Stanley replied, closing the door.

Darby leaned back in his chair to think. *They're never going to allow it. I'll need to push the first units near completion before they dig in.*

Gabriel Carter stood before ten thousand congregants as the applause wound down. As the senior pastor of the Righteous Way Christian Church, he looked after fifty thousand flock members spread across Atlanta, Georgia. He preached five sermons a weekend; televising the Sunday morning service and broadcasting the other services over radio and the internet. Gabriel was a charismatic minister with a Southern sensibility; projecting a genteel persona for the remainder of the country tuning into his ministry—often referencing those Yankee Christian brothers living in Northern states.

At thirty-eight, he enjoyed a following known only to a few in religious circles. Striking a chord of growing disenchantment with formally organized religion, he preached directly from the Holy Bible as an evangelist—granting no denominational credit. Gabriel was well known for his creative use of words and memorable phrases. Tall, thin, and angular, lines of muscle and bone held out his suit like a coat hanger.

"The Lord shall surely bless the giver. Thanks be for these tithes and offerings. You may be seated. This morning, I hope to grab your attention and stoke excitement. Good news is all around. And if y'all behave, I promise the message will be brief."

The audience openly laughed. His sermons went long when the audience was responsive. He smiled, waiting for the crowd to settle down. Gabriel walked to the center stage as he always did at the beginning.

"Thought you'd like that—I want to talk about the Apostle Paul and our magnificent technological age. They kind of go together, if you think about it. Our society has a great deal in common with the city of old Corinth.

"Now, I know some of you out there never cared too much for school. That's just fine. Loving history is not for everybody, but history itself is. It's a free ticket to living a better life by not reliving the mistakes of the past. As I promised, I'll be brief since I don't see

Charles wiggling in his seat."

The video camera panned along the sanctuary's front row, stopping at Charles Ettinger. Charles smiled and waved back at Gabriel to go on with the sermon. Once homeless, Charles was the first congregant to join Gabriel's fledgling church back in 1997, in the basement of a small printing shop in downtown Atlanta. After Gabriel began televising his broadcasts, he often used Charles's inviting smile and jovial nature as a production prop and theatrical foil for his own oft-told and poorly delivered jokes. The audience laughed at their relationship's slapstick comedic nature, which often unexpectedly erupted during a service.

Charles wore his favored outfit of jean overalls, a colored button-down shirt and hiking boots—two hundred fifty pounds of weight squeezed into five foot four of height completed a jolly lampoon. A dark complexion from sixty-eight years of life under the Georgia sun contrasted a grey-white-peppered beard and full head of hair. Charles's toothy smile played on the hearts of those who watched Gabriel's broadcast, and endeared them to his ministry by the continued flow of generous weekly donations.

"As many of you know, Paul wrote letters to the church at Corinth; three to be exact. He also made three separate church visits to discover for himself what went wrong with that port city sanctuary of God. His letters were a rebuke of some behaviors, comprised of suggestions and warnings to the congregation.

"Now, a passel of you are already saying, 'Ahem…yeah, this sounds awful familiar now, Brother Gabriel,' and you'd be right. The Bible is chock-full of lots and lots of examples of one person warning and telling another person or group that they better watch out or else.

"In Paul's first letter to the Corinthian church, called the warning letter, he addresses a great many issues, including: Christian unity, wisdom, ministerial roles, immorality, marriage, the body, idolatry, the Eucharist, gifts of the spirit, love, and the resurrection. We've covered these in other sermons. Unlike Paul, I'm going to let you all off the hook this morning."

Light laughter circulated throughout the audience. Gabriel panned his gaze over the congregation, beaming amusement—smiles were calmly returned.

"This morning's message is about patience. Saint James penned a letter to the early Christians talkin bout the very thing; being a patient farmer waiting in peace, just knowing the rain was on its way and forthcomin crops abaundant. Behold the blessing being assured in the fruits of the sprint. Gosh darn I love that!

"Don't ya know, Saint Paul couldn't help himself here either; had lots to say. He also sent one of those epistles to a number of Jewish Christian Galatians. An epistle is just a fancy word for a written letter. Paul let these folks have it with patience in the fruits of the spirit: love, joy, peace, long-sufferin, gentleness, goodness, faith, meekness, and temperance. Think I got em all.

"Thus ends our short Bible lesson today. Y'all did well. I see even Charles was able to sit though it," Gabriel said, grinning from ear to ear—eyes twinkling for the camera. "Now, I want to tie this down to today's message," he said, pointing to the stage. "God wants you to have patience." Cupping hands around his mouth, he yelled, "What does God want you to have?"

"Patience," the audience rumbled.

"I can't hear you! Come on. Shout out like you know you're God's special children. What does God want you to have?" he urged.

"Patience!" the audience bellowed.

"One more time so God in Heaven knows you love him!" He stomped around the stage to show his excitement to the crowd as he yelled. Gabrie's shoulder-length brown hair fell in his face, and he brushed it to the side with his finger as a stage tool to demonstrate his depth and passion.

"Patience!" the congregants roared. Many jumped to their feet in excitement, clapping and smiling.

"That's what I want to hear. You can sit down now. I think God knows you're present this morning. Many of you may've got wind about a new invention. It's a newfangled electric generator that runs all by itself—reportedly a game-changer—magnificent piece of technology. I'm so tickled that I may need to get one for the church.

"Just imagine how much money Righteous Way can save in heating, cooling, and electricity bills. It would almost seem like a Godsend, given the condition of our economy, and the wars and poverty that ravage society. Only it came from man. Now, that's not to say it's a bad thing because this generator was fashioned by human hands. The Bible says we're created in God's image. But patience has a place too.

"How?" Charles called out towards the stage, as if on cue.

"Charles, I'm so glad you asked me that," Gabriel addressed the camera with a snicker. "He's great, isn't he?" Gabriel added after a brief pause.

"It's just that I think about all the people this little engine could put out of work. Now, it's easy to point fingers at the big oil companies, isn't it? Not a single day goes by when clean air, clean water, conservation, and recycling aren't hashed and rehashed. Oil spills, all that automobile exhaust, and coal-fired electrical plants are the targets of continued concern and complaint.

"Let's say we give every home in America one of those perpetual electric generators. Then what? I'll tell you, one thing's for certain. Lots of people in the oil and gas industries will be out of work. What about all the gas stations and convenience stores who sell fuel? They'll be out of business too. All those with the utility companies will lose their jobs as well.

"How about the money from those people no longer circulating in the marketplace to support our overall economy? I'll tell you what. They won't be spending it at places of businesses. This returns the country to a recession and possible depression—weakening the United States in the eyes of the world, hurting an outspoken society of Christian values since its beginning.

"Patience my friends; in all things patience. I'm calling on this congregation to withstand the urge to purchase one of those generators. I know free energy seems like a dream come true. However, in the near future it creates more of a nightmare.

"Let the non-believers use the technology. Wait twenty years before adopting it. This is God's will.

"Have not the oil companies provided for your energy needs since before any of you were born? Of course! Don't we owe them the same courtesy? Let our brothers and sisters in the oil, gas, and energy business migrate to this new technology slowly over time, so that they can responsibly absorb the methods of energy creation and supply.

"Are they not now standing by you in your time of energy need? So too should you stand by them as they adjust to the long-term transition away from fossil fuels. Will you all stand together and pray with me?" Gabriel petitioned.

Congregants clambered to their feet. Ten thousand hands joined for the oil companies and their stability in a changing marketplace. After the prayer and benediction, Gabriel quickly exited the stage.

"How was it? How did our high-handed ratings group reward us?" Gabriel asked Director Taylor Rourke, as he walked backstage.

"Brice's initial figures say our core demographic is watching. We're level with the same numbers from last week. But those aren't the numbers that really matter."

"Yes, the many souls we've saved."

"Of course, those numbers too. We'll have donation tally within the hour. You'll know then to either pour it on or lay off the engine at the eleven o'clock service."

"Taylor, enough about ratings and this week's offering-plate pocket change. What about the money from Coral and the others?"

"Like I said, Coral Oil's interim chief is making a fifth of their pledge for each sermon like the one just broadcasted. You have two more to go this weekend."

"Good. I'll be in my office until the next service. Don't let any more congregants backstage. That woman who got by your security last week wouldn't leave my office; even after I'd departed for the final sermon. When I got back she was still there. You know, she went through my things while I was away—stole my favorite platinum pen—I couldn't believe it."

"I was on vacation last week and you know it. It's the only time you let me take off all year," Taylor lamented.

"Hey, if you can find a better job for the money I'm paying you then the door's wide open, brother," Gabriel shot back with a large smile as if he were on stage.

"I didn't say that, Gabriel," Taylor replied, lowering his eyes.

"Sure sounded like it."

"I just wanted to explain that the blame was not mine."

"Not yours…who else's could it be? Is this not your show to direct? Do you want my shtick? Do you wanna get out in front of those people five shows a weekend—try pullin' them out of their dead-end lives? I'd be happy to hide behind the curtains and take care of everything else."

"No thanks," Taylor said, waving his hands as if to ward off the idea.

"Fine, then keep your security people trained up. And fire the guy who let her through. Oh, one other thing: Make sure to get with payroll and withhold the money it'll take to replace that pen from his last paycheck!"

"I will, Gabriel."

"And get me those numbers when they come in."

"I think your last piece on Senator Scott was adequate and a direction you might consider taking your stories in the future," Frank relayed to Abigail as they discussed the previous week's stories and future potentials.

"How's that: Short and uneventful? TTN has interviewed him five times this year. If we provide him any more coverage, then he'll begin running for President."

"You have lost me, Miss Sanders."

"There was nothing new to report other than that he had once again been promoted. All the relevant questions have been put to him before."

"That's what I have tried to impress upon you and the others since taking over this network. It's all been said. This is a business. If we are to generate the revenues I have been tasked to produce, then it must be treated as such."

"Frank, this is the news business. Try not to forget that part of the business. The news happens out there."

"Miss Sanders, I have repeatedly asked you to use my surname. Please respect this request. I am, after all, your superior."

"Frank, you're my superior. However, I didn't enlist in your army. Your given name is Frank. I use it to create a more personal rapport. I'm having difficulty making you understand my perspective on reporting the news."

"Miss Sanders, you will not have any better luck by informally addressing me."

"Okay, then. Let's move on. There is a story no one's telling in Houston."

"What story might that be?"

"Fountain Oil's chief is going to release a technology that might altogether change the face of the planet. What's the angle? Why would he do it? This is a high-minded ideal, full of heartfelt and beneficent sentiment. It doesn't smell right."

"What smell might be pleasing, then?"

"Frank…excuse me, Mr. Lambert, surely you can see the confusion? Why would this guy betray his own kind; or his own company, for that matter?"

"Maybe to help the world," Frank dryly replied.

"Do you know anyone in the oil business?"

"I cannot say that I do."

"Forgetting the fact that they have bought our Congress, like others in energy, commodities, and pharmaceuticals; they care for nothing but making large profits for themselves while ignoring the destruction their industry brings."

"That's quite an indictment. Are you sure you would be the right person to report on this story? There is clear—"

"I am the right person."

"But the story has already been covered by the other networks; including our own. There is nothing new to report. All we can do now is wait to see if Fountain actually releases this engine he claims to have invented."

"That's just it. Why would big oil invent a technology that would destroy their business model? That's an angle no one's covered. This is the story that hasn't been told."

"So call him to discuss it. See if he would be willing to elaborate. Why fly all the way to Houston and hold a crew on standby until you know if he will talk? That costs the network money. Our affiliates do not work for free. If you don't get a story worth producing, then we still pay them for waiting on call. Besides, Miss Sanders, we have talked about this already. Your place is behind the anchor desk."

"The story is in Houston. If you want it, then that's where I need to be."

"If you are so certain of this, then why don't you have our Houston affiliate send a crew over and produce an interview themselves? They are an affiliate station. They're required to share their stories with us."

"This is my story; my angle. Plus, there's a reason why their talent is stuck in an affiliate news role. It takes a great deal more to be a network newsperson. Young talent starts off there to get experience. By the time they're good enough to get the tough stories, the network has already hired them away at four times their salary. They can't get the story out of Darby Adams. I can."

"I'm going to say no, Miss Sanders. I am saying this for the good of your career and that of the network. You are our network's most recognized personality. Your place is here."

Pausing for a moment, Abigail regrouped her thoughts while Frank grew annoyed; knowing she was going to come at him from another direction. He was tired of it and wanted her to simply accept his decision. He interlaced his fingers and stared back—waiting for the next salvo.

"Mr. Lambert, what am I good for?"

"I don't understand the question."

"What do I mean to you? What do I mean to this network?"

"A trusted face in news."

"Frank, give me a break."

"Ratings."

"Finally, a little honesty—I respect you more for that answer. What kind of weekly numbers do you suppose we'll make when I uncover what Fountain Oil is really up to?"

"But you can't know that."

"Not behind a desk in New York. That story is happening in Houston. If you want it, then let me go down there and take it from him. Do you think he's just going to hand it over? Whatever he's up to will be covered under layers of lies. It's what they taught us at journalism school: Sifting for the truth."

"I didn't attend journalism school. I possess a master's degree in business management."

"Of course you do. Mr. Lambert, if you want more advertising revenue, then you must lead in ratings. Those ratings come from news coverage. News is our business."

"If it will end this discussion, then do the story. However, don't come back empty-handed."

"It's unheard of that I return without something," Abigail claimed, unable to repress a triumphant smile.

"That's fine, Miss Sanders. But, please refrain from wasting time or money on this assignment."

"This is Houston, boss, not Milan."

CHAPTER

XII

WHAT SHALL THE MEEK INHERIT NOW

After the impromptu visit with Ethan, David had regained much of his confidence and reminded himself of his purpose and destiny. No amount of corruption could bridle him now.

David called an emergency meeting at the CMC's headquarters. The table had been removed from the conference room to accommodate fifty chairs. As they awaited David's arrival, gossip about his reacquired faith quickly spread through the group. The room filled with lively conversations of past CMC successes; and a general acknowledgment that everyone knew David would have eventually regained his footing. After all, he was the President, CEO, and creator of the Citizens' Mandamus Council.

As David entered at the back of the room, all those assembled jumped to their feet and clapped with exuberance that their leader had returned. He swaggered to the front in silence. After allowing the applause to calm, he fluttered with his hands for them to take their seats.

"It's good to have you here. I haven't seen this group together since our Annual Meeting; and never twice in one year. This is quite the time, isn't it? So much has happened; difficult, rewarding and downright peculiar.

"As you know, it hasn't been easy since the government set out to destroy the Citizens' Mandamus Council; the courts rejected our motions straightaway without consideration. Many of you were probably wondering if I possessed the backbone to continue fighting. I understand that some of our own state directors are already looking for legal work with other law firms.

"In many ways, I feel that I've failed you; being unprepared for such a move and how to handle it. Before we begin our discussion of what is to be achieved this week while we're all together, I'd like to extend my deepest apology for falling short. Also, I most sincerely thank you for not abandoning the CMC during this trial."

The directors clapped and nodded towards David. He acknowledged their graciousness with a simple smile. He went on, "Now that my faith has been restored, I want you to know that I am more confident than ever of the CMC's ability to prevail. We have important things to discuss. So, let us to it with enthusiasm and courage.

"The Citizens' Mandamus Council is, in normal times, an organization that observes and reports. I built it to be so. Our government possesses all the tools to implement anything it and our people could possibly need to thrive. These, however, are not normal times.

"As Ethan Scott, one of our esteemed past colleagues pointed out, the Council's not an organization of action. We are watchers."

A light grumble rolled through the audience.

"Now, hold on a moment. Ethan is honorable and hardworking. He needed something different than the CMC could offer and so followed his life's path. We should wish him well. We need more people like him in government.

"Our country's no longer stable. Corruption has reached boiling point and is uncontrollably spilling over. Our leaders no longer even attempt to cover up their outrageous activities. They simply expect us to accept it. Can we let this go on any longer?" he asked the room.

"No!" the gathering threw back at him.

"No is right! We cannot! We must do something; something not mandated in our corporate charter—and it must be now!

"The government ruled that we may no longer investigate or file writs of mandamus; activities free for any law-abiding citizen to exercise. We've been denied our rights. The Constitution has been abandoned by the very government overseeing it.

"We've lost our government and our voice! Today we'll talk about a solution to such a large problem. After I've proposed our new direction, then we'll break off into five groups; all tasked with different goals to achieve this week. This Thursday, our plan shall be announced to the world.

"As we begin, I want you to feel free to offer suggestions or criticism. I by no means feel we have all the answers; just a direction. You'll help in charting a new course.

"Until the CMC's rights are restored to carry on with normal activities, our new business is value! We'll be issuing a note of value. More specifically, we will be offering it to the American public to use as an American dollar alternative."

"David, it can't be done. It's illegal! The Legal Tender Statute provides for 'all debts, public charges, taxes and dues'," Brian Barrette stated.

"Ted," David redirected as another hand was raised. "Brian's right—but so is David. We can't issue coin; however, paper's completely fine. We can issue our own note without breaking the law. The statute you cite recognizes the government providing a currency that can be used for all public debt. However, as a business or a private citizen, you're not required to accept the United States currency for payment."

"Thank you, Ted. Shocking, isn't it? The currency representing the wealth of our nation retains its potency only because we choose to recognize and accept it as so. Its only worth is based upon the full faith of the United States government. That's us. We are the government—at least in theory; and a theory is all that's left.

"Washington representatives are no longer listening to their people. They only hear lobbyists who don't represent us. They stand for the corporations—the new government owners. As we're aware, a corporation is not the government and therefore cannot be voted out of office.

"Our government and our currency are a sham; not worth the promise backing the note. The currency alone is no longer based upon any real wealth. America does not possess the gold or other fixed assets to make good on all the United States currency in circulation. We're lost.

"It's time we take back our land, our laws, and our government. We'll do it through script. What can they do to stop us? You might suggest that they control the military and that's how they'll do it. The military is paid in dollars. Even a soldier must be paid. Did you know that the contract a soldier signs when enlisting in the military states what the soldier will be paid in United States dollars? If that same soldier is not paid, after sixty days has passed, he may abandon his post without becoming a deserter—free of military legal action. General Washington struggled with this same issue during the Revolutionary War. It was only his ability to inspire those who were not required to stay on that saved our army and led to its eventual victory against the British."

"So we're going to revolt against the United States government? How can we do this? They have all the power," Brandon Sutton stuttered.

"Brandon, I hear your concerns. I'll address them as best I can. If I understand correctly, you believe the government has a power we don't; and that the action I'm proposing is a revolutionary move.

"First, the nature of power is quite a lengthy discussion, if we were to do a proper job of it. Since we're lacking time this week, I'll quickly tell you what I think. Agree or disagree as you see fit. Power is merely the motive means to accomplish an intended action or outcome. There is only one power applied in life and nature, in innumerable times and ways. The particular power you made reference to is political power, correct?"

"Yes, that's right," Brandon replied.

"Is this political power available only to the politician or may anyone wield it?"

"It appears to apply only to the politician; even though I know that's not true," Brandon answered.

"And there it is for all to see, and you already knew it. You know that political power is simply power of a political type, but it is power nonetheless. We have power: to act or not act; to think or turn off our minds. Power is only a motive force. Choosing to use power is an act of power in and of itself.

"So these hooligans, the politicians, have simply chosen to use political power while you have not. It's not the use of power I take up against. It is the corruption of power by these swindlers I'm in a twist over. Like politics is a characteristic of power within the context of this discussion, so then is corruption.

"Corruption of political power here is simply the abandonment of accountability to the responsibilities associated with holding a position of authority; like many in our Congress. They wield the motive power to enact laws which govern our lives. We abdicated that power to the politicians when they were elected to office. This power was given only to provide for the common good; not for the good of themselves. In this way they've corrupted the power we gave them.

"We're left with no choice but to take back that which can only be given: the power granted by the will of the people. The only means available to do this is by undermining the currency which backs their legitimacy.

"Brandon, you're correct. This is a bold move; unlike anything the CMC has ever attempted. This was not desired for my life or yours. I only wanted to do my part, make a living, and go home at the end of the day. I wish to make a real difference, to be sure. But what else would you suggest—that we do nothing and simply go away because the corruptors say so? Is that what you want to do, Brandon?"

"No. But, I didn't think my job with the CMC would come with a price like this."

"Nor did I, Brandon. I want you…I want all of you to know this. Issuing a note is nothing new. There actually are many communities throughout the US that make use of a local currency to bolster the regional economy. I am simply proposing that we do it on a much larger scale—to include every state in the union.

"The Godforsaken politicians are not going to turn over their position. They're too entrenched to willingly give up. We'll need to take it from them—but it can't be done by force. This can only be accomplished by bankrupting the currency which pays for the army that legitimizes their existence.

"Has the CMC's history been written by the authors of our society's demise, or do we still have a few passages yet to add? I have much more to say for my part. Let this not be the last word for ourselves, or the greatness that our country still carries in its belly."

"How can we circulate enough of these notes to make a dent with the US population?" Ted shot back at David.

"Ted, I'm glad you asked. In my many discussions with Ethan regarding his newspaper, the printing aspects of the business always intrigued me. After a number of conversations, Ethan laid out the fundamental production process for all printed material. We can design and print billions of notes of our own. The CMC's trust fund of over one hundred fifty million will pay for printing costs and issuance with reserve centers distributed at major hubs throughout the United States."

"So we're not going to try anything less drastic first?" Brandon asked.

"Quite right, Brandon; I was about to get to that. This move would forever change the face of America. The unintended consequences we cannot predict could be severe. If it's possible that we not take this step, then I would much prefer it. To that end I believe we should use it first as leverage to force the legislative branch to act in accordance with the people's will. By threat of this action we require the government to do its job and nothing more. Do it or step down."

"David, we've been taking this action all along, and look where it's gotten us," Ted grumbled.

"Then what would you suggest, Ted?"

"New and immediate elections for every senator and representative in office," Ted replied without considering his words. The look on his face was one of surprise and shock.

"That's a fine suggestion and we should plan for it. Do you know that our government will allow its citizens to file their annual tax returns electronically, but still will not allow internet voting? I find that curious. They gladly take our money but not our votes. The government seems to accept that a virtually filed tax return is valid and yet a virtual vote poses too many security problems. I wonder if the real fear is that the stability of the career politician and lobbyist would be too threatened by such an openly democratic method—

so immediate and final—Electoral College electors knowing immediately how they should vote. Whew; powerful stuff!

"We should hold on to that as a second course of action. I say this not timidly but with prudence. We may have right on our side, but we still should give them a chance to capitulate. You'd be right to point out that this is what the CMC has always done. It is, but not to such an encompassing degree; it's not one conman dressed down. We're going after the lot. Though they don't deserve it, diplomacy should first prevail. Remember, this is a new day; a new CMC."

"How will this offering be backed? Who'd accept a note simply because it's issued? There's no inherent worth!" Jason Morgan bellowed.

To Jason's constituents, he outwardly maintained the most liberal and relaxed leadership style; he was director for the California office. Fiscal concerns were always a weakness, which made this financial question surprising to David.

"Jason, you have my attention. I'm glad to hear you're engaged in the finer points of what I'm proposing. You're correct. This issuance in present form is not backed by anything. All that we really need to do is convince people to use it; and businesses to accept it. How is this any different from the currency in circulation?"

"Well, for one, it's backed by bonds issued by the Reserve Board," Jason stated.

"Yes, purchased by what, more currency? Even if these bonds, which are another form of paper promises, are purchased with foreign currency, the US dollar is still in no better shape because it's purchased with a foreign country's currency. This is simply a foreign government's parchment spit-promise. There seems to be an awful lot of promises being made, in this dialogue alone, not backed by any inherent value.

"Don't you see, Jason? This is the foundation of our currency and our government's problem: no objective worth to base currency or their corresponding governments upon. What is worth?"

"What about gold?" Jason offered in a serious tone.

"America doesn't have enough to back all its currency in circulation.

So, this is yet another promise Uncle Sam can't keep…and gold is really no better than currency from a position of ostensible worth. What good would a bar of gold do a starving man? To him, the metal's useless; a loaf of bread would represent more usefulness than a yellow brick.

"Do you not all see the underlying issue of our government currency? No worth is offered in exchange; just a broken word. Our money is based upon promises and nothing more. It has no worth and offers a weak commitment to make good. Our elected representatives are now openly not representing the people. This eliminates the politicians' worth to the people and is another blatant broken promise to their constituency.

"However, issuing bonds for our new note is something I've already thought about; and a consideration we'll work out this week. I've established five committees, mandated to achieve individual goals over the next two days. We're moving quickly on this. Harbor no illusions, the CMC will be taking action this week.

"The Marketing Committee will work up our presentation to the American people. This'll be a sales pitch as much as sustentative. Once it's begun we'll be spending all our time speaking to anyone who'll listen to what we're proposing. Public speaking venues in every state will become our temporary home. At this point, I believe a lot of people will be receptive.

"Next is the Minting Committee. You'll be responsible for locating and hiring an engraver. You'll also broker the printing job and develop anti-counterfeit measures. And you hold the honor of naming our new note.

"Our third team will be the Reserve Committee; overseeing transportation, security and issuance. Quickly, you'll need to establish reserve depository hubs throughout the United States where the currency can be stored and guarded.

"Second to last is the Underwriting Committee. Jason, since you asked the question, I want you to chair that body. Make sure you switch with someone on that team, as I initially assigned you to marketing. Jason, your committee will research the issuance of bonds, determine if we need them to proceed, and establish relationships with brokers and stock markets around the world for our note's issuance and sale if we so choose to take that road.

"Finally, our Legal Committee will prepare the CMC's defense, as this is sure to upset the entire hive of elected drone-bees. You'll also assemble the list of demands that we'll put forth to the legislative branch. Remember, legal team, we want nothing more than that they simply do their jobs. We do not want to negate the Constitution in any way. We do, however, wish to suggest that legislation be immediately passed outlawing lobbying.

"I'd like all of you to split up into those five committees. Each group has assigned tasks they must complete today. Sasha's passing around committee member lists. Please see that you join your group after we take a ten-minute break."

Abigail laughed, her head tipped back. Sam slapped her shoulders. They and his news crew rode the elevator together at Fountain Oil headquarters. As the doors opened, Abigail said, "Stop, Sam, you're going to make me sweat."

"A woman with your breadth of travel I think would have heard that joke a few dozen times," Sam replied, enjoying his moment with her.

"I have, but not like that."

Stanley greeted them as they emerged. "Miss Sanders, it's an honor to have you here today. Darby is of course expecting you."

"Thank you."

"Why don't you have your team wait in our conference room?"

"That'd be fine. Sam, can you set up in five?"

"Five minutes. Are you sure you haven't been taking notes from our fallen leader?"

"You haven't met the new guy, have you?"

"No."

"He makes Sandra look like a choirgirl. Plus, I don't know what you're complaining about. You lost the weight Sandra asked you to lose."

"Yes, I did. And, darn it, she didn't come this time. I was hoping to show off my new body," Sam mocked.

"I'm fairly certain she wouldn't be interested."

"Sure about that?" Sam asked, batting his eyes at Abigail.

"Stop that right now before I call security," Abigail said with a giggle. "I'm pretty sure. Anyway, the new guy starches his shirts a bit too heavy."

"Is he that bad?"

"Let's just say that Sandra would be a welcome return."

"It must be bad. Guess I'll hold off sending my demo up to network."

"Sam, you wouldn't like it there. You Texas affiliate boys like to play too loose for network."

"You never appreciate me," Sam ribbed as Stanley led Abigail away. Stanley entered the office ahead of Abigail. Before he could announce Abigail's arrival, Darby said, "I know Stanley, she's here. Just a moment." He stared into his computer screen—tapping on the keyboard.

"That's alright. I can wait," Abigail offered, sitting down in front of Darby's desk.

"Miss Sanders, it's good of you to come. I'm running a little late on engine production projections. If you could indulge me a moment, I'll quickly finish."

"Take your time."

Stanley left. Abigail waited in silence while Darby worked. She noticed that framed pictures of oil tankers and derricks were stacked against the wall next to Darby's desk. Bare walls reflected sunshine, bleaching the colors of the undecorated office.

"There…finished," Darby said.

"Your workplace is so barren. The light's quite severe. Are you a minimalist, or moving premises?"

"Funny—neither. As you may've heard, I'm changing a great many things; sweeping away the past and focusing on the future."

"Sounds lofty, but aren't you still one of the world's largest oil producers?"

"For now—won't be that way forever."

"I heard the radio broadcast—quite a bold move."

"Miss Sanders, it seems that we're already doing the interview. I'd like to do this a little differently than what you're accustomed to. Hear me out before saying anything."

"Okay."

"I've watched your interviews over the years. You have a habit of uncovering the facts. I respect the commitment. However, of late you and every other major news personality have transmogrified into sensationalists."

"If it bleeds…" Abigail acknowledged with a smirk.

"That's it exactly! If it's oozing blood, then it's got our attention. Right, but what happened to the search for truth? It doesn't seem a day goes by when one of the networks isn't overdramatizing some poor schmuck's demise. Then all the other networks pick up the story and broadcast it twenty-four hours a day until some ratings company tells you to do an about-face."

"Are you sure you're in the oil business? You know a lot about broadcasting."

"I don't know anything about the information business—just a viewer. What you think about it?"

"We do have advertising and ratings goals; you're correct. And in recent years, many of the things you cited have become commonplace. It doesn't happen in my interviews, though."

"I get that—just wanted to mention it. I'd also like to discuss the questions to be posed. You must agree that no questions other than the ones I've approved will be used while recording."

"Mr. Adams…"

"Call me Darby."

"Darby, I didn't fly down here to be told how to do my job. This isn't a public relations piece."

"Nor do I expect it to be. I just want it clear before we begin that I am not going to be used as network cannon fodder. So if this interview is meant to be anything other than your search for news, then I'm not interested."

"Alright, Darby, I'll tell you the questions I want answers to," Abigail volleyed back with confidence—eager to demonstrate her integrity.

"Wait, not here. Let's go for a walk. I've been in my office all day and would like to get some air."

"Fine."

They rose together. Darby gestured for Abigail to exit through the doorway. As they passed the front desk Stanley nodded to Darby, indicating that he would take care of the production changes.

"I thought we could walk in the garden," Darby suggested as they stepped into the elevator.

"The garden…? I wasn't aware you had a garden on the grounds."

"It's on the rooftop," Darby replied as he inserted a key beneath the touchscreen.

"Of course—where else would you put a garden in the city?"

"Indeed," Darby added. The doors closed and then opened a few moments later.

It was a beautiful fall day—mild temperature and rich blue skies. A meticulously sculptured garden filled Abigail's view. Potted Japanese maples spaced five feet apart encompassed the roof's perimeter. Manicured branches and delicate shapes exposed the gardener's grace. Their bark and multicolored leaves announced that summer had departed.

A maze of white granite walkways stretched out in multiple directions before winding back to the center where the helicopter pad was located. Miniature butterfly bushes lined the paths; their petals a sprightly periwinkle framed by hunter green leaves.

"It's lovely," Abigail noted—completely surprised and disarmed by its beauty, precision, and the secrecy of its existence.

"Yes, it is. I come here to get away from the madness. Today, it's even more handsome a garden with you standing in it. Shall we journey towards the center?"

"I'm sure you know the way."

"I thought it might be fun to follow you while we talk."

"Then let's enter this way," Abigail chose, feeling like a child at play.

As they started out through the plexus, Abigail led them into a blind alley. Darby just smiled, enjoying her trial and error.

"It must be difficult to get to your office quickly when shuttled to work by helicopter," Abigail joked—still delighted by her surprise departure from daily life.

"Oh, I've walked the path enough times that it only takes a few seconds now. It's great entertainment when others land on the roof with me."

"Such a beautiful garden. Why put it here?"

"Two reasons: It's just for me; and it serves as a reminder to slow down and enjoy each day."

Finally reaching the helicopter pad, Abigail released a quick "Ha!" before realizing it was time to return to work. She asked, "How would you like to begin?"

"I'd like to begin by asking you out to dinner."

"Sorry, but I don't date billionaire oil barons. It's a rule that has always stood well for me. Let's just stick to the questions."

"If you say so," Darby replied disappointedly.

"Explain your engine to me. How does it work? How long have you had it?"

"As you know, there's a limitation on the particulars I can provide. The patent process isn't finished."

"What can you tell me?"

"Think about how the ocean's waves undulate. It's the same with the Earth's magnetic field—tiny oscillations caused by the sun's charged particles. Like electrical plants that harness our seas' continuous up and down motion, our engine utilizes the same principle."

"How is that principle applied in your engine?"

"Again, this is as much as I can say about the engine's design."

"When did you get the idea for such a technology?"

"A few years ago; actually, I've considered pulling up oil stakes for some time. Success is a funny thing. It's as difficult to shake as failure; especially when so many others rely on you."

"When will the engine be available for sale? I've heard two years. I've heard six months."

"We're near completion of the first million units in our four plants. You heard correct on both accounts. Initially, I intended on releasing the technology in two years. However, those uninspired by such an innovation will try to undermine its beginning. I have no choice but to go with the units on hand. Once the technology is released, then there's nothing that can be done about its use."

"Who's threatened its use?"

"I'm not naming names. Let's just say that my world is small and there are few who can hurt me; use your imagination."

"Government officials, other oil companies, technology firms?"

"You left out religious zealots and conspiracy theorists. But you get the picture; anyone who stands to lose if the status quo changes is suspect. This doesn't include the average American citizen. In mass, they have forsaken their right for something better."

"Why would you say that?"

"Because they have. How can the average person on the street allow the DC schmucks to get away with the garbage they dump on the population? People have the power by constitutional right to rid themselves of the leeches anytime—and don't. Do you know why?"

"I think you're about to tell me," Abigail said wryly, feeling annoyed with his rant.

"That's where you're wrong. I can't say I know why—not a clue. When I want something, I get it. It's easy to say that now because I have more money than anyone you've ever known. But it was so before I made billions. No one gave me Fountain Oil. I built it myself."

"Darby, sources say the government's going to halt production until they deem your technology safe. Is that true? What are you going to do about it?"

"I'm aware of Bonezo's efforts to protect the other oil companies' bulging bottom lines. The units will be ready before they can enforce any legislation. This is a presidential and congressional election year. The carpetbaggers are too busy selling their wares to worry about me this late on the campaign trail."

"My final and most important question to you is about the future. Have you thought about the impact your technology will make on the world; good and bad?"

"Dead on target; both good and bad will come from the engine. However, I wouldn't release it if I thought the cost far outweighed the benefit. It's going to hurt some. To start, oil prices will plummet around the world. Our currency is tethered to the price of oil. So, when crude drops the dollar precipitously rises in perceived worth.

"Now, this sounds like a good idea. And for a short while it'd be wonderful for America, until the other superpowers lose their currencies value against the buck, throwing their economies into peril. This then filters back to us because we buy and sell from those same countries.

"America can't return to the isolationist ways of its distant past. This only encourages jealousy and war. The political unrest will be devastating. Those same countries' populations will likely lose faith in their leaders like we have in America.

"I can go on. But it's unnecessary. You get the picture. Releasing too many units too quickly will bring about all the things I have said and much worse. A million units will give us a nice snapshot of how it will be accepted; and allow society time to digest it without throwing our world into chaos."

"Have you got a name for the engine?"

"Its name is the Kratometric Engine, after the Greek god Kratos—god of strength, might, power, and sovereign rule."

"I like that. It reminds me of my old boss."

"What happened to him?"

"Her—she took some time off and was replaced by the Greek god of bureaucracy."

Darby laughed and shot back, "That's too much. So do you have enough for the interview?"

"I have a few other questions that follow from the ones already posed; nothing you can't handle. We can proceed when you're ready."

"What do you think about joining me for lunch after we wrap this up?"

"I'm thinking about the same response I gave you for dinner. Come on, Darby, let's get this over with. This time, lead me out of the maze. I didn't leave any breadcrumbs."

All fifty CMC state directors had assembled behind a bank of microphones and video cameras at TTN headquarters. Sasha had arranged a news conference for David to publicly address Congress's moves against the CMC and announce their new initiatives. Also invited were the other three national news networks: VTN, CBN, and the newly formed internet exclusive news network INN.

"Where is he?" Daniel demanded.

"He should be here by now. I've left a number of messages for him. He's not answering his phone. I am sure he'll be here," Sasha assured.

"This is ridiculous. He's wasting my time and further embarrassing the CMC, if that's possible."

Shocked at the slight, a departure from his televised persona, Sasha defended David. "Mr. Walters, I'm sure he'll be here momentarily. Something unforeseen has come up."

While grandly entering the conference room from the rear, David belted out, "Something did come up. I woke today and couldn't find my spine until a few minutes ago. Rest assured I did locate it, and am here now. Please do forgive my delay—and a bit of a nervous stomach."

A general amusement at David's comments gave way to audience laughter as he strode up the center aisle, taking his place behind the microphone bouquet. Daniel stood stone-faced next to David, waiting to moderate the event and impress Frank, who quietly milled at the back of the room. The TTN icon conspicuously hung on the wall behind David, Sasha and the directors—well within the view of the other network cameras.

Ignoring Daniel, David began, "We have important things to discuss. With so many problems facing the CMC, I thought we'd start with the law. Lady Justice is no longer blind in this country. As a matter of fact, she's been peeking from under her blindfold for some time.

"How so, you ask? To start with, the CMC has been denied its daily business activities. These activities are completely legal and available to any American citizen. However, the courts, influenced by the Senate, have, by a writ of mandamus and court order, frozen all of our daily operations—hindering the ability to act on behalf of the American public.

"At present, our case is held up in the appeals court, with the intent of wearing down our will to go on. I assure you that our resolve has never been so robust. We've recommitted in our mission to guard public interest. To this end, I will lay out a new plan of action.

"Government corruption has become so commonplace that it is openly and generally accepted by the average citizen, who feels helpless to make a difference. What corruption do I speak of? It's the fidelity politicians show their corporate masters, while ignoring the will of the people.

"When does the authority conferred upon a representative transmute itself into corruption? It does so when it is used for something other than what was intended. When a senator attempts to push through legislation, which is meant to only benefit fossil fuel companies and ultimately undo alternative-energy legislation that's meant for the benefit and will of the people, then a sacred trust has been soiled with bias, greed and a pursuit of power for its own sake. I could cite hundreds of similar examples occurring every day, but this one makes my point nicely. It cannot stand. This is corruption in commission; knowingly participating in a fraud. A decision was made to benefit a corporate entity and not the people.

"What of omission? That's right. Our government is also woefully guilty of ignoring what large corporations have been doing to the public—this turning a blind eye to the greatest historical wealth transfer from the poor and middle class to the upper class is equally disturbing; and more egregious in many ways because it allows those in charge to claim that they had no idea what was happening. "Of the greatest corporate offenders to public trust in addition to oil companies are banks, mortgage companies, investment and wealth management firms, multi-conglomerate international corporations and stock markets; with the Phillips Stock Exchange here in New York being the most deceitful. The destruction and greed from these entities surrounds us. We are reminded daily of the price paid for their avarice.

"A few years ago, banks and mortgage companies inexpensively borrowed money and loaned it to anyone with a heartbeat. The loan products I speak of were multi-adjustable-rate mortgages that only required the borrower to state their income and assets without any proof—commonly referred to as liar loans. That's how a waitress was qualified to borrow three times the amount she could afford to pay.

"What makes this lunacy bizarre is that after the loan closed, the bank sold the loan to another financial institution. The bank then took their profits from the first loan-closing and lent those to another unqualified borrower. The cycle repeated itself again and again—funding millions of loans that should have never been made, that would very likely default, and finally caused the biggest artificially created real-estate crisis in eighty years.

"Investment and wealth management firms were accomplices in this process. These poorly underwritten and non-verified loans were sold to investment firms who bundled them together into blocks—finally peddling them on the open market like company shares on stock exchanges. They were touted to be collateralized and highly rated investments. An unsuspecting public, that trusted the so-called risk management experts, purchased these investments. Endowments, retirements, pension plans, education funds, and trusts have been taken to the cleaners. This fleecing is second only to the oil companies' stranglehold on an American public shackled to fossil fuel for their automobiles and home heating."

Frank tipped his nose towards Daniel. Daniel rose up from among the seated audience. The other reporters rolled eyes and turned heads.

"Mr. Samuel, could you tell us why you feel the banks are behind this court order?" Daniel probed.

"Excuse me, Daniel, is it? Daniel, I will not be taking any questions today. Thank you."

Feeling insulted in front of the other network reporters, Daniel pressed, "Mr. Samuel, it only seems fair that you take a few questions from TTN—seeing as we graciously hosted you at our headquarters."

Annoyed by Daniel's grandstanding, David replied, "Daniel, I didn't come here expecting to do anything other than to make a public announcement regarding the CMC's new direction; and the reasons for doing so. I chose TTN because Abigail Sanders has fairly reported on the CMC in the past. If you can't sit quietly, then I'm sure one of your colleagues' networks would be more than happy to provide the venue. Now then, would you mind if I continue?"

Daniel sat down without another word. Frank knew David wasn't mincing words, and quietly left the conference room to save face.

"Now, let's get back on track. Where were we? Oh yes, of course, the financial institutions. So, now we have investments that are failing, retirements being destroyed, and the only people benefiting from this were the circus clowns that sold them in the first place. Because our economy is interconnected, the foreclosure rates exponentially increased, exacerbating the downward economic trend. Unemployment rose—further accelerating the country's bleak overall financial health.

"The knockout blow was delivered by the banking industry. These institutions' credit-card divisions arbitrarily increased their interest rates. They shortened billing cycles to ensure more people would be late—so they could charge their customers more fees. In the end, they took as much money as they dared from consumers and then blamed them for borrowing too much—these same citizens that should never have been given so many lines of credit to begin with.

"Modern-day banking is not modern at all. It's one of the oldest gimmicks. They use their scientifically based marketing apparatus to make people want to spend; want to live a life they didn't earn and can't afford. They convince the consumer that they deserve an expensive home and extravagant automobile. Worst of all, the American public is sold on the idea that their lives have no meaning unless they accumulate more than can be used—gorging themselves on consumption.

"It's truly amazing what the banking industry has done to this country. They're the drug dealer that maligns the user for their addiction—lacking the backbone to admit they're the source of all this misery. They destroy people's lives, take all the money, and dispose of the carcasses—making way for the next generation of junkies they can string along and finally discard.

"Our public officials are just as guilty as if they owned the banks themselves. Corruption by omission is more insidious than commission because of the silent way it works itself into the fabric of society. Like a weed, it goes unnoticed until all the healthy surrounding plant life has been choked out.

"If the bank's mortgage debacle is brother to credit-card thievery, then the stock markets are its cousin. How can something so seemingly serendipitous be allowed to exist? Ostensibly, the open market regulates itself. After all, if a company listed on a stock market performs well, its stock price rises. In failure, its worth plummets—it makes rational sense.

"Unfortunately, this is where theory parts with practical application. When the president of a corporation sells off all his company shares six months before posting a dismal earnings report, the system of checks and balances failed. When the futures market overly influences the cost of goods, services, commodities or energy, it's always bad for market stability and honest investors. Wealth and worth are created and destroyed based on speculation, with nothing tangibly generated—nothing valued, nothing affirmed.

"What a sham—creating wealth, not from work or something useful, by scaring your fellow man; or instigating the false belief of a quick and easy buck! It's a system twice as fake and manipulated as our own currency. A dollar is at least representative of theoretical worth.

The stock markets' only purpose is to move money based upon lies, manipulation, and greed so lascivious that Hades lacks room for these souls.

"Today's stock market endgame is the wealth-stripping of the middle class and the poor; one mutual fund and one retirement portfolio at a time. A shell of legitimacy that thin should crumble under the slightest pressure. Yet, it does not shatter. It's actually reinforced by individual investors' wishful thinking—believing they can beat the system and make the highest returns on their investment anyone has ever reaped, never having to risk the money they placed on the altar of false hope.

"Let us also not forget the large multinational companies based in the United States; their boards and officers. There are so many things to rue about a great many behemoth corporations that I must only choose a few comments, lest we spend the entirety of the day lamenting them. I often wonder how such large entities are not crushed under the weight of their own malfeasance.

"Along that line of thinking, I'd like to put up an idea for you in the audience to consider in your own time, while going about your business as newspeople filming this release, making your notes and so on. You're paid a wage for your work, are you not? Your work is important to the news agencies that employ you. I dare say that, if it weren't for you, there would be no news networks; at least not as we know them today.

"A question I'd like to raise is, how would you balance the worth of your work and contributions to your employer compared to that of the board members and executives? Would you say that the network officers are worth four hundred times your salary? If they were to lose their job, would you still report the news? Of course; and the news would go on.

"This is a simple example; clearly demonstrating a severe imbalance of pay and severance benefits when a job is lost, not working in tandem with the worth of the work provided. It seems obvious to me that the top-based rewards structure of many large corporations encourages those with extreme greed in their minds and hearts to provide leadership to those who will ultimately suffer under the boot of tyranny. In this example, no matter what level of service an employee renders, their career and livelihood rest in the hands of a capricious and self-involved megalomaniac. This can only end badly for the employee, while his chief reaps vastly greater rewards; sharing none of the risk the average worker is burdened by.

"These same individuals entrusted to lead such mammoth entities have time and again shown a proclivity for the creative nature with which they account for their profits and losses. This serpentine move to conceal underperformance or overstate revenues ultimately influences their stock price and rating on the various stock exchanges—bolstering perceived wealth, with the added benefit of providing a dishonest justification for executive pay increases and bonuses many hundreds of times the average employee's salary for no concrete reason other than unchecked greed. When the markets discover that the company's books, like the goose, are cooked, the executive has long since yanked their golden parachute's lollipop.

"Before the dark prince has taken his ill-gotten gains, he sullies the market along the way—violating antitrust laws meant to protect small businesspeople from unfair trade practices. These laws were instituted to ensure the general health of the open market by disallowing monopolies. Monopolies like corporate executives such as these stifle fair competition—destroying everything other than themselves in the wake of their own self-delusion.

"Worst of all, these pestilent carriers have forsaken the very people that provided the opportunity to be looted. Many international corporations based in the US were once small companies. Built on the backs, money, and faith of the American people, these corporate leaders shuttle jobs overseas because it's cheaper to buy labor at one tenth the cost. It remains very curious to me that these companies would never have had the opportunity to betray the United States had the American public not spent their money on whatever product or service it provided. These businesses represent a prodigal son who has not and will never return home. This is criminal and should not be tolerated.

"The corporations do not act alone. They have henchmen to do their dirty work. Their hired guns are designated in many circles as political operatives. You know them as lobbyists. Their profession's only purpose is to convince, cajole, manipulate, leverage, and buy every elected official that will aid in their company's long-term financial goals. When the politician capitulates, he or she ceases to be your representative and becomes a traitor."

By now every reporter's face was flat, without emotion. They knew every syllable was true. This truth seemed to hang in the air, wanting a solution.

The directors stood calmly behind David but intently stared into the cameras and at the reporters behind them. David took a sip of water and cleared his throat. After setting the glass down, he grabbed both sides of the podium.

"I needed a break; as did your ears, I'm sure," he joked.

The crowd responded with a low laugh.

"We certainly do have problems that need fixing, don't we? If the government wasn't blocking the CMC's normal operations, then we'd still be filing writs and pressing the public's rights today. Having had the opportunity to step back from our everyday activities, I can see that it would not have done any good.

"As a good friend recently told me, the CMC is not a company of action. Well, that's going to change! Beginning today, the Citizens' Mandamus Council no longer is interested in filing writs of mandamus until our rights to do so have been restored. Starting today, the CMC is in the value business.

"Congress and the corporations I've referenced have thirty days to cease their unlawful, destructive, dishonest and disloyal activities. We are also strongly suggesting that legislation be passed that outlaws lobbying, as it is commonly known. After that period of time, if it is found that to a great extent these behaviors have not discontinued, the CMC will begin representing the will of the people. All of our efforts will consist in circulating a new nationwide note of value."

The reporters all jumped to their feet, yelling questions. Cameras flashed and clicked as they photographed David. Others dialed their mobile phones.

"Please, everyone, calm down. As I mentioned earlier, I will not be taking questions today. There are still a few important points to cover before I finish. May I please ask you to be calm? Thank you."

Daniel barked, "What are you, some sort of a socialist? Money is evil; is that it? How do you suppose things will get paid for?"

"Mr. Walters, I'll ask you one last time to take a seat. If you don't comply, then I'll be taking up with one of your competitors here in the audience; never again granting your network another interview, invitation to future events, news conference, or the time of day. I hope I'm being clear," David cautioned sternly.

Daniel recoiled in humiliation. The other reporters looked on him with disdain for interrupting—Daniel's grandstanding and inflated ego were well known in news circles.

"I'm sorry for that interruption. Let's get back on track. Currency is the source of all this corruption of power, isn't it? The answer seems as obvious as the question. Yet we look upon the American dollar as if it possesses mystical qualities, don't we? It seems so to me.

"The United States dollar's fundamental power rests in the guarantee of the government to make good on the bill. It's not based upon a fixed asset any longer. At one time, our currency was based upon gold, but those days are long past. We are left to assume the government will always make good on its promise. The foreign nations who have bought our debt to keep injecting their countries' perceived worth into the marketplace is counting on the United States to make good on its obligations.

"There's a problem with this promise: It's not being kept. Do any of you in the audience trust your representatives to act in your best interest? All things considered, most would likely answer, no. Our government's word is no good. So, how can we expect it to keep its promise to make good on all its currency. It can't.

"If this government cannot keep its promise to its citizenry and still issue a currency every person recognizes and utilizes, then there is no good reason why the Citizens' Mandamus Council cannot offer up something different; something of worth. We do care about our people. We do want their interests represented. There really is no reason why the CMC's guarantee is any less credible than the United States Government. I would also add that the Citizens' Mandamus Council is in excellent financial shape, can live within a budget, and can pay its bills with cash instead of broken promises.

"I would like to address Mr. Walters's underlying accusation. Daniel insinuated that I'm a socialist and consider money to be evil. Does that just about sum it up, Mr. Walters?"

Daniel said nothing, sinking farther into his chair as his fellow reporters sneered.

"It can't be that I feel money is the root of all evil, now could it? The Citizens' Mandamus Council is a for-profit corporation. I need money to pay my directors, who are all attorneys. They have families to feed and staff to pay for. I must set aside money for my old age when I can no longer work. Does this sound like the activities of a socialist? No, it doesn't. I just happen to have built a corporation with the sole purpose of holding the United States Government accountable. How is this in any way socialist?

"What of money? Is money evil? I don't see how. It's a slip of paper. Its only purpose is to purchase things. In many ways I find great nobility in currency; not for what it can do but in what it represents. A currency note to me signifies an honest exchange between two people: equal for equal. It offers no deception, for none is possible. It forces a truthful discourse between two or more people for the exchange of goods, services and satisfaction of debt. What higher good can there be in organized society than that?

"Currency stands on its own the way two soldiers from opposing forces stand face to face on the battlefield before engagement— offering quarter to the other in exchange for a surrender. Currency is the salute rendered by each to each. Currency, like the salute, says 'I am unarmed. At this meeting I will not harm you. I respect you as my equal.'

"At this time, a fixed amount of notes to be printed has yet to be determined. However, the paper's worth will be well over a trillion in denominations of one, five, ten, twenty, fifty and one hundred. In fact, the name of our new note of value is 'the Worth.'

"That is all for now. I bid you good day and hope this course of action may be averted. Wide is the path, ladies and gentlemen. Wide is the path," David repeated with serenity.

He next motioned for Ted to move from behind him and walk through the central aisle of the audience. One by one the directors followed Ted. There was applause, mixed congratulations, jeers, yelling and reporters demanding comments from directors as they passed by. David stood post like a general reviewing his soldiers; watching with pride as each director paraded with dignity—knowing they were a part of something very human, historic, and requisite.

When every director had made their way through, David stood alone at the front of the conference room and paused for a moment, taking in the commotion. The unintended response would soon show itself and would likely not be pleasant. In his gut, David knew this—but it was necessary and too important not to complete.

He thought of Ethan as he stepped forward to exit, the reporters attempting to gain further comment blurring out of his vision. He gazed outside the conference room windows down onto the city below. A gray haze hung over the streets, filling him with dread for what he was releasing: dread for himself, the CMC, and the country. America must contend with itself, the cost of freedom and the need every so often to shake the tree of liberty loose from its oppressors without destroying itself.

CHAPTER
XIII
THE DIFFERENCE BETWEEN SACRED AND SCARED

Following the CMC's press conference, a frantic House and Senate assembled for separate emergency meetings. House Speaker Delilah Talbot tapped her gavel, attempting to gain order over the House representatives. Before her a chamber of political giants clamored. She was concerned; not for the state of the union as much as the state of the status quo. The CMC's move had far-reaching potential to upset perceived power and strip away assurances once considered implacable.

Vice President Fulton leaned forward in his chair directly behind Delilah and said, "You need to get control of the session. This is ridiculous. How are we going make any sense of this if they keep breaking parliamentary procedure—congressmen openly arguing with each other?"

Fulton's place was with the Senate. However, President Anderson had asked that he, Byron, sit in on the Senate so that he could confer with Ethan. Fulton agreed and so joined the House of Representatives to gauge their attitudes and report back afterwards.

Delilah maintained calm composure while the representatives could see her face, but after swiveling back towards Fulton, she snapped, "Great advice, Richard—I oughta write that down." Nodding to the Vice President as if they were exchanging cordial greetings, she then turned back to face the chamber.

"Madam Speaker, may we have order?" Representative Ruben Conway of Texas, Sixth District, demanded.

"We will have order," Delilah shouted—banging her gavel yet again—finally the angry reddened faces began to calm and the representatives sat down.

Ruben said, "Thank you, Madam Speaker."

District constituents knew Ruben as an affable and fun-loving man—people simply liked him. Having served fourteen years in Congress, his status as an incumbent was solid.

He continued, "What an outrage, my fellow representatives. This self-proclaimed savior is nothing more than a huckster selling his wares. He's putting a gun to our heads and telling us to dance. Well, I for one will not two-step for this cowboy."

Applause and cheers erupted during the pause.

"David Samuel claims that we've sold the American public down the river by working with corporations. How does he expect us to manage the government without help from valued corporate partners? There are some big shoes to fill serving in public office. The United States simply does not possess enough governmental agencies to deal with the needs of the average citizen. We heavily rely on private-sector industries to bridge the gap where we leave off.

"Mr. Samuel would have us believe big business lobbyists are evil. How so? When an individual has a problem and takes it to their state's senators or representatives, are they not lobbying for their interests? Seems so—How's it fair, then, that an ordinary citizen may approach their representative to solve a problem but a corporation can't?

"If I understand David Samuel correctly, he's embittered because the courts put an end to his mischief. He doesn't feel his rights have been protected. He expresses quite clearly his belief that the opposite's true; that his right to file lawsuits all the livelong day has been hogtied. What's behind his complaint that corporations use lobbyists to have their grievances heard? He too is attempting to deny enterprise a right to representation. I put it to you, Mr. Samuel: How are you different?

"David Samuel complains that CEOs make hundreds of times more than the average worker. What then, may I ask, is he asking for at his pep rallies? I assure you it's not a pat on the back. The CMC is reputed to take in millions at these cult assemblies. I task you, my fellow congressmen, to hold Samuel's feet to the fire. What's good for us is good for him. We should take a hard look at what he's done with all that loot."

The audience rose to clap and cheer. For the moment, guilt did not rest on their shoulders. As the applause died down, Ruben concluded, "I yield the remainder of my time to the congresswoman from Illinois."

Ruben stepped away from the podium as Representative Marilynn Maloney, Seventh District, took his place. She composed herself while waiting for quiet. Her appearance was always one of utmost self-importance.

Marilynn was an atypical congresswoman. Strong family ties to Chicago granted her bid for election three terms before. She rarely spoke out for or against anything. Her vote had been bought and sold before she took office. At just thirty-six, Marilyn's dark brown hair and sultry appearance turned more than a few heads in Congress. Yet her greatest asset was the unknown nature of her politics; allegiances of the silent kind.

"My colleagues, I am very concerned by what's happened here today. An edict was rendered by a private citizen to this governing body. When did the tail ever lead the head? If Mr. Samuel has his way, then it will be so. For all his accusations, and that's all they are, he failed to mention the most important thing: true power. What is the House body if it does not represent power? I'll tell you what: a failed state.

"My ancestors built Rome. They also watched it crumble and fall before their eyes hundreds of years later. It happened because they allowed their leaders to be weak in the eyes of their enemies and citizens. We cannot let that happen here. We are the hope of mankind; that democracy can stand as a shining beacon in the darkness.

"If I were an orator, or a woman with keen dialectical skills, then every point Mr. Samuel made would have been countered. Unfortunately, I'm not gifted in forensics. But this is not a loss, my fellow representatives, because we don't need to debate this man. We do not even need to recognize his existence. We carry the burden of leadership. We don't need David Samuel, or his Citizens' Mandamus

Council's support to rule. We are imbued with righteous dominion over this country and its inhabitants. Let us neither recognize his words, nor acknowledge his actions.

"He mocks his own representatives; yet fails to participate in the process. He rattles his saber and cries out for justice. Let him have it. This is the United States of America. If he is filled with such certainty that his cause is just, urge him to run for office and change the government from within. Public officials were still elected the last time I checked."

Laugher filled the chamber. Light applause continued as Marilynn's gaze and curt smile scanned the room.

"I understand that the Phillips Stock Exchange, America's largest, lost nearly thirty percent of its worth after this announcement. So what? The ground will be retaken. This government will not be bullied by its people. We'll burn this fool's useless money after his precious CMC has financially collapsed.

"Time on the floor is ending. I wish to leave my congressional leaders with a parting thought that should warm your hearts. His idea hinges on the belief that the American population actually has a will left. When was the last time any district inhabitant opposed our wishes, power, or vote? Can anyone here remember when a constituent last walked through your doors? I'll sleep tonight in the knowledge that this will be the last we hear from Mr. David Samuel."

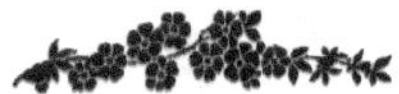

In Senate chambers, Ethan had taken his place behind the podium. President Anderson, seated directly behind him, eagerly awaited engagement to ascertain tempo and attitudes.

Ethan opened, "Fellow senators and Mr. President, for the evening and only this evening, I will be granting a limited departure from typical parliamentary procedure regarding time to speak, and open the floor to immediate responses from the Senate. I feel that it could aid efficiency of shared thoughts during this crisis.

"I must warn you that such an exception will continue only if decorum and mutual respect is observed. Any departure from courteous conduct, and this ad-hoc open forum will end and there will be a return to business as usual on the Senate floor. Also, I wish to explain that this is not a policy change to normal Senate floor procedures. As president pro tem, I'm exercising discretion only for this evening's late-night session.

"The senator possessing the floor will be granted the usual time to speak. The senator may accept and answer questions. I call on the senior senator from the state of Oregon, Arthur Davis. Senator Davis, will you please take the floor?"

Stepping behind the podium, Arthur said, "Thank you, Senator Scott. I'll get straight to the point. This threat is real. It has, within less than a day, shed a third of our economy's wealth. We haven't the time to debate the merits of Mr. Samuel's accusations. We must deal with his actions.

"What I see as the immediate issue to address in contending with the Citizens' Mandamus Council is the legality of this move, and if it violates the USA Freedom Act. Is it altogether legal for the CMC to issue currency? Minting coin is clearly a violation of law. We are currently fighting in many theaters of war. Shouldn't we make it criminal to print and issue any new currency during a time of war for the sake of stability? He's calling it a note of value. But isn't this really wordplay for replacing the dollar?

"This leads to my next point: the USA Freedom Act. We are still in a quasi-state of war. This attack on our government is an act of economic terrorism. We possess provisions under the Freedom Act to seize enemy assets and personnel; and deny them recourse until our country returns to a state of peace. Do I have a consensus?"

"I would give my consent to these suggestions!" Senator Duncan Lungren called out.

Senator Lungren, a man of his own making, hailed from Tennessee. Unjustifiably confident, he was originally elected after a predecessor was caught embezzling money during the campaign. With an incumbent rapidly losing steam, Duncan didn't need to do anything other than promise as little as possible. Duncan had made a career of doing nothing in the Senate. A puffer fish, he was notorious for seizing opportune moments to make a show of power and importance. In the end, he'd take up with the side more likely to win. He personally was unlikely to do anything other than vote.

Senator Lungren went on, "This CMC organization is nothing but the worst kind of rabble. They wouldn't dare snub the dollar with a try at our national currency. Why, it's outright unpatriotic. How can we allow this to happen?

"Surely, at least once in his life, Mr. Samuel recited the Pledge of Allegiance. Every US child starts their school day with the covenant, and has done so for over a hundred years. What he's doing is an affront to this country and a violation unprecedented in American history. The CMC ought be disbanded. Further, we should have one Mr. David Samuel declared an enemy of the state and dealt with accordingly."

Senators applauded as Duncan posed to relish their approval. He nodded and beamed a smile. After the clapping subsided, he took his seat.

"We're wasting our time with useless posturing and rhetoric!" Hubert boomed, as he jumped to his feet.

"I recognize Senator Hubert Riley from the state of Alaska," Senator Davis proclaimed from behind the podium.

"This is ridiculous, what's going on here. Look at the mockery David Samuel's making of this body and the United States government. When someone picks a fight, you knock 'em down so they can't get up again. We don't have time for the inane procedure of passing a bill making it unlawful to print his note of nonsense. It'll take too long to get through the Senate, House, and onto the President's desk—ultimately missing Samuel's thirty-day deadline. We must act now! Senator Davis, I ask you to yield your remaining time on the floor to Senator Ethan Scott from the state of New York."

"I yield the remainder of my time," Senator Davis agreed, stepping away.

Ethan took his place behind the podium and addressed Hubert, standing in the chamber packed with senators, "Senator Riley, you called me to the floor. How may I be of assistance?"

"As a dedicated public servant, I call upon you, Senator Scott, to deal with your ex-employer for the sake of the American people."

"Senator Riley, I'm in agreement; I do not wish to see our country suffer. But what would you have me do? We're a nation of laws. He hasn't broken them. There's no legal recourse to avail at this time; unless you're suggesting that I break the laws we're sworn to uphold."

"Senator Scott, you take my statement too far. I'm not goading you to break anything; only proposing you sway his decision for the good of the American people."

A consensus spread amongst the seated senators with murmurs and head-bobbing. Ethan felt it in the dark and glassy stares. They wanted Ethan to make their problem go away.

"Senator Riley, it would seem like a considerate request if not for the fact that he's within his rights to do what he's threatened. He's pursuing his own happiness. Do you expect him to not act upon his conscience?

"No, Senator. I would entreat your friend to do what's right and good for his country."

"And what's that, Senator Riley? What is good for America? Do you have the answer to a question so far-reaching? Are you really interested in what's good for America, or in what's good for you?

"I resent that," Hubert rebuked, attempting to deflect by false injury. It might have worked, if not for Hubert's heartless reputation.

"It's your choice to resent it. I meant no offense and was simply attempting to get at what you're asking me to do. There's something here that hasn't been mentioned. Given the direction of our discussion thus far, it's not likely to be heard. I'll therefore voice it for the sake of balanced deliberations.

"That something is the question why. Why would a man, dedicated to the US Constitution, wish to issue a quasi-currency note instead of using the dollar? Could it be that he truly believes his assertions? I do know the man. David wouldn't have tendered a warning unless it was intended to be clearly understood.

"If we assume his claims are true for a moment, then we are stewards of our country's malfeasance. And so, what's left to be done as the legislative branch? It's a difficult question. When we accepted the privileges of our office, all the built-in failings came with them.

"We have a crisis to face. A third of our stock markets' value was lost in a day. Repercussion will ripple for some time to come. I wonder, though, if we're not making a mistake in where to place our efforts to avert future damage. Every legislated virtue becomes a vice. Senator Riley, I yield the floor to you so that I may reassume my procedural duties."

Ignoring Hubert's oral musings, Ethan obsessed in his head. *David's within his rights. He's also going to destroy our economy. As much as I despise these people, will one of them please just come up with a legal way to fix this? How we exist as a functioning government is a biblical miracle.*

The day following David's ultimatum, CMC board members and committee chairmen assembled to discuss initial progress. Outward excitement filled the conference room. Inwardly, their stomachs churned with dread.

"It truly is an exciting time for the Citizens' Mandamus Council. The executive board, comprised of David Samuel, Daphne Cook, Trent Mitchell, Betsy Coffman and myself, has assembled this morning to complete a first end-of-the-week committee chairs debriefing," Emily Watson was wrapping up.

"Thank you, Miss Watson. Emily, your public speaking continues to improve. Before long we're going to put you on the road to strengthen our presence," David teased, mindful of her nervous tendency when addressing more than a few people at a time.

"Think I'll pass, David."

"Look, people, we're already defeated from within. Let's see if we can save the CMC in other ways then," David mused. "We'll be meeting each Friday until the deadline one month from yesterday. At that time, if the government hasn't capitulated, then we will proceed as planned. There's quite a bit to do, so to it we go.

"First, ensure your people know what their responsibilities are. During this period, we don't know how many directors may choose to move on, and we must prepare for this. Also, keep everyone well informed. This'll contain speculation to a minimum.

"You've all done admirably in a job you didn't have a week ago. I'll expect the same performance all the way through to the end. You and your committee members will have access to the CMC board at all times. This is a privilege. Take care in calling on them, unless it's absolutely necessary. We're here to help. However, there are more of you than us, and time is short.

"Let's begin with Ted Stevenson, our Washington DC office director and Legal Committee chairman. Ted, where are we at with the Bone Yard gravediggers?"

Ted smiled; not expecting David's common slang usage. "That handle always makes me laugh. Our defense is in the research phase. At the moment, we don't foresee anything the government can come at us with; well, legally that is. I was informed this morning that they've already filed for an injunction to halt any production of our paper. It won't stick and will be thrown out by the judge as it lacks any legal standing. As you cited, there are a number of small communities throughout the United States that use some form of local currency to bolster their economy. Even city transit tokens are considered a form of currency. So, the government is going to find it difficult to deem the Worth *nequam*. With that, it's also important to remember that DC has made examples of smaller entities trying their hand at this."

"Brian, I like the name your committee came up with. The Worth; it's poignant," David interrupted.

"It tickled us too," Brian added.

Ted continued, "The Worth, as we've devised it, is an absolute measure of value against everything: every commodity, service, object—anything that exists; anything as of the Worth's original issuance date; hence being a note of value. It is not a currency note or a banknote. Our note does not represent any bank, government or country on the planet. It is an honest measure of value, and nothing more. It can be exchanged based upon its face value against any commodity or currency as of the issuance date at parity; as a reflection of the established exchange-rate tables set forth on the issuance date. Future commodities, currencies, products, and services shall be added to these tables as they become available. These tables are the Worth's immoveable foundation and critical to its measure of value. As I mentioned, there isn't much of a defense needed at this point. We're not breaking the law."

"Wow…and you call yourself a lawyer. When did an American not need a defense regardless of guilt or innocence? Besides, doesn't your committee have an additional member?" David quipped.

"Okay, boss. Take a cheap shot just because I head up the DC office. It's not my fault Washington gets no representation in Congress."

"Easy there, tough guy; I'm just having a little fun to ease the tension."

"Sure," Ted said with a grin. "We're researching obscure rulings to prepare for anything strange the government may throw our way. We're also preparing a litany of motions and the typical court filings to slow down any assault on our efforts. At this point, the thirty-day clock is already ticking. Every filing imaginable grants thirty days for an initial reply. So, there's no real recourse unless they were to change due process itself."

"It sounds like we're on solid ground. Thank you, Ted. Jason Morgan, with the California office and chairman of the Underwriting Committee, what do you have for us?"

"I have more for this board than it has time to listen. The quick and dirty is that none of the North American-based stock exchanges will allow us to sell on their markets. We expect this to change."

"Why would that be?" Emily posed in a serious tone.

With a triumphant smile, Jason replied, "Frankly, because the Japanese, South Korean, Brazilian, and many European countries have agreed to sell them on their exchanges. All have designated the Worth A-rated if we successfully launch the paper. With that rating, the markets will devour CMC bonds. Our own exchanges will have no choice but to sell them, or miss the opportunity to make a lot of fake money on the initial issuance."

"We never did determine that this was the direction we were going to take: issuing bonds," David injected with a look of concern.

"I know. But once I started talking with foreign exchanges, after the initial defeat with our own, other countries began calling on me. It's exciting, to say the least. I think what's important to consider, in making the final decision, is the legitimacy conferred upon the new note. With foreign backing, it will certainly have more credibility throughout the world, not to mention the effect it will have on our own people," Jason said.

"You put your finger on my greatest concern—what'll happen the day after those bonds hit the market? We merely want our government to act on the will of the people. I wish things to be turned around; not upside down. If the cure is worse than the disease, then what do we gain? In the very least, we should consider this a holdout position—preparing as if we're going to issue bonds. If we need to actually pull the trigger then we will. First, let's see if the Worth can gain confidence on its own before we involve foreign investors in America's domestic interests. Is everyone on the board with me?" David enjoined, as he looked to his leadership for their response.

Everyone nodded. The committee chairs turned about to ensure the others present agreed. It was a solemn and frightening moment.

"David, we're already working with a law firm here in New York that specializes in bonds and initial public offerings."

"Good, keep at it, Jason. Who's next?" David asked.

"I am," Dana said.

"Fine, Dana. What's the Marketing Committee got for us?"

The Denver office director, Dana Roybal, replied, "It goes without saying that we're selling this idea to an eager crowd. We don't need market surveys to know that Americans feel disenfranchised. No matter who's sent to Washington, once a lobbyist sinks their teeth into them, the people's needs are pushed to the bottom of the list.

"Our pitch should be factual with an upbeat message of hope;

followed by predictions of what this new note will do to the status quo. At first our committee felt that a negative campaign was the way to go. These jokers have certainly provided lots of ammunition. However, after working up a few scenarios, the message sounded like the evening news. We don't need fear, like the networks do, to sell an idea.

"The campaign slogan we came up with is 'What's it worth to you?'; with an emphasis on worth, because of its implication of what's important to the people, and the paper's name. In addition to the typical news releases, conspicuous internet exposure, email, viral marketing efforts, social networking campaigns, and posters with people from all walks of life will precede public speaking engagements.

David warmly replied, "Nice, Dana, very nice; though I'd disagree with you on one point. Not everyone in the crowd will be thrilled with our ideas. The top ten percent will eagerly dismiss this message. Ensure, while practicing speeches, you prepare our directors for likely-resistance in the crowds. Still, you've done some fine work. When will we be ready to deploy?"

"By the deadline."

"Excellent. Brian Barrette, from the Kansas City office, let's hear from you next. How far along is the Minting Committee?"

"David, I still find it humorous that you had me chair the Minting Committee. Unlike you, I do believe money, and the love of it, is the root of many evils."

"Brian, the ironies of life never cease; even after you die. It's for this very reason that it had to be you. Only someone who could not be seduced by the lure of wealth should be in charge of the plates and production. How far have we progressed?"

"We've commissioned a Master Engraver in Germany to create the plates, and to work alongside our digital press people. The note will look similar to currency—so people will feel more comfortable. As you requested, we'll make reference to our slogan. We also included the requested symbols.

"We have two South Korean printers awaiting the final order to begin. An initial one trillion can be turned around in three days. We also nabbed an ex-Treasury employee to help us with anti-counterfeit measures: cloth-woven paper, reactive ink, magnetic security strip, reflective watermarks, internet registry, and unique registration numbers. All of these measures will be included in the initial printing. The paper is as secure as we can make it!" Brian boasted.

"Nice work. Whose idea was it to call our fiat the Worth?" David asked.

"Mine. I wanted the name to impart what we're really getting at; the worth of our currency and ourselves. False promises have floated for too long."

"Well said, Brian. Jared, that leaves you."

"So did you leave the best for last or the easiest?" Jared asked with his typically gracious smile.

"You decide," David replied, shooting a warm smile back. David always appreciated Jared Griffith's self-sufficiency as Arizona's state director. He worked hard and went home each day to his family. Jared never caused waves and was a seemingly forgettable man because David never heard from him, aside from progress reports— he never needed help.

"I'll assume the best, as usual," Jared confirmed, laughing at his own joke. "We're actually finished with what the Reserve Committee has been tasked to complete. Nine large post offices have been secured throughout the United States—previously closed due to consolidation. These hardened facilities provide appropriate security for storage. We're awaiting the return of the signed leasing agreements. The nine locations are spread evenly across the United States: three sites located on the West Coast, three in the center, and three on the East Coast. They're also distributed evenly throughout the Northern, middle and Southern thirds of the country. This'll make stealing large sums of the note impossible. Our committee has hired Incubus Security. They're largely ex-military personnel, all with combat experience. They'll secure facilities and transportation of all bulk deliveries."

"Jared, you've sewn it all up for us. Let me know when we receive those contracts. By the way, how did you get the government to work with us, given our move against them?'

"I created a separate company under another name, with the sole purpose of subleasing space to the Citizens' Mandamus Council."

"That's it, then. We've accomplished more than I could've hoped for in less than a week. If the government doesn't heed, then we're positioned to move forward. Does anyone have anything to add?" David asked with pride.

A room filled with confidence and enthusiasm fell silent when it became evident that their rhetoric was about to become reality. They knew the government would not capitulate. Fear of what they would unleash became palpable.

"You can't beat City Hall. Isn't that how the saying goes?" Trent Mitchell tolled, like a bell in the fog of night.

Trent was always the most sober in leadership. As a tax attorney by trade before joining the CMC's executive board, Trent's voice typically reflected cold, hard facts. While he could be moved by David's words, his pragmatism could not let go of the truth; this was going to be a painful fight. Their lives were about to change and it scared him.

David reverently explained, "Trent, you know that during our Revolutionary War, General Washington's greatest asset wasn't strength of arms. In fact, the British often outmanned and outgunned the General's forces. Yet, he prevailed from the outset: at Concord and Lexington. It was for this reason that George Washington eventually took Boston. The British simply didn't believe he was up to it. The English should have easily routed the General. The opposite occurred and rewarded George with stores of gunpowder and cannons later used against their former owners.

"What I narrate is an ignorance of enemy capabilities: the colonies' then and ours today. The US Government has known for years that the Citizens' Mandamus Council stood its post against every move which served political greed. They knew then like they know now; we might eventually do something. That they're uncertain we can actually follow through is our strength, and could serve as an change agent before we're forced to do this difficult thing. The government still has time. We'll know at the end of thirty days, won't we?"

"So what does this mean; that the hardest part is committing to action? Isn't that a little naïve? Regardless of the best-laid plans, unintended consequences bear on every decision. Are we really ready to throw our lives away for fellow citizens? We've been doing this for years without so much as a thank you from the average American. The commitment and sacrifices have been enormous," Trent lamented.

"Trent, I wouldn't insult you by claiming the road ahead will likely be smooth. I can't predict, with certainty, the outcome for every particular of this plan. What I know is that it must proceed," David insisted.

Jared roused, "Does anyone ever wish to live in times such as these? I certainly didn't want this. I had a different set of plans for my life. But here it is; and here I stand. Insupposable and possibly horrible days are ahead. Someone must face them. We're as good as any to take on the task. Hell, I'm excited for what's coming."

"That's what we're going to need in the coming days if the government doesn't change its policy on corruption. Thank you for that, Jared. With this kind of spirit we're sure to prevail.

"Listen, Trent, life could become dicey for us—professionally and personally. There's good reason to be scared. This is the stuff of greatness: staring down fear and forcing it back into the shadows where it belongs. Courage doesn't exist in a vacuum. It can't live without a reason or need. It's days like the ones we're now living which define human eminence. We didn't pick our days in history. But we can choose how we face them. Do we run and hide, allowing the few to take from the many? Do we stand by while thieves steal our birthright to dignity because they claim to have dominion over us? Do we choose to exist on our knees instead of our feet?

"I say we have a right to better. If we must endure their corruption and perversion of a well-conceived institution, which the United States was designed to be, then they must accept and receive the wrath of those they would rape!" David shouted.

At the news desk, Abigail agonized over Daniel's rattling off the evening news. Frank Lambert's regime condemned her to seldom leaving a well-gilded cage to cover an event on location. Abigail's journalistic tools dulled moment by moment, like a scythe that no longer cut—wasting away beside a blue-footed booby bird.

Her drudgery demanded a recitation of poorly written prose; prompter-scrolling along a three-count rhythm. A child could do it. She detested this most—losing professional credibility with each broadcast. Her life and career had become a joke.

TTN had ceased to be a news-based organization and was now a mouthpiece for the highest bidder. As time marched on during the presidential campaign, less was run on important issues and more about gossip; and problems generated from their spread.

The CMC was Abigail's balefire. After issuing Congress their ultimatum, it became increasingly difficult to showcase business-as-usual segments—there were far too many affected by the failing false impression that all was well in America and nearly every story directly or indirectly related to David's move against the House and Senate. Her only comfort in missing such an important event was David's public chastisement of Daniel.

Daniel began closing a segment on joblessness as Brian Calvert, the evening producer, fluttered fingers towards Abigail, indicating the camera would be panning to her. Abigail's prompter lit up with text. Brian mouthed a countdown and then pointed to Abigail.

"Good evening. I'm Abigail Sanders. In a related story, President Byron Anderson addressed a group of unemployed numbering in the hundreds at a closed Pittsburgh steel factory this afternoon. The President suggested that our country should cease providing jobs once held by American workers to underpaid overseas laborers. He spoke at great length about the need for an employment bill; and promised this would be the first issue he and the Blue Coats Party would address if reelected.

"At the outset, the crowd responded well to the President's speech. However, by its end, many were outwardly frustrated—yelling obscenities towards Anderson. Pittsburgh police were on hand in riot gear, though no violence was reported.

"Presidential hopefuls Michael Bishop, Governor of Oklahoma, the Liberty Party's nominee for this presidential election, and Senator Heath Slaughter from Nebraska, the Britches Party presidential nominee, squared off against each other in Omaha this afternoon. From the debate's outset they seemed more like friends than campaign adversaries, jointly siding against the incumbent for allowing the true jobless rate to reach thirteen percent and failing to keep a campaign promise from Anderson's first election to do away with lobbyists. Lack of government and corporate accountability was a topic both felt was directly to blame for the decline in our gross domestic output.

"After Bishop and Slaughter ceased addressing sustentative issues by making President Anderson the scapegoat, they retreated to party dividing lines—continuing personal attacks on one another. The Liberty Party, generally considered to be intellectually and socially conscientious, claimed that many new governmental and social programs were needed to solve the country's biggest problems. The Britches Party, regarded as the strongest of the independent parties, touted fiscal fundamentals and government minimalism as their platform centerpiece. Like President Byron's speech, the debate started off with an enthusiastic audience, only to lose viewer-following as the debate trudged on. A large portion of attendees departed before closing arguments were made."

"That's quite a story," Daniel interjected, knowing this on-air sarcastic jab could not be counterpunched. Having her sit so close provided him sweet revenge, after her many outward rejections.

"Thanks, Daniel. You have something related to a story I produced a few days ago, don't you?" Abigail continued, smiling into the camera.

"Yes, I do. As Abigail mentioned, famed oil magnate Darby Adams has in recent weeks announced the invention and imminent release of an electric generating engine that needs no fuel of any kind. Just this morning, Mr. Adams announced that he will give away the first million units, allowing those willing to test the engine in their own homes and quelling any concerns or objections Congress and other fossil-fuel companies have raised. If this is not some kind of a hoax or scheme to run up oil prices, then the oil and gas industries will have a tougher contender for the power market than solar panels and wind turbines combined. As of the stock markets' close today, oil was trading at seventy-one dollars a barrel.

"Other oil-producing nations are quickly responding to Fountain Alternative Energy's innovation by drastically slowing production to stave off price declines. Speculators have been making hay since the markets opened this morning, causing extreme gyrations in oil futures; ultimately driving up the cost of crude at the close today. Needless to say, the message coming out of the Middle East is that they're not happy with Mr. Adams.

"A Senate bill was presented today for consideration, seeking the halt of Mr. Adams's motor. Public safety concerns were cited as a chief consideration for the legislation. Sources close to the Senate claim other US fossil-fuel companies are objecting to its release, claiming it would unfairly burden an industry already under stress—the same group opposed to the Alternative Energy Bill. The Senate committee overseeing the Alt-Energy Bill's implementation has already issued thirty million in grants and loans for a myriad of technologies in development or near completion."

"Thank you, Daniel. As tonight's top stories are all seemingly related, our dollar bound to the price of oil has China worried and angry with the United States. Though every economist will explain the dollar's fluctuation differently, the result is still the same: The value of the dollar is dropping. Is it because of the many alternative-energy technologies threatening oil companies' profits? Is it the ongoing undeclared war in the Middle East running up our country's debt while soldiers are still dying there—and an ever-increasing number of United States military installations being built? Could it be the Citizens' Mandamus Council's announcement to issue its currency, or possibly a different story altogether? Depending upon who you ask, the explanation is one of these or a combination thereof.

"The Chinese government's official comment is that there's no comment. However, there have been strong warnings from Beijing to the White House today that if the value of the dollar drops much further, contributing to the driving up of the cost of a barrel of oil, then the Chinese will cease buying United States Government bonds. The effects of this move by the Asian government would be felt immediately and painfully in every currency market around the world.

"Unofficially, the Chinese Premier suggested that America should do away with the CMC; and if leadership cannot find the courage to crush something so destructive to our national security, then North America's future is bleak. Confirmation of this could not be made. TTN's requests for comment left with the Chinese Embassy in Washington were not returned."

"Thank you, Abigail. In our final story this evening, a new bill submitted for consideration by Senator Ethan Scott seeks to end market churning on all American stock exchanges. Senator Scott is quoted as saying, 'The market gyrations are largely but not completely caused by margin trading and speculators. These activities greatly affect pricing and are directly related to the economic bubbles that burst in America every few years. The continual destruction of the average investor's retirement accounts alone justifies ending these business practices. Bubble economics are not necessary in America. It's ridiculous to endure more frequent and unnecessary recessions because we allow market-economy wildcards in play. It's time to reexamine so-called expert methodologies—ushering scads of consumers into negative territory, while those few influencing market conditions quietly strip away wealth from an unsuspecting citizenry.' Senator Scott went on further to say that there would be Senate inquiries into these business practices on the Phillips Stock Exchange and the other American stock exchanges as the bill continued in the process of passage.

"There's been some initial objection to Senator Scott's proposed bill. However, no congressman would comment for the record. It's been some day, hasn't it?" Daniel bantered before the cameras.

Ignoring Daniel's endeavor to appear to be a close colleague, Abigail said, "That's right, Daniel. Finally, in an unrelated and more upbeat story, we take you to Houston for a few video updates of the Mission to Mars project, still slated to launch in a little over four years. The spacecraft's construction appears to be back on track. This is what the Mission Director had to say."

The camera switched off as the video played for the audience. Daniel stared at Abigail like a child with a bruised ego. Recently, he had abandoned petulance to try and forge an alliance. Grasping Daniel's motive, she detested him only a little less. At least his maneuvers were not machinations.

As the video played out, Abigail began to think about the gloomy content of their broadcast. *The world must really hate us. Our markets and military continue to rain down destruction. And yet, if America didn't take up the fight against tyrannies throughout the world, then who would? We'd be even more despised in failure.*

Brian pointed to Daniel. Daniel returned to the dummy prompter. Abigail regained her concentration and the tedium went on.

CHAPTER
XIV

THE CANNON REPORTS

It was Friday afternoon. A week had passed since Darby's controversial announcement. Calls for additional interviews had not ceased as a circus atmosphere formed. News organizations were not resoundingly interested in how the technology worked; or even if it improved people's lives. They wanted his opinion on hearsay regarding the government's response, and that of the other oil companies.

It bothered Darby to see his humanitarian efforts reduced to intrigue for talkshow channels and news fodder. At his desk, he burst out, "Stanley, why is it human nature to ruin everything that's good?"

"I don't know for certain. It seems that to rise above mediocrity is still the same social sin it's always been," Stanley offered.

"But why—does not humanity benefit from an engine that provides electricity without a fuel source? This takes us one step closer to true freedom. Why is the turmoil this innovation creates amongst the chosen class more important than the positive impact it will make for the average person?"

"I think you answered your own question, Darby. I come from the top rung, and know what it is to be of the elite class. Choosing to make my own way in life was a personal choice. It takes me one step closer to personal freedom. My parents are still upset with me for not remaining in New York to work for the same stuffy, self-indulgent set I was raised among. It's about power and control—it always has been and will never change."

"But that's exactly what I wish to accomplish: empowerment of the self. Why must those who have power over others have it? They don't need it to exist. In the United States, a person given enough financial wealth can have enormous influence over many, but to what end? Why have it? The wealthy man's life is just as wealthy if he does nothing against or on behalf of another."

"In my experience, Darby, it seems to a great many of privileged stripe that it's the only way they may enjoy their good fortune. Power over others is salt for the meat—without it life has very little flavor."

"Stanley, I'm once again taken back to the same question: Why?"

"On that score I can't say for sure. It may be guilt for possessing so much while others have so little. It could be so that they may actually feel something. Darby, you don't have to imagine what it would be like to have anything you want simply by asking for it. You live that life. What if you felt guilt or anger when near those who live in daily need? How might that affect your personality? Would you be charitable to extinguish your own guilt, or brutal to douse the anger and disdain you held in your heart?"

"I feel neither of these."

"That's because you built wealth. You didn't steal or coerce it out of someone's hands like our politicians do. It was not passed onto you by a previous generation, as a nepotistic mechanism to ensure immortality; attempting to keep separate one's perceived superior genetics from those of the inferior class.

"You possess the understanding of risk and reward. There was nothing given you on your journey; no conduct provided. You could have easily been obliterated dozens of times along the way. You weren't destroyed. You survived and bought a life with your own hands.

"So few of the ruling class are cognizant of what you know. You own your life. You make no apologies for it because you don't need to. That's what I want for myself and why I work for you."

Darby reveled in Stanley's words, knowing their truth. Just then, a sharp pain stabbed his heart—the joy of his accomplishment, having built an oil company from the first contract upward, was split in two by the knowledge of how his electric motor was acquired.

Angered by the idea of greed destroying his legacy, Darby's mind turned to business. "Stanley, let's get back on track. Has anyone called today worth talking to?"

"By worth, are you referring to gossip rags trolling for comments on your plan to stop the congressional juggernaut from bringing an end to this new-fangled gadget? Yes, the *DC Examiner* called again, just in case you changed your mind after rejecting them a few days ago."

"I love to hate people like that, Stanley. They beg you detest their existence. Pass. Are our filming crews ready for the big day? We're down to less than two weeks."

"They're on call and waiting for your order. As soon as the delivery trucks roll, they'll follow to capture responses. Are you sure you don't want to wait for consumer campaign response; some sort of through-the-mail or internet announcement that they'll be receiving a free unit?"

"We've covered this. There's no time. If we wait, Bone Yard boys will set a picket fence before the first engines leave our production facilities. Just have the delivery people go door to door. If they're not interested, then move on; though I don't imagine many will. Free and fear are the words that prod underdeveloped psyches to scramble."

Darby continued working at the office through the weekend, ensuring final unit assembly continued as planned. Engineers repeatedly called to relay unplanned problems they needed a decision on. He could have taken those calls anywhere in the world. However, this desk was his sanctuary; where he felt most at peace. At times he grappled with the urge to leave for the plants; Darby could move his employees faster in person. However, early in his oil career, he had learned through trial and error to allow his foremen to do the job. Back then, Darby was involved with the entire operation when he was on a drilling site. Many good leaders were lost to his dogged nature not to stop until the goal was met. Letting go and delegating to people he hired was a difficult transition. After learning that particular lesson, his business profits and success exponentially accelerated.

The weekend crawled as one call stacked atop the next; he fought to keep delivery on schedule. *One million units have gotta go; not a one less. I've never missed a deadline. This time will be no different.*

Sunday night, Darby ate a meal sent over from home. Darby's tightened jaw chewed his food, waiting for the phone to ring. From the darkened city below, street lamps and other buildings reminded him that he was not alone. The elevator door dinged outside his office. *Must be the cleaning crew—I'm the only one on this floor*, he assumed. Darby continued eating, tensely anticipating the next catastrophe.

Footsteps approached. A distorted peopled-form grew distinct through the opaque glass. Outside his office, it abruptly stopped.

One whispered in a cadenced tone, as if counting down. The door burst open, slamming against the wall. Two men rushed in, pointing small assault weapons at Darby. They began screaming. Darby couldn't understand, but knew they wanted him to rise as they motioned their weapon muzzles upward.

The intruders were in their early twenties, one stocky and one taller, wearing grey shirts and ill-fitting black pants. Spiced body odor trailed their malnourished bodies.

Darby stood up, fork and knife dropping onto his plate—the clanking flatware startled both men. One yelled, "Kosmaghz!"

Darby screamed, "I don't know what you want! I can't understand you!"

They ceased their clamoring, glaring at Darby; responding to strength with submission. Realizing what Darby was communicating, one man sat down in front of the desk while the other slapped Darby, annunciating with a Persian accent, "Raise your hands, if you please."

Darby did so, purposely knocking the plate off his desk as he lurched at the top drawer—grasping for a pistol.

The seated man hollered, "Be ruye cheshm!" The other pressed the muzzle of his gun to Darby's chest. Darby froze, but his hand fully grasped the hidden pistol handle.

The nearest assailant looked to the ceiling and began chanting, "Khcoda chkoobe!" Darby yanked out his pistol and squeezed the trigger, hitting the seated man center chest. Time slowed Darby's perception. As the wounded man fell backwards, a barrel repeatedly cracked, its rounds drilling into the ceiling. The other intruder's dirge ceased and his eyes turned cold. Rapid fire spewed from the attacker's gun faster than Darby could bring his pistol to sight. Bullets struck Darby twice above the heart, swiping his sense of balance—his knees buckled and the floor rushed to his face.

Darby used what little strength remained to pull his trigger; hate still bonding to his slipping life. As the world went dark, Darby's ears filled with his own screams, and that of a handgun discharging.

Gunpowder and the metallic pungency of blood menaced the air. Pain demanded Darby's mind. He blinked, and the blurry image of a uniformed stranger appeared above; seemingly only seconds after the shots were fired.

The paramedic yelled, "Darby!" A muffled and distorted name he knew. Darby felt tired and wanted to sleep. Suddenly, pain stabbed his chest. Overwhelmed, he vomited on himself.

The paramedic wiped Darby's face before fitting an oxygen mask. "Darby, can you hear me? My name is Jeffery. I'm here to help. It is very important you listen."

Darby rolled his head back and forth like the stringed gestures of a marionette; unsure if he was making the movement.

Jeffery continued. "Good. You've been shot twice in the chest and once in the neck. We've stabilized you as best as we can. You're losing too much blood and so we can't wait any longer to make things better here. You're lucky you have a landing pad on the roof. Our helicopter is already topside. Mercy One Hospital is only a few miles away. This is the important part. Are you listening?"

Darby nodded, as he began to drift away.

"If you don't stay awake, then you're going to die. You're in shock and there's nothing more I can do. It's up to you now! Do you hear me? I understand you're one tough customer. It's time to live up to that reputation. I'll be with you during the flight. I'm doing my part. You need to do yours! Are you with me?"

Using the only strength he had left, Darby winked. As the gurney lifted upward, he suddenly felt faint; as if he were floating, while his skin flushed warm and cold. Blood began leaking through one of his bandages. Jeffrey grabbed Darby's neck and clenched as tight as he could, holding the wound closed. They rode the elevator to the roof and loaded Darby into the helicopter; the roar of its engine barely audible to him.

Blackness took him again. Nothing entered Darby's mind until the emergency room examination lights penetrated his eyelids. Palpitating agony drew him out and he surfaced into awareness. Urgent conversation volleyed across his prone body. A sudden crack, like a discharging gun, rang in his ears; followed by clear vocalizations of his own screams.

A woman's voice emerged from a hovering face, "Darby, I'm Doctor Templeton. You've been shot multiple times tonight. We have your blood type and are replenishing your supply. You arrived just in time. Someone above must love you. As soon as you're stable, we're going to remove those bullets."

"Pain," Darby mumbled.

"I know. Your pressure is still too low to give you anything. We'll be in a safer place in a few minutes. Just hold on a little longer. The pain will soon be gone.

"Stay with me, Darby." Her voice echoed as he fell asleep. Knowing he would be alright, Darby set his mind to childhood memories. Fishing with his father enchanted his mind, as Doctor Templeton performed surgery.

The following afternoon, Darby opened his eyelids for the first time; squinting at the attention-begging sunlight. He strained against it, raising a hand to cover his eyes. Footsteps closed on the bed.

"Darby, it's good to see you awake." Stanley assured with true concern.

"How long have I been asleep?"

"It's four o'clock now. After a five-hour surgery the doctor finished a little after four this morning. You've been under since."

"Were the two men caught? They came out of nowhere—thought they were from housekeeping. Before I could do anything, they started shooting."

"The actual cleaning crew arrived a half-hour late. They found you and the others in a pool of blood. Both men are dead. You shot one dead-center and the other multiple times in the torso. Don't you remember?"

"I think so. Yes, I fought back. That's right; I shot the first guy almost straightaway. Then the other one got me. The only thing I could think of was to fire. But I don't remember shooting the second one. He was chanting something—not sure what."

"The police have come and gone twice today. They need a statement. Do you feel up to talking with them?"

"I can talk."

"The media have also been bugging me to get a few words when you woke."

"No news people," Darby groaned. *What do they expect to see? Maybe I'll die on camera, answering a mindless question.*

Drifting, Darby ruminated. *What were they after—obviously my life; but why? They could be zealots or somehow connected to one of the Gulf's oil producers. It must be the engine—and the list gets longer. It might be somehow mixed up with George. It could also be nearly anyone in Washington. There are simply too many people who stand to lose influence, power and money by allowing an average human to take another step towards self-reliance. This isn't the end of it. They'll continuing trying to derail the effort. My only option now is to release the damn contraption—I won't be safe until it's done.*

"Stanley, strike that. I want every Houston newspaper, television, radio, and internet news agency here in an hour."

"I'll see if we can borrow a conference room. I'm sure they have one at this facility."

"No. Here…in my room. I want them to see the tubes, the wires, the bandages and the man. Do it."

"Right away," Stanley replied, as he rushed out.

An hour later, his room was gorged with reporters, cameras and sound equipment. The hospital administrator followed Stanley into Darby's room. "Mr. Adams, this is completely inappropriate. We're a hospital, not a social club. These people need to leave."

Annoyance, pain and then consternation passed over Darby's face.

"Look…if you go away, now, I'll settle all the hospital's outstanding debt."

The administrator's blank expression contorted into confusion. Without another word, he turned and exited in haste—not to be seen for the remainder of the day.

"Mr. Adams, you were shot at your office last night. What can you tell us about it?" a young Hispanic female reporter asked, extending her microphone close to Darby.

"Stanley, help me sit up," Darby instructed. He was already beginning to tire.

Stanley assisted him and then stepped away. Darby said, "I was shot in my office last evening. Why the two men attempted to take my life I can't know for certain. What I am sure of is that they were not working alone. This was the work of a coward. There are those who do not want to see my new technology released to the open market. Many fear their way of life will change and would do anything to keep that from happening."

"Who do you think was behind this attempt?" another, male reporter asked, squeezing his way to the front.

"Son, I don't know. If I were ten years younger, then I would make it my business to find out. I'd locate and destroy them. Today though, my choice is different. I don't care. I do want those who are responsible to know this: You are spineless for doing this. You will not stop the engine. No matter what you do, this will come to pass. This is all I have to say."

Darby's face modeled alabaster white as he sank back into bed. His frailty was clear to see; the brief exertion nearly causing him to faint. His eyelids fluttered and began to fall; obvious to all that the news event was over. Stanley began guiding reporters out of the suite. After everyone had left, the room was once again silent.

Moments later, a frustrated police detective entered. "Mr. Adams, I'm Detective Tom Goodwin. What are you doing? We haven't taken your statement yet. Who gave you permission to talk with the press?"

Darby held his eyes open long enough to say, "Detective, it's so good of you to come. Maybe you might consider doing a better job of keeping men like that off Houston's streets. Then I wouldn't be forced to confront my attackers using media personalities."

"There is procedure for a homicide investigation," Tom informed with petulant anger.

"Tom, the taxes I pay more than cover your salary. I'll talk with you tomorrow when I have the energy to tolerate bad behavior. Goodbye," Darby dismissed him as he relaxed. The detective faded away— aching wounds leashing him to a detached world.

Julia entered Hubert's office to announce, "Senator, a Miss Preston is here to see you."

Surprised, Hubert boomeranged, "Send her in."

"Right away."

Anne walked in a few moments later; Julia trailing behind her.

"That'll be all, Julia," Hubert settled.

"Pretty little girl…really, Senator, is that necessary? Can she even vote yet?"

"George told me about your direct nature."

"Stock-in-trade," Anne replied, flashing the smile of a confident, mature woman. "Yes, George was fond of me."

"Fine…Yes, she can vote. Now to something more serious: Why are you here? On the phone, we agreed you would let me know when you were in Washington."

"I'm here, Senator," Anne stated, cupping upward hands. "Don't tell me; Don Giordano's? By all means, do let's wax cliché?"

Embarrassed that it would have been his first suggestion, Hubert said. "Not necessarily. However, I have a meeting in a few minutes and would have more time to speak with you over lunch."

"I'm here now. Why don't you simply say what it is that needs to be said and save our taxpayers the cost of a meal? You know John Stanton was always funny that way. He worried someone would see us together."

"Nothing worries me, Miss Preston."

"Excellent! I couldn't stand John's whining. Call me Anne. If we're going to do business together, then we might as well get cozy."

"Anne, I know you had dealings with John, though he didn't share details."

"Good to know."

"Am I mistaken or are you a problem? John ups and leaves town. He's not been heard from since. George Weatherby dies in a plane crash. You must be dangerous or unlucky."

"I don't believe in luck—depends which side of the gun you're on. So, Senator, why have you called on me?"

"You worked for George Weatherby."

"So?"

"You did things for him. I want you to do the same for me." A faint hint of sulphur suddenly filled the space between them. Aware that his dark potent was mindfully present, Hubert attempted to redirect his thoughts back to Anne.

"Things, Senator?"

"Call me Hubert."

Grinning as if she were about to viciously beat a chained dog, Anne extrapolated, "Hubert, you want me to bribe. You want me to coerce those you wish influenced with whatever brutal means I have at my disposal. You want me to assassinate people you need eliminated. You want me to do all the things you cannot have your prints on. That's what you want."

"Are you out of your goddamn mind? I'd be finished if my office were under investigation."

"It's not. If you were being watched, then I'd know. I've been told you couldn't be spooked; sure heard wrong. Politicians are funny that way—never say what they mean, even behind closed doors. If there's one thing I'll miss George Weatherby for, it's his blunt nature. What he wanted never needed clarification."

"Anne, I don't think you realize who you're talking to. I am the chairman of the Homeland Security and Government Affairs Committee. When I want to be heard, I am heard. I can take away your civil liberties as if they never existed. I can open and close doors the President doesn't know exist. Watch your tone when addressing me."

"Hubert, darling…look into my eyes. Do I appear concerned? It's why I'm sure you're full of crap. One as powerful as you allude to being would never say so. You make me smile, Hubert. Did you know that? I like you. I liked George more. George was a bastard. Everybody knew it, too. He didn't hide behind pretence. He lived outwardly as a villain. If George wanted something, he just took it. Your kind steals under the cloak of legitimacy and then calls it law. How much legislation have you passed with the singular goal to serve your own needs? A criminal calls his booty loot. Your shell game is called taxation."

"All of them served my needs," Hubert affirmed in a stern voice.

"That's more like it, Hubert—better stop; I'm getting wet. We can do business now."

"And what of you, my dear?"

"I'm a shark. I am at the top of the food chain. I don't make excuses for why I do what I do."

"Let's get to it, then."

"Thought you'd never ask. What do you need me to do?"

"You're close to Senator Scott."

"You do your homework, Hubert. Yes, we know each other."

"Good. I want you to persuade him to propose a bill to quash the Citizens' Mandamus Council's right to exist. I want them out."

"Why don't you do it? You're the HSGA Committee chair."

"It'd be too obvious."

Hesitating for a moment, Anne looked him in the eyes, studying his facial expression to determine commitment. She offered, "Five million."

The faint sound of a lion purring sounded in his ears. *What is that?*

"Fine."

Anne stood up with a look of excitement as she said, "Well, I must be off then. A girl's gotta eat. Ethan's office is two floors down, correct? Don't get up. I'll find my way—call you when it's done."

Hubert began to stand as Anne turned to walk out. He raised a hand and began to speak but stopped himself, letting her go.

As Anne rode the elevator towards his floor, Ethan was at his desk reading the news. He was happy for David to have found his voice again.

If David's terms aren't met, would the CMC really follow through?

As Ethan pondered questions, a door knock sounded.

"Yes, Jane," Ethan annunciated, peeking over his flashing computer screen.

Anne opened the door and sauntered in. Eyes widening with surprise, Ethan smiled, stood, and rushed to kiss her—quickly closing the door for discretion's sake. "Sit down. It's good to see you. Where've you been? We've traded phone messages and texts for six weeks. I was certain you left me for an oil baron."

As they sat, Anne said, "That's sweet, but no—I wasn't that lucky. No new fossil fascist to pick up where George Weatherby left off. Still, we mustn't lose hope. He'll be a tough client to replace."

"Did they ever determine what caused the accident?"

"Still a mystery; but that's not why I'm here."

"You were thinking about sweeping me away from Washington for a week?"

"If you'll let me talk, then I'll explain," Anne zipped.

"Go ahead," Ethan replied, interested in what she had to say but more happy to see her.

"I'm here in an official capacity. I want you to author and sponsor a bill making the issuance of a note of value illegal. I want the act to be treasonous and a felony. I also want you to present it to the Senate in two days. If you need my assistance, I can help draft it right now."

Color drained from Ethan's face; his joyful flare vanished. Outwardly sapped, his body slouched. "I can't do that."

"What do you mean you can't? Senators do it every day."

"Who put you up to this? Who do you represent? Why?"

"Ethan, I told you not to pump me for shoptalk. Look at you. You followed my advice. You made powerful friends. You've only been in Washington a short time. Consider what's been accomplished.

You're a committee chair, the Senate Majority Leader and president pro tem. You've done the impossible. Time to make an even greater difference—it's what you wanted."

"I didn't ask for most of this; much of it is still confounding. Why me? And it was given; nothing earned. In the world most any person lives in, nothing comes without sacrifice. I haven't suffered here at all, except for the fact that nothing gets done. It seems, with each step, when control of my calendar is gained, I'm burdened with more bureaucratic responsibility. I've done nothing useful since setting foot on the Hill. Tell your boss that I won't do it."

Anne slapped the desk. "You're joking, right? You can't be this much of a sugarcoated nancy. Your head's always been parked in the clouds; but this is beyond comprehension. You're not a Boy Scout any longer. You wear the uniform of a soldier. Act like it!

"This must be done; not just for whom I represent, but also the good of the country. You've heard the news and seen the reports. Look at the havoc your friend has caused the United States in just a few days. Our allies are already wavering in military commitments that were firm only days ago.

"You've witnessed how it's affecting the stock exchanges. Forty percent in the first day: That's never happened. All the major stock exchanges opened three percent lower at the beginning of business today. Ethan, panic's gripped the streets. What's next is not going to be a surprise. Unemployment numbers that are already high will go higher. Oil prices will climb, and the cost of gas and groceries will follow. The other market segments will constrict, exacerbating current problems while creating new ones.

"Let's not even delve into what the emerging markets are going to do us. They're already positioning themselves to cut out the United States in the next ten years, decoupling our leverage over the world. If that happens, then the chasm we may tumble down will not be a rabbit hole. Ethan, have I got your attention? You need to do this and I mean right now!"

As Ethan took in the diatribe, the words left out entailed a need for justice. *Can't believe I'm even entertaining this, but she's right.*

Normal channels won't work—we're out of time. Hal's the only one I know, other than Anderson, that can immediately help deal with this. God, what's it gonna cost me?

Ethan's long-awaited desire for a deeper understanding of their relationship's nature had been satisfied; and he didn't like it. He knew it had to end although he didn't want it to—staying with her would make him a fraud.

"I don't agree with your politics, Anne; never have. However, I'll consider what you've asked. Let's talk about it in a few days."

"A few days? We need to act now! If you don't…"

"I said I'd consider it."

Sasha's voice sounded from the speaker on David's desk, "David, every director has logged onto the video conference call and is ready to begin."

"Thank you, Sasha. What an impact a week has made! Our committee chairmen and executive board met last Friday after the remainder of the directors had departed for their home states. It appears that our working pace will allow for goals to be reached, in the event our demands aren't met.

"I think I can speak for all who attended the meeting that we have reason to be excited. Without wishing to dampen enthusiasm, there are some sacrifices required to stay on course. These difficult choices we are about to discuss will be implemented with the understanding that they're not permanent changes, but ones we must make to prepare for what's coming.

"The most painful of these will start at the top. Every director, every board member, including myself, must take a thirty percent reduction in pay, beginning immediately. Let me state again that this reduction is only temporary. If we move forward with the issuance, the amount in dollars your pay has been reduced will be replaced in Worth note."

David paused to allow for dissenting opinions. Silence filled the moment with a cringeworthy pause in the directors' minds.

"The temporary changes do not end there. I must ask that you lay off half of your staff, unless you can convince them to donate their time. When this crisis has passed, they will be offered their jobs back.

"The engraver has provided a preliminary date of seven more days to have completed the digital designs and plates. The printer has set aside press time for the week we will announce the printing and issuance. The CMC will take secret delivery of fifty billion impressions of the new notes worth over one trillion in Worth paper at a cost of forty million in United States dollars. That money has already been set aside in trust to be released once we have taken delivery of the notes at the nine CMC reserves positioned throughout the United States. We're also nearing the end of a bond issuance for an additional one trillion in Worthbyte digital notes of value—China and Europe have a large appetite for them."

David paused once again; providing the directors a chance to speak. After a brief delay, various directors began talking over each other. A mixed response of excitement, resentment, anger, and fear percolated. Not everyone was at peace that a time of change had arrived.

Ed Castor, director of Delaware, won the contest to be heard—verbally trampling the others until they had quieted. He stiffly contended, "As I was saying, it's high time we act on the country's behalf. What our representatives have done to its citizens, let alone the Constitution, is deplorable. How long do all of you sniveling in fear think we can go on wasting resources and depleting wealth before a collapse of our monetary system occurs? I am glad for this. I proudly take a pay cut and can promise that my staff will not desert our effort in this time of need."

Nathan Braun, director of Georgia ribbed. "That's big of you, Ed. But are you going to be singing that song six months from now? Ladies and gentlemen, this is our country we're talking about. I agree with all of you that we have real problems to solve. I think that if David's idea to bamboozle those Washington scoundrels into doing their jobs works, then we've won. However, if they call our bluff, then are we really ready to poison our country's money supply? I know what's going on isn't good. But this looks like we're about to pour gasoline on a fire."

"David, this is Ted. I'd like to add to this discussion if I may."

"Go ahead, Ted," David offered as Ted's face appeared on David's monitor.

"Everyone, Ted Stevenson here, director from the Washington D. C. office and Legal Committee chairman. After listening to the last two comments, I was struck by one invariable truth: You're giving the politicians exactly what they want. They do this every day to us under the guise of public and political discourse.

"The career politician only engages the public on loss leaders. You know what I'm talking about; an item a retail store is willing to sell at a loss, costing people very little to purchase or sometimes nothing at all. The operator lures a person into their store or website to gain this inexpensive item, only to trick them into spending more money on other items. The unwitting customer engages the retailer, thinking they're going to acquire this beloved item for little or nothing. Instead, the dupe leaves, having spent much more than they intended or should have.

"Our representatives use this tactic to appear as though they're serving our interests, when really nothing that truly means something to us is ever addressed. They deploy hotly debated issues that are impossible to fairly legislate and can only be used to separate one segment of the population from another; thereby turning our focus on one another and not their performance.

"Take the issue of abortion, for example. This topic raises some sort of emotional response from nearly everyone. We are, after all, talking about the sanctity of human life. But whose life do we put more importance on—the unborn baby having not experienced life yet, or the pregnant woman to do with her body what she wishes?

"In our *so-called* free society there can be no absolute answer to the question: Is abortion right or wrong? By granting either the unborn baby or pregnant mother their absolute right over the other, a freedom is sacrificed, which isn't allowed under the US Constitution. The right to life and the right to choose can only be debated in a land of laws. It cannot be fairly solved; someone loses with any decision.

"This is how the politician keeps people distracted from real issues, like taking up with corporate interests over the people. We've been indoctrinated in this bureaucratic tap-dance for so long that we willingly go through the motions of voting every few years and then forget about the baby-kissing hacks and what they're doing in Washington, so long as it doesn't affect our individual lives. But, we can't ignore it anymore—it's affecting everyone.

"Because we've been brainwashed by political trickery, we're programmed to take our own personal views and turn on each other instead of the Bone Yard dirtbags responsible for the problem to begin with. I say this because we're doing it to each other right now. Ed, I understand you're tired of corruption and glad to take on the patriotic fight. Your loyalty is appreciated. Nathan, I hear prudence in your position, If our government had the courage to maintain prudence all along, then our country wouldn't be in its current position.

"Don't lie to yourselves—they're already working us and we can't let them. Trust me on this. I office in the most corrupt city there is, second maybe to New York. And yet these are also places of great nobility and rich history, birthplaces of freedom and hope for all mankind.

"In Washington DC nothing is as it seems. Complex human issues are not solved; they're negotiated. We as people, like the issues they were elected to solve, are not looked upon as real; in person or issue. We are simply a means to an end; a necessary evil to tolerate so they may rob citizens of their wealth and birthright.

"I live at ground zero. This is where our fight must start and stop. Whatever side of whatever argument any of you stand on this conference call, the war must be waged—and it must be now! No one wishes for these days to befall them. But they have fallen, and at our feet do these problems lie. So, let's end the needless debate over selfish issues and get to the ugliness."

After a moment, David broke in, "Ted, that was amazing."

Stunned by his own words, Ted acknowledged, "I just felt it needed to be said."

As before, directors abruptly spoke together, attempting to make similar points. Generally, voices were positive and hopeful. Some even began to share thoughts of courage and conviction; as if the others were listening.

Nathan belted out, "David Samuel!" The directors heard someone utter David's name but continued talking over each other. Nathan stated again, "David Samuel!" The other voices trailed off and quieted. Nathan repeated, "David Samuel!" This time every director heard Nathan.

"Yes," David responded.

"Since determining this course of action, you, the other committee chairmen, and the executive board have taken this organization in a direction some of us cannot follow. I regret to inform you that Director Jim Price of Florida, Director Walter Hill of Kentucky, Director Benjamin Whitfield of Tennessee, and myself immediately resign from our respective state offices. Our reasons for leaving differ, but hinge on the commitment to go forward with the note issuance plan. We cannot contribute to the demise of our own government. Goodbye to you all. And good luck."

Four conference video feeds went black. Silence found their gathering again; elation choked by unexpected casualties. No one could think of anything to say.

After allowing the darkened screen connections to resonate in the minds of the remaining forty-six directors, David confirmed, "For the time being, the Georgia, Tennessee, Kentucky and Florida offices will remain closed until the crisis has been dealt with and suitable replacements have been hired.

"Do all of you feel it? That sense of despair at the loss of our friends? This is not the end of what we'll lose. Our pain has only begun. If those we've elected do not get our house in order before the deadline, then more blood will be spilled. This is war! And we're fighting to take back our country. That's right! It's our country too! They may be Americans. But they stopped being citizens the moment their seat was sold to the highest corporate bidder. When the government stopped being of and by the people, those holding political office ceased to be anything other than combatants. They're the enemy of the people.

"Difficult times lie ahead. Wonderful days also stand waiting for us to seize if we only maintain fidelity. You must not waver in your commitment. Know where your heart is at all times; so that when doubt and depravation strike, you may beat them back with conviction. This is our fight. It can work if we stand fast. There's no more ground to take—we already own the land and only need to hold the line. This is our home, not theirs. This is our country, not theirs. It is our army manning the watchtowers of our borders. It's our birthright; and we're not required to give it up.

"All of you have recently seen or heard about my crisis of faith. I suffered and lost belief in my fellow countrymen, and worse, myself. I was adrift, my brave friends. It was only after resting on the bottom of a pit of anguish that I began to look up. I saw possibilities again and was hungry. An inch at a time, I crawled out of a hole that existed inside my heart. And unless we stay together, walking the Citizens' Mandamus Council and our country out of this hell, we will fall as a people.

"Now are you with me? Are you willing to fight? Will you fight? Will you stay loyal, keep the faith, and act as humans with a destiny? Will you do this?" David yelled.

The conference call exploded in cries of courage. Cheers and roaring jubilation echoed through David's computer screen as tears flowed down his cheeks. The sound of human anguish crying out and the heart to take back what was stolen touched every director. David's shaking hands tapped his keyboard to block the video feed, and then he erupted in outward wails of suffering and victory—cries for himself, for his people, for his beloved CMC.

CHAPTER

XV

A DAGGER FOR DEAR BRUTUS

Daniel squeezed in next to Abigail at the start-of-the-day briefing—a Frank-instituted measure to boost TTN headquarters proficiency. Try as she might, Abigail was not always successful at maneuvering so Daniel could not squat nearby.

Frank droned on about the new production matrix maximizing quality and minimizing editing time. Abigail attempted to follow the lecture but became distracted by its tedious and minutely narrated details. Frank's voice withered into white noise as Abigail suffered. Daniel leaned over and whispered, "I bet you miss Sandra. You were always her pet. Those days are gone now. I like Frank. He seems to know what he's doing."

Abigail turned to Daniel and impulsively shot down his vacuous comment with a sarcastic, "You think?" Immediately, she wished she'd said nothing.

"Frank always knows the best way to do everything. You've gotta agree that things are running more smoothly than before."

"Sure." Abigail falsely indulged.

"Instead of berating the staff, as Sandra did, Frank actually takes an active interest in our suggestions."

"You don't say."

"Come on, Abigail, you can't deny it's true."

Abigail turned to Daniel and demanded, "If I agree, will you stop that claptrap?"

"Is there something you two wish to add?" Frank raised his voice pointedly, as if addressing troublemakers chatting away at the back of the class. "I am serious. Since you both seem to feel more important than the rest of us, why don't you two run this meeting?" Shocked, Daniel lowered his head. Frank looked to Abigail and repeated, "Abigail, do you want to take charge?"

"Actually, Frank, I do," Abigail stabbed, as she jumped up. She stepped back from her chair, smiling, and strutted to the head of the table. She momentarily faced Frank and then turned to address the staff.

Abigail cleared her voice. "Thank you all for attending this daily briefing. Frank asked that I take over. So, let's get started. Meetings like these are largely a waste of time; ultimately you're going to do what Frank says. Enduring half-baked rationalizations is unnecessary. It doesn't matter why—Frank says, you do. He's not interested in your opinion and is not going to act on it."

Her face relaxed; she felt a rush of joy after confronting his poorly deployed management style. Flustered by Abigail's manner, Frank intended on giving her a good talking-to. Before he could interrupt, Abigail continued. "This new matrix is to be scrapped! Okay. Now that this is out of the way, let's talk about the business we're in: news. Daniel, what do you got?"

"Uh, um, Frank, what are we doing here?" Daniel asked, turning to Frank.

"Don't look at Frank. Look at me. Frank told me to take charge. So, let's get on with it. Daniel, what stories are you working on?"

"I'm following the CMC's progress with the ultimatum issued to Congress. So far not much has changed."

"Not much has changed, Daniel? The CMC is stepping up, toe to toe with the government, and telling the Congress to get with the program or else; and you're telling me nothing else has happened! What are your sources saying?"

"There are no sources. David Samuel came to us. If he has anything else to relay then he'll tell TTN first."

"You know that for certain, do you? David Samuel made that promise. Daniel, did David Samuel ever make that promise to you?"

"Well, no, but…"

"No!" Abigail yelled. "No! Daniel, David Samuel gave TTN the opportunity to host that news conference because of me. It was not for the love of TTN or your presence. And from what I was told, David made it clear that he wasn't interested in answering your questions.

"Don't worry, Daniel, I'm not going to take the story from you. In fact, I expect to know by broadcast time how close David Samuel is to following through on his promise to issue currency if the deadline is reached and the CMC's demands are not met."

Daniel looked to Frank again.

"I said don't look at him, Daniel! Look me in the eyes. Get it done and check back with me by broadcast. We're going to run a thirty-second spot on the CMC's deadline.

"In fact, all of you here start tying in whatever stories you're working with the CMC's deadline. We're going to run a twenty-day network special. If it's not related to the CMC, the presidential or congressional elections concluding in the next three weeks, then put it on the back burner."

Abigail's hands became animated as she grew excited with the momentum. This kind of activity had gone missing for some time. Observing the staff's growing engagement, Frank stepped to the side, dismayed that he had not been received in the same way.

"We need a campaign theme for this initiative. Anyone…throw your ideas up here!"

"The CMC Countdown," a staff runner said from the back of the room.

"Good start, but too obvious; and not quite what we need. Let's keep this going."

"Political Terrorism: A Possible Future for the United States," Daniel suggested, trying to please Abigail.

"No, no, no! That isn't even obvious, Daniel. You're trying to use fear to gain viewers. The CMC is not a terrorist organization. They're Constitutionalists. TTN would look like they were running some group's political agenda if we tried to sell a news series special with that. However, I give you credit for boldness. Next…anyone?"

"The CMC's Constitutional Convention," a cameraman offered.

"We're getting warmer here, but a little borrowed. Come on people, we're on track. Let's go! What's it gonna be?"

"The Buck Stops with the Citizens' Mandamus Council. I see

dollars falling on screen from top to bottom as a wipe and fade in and out of the United States Constitution, finally blurring in and out of an American flag waving in the wind," Brian Calvert, the evening broadcast producer, said.

"That's it, Brian! You nailed it! Get something to me by mid-afternoon. If you have finish quality by airtime, we'll run with it tonight. Have one of our staff writers put together some accompanying copy that could run continuously with this presentation. I was wondering when you'd speak up. If I had a dollar for every time you saved a broadcast when a prompter went down, a lead story was not ready, or a satellite uplink was lost, then I wouldn't be working for TTN; I'd own it. Nice job, Brian, and nice effort from the rest of you!

"Did all of you pick up on the stories we ran on last night's broadcast? All of them were related in some way to the CMC. I don't think the other networks caught it. Their stories were varied. What does this tell you? What does your nose smell here? I'll tell you what mine's getting a whiff of: The CMC's put their finger on what people are thinking. Everyone's wondering what our country's next move will be. Underneath it all, I think we know that this nonsense cannot go on any longer. We're going to push this theme until it's played out. I bet it'll take the other networks at least two more news cycles to catch on.

"Alright, let's run with this. Department supervisors, check back with me by three this afternoon to discuss the stories you intend to run tonight. That's a wrap. Get to it!" Abigail bolstered, as she locked eyes with Frank, not diverting them to make plain her confidence that she could better lead the network.

Everyone stood as Frank retook the center front of the conference table and said, "Wait, everyone, sit back down. This is not what we are doing. Just wait one minute."

From a speakerphone next to the podium, Xavier demanded, "No, Frank, you wait! Run tonight's news and let's get started immediately with the Buck Stops Here campaign. That was really good, Brian. I'm still chuckling about it. We're going to pick up an additional quarter-billion dollars of ad revenue. Abigail, are you with me on this? You haven't been as active with the revenue stream before. I want you to get with the Vice President of Advertising Sales on this. You're responsible for ensuring the seamless process between marketing and the folks following the cock-and-bull. It's a good game plan. Make sure to squeeze every penny out of this."

"Xavier, I didn't know you were joining our meeting," Frank buzzed, attempting to cover his nervous surprise.

"I was told about a great many of your changes to network procedure; wanted to make your morning meeting, but couldn't get out of Aspen in time. I'm in the air on my way back to New York. Listening in was the next best thing."

"Well, that's great. Xavier, about this campaign…maybe we should look at the entire picture before moving forward. We could meet when you get back today," Frank suggested.

"Wait!" Xavier's scream echoed round the room, shocking everyone present. "Frank, you told the young lady to take control of the meeting. She did. Live with it."

"But, Xavier, I was only making a point—attempting to shame the two of them for interrupting."

"You're kidding with me, right? Are you a child, Frank? For Pete's sake, say what you mean or say nothing. If you had no intention of having her take on your responsibilities, then you shouldn't have invited her to park her behind in your chair. I don't know, Frank. I like Miss Sanders's ideas. Don't you?"

"Absolutely!"

"Good. Then we're all on the same page. Get it done," Xavier demanded, ending the call with a loud bang.

"After your department meetings this afternoon, I want you to report to my office," Frank sniped with a scowl on his face, before stomping away at a brisk clip.

Abigail left for the editing room. She had a few ideas to develop from video footage of David Samuel's past work: A collage of news reports, speeches and TTN interview video would provide a great lead-in segment to the series.

Daniel caught up with Abigail just as she sat down at the editing console. Daniel leaned against the doorway and looked at her with a grin.

"What is it now?" Abigail asked, bothered by his presence.

"I wanted to thank you for those kind words."

"You're welcome—there you go. Now, I need to get started. So, if you don't mind…?"

Disregarding Abigail's sarcastic request to make himself scarce, Daniel continued, "I always knew you had a soft spot for me."

"Yes, Daniel, I do have a soft spot for you; like a weak arterial wall moments from an aneurysm."

"Abbey, I can't understand why you don't like me. We're colleagues, after all. Don't you think things would be easier round here if you'd just try getting along?"

"Daniel, if you call me Abbey again, I'll break your tongue. Our getting along is not a job requirement. In fact, I prefer not getting along. It allows me to be true to myself."

"Why's that so important? Don't you want to fit in? Don't you want to be liked?"

"Liked by whom?"

"By everybody."

"If everybody includes you and Frank, then I'll just go on this way."

"I don't understand why it's gotta be like this," Daniel whined.

Abigail's eyes rolled back as her head began to ache. Family or not, she still could not fathom how Xavier tolerated Daniel working at network.

To complete the lead Abigail wanted in time, she simply ignored any more questions. She met with the department leaders at the scheduled time and assessed all the stories presented her for the evening broadcast. She then reported to Frank's office as ordered, letting herself in and taking a seat in front of his desk; not waiting for the secretary to formally usher the moment.

"You asked to see me after the three o'clock department chiefs' meeting. The meeting took place. All of tonight's stories have been approved. The work is excellent. Even Daniel is providing quality insight into what the CMC's up to. They must be feeding him information just so he won't stop by their office. I know I would. What was it that you needed?"

"First, I frown upon your disparaging a fellow colleague. Second, just what did you think you were doing with this morning's meeting?"

"Ah…I see. Let me say that I agree with you. Only I don't consider Daniel a colleague. What he does isn't journalism; barely qualifies as work. To address your second question, I did exactly what you asked me to do: I took charge of the meeting."

"That was not the point."

"But that is the point, Frank. I did the job you're assigned to do."

"It was not what I intended—you know better. So please discontinue the cretin charade."

"And you thought shaming was a good idea? What are you, Frank, fifteen?"

"I will not be spoken to this way by a subordinate. Consider yourself…"

"What? What should I consider myself?

As Frank searched his mind for the right words, knowing he could do nothing with Xavier's darling, Abigail waited with bated breath for the next nonsensical comment. As the silence went on, Abigail thought, *Maybe I should've taken Frank's job. At least this idiotic behavior could be minimized.*

All the years and commitment it took to reach her position would be sacrificed too soon. She wasn't ready to let go and move into management. There were still too many important topics to cover. Yet, life could not continue in like way; working a circus act with clowns that don't perform well.

For the first time, Abigail began to seriously consider the option. *Why would I need to give up the desk to be TTN President?*

The physicians wanted to keep Darby another week. Unwilling to accept their diagnosis, he released himself from the hospital. Ten days recovering in bed filled Darby with a mixture of excitement for his engine's future, hatred for the past, and conflict over the collision of the two. During this infirmity, he couldn't shake the price or wish to be different—finally finding acceptance in a realization that to truly set loose the ruthlessness which built his empire, he would be required to let go. Surprisingly, this was not a tragic thought. He felt ready to allow whatever unknown cosmic force that seeks to balance all things to have its pound—*it was good.*

"Stanley. Yes, I'm home. I told you yesterday that I wasn't staying another day. I am alive, aren't I? What about the doctors? I heard that from them too. Look, I can stand on my own two feet. Yes, but only a little dizzy. No, you don't need to do that.

"Listen, I want you to call that Morgan fellow who interviewed me. That's the one—I want to talk about tomorrow's event; and some other things. Like what? Like it's none of your concern. Just get a hold of him to see if his program is on today. I have a few things I'd like to say before the wheels begin turning. Of course I'll be here. One more thing: Will you call the maid and give her the day off tomorrow? It's a big day for us all. I'd like to spend it quietly alone at home. Thanks. Call me when you know about it."

Darby sat down at his kitchen table, overlooking the river. A silt and muddied body followed the inlet to the ocean. He was calmed by this water moving along without a thought at all—purpose and form devoid of intention, as it merged into the distant sea. The quiet of his home made loud Darby's anguish over a lifetime of effort for what and for whom he was now unsure. The prize for all his work could not be had.

The phone rang. Darby asked, "Is it done? Good. Have them come Tuesday. That's fine. Morgan's on in an hour—wants me for the entire show? You're right about that. I may be strong enough to go home but making any more trips today would be foolish. I don't have the energy for it anyway. He would? That's great. So he's going to call me here and host his program that way—fine by me. Yes, I'll make sure to mention that too. Call me after the program."

An hour later, Darby's phone sounded out. "Hello?"

"Is this Darby Adams, President and CEO of Fountain Oil?" Morgan asked.

"Yes, it is; and Fountain Alternative Energy."

"Darby, it is awful good to talk to you again. Your assistant spoke to our producer and asked if we could spare some airtime to go over that new motor you're selling tomorrow. He about lost his lunch—and then cleared an entire hour. I hope we have enough to talk about."

"I'm sure we'll fill up your slot nicely. Are we broadcasting now?"

"Yes, we are. The program just began a few minutes ago."

"I'd like to clear up one thing from the outset. We're giving away the first million units tomorrow. We'll be issuing them to the residents of Houston as our test market. Going forward, the motors will then be sold on the open market."

"That's quite a generous gift to the people of Texas. May I ask; why so charitable?"

"There are a few reasons. I'll admit the initial impulse was not altruistic. But after having the chance to ruminate over the idea, I thought what a wonderful gesture it would be to provide a million families with free electricity.

"To be truthful, Congress has already assembled an oversight committee, and is winding up the bureaucracy needed to keep my motor from being released at all. I had no choice but to make the technology available as swiftly as possible. The fastest way to get it into the people's hands is to give it away. Once it's publicly acknowledged to be safe, the other energy companies, and their lobby-monsters, would have no choice but to accept that it's here to stay. The era of energy dominance is coming to an end.

"There's also the blessing of the giver. As I mentioned, it was not my original intent to give away the technology. However, I can say now that doing so fills my heart with joy."

"Darby, that's amazing. Now, as most listeners know, you were shot over a week ago. Can you tell us what you've gone through? Do the police have any idea who's behind it?"

"What have I gone through? I would say that what I went through was what went through me. I was gunned down."

"Sorry, that was insensitive," Morgan replied.

"That's okay, Morgan. I'm feeling a little punchy. The police have no idea who did it; but I do."

Morgan waited, thinking Darby would explain, then carefully asked, "So who do you think did it?"

Darby hesitated. After this, he could not go back. Darby wanted peace more than anything; but could not have it without letting go of everything he ever worked or fought for. His stomach painfully knotted as he clenched the phone.

"Darby…" Morgan broke the silence.

"It was the Moborak. They sent two assassins," Darby explained, allowing relief to fill his body with warmth.

"How do you know? Aren't they the same group responsible for the short offensive against our military bases in Afghanistan? What do they want with you?"

"The very same group—they wanted money; and I refused to give it to them."

"Why you? Was this some sort of blackmail scheme?"

"Not blackmail—they simply demanded more of it."

"So you've given this extremist group money before?" Morgan asked with bewilderment.

"Yes, but unwittingly. See, the more money I made, the longer the line of politicians grew outside my office, creating ways to leverage any wealth they could take under the illusion of legal right. This time though, it wasn't someone in Congress threatening to turn a drilling site into a protected wildlife refuge. It was another oil company wanting to ensure that fossil fuel remained on top of the energy-producing mountain. I was forced to pay millions; which ultimately ended up in the Moborak's hands. When I made it clear I would not be shaken down any longer, they sent a message."

"Darby, that's right out of a spy novel. Do energy companies leverage each other as often as you seem to indicate?"

"What do you think? Of course—though this is the first time I've become entangled with religious extremists. Futures markets and refinery output is the standard operating procedure for internecine fossil-fuel squabbles—forcing each other's hands or cuffing them behind. However, different issues were at play this time. Rest assured, the intent was to maintain energy status quo."

"This is exciting and frightening. We'll talk more with Darby Adams after hearing from our sponsors." Darby shifted back and forth in his chair; attempting to find a comfortable posture to hold. The bullet wounds pulsed a dull repetitive ache during the pause—drawing out the moments until his attention could be diverted back to their discussion. Morgan said, "We're back, program listeners. I'm continuing my interview with billionaire oilman and alternative energy leader, Darby Adams. Before our commercial break we were talking about the Moborak hitmen sent to take your life. Is there anything more you'd like to add to that?"

"They came for me and failed. What I find most interesting about the Moborak, from what little I know, is that their group is only a few years old. Until recently, they were largely underfunded. The moment money fell into their hands, key American military installation information was provided to them. Their strikes on our bases were made in concert and executed with a precision well beyond their capabilities. It's an inexpensive way to create an incentive to divert money away from any other major projects like the Alternative Energy Bill and the Mars Mission Bill."

"Are you saying there are ties between the American government and terrorist organizations?"

"I didn't say that. It just seems curious how a low-technology radical organization could've completed such an intricate battle plan without a lot of logistical help. Put the puzzle together and let me know what you find."

"If I ever get wind of anything like that, Darby, then I sure will. So far you haven't disappointed our audience. Demographic feedback is topping the metric charts by the number of listeners tuning in. Without sounding too judgmental, is there any way you could be wrong about a government plot, or even Moborak involvement, in your recent brush with death?"

Smiling so hard his cheeks hurt, Darby replied, "Oh boy, Morgan, how I wish it weren't true. Until recently, I dealt with adversaries like I deal with insects in my home. They're eliminated and given no further thought. If it was in my way, then I'd kill it and sweep it aside. Sounds ruthless, doesn't it?"

"Respectfully, yes."

"In all my years, I never raised a hand to another or took to destroy another business without having good cause. If you're a businessman, then you know, at some point, a choice has to be made; it's you or them left alive when the scuffle is over and the dust settled. I never lost any sleep over those choices—they came with the path.

"The America that I knew as a child, which helped end the tyranny of Nazism, is not the same country today. There's no dignity or pride left in being American. People have lost their will to fight. It isn't the villains or our country's enemies we lack the stomach to face. It is the corruption that has found its way into nearly every seat of government across the land—a pity too. America holds in its people a birthright to greatness; much like the rest of humanity shares in their cultures. This corruption doesn't stop with the politics. It filters down to the individual lives of our population; infecting all with the pestilence corruption carries. In the end, it annihilates the will to hold accountable those who hold power over us.

"Washington DC is robbing its citizenry of their authentic humanity. One not dare show any sign of character in society, lest they be convicted of having a soul. This is the true crime now to offend our rulers: possession of human dignity and the ability to hold one's chin up with pride. We are a defeated people—invaded from within by apathy and indifference to the belief that we possess an existential right to something better than living as state-controlled robots."

"That's a little too arcane, Darby, don't you think?"

"Please don't interrupt. I'm not finished."

"You're in charge, Darby. Please continue."

"We're born with a sense of power in our minds. We intuitively understand from the first scream emerging out of our tiny mouths that we're alive and must be heard. A newborn knows this truth. This power we access is limitless. A person can accomplish anything—if their will and belief holds.

"What is this power if not the ability to move an object or idea? To live in a society of movers who've relinquished a portion of their will and freedom to be ruled over by another for the sake of social order is what it is to be civilized. We possess this power; all people do. Those empowered over us are temp-employees. It was never meant to be a permanent position. Our country could be a better place if we simply remembered who we are: the landlords of our own power. I'm certain there are a few tenants in Washington needing eviction. The world needs reminding of this, regardless of the fashion with which a government oversees its people. Abiding authority over a population cannot be taken—only granted.

"I think most tragic is that it's unnecessary. We're not required to idly sit while our lives are stripped away by the few. It can be very different.

"Socialism and communism attempted to take humanity to the next place in our social evolution. Those social constructs theoretically offer much to humanity. It is in practical application that they fail as reliable societal institutions. Their downfall lies not in their individual intent, but in our humanity. We are a lazy bunch, we humans. We want something for nothing, if we're honest. The more we're given without effort, the more it costs our hominal dignity and empowerment. We are meant to be empowered, using that endowment to better our lives; anything less is discarded legacy.

"Capitalism isn't faring much better for us. Oh, it's made me very wealthy. It's taken mankind through the industrial revolution and ratcheted efficiencies to a state where men, not machines, are becoming obsolete. Technology, for all its magnificence, is eliminating more jobs than it's replacing. As time passes it'll only get worse. The open market economic system brought us this far; just as every other social and economic paradigm served its purpose and then died.

"Unchecked capitalism is dead. It's no longer producing enough to sustain the vast majority as it once did. I, and others like me in the privileged class, will be protected for a while yet; but it's coming for us too.

"What must we do then? Isn't that always the question repeatedly posed throughout history? We must change. Capitalism has served as the most pervasive economic force in human history. It's taken us as far as it can. It still provides for a wonderful motivation; the individual gains reaped by one's own effort. This we should not forsake.

"However, the next question to ask ourselves is, how much wealth should one possess? What's too much or not enough? Lacking Solomon's wisdom, I'd suggest a person has accumulated too much when their available sum circumvents any regard for the laws governing their lands. At the point where judges and politicians can be bought to look the other way, then too much has been amassed, and should be contained. It sounds like many of America's largest corporations—which no longer fear to cross laws governing their business activities."

"Darby, I hate to point out the obvious, but as you said a moment ago, doesn't that include your oil empire?" Morgan sheepishly asked.

"It does."

"So what do you plan to do about it, then?"

"I'll tell you in a minute, Morgan. I have just one more thing to say about this subject. I know I've touched on a number of dark topics, with implications that seriously impact the average American citizen. However, I also want you to know that I have hope for America and the rest of humanity. Look how far our species has come. We've overcome obstacles much worse than this. We will prevail; even if the answers are not yet obvious. Exciting days are ahead. Solutions to some of our most fundamental problems are closer than we could imagine: hunger, homelessness, education, healthcare, and so on. The reason I say this is simple. What else are we going to do with our time? How much more efficient can we become before humans run out of things to do? It's not support or services we lack. It is humanity's financial and social superstructures that must change to support the new technological realities.

"You asked what I intend to do—my Kratometric Engine is a start. Trucks are loaded and ready to begin delivery tomorrow morning.

Our goal is to give away all one million units by sundown tomorrow. The residents of Houston need only to accept delivery of their free unit. If they do not wish to receive the gift, then we'll simply offer it to another family.

"I also intend to leave this world with a clear conscience. To accomplish this, I'll shut down Fountain Oil within six months. All the oil wells will be sealed, and the fields will be chemically spoiled to render them commercially useless. I intend to make wealthy those who have done so for me; and therefore will be dividing Fountain Oil's money amongst its employees. Every worker will receive an equal severance and retirement. I'll provide as much comfort as I can to those who have suffered at the heel of my boot. I also want to say…" Darby faltered, as he struggled to continue.

Silence filled the airtime. Darby began to weep, then stopped. He cleared his throat and attempted to speak, but again stumbled.

"Darby, what is it? What can be so terrible after making such fine gestures?" Morgan asked.

"I can no longer do this."

"What can you no longer do?" Morgan whispered.

"I can no longer be a part of an economic system that enslaves the vast majority by a small minority. I'm releasing the patent for the Kratometric Engine to the world. Diagrams, principles, research and instructions for its construction will be available on Fountain Alternative Energy's website for anyone to download and make use of. The power of self-sufficiency will no longer be held by the few over the many.

"Morgan, that technology does not belong to me. I killed a young inventor and his family for it years ago. I wanted the idea. He wouldn't sell it to me; and so I took it with as little regard for his property as for his life. This is what unchecked greed looks like— it's voracious, insatiable, and ultimately destroys its master once all others have been used up and cast aside. This appalling secret can no longer abide. It's eaten me alive and now there's little left of what once made me human. I'm an empty shell and only seek peace. Wealth has been a noose pulling ever tighter about my neck. Morgan, there's nothing more to share with you. I don't know what will become of me. If my enemies are to assume the role of executioner, then I hope they do it quickly. Goodbye," Darby entreated, ending the phone call.

Darby painfully rose and walked directly to his desk, where he wrote down instructions on company letterhead for Stanley to follow. After signing off his final wishes, he faxed the documents to Stanley's office computer.

The phone rang out, shattering the silence and disrupting his relief that veil and grotesquery no longer obscured his life. Darby made his mark; his was a life once lived in great achievement. Horrid also was the darkness; having wronged so many on his journey.

"Stanley, did you get the fax? Good. Yes, all of it. Yes, just as I said on the program. Make sure Legal takes the lead on the cash distribution and company stock transfer. The paperwork stipulates who and where. See to it that the engine specs are on the website within the hour. Just as it stated; Fountain Alternative Energy is yours to run. You're the chief now. Because it's what you said you wanted.

"Regardless of what anyone says, no one gets where they're going on their own. Every successful person took help from someone. Take that fire to make your place in business and do something good for humanity.

"Yes, but what you don't know is that once we started to develop the Kratometric Engine I had Research and Development work on other technologies we've quietly patented. No, he and his family were the only ones killed. I alone will carry the burden and face whatever punishment comes.

"Giving away the engine is my gift to the world. Take the remainder of your company and make a difference, Stanley. I've never said this to you, but I'm proud of the work you've done and know you have a brilliant future.

"No, I won't be there tomorrow when the deliveries are completed. It's your company after the tasks I have set out for you are completed. You talk to the employees. Explain to them the importance of what they do, and inspire them to follow their new boss.

"Stanley…Be good," Darby softly requested as he hung up the phone.

As Darby slouched over his chair at the kitchen table, a door-knock sounded. The police moved quickly. He got to his feet, calm in the knowledge that it was finally over and he could simply allow this to happen.

Darby shuffled to the door, hesitating for a moment before turning the knob. The door seemingly opened by itself—Darby not feeling his arm pull it. Standing before him was a man wearing a white chef's uniform.

"Mr. Adams."

"Yes?"

"Mr. Huffington arranged to have your evening dinner sent from our kitchen. May I bring in the meal?"

Surprised by the gesture, Darby replied, "Uh, yes. Please set it down on the kitchen table."

"Right away."

The brown-eyed young man set out the meal and then explained, "The presentation consists of smoked quail with our signature demi-glaze drizzled on top, a garden-picked medley of seasoned steamed vegetables, freshly baked dinner bread, and for dessert our signature chocolate soufflé."

Darby reached for his wallet. The young man interrupted, "Everything's been taken care of. Please enjoy yourself." He bowed and departed, closing the door behind him.

The food's aroma was especially delightful days of hospital fare. It brought warmth to Darby's heart like he hadn't experienced for some time. Stanley's duty was to ensure Darby received what was needed. This was different. Stanley would soon be his own man. And so Darby could enjoy this gesture not as a boss, but a kindred spirit.

Darby sat down to eat. As he took the first bite of quail, the smoky flavor excited his taste buds. Delicious, Darby thought. The fowl's earthen colors against the asparagus and bread pleased his eyes, as did the textures and tastes over his palate. It was pride in the meal's excellent preparation Darby enjoyed most. A stranger he would never meet again had respected themselves enough to provide a person they may never know their best effort. Darby was endeared to distinction in all its forms.

After finishing the entrée, he moved the plate aside to make room for dessert. As his fork broke through the confection, his delight withered as he remembered that he would likely soon be interrupted by someone from law enforcement. Warm, sweet chocolate melted in his mouth, while the bitterness of incarceration and eventual execution soiled his mind. Each bite becoming more bland than the last. Although he was now free of his burdens, freedom would no longer be Darby's, and the meal lost its appeal.

Darby stood up, exhausted by his fresh-aching wounds and needing rest. He carefully gaited to the living room and settled into his favorite chair. As he bent over, moderate discomfort became stabbing pain and he accepted he would have to stay put for a while.

God, I'm tired. Will the cops be decent? Will they respect what I've done, and the power I once wielded? Will they show me the same cruel indifference the killers I hired provided? Haven't I earned the right to be revered? What can anyone claim that rivals my accomplishment; a life as rich and full of reward? Only a few may boast they are equal! How about that engine? Such a fine piece of engineering!

"And I took it!" he yelled out loud. "It was there. I wanted it—and took it! For the love of…why did I take it? That boy was never going to make it work. He would've found his way to me eventually. Why?"

The room fell silent. Darby suddenly grew angry and ruthless in the way George Weatherby noted so many times. He screamed, "I was fine before I stole that damn machine! I had it all! I could buy anything or anyone! Why did I have to take it too?"

His body throbbed as he sank back into the leather chair. Each painful surge reminded him that his choices had brought him to this point. *I'm such a sick bastard! I never wanted this…to be a better man…*

for the sake of goodness. Damn it—I murdered that innocent boy, and have been trying to kill off the self-hatred of destroying the best thing in me. I took something I could've built with my own hands. When did I become a politician? I wish they'd hurry up and drag me away in chains—whipped and tortured—a slow, painful death.

"Please, someone come and be done with me," Darby sobbed. "Why did I stop the gunmen?"

As self-loathing seethed, Darby's skin crawled. He couldn't stand the life he inhabited. He had committed the greatest act of evil against the self. Darby reached into the table drawer next to the chair and gripped a pistol. He pulled back the slide and released it, chambering a bullet, and then pressed it against his head. The steel muzzle felt cold.

He wanted to die; wanted to pull the trigger. He hungered for his anguish to stop—but couldn't do it. His need to live taunted him.

What if I recanted my statements? They'd understand. I just survived an attempt on my life. I'm delirious and weak. The doctors practically demanded I stay in the hospital. In a crazed state I left the hospital, ignoring the advice of those who cared for me. But I'm still a thief; no better than a DC bootlicker. I can never again hold my head up and say I did anything—only that I'm a fraud.

"Do it!" Darby yelled. His blood pressure surged and his chest wounds began bleeding through their stitches. His head ached and the gun shook. Darby began thinking of a beautiful girl he knew in high school. She was sweet and spoke often of their future together. At that age, the conversation annoyed him. Now Darby treasured the memory of someone who cared for him while still whole and unmolested by the world of money and power. Where did that boy go? he thought. "I'll tell you where he went—Brazil to take the life of an innocent and throw away everything he'd ever worked for! He even killed an old business partner to cover the crime! George Weatherby will never be missed; but he still had a right to life no matter how he chose to live it. Where is that boy? He's gone missing, never to be seen again. He is nothing to no one!"

Youthful images flashed in his mind. Moments of elation flooded his consciousness. Infatuations and romance of a tender sort came forth, as the feminine qualities of those experiences soothed his mangled and destroyed heart. Then Darby contemplated his first business success; the thrill of victory, and fidelity shared with young men naïve to the corruption that would soon fill their souls with lust for self-gratification and control.

His life's narrative played out, memory by memory, as he began shedding tears, knowing it was coming to an end. Darby rocked back and forth as his mouth gaped; attempting to let escape the agony of the assault on the totality of his life. It was he who had fatally wounded his existence; laying waste to an excellence no other human could touch.

It was about to be extinguished—he struggled with the letting go. Darby wanted to live, and suffered the wanting and the leaving. Beaded sweat rolled down his face. He began to shudder and wail as the trigger was squeezed and the hammer fell.

As the bullet entered his brain, he experienced a lifetime-collage of images, sounds, smells, laughter, fun, joy, and sorrow. He loved existence and did not want to stop. He hungered for more life but could not live with himself another moment. He was a man who once existed and now was no more.

A final poetic memory emerged before Darby's light disappeared; when he and George were just starting out on their journey. They often sat on a park bench near a stream and skipped rocks as they planned future businesses together; fifty-fifty. Then, their friendship was more important than money. They shared everything; a bond fed their hearts with a closeness they never knew again.

Darby died and found peace.

Ethan cleared his schedule for the day and flew to New York. A week had passed since Anne pitched the bill to reign in the Worth.

Anne's apartment doorbell rang; not expecting company, she assumed it was a delivery. She opened the door in a pink and black thigh-cut silk dressing robe. Ethan stood at the entry, clad in a coat, dark blue suit, and red tie.

"Can I come in?" he asked with a forced grin.

"Get in here before I drag you through the doorway. You're looking especially handsome today—sit down. I'll pour us some coffee."

"Thanks," Ethan replied as he sat. It felt familiar and pleasant, as had their relationship been before he left for the Senate. For a moment he forgot why he came.

"So what dragged you away from the Bone Yard?" she asked, expecting capitulation.

"I hate that moniker. Might be true, but it doesn't help our country to joke about rampant corruption."

"Rampant corruption," Anne mocked, sliding next to him on the couch and setting his cup on the table. She flirted, "Tell me something, Ethan. You've been in Washington a few months. In all that time, can you honestly tell me you've personally experienced rampant corruption? This is a direct question. Tell me."

"Have I watched a politician ripping the retirement check out of Grandma's hands? No. As a matter of fact I haven't seen much of anything resembling something that could be considered accomplishment. Seems its only purpose is to feed. Haven't witnessed any brazen thievery—what I have seen is a constant battle over perceived power; little children bickering for more. Don't see anything of the American people represented there. It's as if Washington is its own little country, treating the remaining electorate as indentured servants. As I said, it's a mystery why I've been given position and title. I did nothing to earn it. One thing's certain—whoever's behind it wants something. I can't help but think it's the same person or group using our relationship as leverage."

Alarmed by his keen intuition, Anne put down her coffee and kneeled between his legs—allowing the dressing gown to fall open and expose her breasts. She diverted him playfully, "You never did tell me why you're here."

"You first. Who are you working for?"

She guided his hands to her exposed body and blithely reminded him, "Ethan, this wasn't a part of the bargain; we don't diddle in the shop."

Ethan stopped her from moving his hands any farther and asked, "So you're not going to tell me?"

Slightly annoyed, but maintaining a mischievous tone, she replied, "No."

He retracted his hands to his lap. "Then we need a new bargain."

Resting her hands on his knees, Anne's face turned serious. "What does that mean?"

"It means if honesty does not exist between us, then we can no longer be together," Ethan explained with a blank expression.

"What's going on here? You're carrying on as if we're teenagers breaking up because you really want to date a girl from the cheerleading squad. But that's not it, is it? You want something. You've pressed the question of who I work for too often for it to mean nothing."

"What's going on here is that this isn't the relationship I hoped it would be. I'll admit, when we first met, I was attracted to you. More than your physical appearance was the way you carried yourself. You emanated personal power and confidence. As we got along, I admired more your ability to do a difficult job with a nonchalance and composure few soldiers experience facing down their demons. There was great respect for what I thought was a woman of enlightenment. Early on you seemed to command an understanding of existence, strength, and your purpose. You appeared to own your inner self.

"However, as time has passed, I've witnessed many instances of intentional brutality in the way you interact with others and sometimes even myself. I now know that it's not power I saw in you, but cruelty, making impossible your capacity to love anyone… even yourself. What you wield is ambivalence; often mistaken for power. But it isn't related to power at all. Power is motive. Cruelty is the vice of the cold-hearted. It can only affect and move those weak enough to accept its lies. Now that the difference is obvious, our relationship can only be pretense. I'm losing too much as it is in DC. I'll not anchor my life to one who would choose this for themselves."

"You have no idea what power truly is!" Anne shouted as she stood, allowing the dressing gown to fall at her feet. The angles of her arms and legs contrasting the curves of her hips, breasts, and lips briefly entranced Ethan. Anne then forcefully declared, "I'll show you what true power is. Take your clothes off and climb on my bed!"

Ethan stood up, not touching her body, and stepped away from the couch to reach for his coat. "No. I'm sorry."

Anne's face distorted as she screamed, repeating his response disbelievingly, "No? Do it now! I'm not asking!"

"I'm leaving," Ethan announced, as he put on his coat.

A bottomless pit of hate filled Anne's mind and she seemed to feel the forward shove of a steel-clad glove at her back. She leaped onto Ethan, wrapping her naked legs around his waist and holding his shoulders with her hands. She screamed as one who had lost her mind, and began punching Ethan's face.

Ethan grabbed her wrists as his nose began to bleed. Anne wrung one arm loose and clawed at his face with her fingernails. "Ah!" Ethan yelled out in pain. Anne's other arm wrenched free from Ethan's grip and began pulling his hair before continuing to claw and gouge his face and neck.

Ethan's mind raced towards defense—not wanting to hurt or be hurt. Anne continued her attack. Ethan finally grew angry, grabbed her by the torso, and threw her across the room—her body broadcast a slap as it hard-landed on the kitchen's tile floor. She quickly stood, naked, one of her wrists clearly broken.

Anne, showing her teeth, screeched; primal, vicious, and devolved. Gasping for air between screams, she ordered, "Get your bloody and beaten body into that bedroom now!"

"Not on your life," Ethan replied, breathing deeply.

Anne howled again and charged Ethan, baring her teeth and fingernails. Ethan struck her jaw with all his strength, as she closed the short distance between them. She made a sharp, high-pitched squall and fell to the floor.

Ethan stepped away as adrenaline coursed through his body. She lifted her head and laughed aloud while blood poured from her mouth. Ethan's hands trembled as he reached for the doorknob and turned it.

"Good. A Boy Scout couldn't last in the Capitol. You're now ready to assume real strength. You're willing to do what it takes to get the job done, Ethan. Don't you see? This was what I've tried to draw out of you since we first sat together on that plane.

"Look at how powerful you became when called upon. Ruthlessness was necessary and you mustered it to serve your interests. This doesn't need to change what we are to one another. We can still go on. I'll have a draft of the bill tomorrow morning ready for you to sponsor and submit to the Senate."

"That was not power; it was savagery for the sake of self-preservation. I feel neither pride nor shame. I have a right to protect my life. I would not wield it against anyone for the purpose of personal gain. You're right, Anne. This doesn't change what we are to one another. It clarifies it. I'll see you on the battlefield."

Ethan opened the door and walked out. As the door began to close, Anne stood and rushed at the door. She slammed it shut with a loud bang.

A half-hour later, a doorbell rang. Ethan stood in the entryway, awaiting a response. He wanted it to open. There were things that needed to be said.

After a few moments it unlatched, to Abigail's surprise. Ethan hadn't been sure where to go, but needed a friend—so he had crossed Central Park to Abigail's Upper West Side residence.

"Ethan, what happened?" Abigail asked gently, her expression shocked.

His swollen and bruised face still bled and his hair pulled in several directions. Nail lacerations marked him from chin to chest. His left lapel was torn and dangling from his suit.

He smiled. "I just wanted to tell you that I am no longer dating Anne."

Understanding that Anne was the likely culprit for Ethan's

appearance, Abigail replied, "Good."
They stared into each other's eyes and knew what it meant. Abigail reached out to touch his cheek. Ethan didn't move, but simply closed his eyes. As he did, Abigail leaned in to kiss him.

CHAPTER
XVI
A QUESTION OF HONOR

On an early November Tuesday, radio, television, print, social media and internet news agencies were busy covering the three major elections: Presidential, House of Representatives and a third of the Senate. As had occurred for over a century, the tug and pull between the Blue Coats and the Liberty Party was the primary challenge to the presidential seat. The Britches Party, having survived nearly as long, never gained enough momentum to elect a candidate to that high office. In the end, Britches typically sided with one party, serving as a swing vote mechanism—often deciding the final victory—receiving political favors and discreet payoffs in return for its complicity.

Abigail and Daniel had been at the news desk all day. By three o'clock, a majority of the senatorial and congressional elections had been won. Incumbent Byron Anderson led the presidential race. Frank assigned Abigail to report on the Blue Coats Party's progress, and generally to promote their campaign. Daniel covered the Liberty Party and talked up its merits. The Britches Party was only mentioned occasionally to keep the public up to date with their performance. The Britches lacked the advertising budget of the Blue Coats and Liberty Party to buy preferential promotion. Frank drove his advertising staff like slaves in the weeks approaching election day; leveraging both parties into paying outlandishly for campaign coverage. The other major news networks did so in kind.

Abigail continued, "With hours left at the polls, the political races are holding ground with their parties' current share of congressional seats. President Anderson commands a lead of forty-one percent of the registered voters; followed by presidential Liberty Party hopeful, Governor Michael Bishop of Oklahoma, with thirty-six percent. Trailing by a large margin in third place is the Britches

Party candidate, Senator Heath Slaughter from Nebraska, with five percent of the registered vote."

Daniel added, "That's quite a close race. It looks like this could be a squeaker."

Annoyed by the required on-camera repartee, Abigail replied, "It would seem so."

"Why do you suppose this is so close, Abigail? Preliminary polls tapped the President with a comfortable lead coming into election day. It doesn't seem that your candidate's assured a win at this point."

"Daniel, as you know, the Blue Coats Party's conservative nature supports big business enterprise and the open market. They deplore any regulation on corporate profits. A large military presence throughout the world is also an integral part of their foreign policy. President Anderson, being a member of the Blue Coats Party, has been blamed by many as the man responsible for the recent recession, allowing energy companies and stock speculators to largely influence the market for their own financial gains.

"Tell me, Daniel, do you think the Liberty Party will do a better job for America? And if so, why?" Abigail asked, putting Daniel's uninformed opinion on the spot. In general, Daniel didn't write or research the stories reported. He simply read the prompter.

"Abigail, the Liberty Party is predominantly thought of as highly educated academics. The party's first concern is for the people, and social programs supporting the needy in America. A much more robust government with a diminished military presence is iconic Liberty Party policy. Governor Michael Bishop, in fact, was a law professor before being elected to office."

Surprised by Daniel's command of the subject, Abigail noticed Brian mouthing the words to Daniel—helping him through a tense unscripted moment. After getting Daniel through a near on-air debacle, Brian looked at Abigail and mouthed the words, "Stop now."

Abigail contained a smile as the camera returned to her. She asked, "Daniel, do you think the Britches Party's Constitutional fundamentalism, fiscal conservatism, and national isolationism will pick up any more votes?" She fiercely fought back the urge to burst out laughing.

Brian mouthed the words, "I'm going to kill you."

Momentarily alarmed while Brian switched back from Abigail, Daniel replied, "It's not likely, Abigail. They may see an additional percentage point of support. However, this is as high as I expect them to go. They're currently two points higher than the polls indicated. The real question is, which party will gain their support in last-minute horse-trading? The jury is still out, Abigail," Daniel assured.

"We'll be back after a few messages from our sponsors," Abigail closed.

Frank glared through the control booth glass—stoking Abigail's pure frustration. Brian's exhausted shoulders dropped as the commercials ran. Daniel scowled at Abigail for attempting to make him look ignorant.

"Abigail, I thought we were friends. Are you trying to get me fired? You see Frank up there. He's not going to fire you. You're his cash cow. He'll make an example of me just to vent his anger. Please don't do that again," Brian pleaded. He looked sincere but could not completely conceal a smirk—secretly enjoying Daniel squirming.

Brian stopped talking as he listened to a voice through his headphones. He said into the microphone, "Is that confirmed? Who verified it? Are the police there yet? I don't know. Yes, she's right here. Alright. "Abigail, Sam, from our Houston affiliate, is on the line. Darby Adams is dead. Looks like a suicide. The police don't even know yet."

"Give me your headset!" Abigail demanded, like a predator catching its prey.

"Sam, it's Abbey. What's your source? Will the cleaning man keep quiet until we get a crew over there? Yeah, I imagine he's nervous. Will a hundred thousand buy a little calm for about an hour? He can call the police after that. Ask him. He will. Good. Have your crew there in fifteen. You'll have a short window to get the shots you need and prepare your reporter to go live. I'll handle the feed at this end. Get back with me in five. I'll be here," Abigail assured as she pointed to Daniel to give him sole charge of the anchor duties, and stepped out from behind the news desk.

Frank had noticed Abigail was talking on Brian's headphones and left the control booth to find out what the problem was. Brian fingered his temple to signal a free crew member to find another headset. Brian then pointed at Daniel, still seated behind the news desk, to start reading the prompter. Like an obedient child, Daniel began talking into the camera.

"Miss Sanders, what is it that you think you're doing? Why are you not at your post? This is a presidential election broadcast. Do you know how much money we'll lose by the minute if you're not in that seat?"

"Frank."

"I do wish you would call me Mr. Lambert."

"Frank, Darby Adams is dead in Houston from an apparent suicide!" Abigail exclaimed, expecting excitement from Frank that a major story was breaking.

Frank's face remained blank as he replied, "And this means what to me? We're on the hook for millions of dollars in campaign advertising revenue. Your face is a part of TTN's brand. Let our affiliate handle the story. It will eventually filter its way to us. Have you lost your sense of priority?"

"Did you not hear me? This is Darby Adams, the wealthiest oil executive in America. He just killed himself. Did I forget to mention that this is the second American oil CEO to die of unnatural causes in less than two months? Was it not relayed to you that this is the same man who only yesterday released a million free units of his Kratometric Engine? You know, the engine that needs no gas, electricity or fuel of any kind; that guy? He's dead! Don't you think that's somewhat newsworthy; even on an election day? Some of the candidates knew him personally. I think President Anderson and Darby played golf together."

"Okay, so we'll be sure to give it some airtime when the story gets to us. Now, get back behind the desk."

"Frank, you need to listen to me. I have Sam Hefner, our Houston affiliate producer, on his way to Darby's house right now."

"So?"

"No other news agencies have been tipped off. The police don't even know."

"How do we know?"

"The cleaning man was greedy enough to realize he could make big money fast by calling our Houston affiliate first. Apparently, he likes TTN's coverage of illegal alien abuses. He's at the house right now—next to the body—waiting for our film crew to arrive. We need a confirmed satellite signal now; and spin up the writers and emergency newscast team to go live in fifteen minutes!"

"Live!" Frank replied in a shocked tone. "We don't put dead bodies on live television. And what big money are you talking about? We don't pay for news."

"We do when it's happening now. We do it when we're the only national news network covering it. And it's only going to cost us a thousand Benjamins! I was sure this guy would try to negotiate. You wouldn't believe how many times I've been extorted several hundred thousand for this kind of break."

Frank looked astonished while she finished discussing money issues, as if Abigail had insulted his mother. He posed, "Miss Sanders, who authorized the use of company money for inside information? After responding, then kindly tell me where you think you work. If behavior like this continues, Miss Sanders, it may serve one day soon as a reason for your dismissal."

"I've had the option to offer cash for the right stories going on ten years. Sandra gave me free rein over the company check-book, and would tell you that I never wasted a cent of the network's money. The ratings we receive for truly great stories are worth thousands of times what I offered this guy. Frank, we're in the news business. If you continue forgetting the news part, and focus only on the business, then there'll be no TTN in a decade.

"For the record, Frank, we do put dead bodies on the news. I was in Afghanistan eight weeks ago and filmed dead GIs. They were all over that report. Where do I work? I once worked for a world-class news organization. It was a brutal environment. But we were the best and that was the price. Of late, we're little more than an entertainment venue. Now, if you don't mind, I need to call Houston to ensure he'll be ready in ten minutes. We only have that time to prepare our team to receive at this end and go live. Is there anything else?"

"Miss Sanders, that money was not authorized by me," Frank stammered, his ego bruised.

Aggravated, Abigail asserted, "Frank, Xavier will approve it. If you don't believe me, call him now and explain the story. And if he doesn't, then you can take it out of my yearly bonus. If the story is a hit, though, and my dollars paid for it, I expect thirty percent on increased ratings ad sales for the segment. Frank, the clock's ticking."

"Miss Sanders, I want you back behind the news desk. Brian Calvert will handle the particulars of this story and prompt you when it is ready. Now go!"

Abigail begrudgingly returned to her seat at the desk after the network went to commercial break. Daniel sounded, "Hmm"—gratified she was finally being punished in school for acting the part of a showoff. He felt superior; not the one in trouble with his teacher. Abigail looked at Daniel as if he were a child. The network began broadcasting again and Abigail read news about election results across the country as it passed by on the prompter screen. Daniel tapped lightly on the desk, gloating over his perceived victory.

At Darby's house, Miguel, the cleaning man, had already let Sam and his crew into the house. Darby's decaying corpse crowded the air with a putrid odor of dead human flesh. The curtains were drawn. A sliver of light from the windows highlighted the entry wound on Darby's temple. Blood had sprayed onto the wall behind his chair. The pistol remained in Darby's grip; his hands resting on his lap. Eyes, fixed open and dried, expressed the horror experienced moments before life ended. His mouth held frozen in a painful grimace. The face, a pasty light green-blue, wore the color every human would one day don.

After taking photographs and checking for any obvious evidence, they began to set up lighting and sound equipment for the news spot. Duties were carried out in a business-as-usual manner, as if it didn't matter that this inanimate thing had been a live person only days before. While assembling the set, the rancid awfulness of rotting meat and feces forced the living to cover their mouths. Susan Parker, the newly hired youth-beat reporter, fell to her knees and vomited at Darby's feet.

"Susan, are you going to be alright?" Sam asked.

"I don't think I can do this," Susan moaned, looking up at Sam with pathetic fear.

"Susan, don't think about what this is. Right now you have a job to do. A lot of people are counting on us."

"I can't," Susan pleaded as she started to cry.

"Alright," Sam relented. The cameraman tapped on his watch and flashed two fingers.

"Susan, we have a couple minutes and this feed goes live. You need to pull it together and do your job. Let's go. You were hired for this."

"Sam, I can't!"

"One minute," the cameraman relayed.

"Perfect! Susan, get out of here! Wait! Give me your microphone and power pack. I'll do it myself."

"Sam, I'm sorry."

"Just go," Sam consoled, as he took the equipment.

Sam quickly attached the microphone and earpiece to the power pack while positioning himself next to Darby's chair. The cameraman flicked five fingers twice. Sam squared his posture, pulled in his stomach and looked into the camera's black lens. The cameraman pointed at him.

Through the earpiece Sam could hear Abigail in New York. "This is Abigail Sanders with a TTN exclusive news alert. Billionaire oilman and inventor of the Kratometric Engine, Darby Adams, has died from an apparent suicide at his home in suburban Houston. It appears, from our reporter at the scene, that he shot himself in the head. On location is our TTN Houston affiliate reporter, Susan Parker. Susan, can you tell us what you see?"

"We're afraid that Miss Parker has become incapacitated. I'm Miss Parker's producer, Sam Hefner. I'll be covering the story now."

"Sam, we thank you for staying on the job in such difficult circumstances. Can you confirm Darby Adams is in fact dead; and any other important information you have been able to find?"

"Abigail, you can see, as the camera moves in closer, this was Darby Adams of Fountain Oil. You will also see the star-pointed entry of the bullet wound to his temple, evidencing a point-blank shot to the head. Sitting in his lap we assume is the handgun used in the suicide," Sam narrated, as the camera pulled back to include Sam and Darby's body in full view.

"Sam, have you been able to piece together any clues or leads that might make it a homicide instead of suicide?"

Sam replied, "As you can see from the feed, we have filmed the entire home and found no evidence of struggle or forced entry. There doesn't appear to be anything taken. It's quiet and undisturbed here."

"Sam, was there a suicide letter found?"

"No, Abigail, not that we uncovered."

"Darby just released one million units of his new invention for free onto the market, in a day-long marketing strategy to use Houston as a test for the remainder of the country. An atmosphere of excitement and outrage has surrounded Mr. Adams regarding his radio address, in which he admitted to the murder of a young Brazilian over his invention, and of course the release of the engine's design on Fountain Alternative Energies' website. Were there any technical drawings or other pieces of information that could provide some answers?" Abigail pressed while transitioning to video footage of engine deliveries to Houston homes the day before.

As Sam was about to reply, a police officer stepped through the open door, sidearm drawn, and shouted, "Put your hands up where I can see them! Don't move! You're under arrest!"

Frank immediately cut the feed. Brian looked at Abigail mouthing the word, "Talk".

"Ladies and gentlemen, it appears we are experiencing technical difficulties with Houston. We'll bring you more images as they come in from the home of the late Darby Adams. You saw it here first. Once again, Darby Adams, president and chief executive officer of Fountain Oil, was discovered dead in his home from an apparent suicide."

Daniel cut in, "I'm sorry to interrupt but a determination has been made. President Byron Ulysses Anderson has been reelected to a second term! He just picked up thirty-six key electoral votes from the Britches Party, in a last-minute show of support for the Blue Coats over the Liberty Party."

A day after the elections, Vice President Richard Fulton landed in Houston. He was chauffeured from the airport straight to NASA headquarters. As a caravan of security vehicles and Richard's car entered the parking lot, Shane Ashby waited in front of the main administrative office building near the sidewalk's edge.

The motorcade stopped next to Shane. Two black-suited Secret Service agents approached; dark sunglasses and starched shirts completed the clean-cut governmental patina.

"Shane Ashby?" the first agent belted out.

"Yes."

"Where will the Vice President meet with you? We need to sweep the area first."

"That's dependent upon Vice President Fulton's needs. He's head of the program."

"Wait here," the lead agent instructed, and then walked off to confer with colleagues.

The remaining agents were poised, stern and emotionless. Shane's reflection stared back from the nearest agent's glasses—cold eyes pushing his image outward, making Shane uncomfortable.

The nearest agent lifted his coat sleeve and spoke into a small device, "Yes, right away." Then he motioned with an outward palm for Ashby to walk with him towards the convoy. "Mr. Ashby, will you come with me, please."

 Richard stepped out of the center car as agents spread out to secure the immediate area around the car. He stepped away from the motorcade and walked directly to Shane. Shane was nervous enough about the surprise visit that he forgot to extend his hand.

"Congratulations, Mr. Vice President, on your reelection. Forgive me for being forward, but is there a problem? I didn't expect your visit today."

"The project's timeframe has been a constant concern since I was assigned its completion. I've been too busy with the campaign to get down here any sooner."

"Why don't we go to my office? I have all the data there to update you on our progress."

"Let's walk instead. I don't need particulars right now. Just gimme the unvarnished version; where are we? The boss wants an update."

"Alright, Mr. Vice President. Why don't we walk along the park where past space vehicles are on display? Is there a specific spacecraft you'd like to see?"

"No, you pick one. Let's just get moving. I've been cooped up in transit and need to stretch my legs. I'm on a tight schedule; airborne in an hour.

"Right this way, then. I like the shuttle exhibit. It demonstrates our highest achievement in spacecraft technology until now."

"Fine."

They began walking; suits ran ahead to clear the sidewalk of anyone along their path. A trailing team provided rearguard. They moved like an accordion, expanding and contracting—ensuring no one could approach the Vice President from any direction.

"What would you like to know, Mr. Vice President?"

"Are we going to make the initial launch window in four years?"

"It looks to be the case."

"What about the Russians? They got their money. Sources say they're back on schedule."

"Yes, they are."

"Have you seen their famed fabrication process?"

"No. It appears the reports of improved production time are correct. They've split it in half."

"Great! That'll buy us more time. When can we and the other countries implement their breakthrough?"

"What do you mean? The Russians don't want to share the technology."

"You can't be serious."

"It's complicated, Mr. Vice President. I have my best man on the issue: Charlie Burns."

"I know Charlie. So Charlie said the Russians won't play with us?"

"At this point it's a matter of pride. If we fall behind, then the Russians, theoretically, will share it with us. They would be the ones providing help—further face-saving, Mr. Vice President."

"Russians…if we didn't need to work with them then…"

"Mr. Vice President, I don't mean to pressure you about the deadline. But why don't we simply delay launching an additional eighteen months? We would be in a better launch window for a shorter trip at that time."

Before Richard could respond, fear surfaced on his face, but he quickly contained it. "It is simply not possible…according to the Mars Bill."

Shane understood, for the first time, that something beyond legislation was driving this mission. "Yes, sir," he acknowledged.

"Fine then," Richard added. He stopped walking and turned around before reaching the shuttle.

Shane did an about-face to catch up—Richard having already moved away with a brisk stride. The Vice President was swarmed by the Secret Service detail as he made his way back to the car.

Shane stopped walking and took in the moving mass of black suits. He had been abandoned on the side of the road. Richard suddenly turned back towards Shane and ordered, "Shane, have your department heads' progress reports sent to me tomorrow morning."

"Yes, Mr. Vice President."

Sunday morning was like any other for Gabriel Carter. He had embarked on the third weekend service at ten in the morning. The offering had been collected; exchanging music and inspiration for cash and check.

At the control booth, Taylor Rourke spoke into his microphone, "Live in three seconds."

Charming the camera, Gabriel said, "America, it's good to see you again. Here at the Righteous Way Christian Church we're happy you're with us, and consider you a part of the family. So, if you're watching our service from home, then I hope you are comfortable. I think you'll be jumpin' outta your seats in short order.

"A few weeks ago I spoke to you about patience. I talked about the city of Corinth, the Apostle Paul and his warning letter to the church there. I then cinched it all into his message of patience; patience in love, with each other, and with new technologies that threaten our country's financial stability today. I'm talking about the Kratometric Engine we've heard in the news recently.

"Old Darby Adams gave away one million of those engines to the good people of Houston. Can you imagine: one million engines, just as easy as pie? I heard the initial scuttle about it actually doing what he claimed it would do. Seems an awful shame what became of poor old Darby—or is it?

"Ya see, friends, God knows what's in the deepest part of your heart. I wonder what was in Darby's heart when he doled out all those machines. Do you think it was for the good of mankind or his benefit? It certainly seems something was awry for a man of his accomplishment to kill for that technology.

"He even went so far as to put the technology's plans out on the internet for everyone to have. It's confusing to me. I still can't get my mind around the inconsistencies surrounding the man. In the end, all that applied science could do nothing to save the man from himself. Darby Adams sat on his own bench before he could be judged by fellow countrymen for admitted crimes; and convicted the defendant. He's being judged by God now. I want all of you to remember that as we talk about today's message on the perils of idolatry."

The camera pulled back and panned over to Charles Ettinger. He wore a look of sadness after receiving Gabriel's words. As he faced the floor Charles's beard rested on his chest.

The camera transitioned back to Gabriel as he painted on a smile, "Now, Charles, don't be that way. Come on now, smile for your brothers and sisters, knowing God is just and loves you. You can do it!

"Friends, Charles has the look of a papa bear and the heart of a mama bear." The audience laughed and clapped. "My church family, we don't know where Brother Adams's heart was when he committed his final and awful sin. We do know that God saves. Let's rejoice in that knowledge. Do you hear me? Then let's show Brother Charles his grief is misplaced. Can you put your hands together for me? That's right, clap if you love the Lord."

Soon the auditorium clapped in cadence as Charles raised his head and joined in. His smile was pulled into the camera. Gabriel raised his arms into the air and lowered them to quiet the audience.

"Whew! Don't you just love that; witnessing for the Almighty? It makes me glad to be up here today. Okay, let's get started. Why don't ya'll reach into your Sunday School lessons of the past. Old Moses is sure to come to mind—makin his exodus out of Egypt and taking God's people with him. He also pounded out the Ten Commandments. That's right, the actual Ten Commandments.

"Power stuff, isn't it? It sounds an awful lot like what Darby Adams was attempting to do before he went to be judged by his maker. He fashioned a modern-day calf for us; so we might turn our backs on God and our brothers in the fossil-fuel industry who have provided all the energy we've ever used.

"Let me try to tie the whole story together for you. Then you'll understand my point. You see, at that time, Moses had just led the Jews out of bondage. When you've heard of the Jews wandering in the desert, it referenced this time period. Moses was called by the Lord to come alone to the top of Mount Sinai; to pray and receive the Ten Commandments. Isn't that exciting, everyone?" Gabriel prompted with a smile.

"Now, while Moses was away, the people started to worry what had become of him and who to pray to. Aaron, becoming alarmed by the people, collected all the gold they had and fashioned a golden calf for the people to pray to. Don't you know it, when Moses returned from the Mount and saw the people praying to a calf he actually dropped the tablets the commandments were inscribed on? Moses had to climb all the way back up Sinai once more to receive the commandments again. They didn't have a copy machine in those days," he kidded as the audience giggled and then quieted.

"It was a horrible thing that happened. Aaron admitted what he did. Moses had the calf destroyed and cast into the water. Moses had three thousand men slain by the sons of Levi. Even after that offering and sacrifice, it seemed God had decided to burden them with a plague.

"Such sadness and needless suffering—many theologians consider the golden calf and especially gold to signify idolatry of wealth. Money in and of itself is not evil. However, the love of money is evil.

"Look at what a lack of patience and the idolatry of wealth brought Mr. Darby Adams. It delivered him death. He has been judged. Only our maker can know what his sentence was. We must pray that the Lord was merciful on Darby's soul; as we hope he is with our own.

"Is this what you want with your lives and souls—a living death?" Gabriel charged the audience, as he stared into the camera with conviction.

Cries of "No" emanated from the audience.

"I'm not sure I heard that. Do you want salvation?" he asked the audience with greater intensity.

"Yes!" hollered up to the stage.

"I still can't hear you. Do you want to die in your wealth or live in the Lord?" he petitioned, raising both hands. The audience roared cheers as they jumped to their feet.

"This is a choice you must all make for yourselves and your family. Reject the technology. Look at what it did to its maker. The Kratometric Engine will only bring death. Just take a gander at what it's doing to our marketplace. People are already clamoring for the new owner of Fountain Alternative Energy to produce another million units. People are growing agitated with their utility companies and gas stations for charging money for something they now may have for free. Not thirty days ago, they were pleased as punch to pay their light bill and gas up their cars at the filling station. Now these businesses who've diligently served our interests for years are hucksters in the eyes of the people.

"This engine is the golden calf of our age. It promises and delivers something for nothing. It's going to cause destruction in all our lives if we don't refrain from its use. You must promise, my brothers and sisters, not to accept this technology. God will judge you harshly if you do! For the sake of your souls and your children's, do not be tempted by the engine. God hates the Kratometric Engine.

"Like Moses of old, you must destroy the engine if it falls into your hands." Gabriel then looked off-stage at Taylor and said, "Do we have it? Good, let's take a look. My friends, I want to show you the heart of faith in this video clip. See what some of our Houston brothers and sisters are doing after having received a free engine from Darby Adams. Take a look at Jackson's family here."

The auditorium lights dimmed. On a cinema screen, a man, woman, and two grade-school-aged boys stood in front of their home. A crated box, three feet high, three feet wide and four feet deep set next to them on the driveway.

The father, asked his son, "Jeffrey, what should we do with the misguided man's evil engine?"

"Smash it like Moses!" the little boy cheered.

Jackson turned to his other son and lobbied, "John, do you want to help your brother do God's work?"

John replied, "Yeah!" and ran past the camera's view to return with two steel pipes.

Jackson detached the retaining pins holding the box together. The boys tapped on the wooden crate as their father worked to open it. With one final strap untied, the sides of the box fell to the ground and the top slipped off to one side. Packing material mushroomed to the ground. The engine's two horizontal cylinders, one positioned behind the other, were connected by a transmission module. The generator was mounted at the front of the engine, with the drive component attached behind it. It was gray in color and attached to stainless steel legs. A computer control panel at the back supplied an electrical lead connector. Small pressure gauges lined the exterior of the drive component.

The children began jumping up and down, awaiting their father's permission to begin. Both boys nagged, "Please, can we start? Please, Dad."

"Alright then…But before we begin, John, I want you to tell Pastor Gabriel what this machine really is. Go ahead. It's okay."

John walked up to the camera. He announced in a happy tone, "This is just like the golden cow from the days of Moses. He didn't like the cow because it was bad and made people do bad things. So, he smashed it up and then things were better."

"That's right, John. Now you and your brother go ahead," Jackson urged.

The boys danced about and then began striking the engine. The pipes made loud cracking sounds when impacting the machine's composite casing. Jeffrey struck the panel. It exploded upon impact, sending plastic and glass shards in every direction.

John's pipe made a deeper thud, finally cracking the drive component casing. His brother continued to beat on electrical leads and gauges; popping instruments off their fittings. All the while, the husband and wife approvingly looked on, displaying proud smiles for the camera to capture.

After the boys had destroyed as much of the engine as they could, Jackson asked, "Son, why don't you let your dad take a few swings. Stand back now!" Jackson cautioned as he took the pipe from Jeffery—swinging and grunting with all his strength. The transmission unit began to loosen from its fittings.

Jackson stopped swinging to catch his breath and then asked his sons, "Boys, what've we learned here today? We learned that the Lord does not want us to make an idol of our own power. God wants us to leave the domain of power to him."

The family gathered together as the recording faded out. Auditorium lights brightened from dim. All was quiet.

"Brothers and sisters, what did you think of that? They are a family of God, to be sure. Can you show Him you're hearing my message today? Put your hands together to show God you understand His message."

Charles jumped to his feet as the camera zeroed on him. Tears streamed down his cheeks as he beamed a joyful smile, nodding his head in agreement. The audience followed suit, standing to fill the auditorium with jubilant approval in their claps and whistles.

CHAPTER
XVII
PREMISE

"Ladies and gentlemen, the president pro tempore."

Applause emanated from behind the entryway. Ethan sighed in resignation at the decision that had bothered him since election day; then a strange ease hollowed through him. A nod at the two doormen indicated it was time to enter. Historic, dark-paneled doors swung open. Rushing air blew back against his face and the forced false smile curled; a dictate of senatorial position.

Claps and whistles filled the chamber while Ethan reflected on a conversation had days before. Seneca had been hunched outside near the senatorial offices. Ethan pulled over that morning, leaving his car parked on the street to take a bench seat next to him.

The sun had not yet risen. Pale-blue early winter skies waited for daylight to tuck away distant stars. A light snow-dusting had blanketed and passed through the city in the middle of the night.

"So, are you still of the mind that this cold has nothing on law school?"

"Ha! The numb from this sorry excuse for an early winter storm holds diddly over a first-year law program. Your only purpose in life is simply to survive the amount of reading and memorization required to move on. That's numbing work," Seneca recalled, laughing out loud. "It's good to be a senator isn't it?" he ribbed—pointing to Ethan's car on the street, hazard lights blinking, not being towed away simply because of his title. A police officer happened by on foot, tapped the hood, motioned with his finger toward the traffic, and moved on. "I enjoyed that privilege once."

"What?" Ethan exclaimed in a whisper.

"It's true. I know you had a hard time swallowing all that about law school, given my current state of affairs. But things were not always as they are."

"What happened? How?" Ethan asked—even more stunned than a moment before.

Seneca took a deep breath and exhaled, spewing a steam-plume aloft to part the crisp air. He said, "My name is Barry Hammond, former senator for the state of Indiana. It was my freshman year; and also Hubert Riley's when we first met. From the outset, he and I had different ideas about our country, and conflicting views on an important piece of legislation.

"At the time, Hubert wanted a name for himself; don't see as anything's changed. Hubert got into his mind that he'd impress or intimidate the then old guard by making an example of me. That way the other senators and representatives would fall into line with his future designs. Hubert came to town to dominate—and nothing less would do.

"His plan worked. The short version is that he framed me with a scandal involving prostitution and drugs. Shortly after it all came out, I was impeached and disbarred from practicing law. My political career was destroyed just as it began. I thought my life couldn't get any lower. Then the bottom fell out.

"Hubert didn't simply want to eviscerate my professional life. No, sir. He wanted to punish me for defying his will. The day I left town, he had some thugs stop my car by standing in the middle of the street. After I got out to see what the problem was, they mugged me; took my wallet, money, car, and followed the moving truck out of town. I never discovered what became of my property.

"The police wouldn't help. Every time I tried to file a complaint, they literally threw me out on the street. Not a single government agency would take a meeting. I was shut out of every option in this city, but to walk out on foot. Every attempt I've made since to leave with these two legs has ended in a brutal thrashing. Then I'm returned to town, and dumped on the sidewalk in front of the Hill. The Hill!" he screamed. "So here I sit, on this bench, as a cautionary tale; warning everyone in Washington that Hubert will do anything for power and control."

Ethan didn't think he could be any more shocked that Barry was a former senator until now. He knew, without having any proof, that this man was telling the truth. Now he realized why Hubert's explanation for Barry's access to a private senatorial office garage didn't make sense. Because Ethan could say nothing that would make any difference to Barry, he asked, "So why call yourself Seneca? How's that come about?"

"Why? Hmm. Well, Seneca was an important advisor to Nero. Some would say he was a wise man, although others branded him a hypocrite. In the end, Nero ordered Seneca to commit suicide by poisoning and cutting open his veins. Hubert ensured this would be my nom de guerre; possibly to make a mockery of my short-lived political life, or maybe in hopes that I might choose to finally do myself in."

"You don't plan to give him what he wants, do you?"

Barry chuckled and replied, "No. No. I've wandered throughout DC talking to myself, looking the part of a village fool; all along quietly watching for an opening. Ethan, you and your CMC turned out to be that chance."

"You know I'm not with the CMC anymore."

"But you're for them. And they're for us. Ethan, now that you understand, you can't get lost in the corruption. You must fight it any way possible. America is almost gone now. We can't go back to what we once were or forward in the direction we're going. Knowing what is worth fighting and dying for is to know America. *Silent enim leges inter arma.* In times of war, the law falls silent—not my words, but Cicero's. The Congress is no longer regarding the law or the Constitution as anything other than an ancient meaningless document. They're using our military conflicts and the USA Freedom Act to disregard our citizens' rights and this country's future. Whatever you do, it must be bold; it must be without regard for your future in Washington; and it must be soon. There's very little time left."

Before Barry could say another word Ethan said, "Come with me." Ethan bolted toward his car; Barry trailing. They got in, and quickly sped into traffic. Barry's eyes bulged as his neck swiveled to scrutinize every pedestrian and any vehicle appearing to be government-owned. Ethan's complexion turned red with exhilaration and fear as he mindlessly shuttled Barry away. *I don't know what I'm doing.* Seneca's body odor was immediately obvious to them both—knowing the indignity, Ethan did his best to ignore it.

On their way, distance and passing street intersections calmed Ethan. *We made it.* In the rearview mirror, he caught a glimpse of a black sedan two cars behind as it swerved into traffic; Ethan's throat swelled and his heart raced. Attempting to dismiss it and calm down, Ethan cleared his throat.

Barry interrupted the silence in resignation. "They're never going to let me go."

"What are you talking about?" Ethan dissembled, his eyes catching another similar black sedan in a door mirror emerging from a side street. "Alright, Barry, where can we go? There's gotta be a way outta here."

Tears began to fall from Barry's cheeks. He sobbed, "They'll set up a roadblock just outside the city limits if you stay on this road—can't beat the satellite. They're everywhere."

Ethan pounded his fists on the steering wheel. "This can't be real! This is not happening!" His mind reeled, needing a solution that wouldn't come forth. "No!"

Ethan suddenly jerked the car onto an adjoining intersection; heading west. Tires screamed from his pursuers; one car overshooting the turn and going on. The second followed; but further behind, allowing other cars to fill the open street space. "We've got to shake this guy."

Closing on traffic ahead at a stoplight, there was nowhere to go but straight. To Ethan's right, an alleyway provided a chance. He took it; speeding past buildings close on either side. His tagalong had yet to make the turn. Another quick right into a parking garage as the entry door began to lower, and then straight, right, straight, right, an open parking stall, and stop; both men were thrown forward into the dash after Ethan stamped onto the brake pedal.

They gasped, trying to catch their breath. There was only sucking air and the sound of the engine. After a still minute and huffing for breath, Ethan turned off the ignition.

They looked to each other, anticipation gnawing at their guts. "I think we did it," Ethan ventured.

"Could be waiting out there."

"I don't think so. He didn't make the turn before we ducked in here. We may be in the clear."

"They're still lookin'."

"But not here. We'll wait 'em out and move later." Ethan's eyes began searching back and forth. He grabbed his mobile phone off the floor and started tapping the screen; muttering to himself, "Not fast enough. They got that covered; that's their weakness." Ethan fiddled some more on his phone. Barry watched.

"Yep, that's it. They'd never see it." Tap, tap on the phone and his head raised in triumph. "You're going to take the slow train home. Well, bus." Ethan smiled and turned his screen towards Barry.

"They'll never fall for it."

"They have to; there's too much ground to cover. When a superior force moves swiftly to invade, lacking the ability to retreat, one must become an irregular fighter and move slowly, in disguise, into safer territory. You'll win by evading and crawling your way out."

Barry, filled with doubt, reclined without saying another word. Ethan, uncertain, also rested his eyes.

After a few moments of awkward silence, Ethan offered, "I was compromised. I didn't break the law; but I sure as hell bent it to the point of distress. I used my influence to encourage others to meet my agenda. I just wanted to get something, anything meaningful accomplished. The more authority I was given, the harder it was to keep my position under control without swaying to meet the needs of others. My committee members were all too willing to be a part of it; it's what they knew and made them feel safe around me. I know it now. I was willing to allow a political opponent to believe they could influence my decisions if they only did my bidding. I corrupted myself; conveniently justifying that it was all in the name of doing good for the people. What a wretchedly overinflated ego. I became what I reviled."

Barry patiently considered Ethan's words and simply offered, "But you didn't break the law—and that's what still makes your soul redeemable. Politics is a messy business. It's not for the pure of heart. The razor-thin line between right and wrong is also as grey as the whitest white and the darkest black. You didn't break the law. For the Bone Yard that's an accomplishment. So, with full knowledge of this, what are you going to do about it?"

"Fight!"

Hours later, after dark, they motored their way to the closest bus station. Barry watched Ethan leave the sanctuary of his car to cross the parking lot. At the purchase window, Ethan transacted while Barry scanned for Hubert's men—heart pounding in his throat— knowing at any moment he would be yanked from his seat and beaten without mercy. An audible but contained high-pitched shriek gurgled from his mouth.

It was done. Ethan made his way back, ticket in hand, continually panning the surroundings for anyone suspicious.

The door opened and the car sank as Ethan sat down. Barry was still mesmerized with fear. "Barry…Senator Hammond, I know this must be hard. But you can't stay here any longer. What more can I do to help?"

Barry moved to meet Ethan's eyes. "You can be a senator. Keep your oath to me, the people, and most importantly, to yourself. Thrash them; do your worst. I've got nothing left; I just want to disappear knowing someone will be tending this rotten place."

Nothing else was said between them. They waited, staring ahead, living in their own thoughts. After what seemed an eternity, the nine o'clock bus arrived. Without a word they got out of the car, made their way over to the loading station and faced each other to shake hands. Barry's eyes were dull and lifeless. The spark of joy that had been present in their discussions was gone. A fatigue had taken hold and now all he wanted was to shut out the world.

Barry turned away and hobbled to the bus's open doors. Ethan witnessed lifelessness ambulate; and his hope withered. *Maybe*

Hubert won after all. Barry climbed aboard, settled in next to a window, and zeroed in on Ethan. As the bus departed, Ethan stared back—aching inside. The doors closed and the bus lurched forward towards the exit. Just before Barry disappeared out of sight, he held aloft a shuddering clenched fist to the window.

Seneca's story would forever be etched into Ethan, like a rut dredged over the surface of his heart. Ethan began to think about what he might do—knowing it was radical, impulsive, and right—Barry would be proud to call Ethan by his title.

Applause continued as Ethan walked the aisle crowded by senators and representatives outwardly bearing contrived approval while hiding disdain and doubt. He shook the hands of those who made working in Washington difficult. At last he reached the platform and felt the relief of space; he placed his hands on the podium for support. Vice President Fulton and Speaker of the House Delilah Talbot were seated directly behind him, facing the audience, with President Anderson stationed to the right of the Vice President.

Cameramen at the back of the chamber communicated through headsets with their network control rooms, taking cues and repeatedly nodding. One smile from Ethan and a raise of his hand created one last rumble of cheers and applause before diminishing into silence.

"Fellow congressmen and congresswomen, thank you for attending this emergency joint session of Congress. It is appropriate that I should recognize Vice President Fulton and Speaker Talbot for successfully assembling this body on such short notice. Much needs to be discussed and the time for waiting is at an end.

"Before we begin I'd like to absolve the President, Vice President and Speaker for any political fallout that may come as a result of this evening's proceedings. I explained my concerns in general to them all, but did not specifically address what would be discussed. My hope is that you, the governing body of the United States, deliberate wisely over what is said with an open mind.

"The reason for this meeting is quite simple: Our country's in trouble. America's economy is supported by an open market and a democratically elected republic. We are a magnificent nation;

but that grandeur comes with an affliction—hubris. Arrogance has blinded our people to what made us great, while unchecked greed and corruption of power flourishes.

"That's an awesome thought when considered. This culture is one of fiercely independent resolve, born of forefathers who would not stand for taxation without representation. We Americans sacrifice a small portion of what's held most dear to be fairly and prudently ruled over. That's about as much as the US psyche may accept in the dominion of another over their sovereignty. And we are failing our citizenry with every corrupt agreement forged in obscurity to favor the moneyed few over the remainder making their way through this social experiment called the United States of America.

"America is raising its voice again—not because of the tyranny existing outside our borders, but in defiance of the corruption existing within them. We cannot continue down this path of two-sided government: One rule of law for the commoner and one for the wealthy elite. Evolution and revolution are born of necessity and America is in dire need of change. So with my concerns raised for your consideration, let's ponder the most egregious tonight to drive home this point.

"It's important to make clear, before beginning, that I do not have an axe to grind. The Senate, in its wisdom, has violated the United States Constitution through the judicial branch of government to quash the civil liberties of the Citizens' Mandamus Council by court order, disallowing the organization, its officers, and employees from making grievances known by means of the United States Justice System."

Many in the audience began to speak under their breath as Ethan made this assertion. Their disapproving and angry faces demonstrated displeasure in publicly discussing what everyone in Washington knew to be true. Nothing could be offered to defend the practice; and so it had never been openly addressed.

"Countless of the socially conscientious have felt disenfranchised the entirety of their lives in America. Feeling that, with so much corruption centralized in the legislative and judicial branches, there's nowhere for a law-abiding citizen to turn; that jail may be the only place to find the company of honest and decent human beings. The injustice perpetrated on a seemingly powerless electorate would explain why large numbers of our population can commiserate with this sentiment. Unjust laws favoring business over people; capricious taxation as mismanagement of public monies continues unabated; and the unwillingness of elected officials to represent its citizens' interests would all appear to be just cause for a lack of faith in this country's leadership or future. Ignoring one's conscience destroys the self. And yet, attempting to force change in the current administration also yields the same results.

"This Congress cannot deny, even a day longer, by court order the Citizens' Mandamus Council, its officers, and employees their civil right to seek redress with the state. I would like to call on my fellow senators to put this to an immediate roll call vote. We must do this or America will cease to be a nation of laws. I, therefore, make a motion to dismiss this court order that handcuffs the CMC."

"I second the motion!" Senator Placher Lathrop shouted.

"Will you please stand, be recognized, and answer Yea or Nay to the question: Should the Senate make a motion in the District Court of Washington DC to dismiss the lawsuit in process and request the cease and desist order be rescinded? On the issue of the dismissing the court order curtailing the Citizens' Mandamus Council's business activities, the clerk will call the roll."

The cameras pulled back to bring the full Senate into view. Mindful that scores of millions of Americans were watching the broadcast, given Ethan's words, one by one every other senator begrudgingly voted Yea; knowing what it meant for them. Representatives from the House, seated across the aisle, silently witnessed this in pity and awe, all secretly relieved they themselves had not been forced to capitulate under an unforgiving public eye.

After the voting ended, Ethan enthused, "Good. It's near unanimous. Secretary of the Senate, please note for the record ninety-six votes for Yea and four votes Nay on the matter regarding the Citizens' Mandamus Council. Please see that the proper motions are filed with the District Court Monday morning.”

Silence screamed during a brief pause. “Since we’re here, let’s continue discussing the most pressing problems plaguing our government. We are the government. This is our pestilence. Are we the cause, or did this body merely idly sit by and allow it to happen? Hard to determine, in my view, but I would venture it’s a bit of both.

“Let’s start with the most obvious problem: this dreadful class war we’re in. You in the Congress might say, ‘But we didn’t cause the rift. Why would you insinuate such a thing?’ Every conflict has a cause. This one screws the rube to the wall; the great wealth transfer from lower castes to those on high. But, why? There’s plenty of oil, natural gas, and coal available in the foreseeable future. Oh, it’ll run out eventually, but not in the next ten years. Without a foreseeable shortfall in supplies, why the sudden cost run-up?

“Could it be that the commodities traders wanted to artificially inflate market pricing by speculation in the futures markets; thereby influencing shareholders’ perceptions of market conditions? Could it be that major oil, gas, and coal producing companies realize alternative energies will one day, in the not-so-distant future, replace their energy products? Might it even be the political push and pull on this body itself by those same energy companies and traders; or even going to war with other foreign oil-producing nations in a ploy to either increase or decrease the cost of imported energy, depending on who is lining the politicians’ pockets and in which direction they wish the market to move? Could all of this simply be greed so engorged by its own appetite that everything connected with it is devoured?

“While on the subject of war, I’d like to remind all of you that we are currently in two armed conflicts, and have been for years—the longest we’ve been at war since our founding. We only know that our military will be there indefinitely, obviously so, and yet it is easy to forget, given the battles and destruction are waged on the other side of the planet.

“And what of the 2015 USA Freedom Act? This bill was ratified before entering the first war we’re still fighting; with no end in sight, no way to win, and no way out. This Freedom Act, or should it be edict, criminalizes anyone the authorities see fit to brand a terrorist; non-American and American alike. I ask you: Is this the kind of justice one would expect from a government purporting to preside over a country of laws? Certain lawmakers in this chamber have used the military conflicts we're waging to make war on our US citizens' civil liberties.

"If these conflicts go on long enough, our children will have been born into, and grow up in an America where police could enter their home without a warrant at any time of the night. These young people would grow up never knowing the difference between freedom from tyranny and the version we're selling them. The USA Freedom Act reduces America to a despotic state; and does so under the false promise of protection during a time of war.

"Many of you may argue that I am ranting, and that this is some grand exaggeration. Is it? You might say that if the people cannot trust their elected officials, then they can be voted out of office. How?

"We own the electoral process. The large corporations pay to put us in office, and we do them favors. It takes millions to make it happen. In the face of vast wealth, how can an average citizen ever be heard?

"The large corporations, and their armies of lobbyists, are the voices harkening to our Congress. Their bribes, in the form of campaign contributions, drown out the cries of the people from states you represent. How can you expect to hear anything with the ringing of money in your ears?

"Money seems to be our biggest problem in Washington DC. We can't seem to hold on to it for very long. I have a question for all of you: Have you ever known a tax raised for a particular purpose or program, limited to a given number of years, ever go away?"

The audience laughed, knowing it was one of the oldest jokes in town.

"They never go away. The tax just continues to magically renew and the government grows to accommodate the new cash coming in, necessitating more taxes to be raised later. Where is this money going? I've looked at the budget before and I still can't understand how it works. If I ran my newspaper business like the budget office handles our money, then I would've been out of business.

"If this is too difficult a subject for you, my constituency, to discuss, then what about the simple withholding tax taken from each wage earner every pay period. Oh, it makes perfect sense to do so. Only what's troubling to me is the interest-free loan the treasury takes out from the American taxpayers when they are issued their refund check every spring. That's right. We the government withhold too much of our citizen's money for up to a year and then return it without interest. Does this strike any of you here as curious?

"These problems are just scant examples of the bureaucratic mountain—we know all about it. We created it. But now our system of governing is failing its people at every turn. So what are we going to do about it?

"I can see, looking out into the ocean of faces, that you, my fellow senators and representatives, are put out with me. I see it and understand. I've used some terrible examples here and made you complicit.

"I'd like to take a look at our problems from a perspective that doesn't involve blaming you for a moment; to gain some insight and possible agreement. Technology is the simplest example to drive home my point. We live in an age of wonderful advance, much of which has only been with us a few years. It truly is amazing that in the pockets of every politician in this room is a tiny communication device called a smart mobile phone.

"The portable computer is another marvelous illustration of technology turning one skillful person into forty: word processing, calculations, management, delegation, information storage, communication, shopping, and many other tasks once employing a multitude of people—all now in the hands of an individual. When this kind of efficiency is applied to an industry, its true marvel shines; eliminating hundreds of workers per task to replace them with one tiny device. Profitability and prosperity pass into the hands of a few at the top, leaving those at the bottom even more powerless, and unemployed to boot. Those same computers connected to the internet magnify this effect a thousandfold.

"This would seem a grand exaggeration if it were not true. Look at what's become of the automobile, print media, retail, and manufacturing jobs of all kinds in this country. They've been eliminated by a motherboard, or have been sold off to foreign countries with inexpensive labor. In either case, a great many jobs are gone and not returning.

"These people shouldn't worry, right? They can simply learn modern skills and acquire newer jobs. But ingenuity has already done away with those positions too, rendered obsolete before the digital ink has dried penning the position's description. Professions are now eliminated faster than can or will be replaced. All this begs the question: What good has come? Inherent obsolescence of the carbon kind within the job market has arrived!

"I would by no means advocate turning about; marching backwards into history and abandoning human achievement. But what must we do? How shall we do it? Our system of governing will one day require all people's money to afford every social program—a tax-base bonfire—the average American citizen financially unviable to their government.

"How do we redirect a system of governing rooted in the notion of abdicated authority? How do we foster an environment where it's impossible to cheat? How do we create a country where politician and citizen alike assume a more balanced approach to life? Finally, how do we put to rest the balance between power and accountability?

"Trust; I can just hear the word sold to the people. We politicians will simply need to earn back the people's trust. It's laughable when I think about trust and politics in the same context. I know it's obvious to you too. Trust shouldn't be a five-letter word in the English language; it oughta be four—dirty, repugnant, and offensive to all. Citations should be issued for its use in civil society.

"When applied to government, trust ought never be circulated. In fact it's inherent to most every American not to trust the government. I dare say the Freedom Act was foisted upon the American people for that very reason—to force the lie of trust onto its citizens. If a citizen fails to blindly go along with the government's plans for their money, property and lives, then they're branded terrorists, shackled, and hauled off to jail at the whim of the politician.

"No, ladies and gentlemen, trust should not be allowed in making reference to any form of governance. Accountability…now there's a notion that can sink its teeth into a politician's backside. Accountability and governmental power are opposing weights of a scale, one balancing the other. In fact, all power, in a state of nature, is brought to heel by force accounting to form.

"This is the next step for America to take in ruling over its people. It must be so. There's nowhere else for the United States to go. A little clarity might help simplify what I am saying. If everyone here would look around this chamber, you'd find the most politically positioned people in the United States. Please, why don't you do this for me and for yourselves?"

The senators and representatives turned about, slowly at first, then more quickly they began to rise and shake hands with the people nearby. A low hum of soft voices filled the chamber with conversation. All the while cameras panned through Congress, capturing live video of seemingly friendly political leaders sharing goodwill.

Ethan turned around to see Speaker Talbot scowling, while Vice President Fulton shook his head from side to side in disapproval. Ethan walked over to the President and extended his hand. President Anderson grabbed it and smiled, attempting to contain his laughter.

"I knew you were destined for politics that day we met for lunch. I just didn't guess it'd be such a short career. You sure this is the way you wanna go out?" Byron asked with a jovial tone.

"Wouldn't have it any other way, Mr. President—hope I haven't offended you."

"Not at all—you just like to call a horse a horse. Nothin' wrong with that. It doesn't matter much either way. They hired me back for another four years. I won't be much use after that. You go on and finish sayin' what you came here to say."

"My thanks, Mr. President," Ethan offered, and returned to his podium, nodding at the Speaker's scowling mug.

"Please retake your seats. I was right, wasn't I? There are a lot of powerful people in this room: four hundred thirty-five from the House of Representatives, one hundred senators, one President and one Vice President. That's five hundred thirty-seven American citizens from a population of over three hundred thirty million; an awesome ratio when you think about it. For every six hundred fourteen thousand five hundred twenty-five US citizens, there's one of us—making our position pretty unique. All that authority in the hands of one person calling the shots for those they represent. It seems an imbalanced way to fairly distribute power, don't you think? You have the ability to influence a great many in a way they cannot influence you.

"This form of governance would work well if it were not for corruption. So what can we do with this, knowing it's true? Use it to accommodate the change that's coming; evolution or revolution. In plain terms, power must be redistributed or we'll be destroyed by the status quo.

"David Samuel's much maligned philosophy, at the very least, provides another choice. His inverted pyramid demonstrates that the higher one goes in this power paradigm the more people one would find instead of fewer, making it easier to hold leadership responsible. Corruption cannot exist without a majority conspiracy, which then ceases to be corruption, but instead is political will. That's the strength of this power shift.

"Empowering more people ensures a balance between power and position. Our society finds its next step to take and saves us from ourselves. It also works in any society because it's not a form of government. It's a state of being—"

"Communist!" a man's voice antagonized from the Senate side.

Ethan urgently scoured the crowd, attempting to identify the disrupter. Stacked rows of stone-faced heads, perched atop identical suit-and-tie ensembles gawked back. "I'm not a communist! You don't work! You don't eat! Is that enough down-home, bootstrap, Old-Testament Americana for you? For the love of..." Ethan stalled, bestowing his own lost look towards the statues before him. One hand grappled the podium for stability and the other covered his mouth. And then, in defeated conciliation, he went on.

"You know," he started, and then turned a frown into a propped smile, "I prepared a fine speech, intended to inspire change; appealing to your finer natures—maybe even taking positive steps on behalf of your people. Heck of a salesman, eh? You gotta sell yourself first."

He squeezed out a tighter smile and shook his head back and forth. "My intention is not to uproot capitalism, but to unseat monopoly. This republic was well-conceived; I have no wish for it to be an oligarchy."

He turned down to the notes on his cell phone, and then slapped the screen. "What are we doing here? What is this? You know, let's just get at it!" He snapped his head up with renewed vigor.

"Yes! Let's talk turkey—love that euphemism, don't you? You want their money, don't you? You want their blind obedience too! It's what you want. Why not admit it? There's nothing they can do about it, right?"

Audience faces froze and eyes widened, darting around, trying not to meet Ethan's gaze. Silence banged like a noisy gong.

"Not just you, but your corporate buddies too. Have you ever noticed that, just as society gets a break, and weeds out an unnecessary expense, those same companies find new ways to separate more money from the consumer? They call it fees; we call it taxes. Great, huh?

"Take for instance the television cable companies, who also happen to be the local internet providers. Once again, we're debating whether or not to allow the internet providers to allow more or less speed and amount of access; charging according to usage volume they currently enjoy at one low price. They claim it's because the amount of data bandwidth required is much higher now, burdening their companies' infrastructure. At the same time, the individual consumer is using far less cable TV in deference to the limitless internet choices available; this is not under control of the internet service providers. So, lacking the ability to monopolize the entertainment sector any longer, they're seeking to control the accessibility high ground; getting their loot by hook or by crook.

"Many of you out there support this move. It clearly favors the very few internet servicers while shorting our citizens. They claim it's all about infrastructure. Some of that infrastructure is ours! Arpanet was paid for by our citizens' taxes decades ago. ISPs just monetized it—fine—but you can't have all our blood! Another example of private investment improving the lives of its users! They've made and shined their pretty penny. But it's far beyond profit now; it's control of information flow, the ability to starve out a well-informed electorate. It's gone too far!

"I don't know what to say. We're screwed! What are we going to do? Do you know? Do you even give a damn! How about that? What do any of you think we should do?"

Ethan donned a bewildered face, and began pacing back and forth, waiting for a response. Shocked camera operators were glued to their view-screens, capturing the emotional meltdown. Not one suggestion rose from below.

Ethan halted his wandering behind the lectern and peered ahead. "Let's do this; right now! I'm gonna spitball here. Why not? No one else's got any ideas, so I'll just throw something up there—can't be any worse than this. And if you come up with something better, I'm all ears.

"The wealth disparagement has to stop. You're either rich or poor now; there's no in-between left. It's no longer about whether a person will work, educate, or invest in their life. Technology has destroyed more opportunity than it's created; ushering lightning-fast efficiencies while destroying the need for human intervention. A wealth network distribution model might be one way to go, based on individual effort: no work, no wealth. Top-tier wealth only allowed to accumulate so far and then no more. Any cheating of the system would result in sacrificing everything; being forced to start again at the bottom. I have no idea how much is too much; but a person who commands more than the state where they reside might just have a bit too much on their hands. I don't know; just a thought.

"Wow! Did you feel that? It was a solution! Maybe it was good. Maybe it won't work, but at least it's movement. Let's keep going! In a newer-fangled government model, the more stuff one has, the less political power they may wield, because with much wealth comes greater choice. Why would anyone need political power with the ability to choose anything except to wield it over others; to manipulate for their own selfish ends. No good comes from this. Either great wealth or great political power—one can't have both— let's keep the republic and ditch the Good Ole Boys!"

"Since money's such a hot topic, let's go with it a little longer. For the record, I'm a big fan of an open-market economy. In general, it's healthy, self-correcting, and provides unlimited opportunity. All one needs to do is participate. A win or loss is based upon the worth of the product or service offered. What we're doing isn't that— we're not an open market. We're a monopoly dressed up like a fair market—the fortune cookie that pops out the same message: 'Sages say, don't play a game that can't be won.'

"How could I make such a statement? Because we're failing, and miserably, from the big fat lie floating all around. Our market model is a failure—embrace that fact like a lecherous, hairy uncle that hugs on you every Christmas…creepy and leaves the kids feeling dirty. Not just that, but the fiat required to participate in this charade is a lie—a concept at best, with no value. And the final insult to keep folks from questioning why our currency isn't worth the cloth it's printed on is the propagated fear; worth based upon the scarcity principle that some must be poor for some to be rich; to encourage hyper-productivity; to keep us distracted while at each other's throats—further cementing the 'us versus them' social policy. My suggestion is not utopia; but rather utility. A fair exchange should be considered the highest good, equal for equal. The powerful lose their leverage over everyone else, and everyone else does more for themselves, positively contributing to humanity's condition.

"If you had to choose a group that'd have a tougher time giving up what they've got right now, which would struggle more: the rich and their immutable towers of prestige and influence, or the poor and their seeming lack of nearly everything? I'm thinking the hobnobs would suffer most, and fight harder to keep what they possess—and dare I say might even enable those in lack to stay put where they are, making it near impossible to affect change. Does this sound at all familiar?

"Stalwart open-market economists would argue that the boom-bust nature of our policy destroys the weaker players, allowing the truly strong to survive; and this might be so in a state of nature. But in a state of nature there's no skullduggery, only brute force and truth. In our economy, the weak and corrupt can and do thrive by contaminating and manipulating the monetary structure. In our system good and strong potential are only allowed to grow but so big, and then are cut down by the self-created disease of recession, allowing those who in a state of nature would have died off for lack of true strength to lead the pack. No, our way is not self-correcting or self-cleansing. It's rotten. It's broken. Winner-take-all capitalism destroys the loser, and then soon after takes the winner as well.

"And before anyone says 'disruptive technologies', can we put this false narrative to rest? Sounds fantastic though, doesn't it?…For a mouthy crowd, you sure are quiet. No comments? Fine—this idea alludes to the promise of wondrous future innovations that will make our lives even better. While specious, it harkens to humanity's love of fairy-dust. All the while, profitability and distribution of wealth among many market players is also disrupted, concentrating the majority of market gains into the hands of the few controlling the economic game. Local wages and economies are cleared out to make way for the big-shots; who, in turn, employ fewer and fewer higher wage positions."

Ethan's shoulders suddenly sank; he felt throttled and lacking in anything good to say. The crowd abruptly became riled with a sense of confusion and anger. Non-descriptive shouts erupted. The disturbance quickly dissipated, and once again all eyes lay upon Ethan.

"Our power, as members of Congress, has been granted by the only source that can issue it: the American people. This power was conferred with the commission to act in the best interests of those we represent. Any other use of this facility is a debasement of authority; a corruption. We have abused a sacred pact born of the sacrifice of a people's abdicated free will. We have betrayed this gift, and have collectively destroyed a solemn commitment.

"Power no longer lives here. A thing cannot be alive and yet dead. We are corpses where once stood the mighty. We, the United States Congress, are dead.

"I'm leaving this place and returning to the Citizens' Mandamus Council, if they'll have me; an institution which does not require a solitary soul to sacrifice their freedom for my leadership. My actions on their behalf are either good or bad, based only on their intention and outcome.

"I therefore resign from the United States Senate, a body that is no longer politic but incorporeal. This action I deem immediate and a final epitaph to my public service. To you all, I say, rest in peace."

A silence, like death, seized the assembly as Ethan stepped down from the podium. He turned to walk past the President. Byron winked and patted Ethan's back as he made his way past and down the aisle. No other congratulations, farewells or smiles were exchanged. Not a single representative raised their eyes to meet Ethan's. As he exited, the chamber doors slammed shut, as if they were sealing in a tomb for lost souls.

A Saturday afternoon CMC rally at the Phillips Stock Exchange front steps was about to start, a day past David's deadline. The thirty days had rapidly passed. His hopes dashed, David secretly prayed for a last-minute stay from the dogs he was about to unleash. Ethan's emergency congressional session speech, while eloquent, did nothing to stem Beltway corruption.

More disturbing still was David's two-sided Washington enmity. Though he had never supported Ethan taking up with DC politics, he knew his former colleague was the only politician that could make a difference. David harbored no doubt that what he was about to do was right. The real internal struggle was due to the economic discomfort endured during the recent recession; it would be small in comparison with how difficult times might become once the Worth entered circulation.

David quietly sat atop a platform erected before the sidewalk in front of the Phillips Stock Exchange. Thousands of onlookers, supporters, and protesters moved below in a mass of low, humming conversation—all waiting for David's speech to begin.

As David took in the spectacle, all that mattered to him spun through his mind: the people before him, and their reasons for attending; his intentions in starting the Citizens' Mandamus Council years before; and the challenge of taking on a worthy cause. It all made sense now. Suddenly something arrested his musing—a misplaced stranger with a flowered lapel, positioned across the street to observe the crowd without participating in it. He didn't belong there. Leaning against the building, he just stared in David's direction. The crowd made sense. The electricity in the moment made sense. The man did not make sense.

Police barricaded both street corners, blocking traffic so that people could fill the roadway to listen. Occasional fights broke out between those of rival political views. Officers quickly arrested the unruly, maintaining a civil assembly. Generally, the crowd was eager to hear what the man who forced the hand of Congress had to say.

Sasha continued running on and off stage, ensuring the sound system was functioning properly and that they were on schedule to address the attendees at noon. Cameramen from every network and internet news group wiggled their way through the crowd to set up equipment at the best vantage points. Cameras clicked as David stoically sat in his chair, awaiting the cue.

Ethan had flown into New York early that morning after clearing his senatorial office of personal belongings. Hoofing it up the subway exit steps near the Phillips Stock Exchange, he hurried along, eager to hear David orate. Ethan smiled as he approached the swarming crowd, reminded of his time behind the microphone.

People enveloped Ethan as he made his way through the congestion to be near the platform. Halfway to a good spot, a stranger recognized him, calling out, "Ethan Scott," and began clapping. Others looked towards the sound, also recognized Ethan, and joined in the praise. As Ethan continued to close on the platform the vast majority became aware of his presence and eagerly applauded.

David noticed the crowd's applause and traced its attention back to a man moving through the throng below. He finally recognized the top of Ethan's head and broke out in laughter—standing to join the clapping for his friend. When Ethan finally reached a place near the platform, he looked up at David, smiling back at him in gratitude for the acknowledgement. After a moment, Ethan raised clasped hands in thanks to the crowd and then motioned toward David. People began clapping even louder.

Waiting momentarily to see if the throng would quiet on their own, because it was not yet time to speak, David stepped up to the podium and fluttered his hands up and down for the crowd to calm down.

"Thank you for your gracious welcome, and for attending. We're a bit early, but that's alright. I don't think there would be any harm in an early start. Though all of you do realize this was only meant to be a press event," he joked, and the crowd reciprocated with laughter.

"If you promise to behave, I don't think the networks mind your company," David further humored as he gestured to network personnel feverishly completing last-minute equipment checks.

David peered at Sasha off-stage. She turned to her producer contacts for a decision. All nodded to Sasha; she did the same towards David.

"There are so many dire circumstances having brought our country to this place that I hardly know where to begin. So let us start here: We must stand up to a government no longer listening to its people— we've ceased to be a republic, and now effectively engender an oligarchy—rule of the many by a few.

"Our warning was not heeded. We offered the government a month to take definite steps towards stemming the tide of corruption. Nothing! For this the Citizens' Mandamus Council is left with no choice but to issue the Worth.

"Now, as many of you know, last night the Senate voted, before a joint session of Congress, to reinstate the CMC's constitutional rights—quite big of them to give back what the Constitution already provides. I say this facetiously, knowing that had that vote not broadcast live, the results would likely have been different. Still, I give the Senate credit for doing what's right; even under protest." Light laughter momentarily choired through the gathering.

"Aside from that half-hearted gesture, nothing's changed. Not one triangular bribe has been undone between K Street, their corporate masters, and the politicians. Not one biased and ineffective piece of legislation has been repealed. There hasn't even been an apology to the American people for the despicable job rendered in the name of public service. No, my friends, nothing has changed, and nothing will until we act.

"It's become glaringly evident that the steps we've prepared for over the last four weeks must be taken. They're drastic to be sure; however, we're left with no choice. The architect of the present state of affairs, the United States Congress, clearly is unable or unwilling to represent its people. We therefore march onward in the belief that a great difference can still be made for the better.

"Initial note issuance, valued at over one trillion, in denominations of one, five, ten, twenty, fifty and one hundred will go forward. Exchanging the US dollar on a one for one basis from our nine reserves throughout the United States shall commence next week. National, state, and local banks have agreed to carry the Worth. As the dual economy presses downward on the dollar's perceived value, the Worth exchange rate will increase the number of dollars it takes to reach parity.

"I'm not suggesting that Americans trade all of their dollar currency for the Worth. However, dependent upon how the overall market accepts the new note of value, the dollar could lose considerable exchange rate in the near future. Our goal is not to diminish Americans' wealth. We simply wish to devalue Congress's significance to a point where their stranglehold on our freedoms, laws, and lives is eliminated.

"Be assured, a number of American retailers have already agreed to accept and exchange the Worth. Buyers General, our nation's largest discount retailer of goods, sundries, groceries, and gasoline, with over five thousand national locations and eight thousand locations worldwide, has agreed to begin accepting the Worth Monday morning."

Abigail stood next to her camera crew near the front of the crowd, opposite Ethan's position—neither knowing the other was there. Thrilled and disturbed by David's words, Abigail checked with her cameraman, "You getting all this?"

"Loud and clear," the cameraman replied.

The swelling swarm suddenly roared with jubilation and clapped as David paused, allowing the reaction to peak and recede. He then said, "With many challenging days ahead for us all, I would like to take in this calm moment before the storm to thank a former employee of the Citizens' Mandamus Council, Mr. Ethan Scott.

"Ethan, would you come up here for the public to recognize you?"

Ethan smiled and waved at David; mouthing the words, "No, thank you."

David insisted, "Ethan, please join me. People need to see you."

Once more, Ethan smiled and waved back. Suddenly, an enthused flock swept Ethan off his feet and ferried him over to the stage. Six strong men carried him atop their shoulders, traversing the platform stairs and setting him down in front of David.

Ethan laughed the entire way up the staircase. He shook their hands and the six filed off as David and Ethan stood before a mass of exhilarated citizens.

Ethan waved to the people. They waved and screamed in return. Applause, whistles, and smiling faces washed over Ethan. David handed him the microphone and stepped away—applauding and gesturing for the crowd to continue their praise.

"Thank you," Ethan offered humbly, touched by their well-wishes and astounded by the imparted sentiment. It should be the CMC's moment—he felt ashamed, as if he were stealing David's recognition. While Ethan faced the crowd, David joined the executive board, circled at rear center-stage; facing inward so that no one outside could hear. Heads nodded, and then they took up their places; standing shoulder to shoulder behind Ethan.

The crowd stilled; sensing something was about to happen as a line formed before them. Ethan turned around to see his old friends standing together. David stepped next to Ethan and was handed the microphone. Ethan moved off to the side, yielding center-stage to David.

"The executive board of the Citizens' Mandamus Council has unanimously decided that I must step down as president."

Ethan looked to David in shock. People shouted: "No" and "Don't leave!" David let the anxiety momentarily build before speaking again. "I've been authorized to offer this job to former senator Ethan Scott."

The crowd exploded again—cheers, applause, and even laughter rose from an undulating human sea. "Yes, yes, yes," was chanted from below as Ethan looked to his colleagues with gratitude.

Ethan then paraded from one end of the row to the other, making eye contact and shaking each person's hand. He was touched—fighting back the emotion welling in his chest. When he reached to shake Emily Watson's hand, she leaned in close to his ear and said, "Ethan, we're so proud of you. Say yes."

In that moment, joy, camaraderie, and surrogate family stole away Ethan's composure, and tears poured down his cheeks. Friends and complete strangers overwhelmed him. As it unfolded, David and the board stepped down from the platform, leaving a now openly weeping Ethan to face the crowd. Many below responded in kind. Abigail found herself giving way to a teardrop—ceasing to be a reporter for a moment and joining the crowd's love for this man who had spoken up for them the night before. What Abigail felt for Ethan was much more than she dared to admit to herself.

For as long as could be remembered, Ethan had wanted nothing more than to make a positive difference; to matter in a deep meaningful way—a final acceptance of the self as one who lived up to their own highest held standards of excellence. It was here, in this place, at this time, that his wish had been granted.

After emotions had moderated and the crowd quieted, Ethan offered, "I accept under one condition. David must keep his position as CEO."

Applause followed as Ethan smiled. He then motioned with his hand for David to rejoin him. David made his way back up the stairs. Ethan turned off the microphone to speak privately as David approached. They warmly shook hands.

"David, I wanna know one thing."

"What's that, ya commie?"

Ethan looked out into the gathering and then back to David. "Funny. Everything you've done: Was it worth it?"

David grinned in silence. Ethan stepped away to make David the center of attention, and descended the stairs off the stage.

Alone and after a brief pause, David spoke into the microphone, "I accept your offer, Mr. President."

The crowd applauded; David became lost in the clapping. Their faces blurred into a colored collage. *Yes, it was worth it*—he was certain now that his twenty years had not been wasted. They were validated then and there, and this moment would sustain him in the darker days to come.

Off-stage, David was immediately surrounded by those wanting an autograph—public speaking was always so thrilling, but he never cared to be besieged by strangers. Ethan slipped into the crowd, making his way through to the perimeter. As he passed a cluster of news crews, he saw a familiar face.

"Abbey, I didn't know you were here—I should've expected you. It's good to see you," he anxiously expressed.

"I see your face is healing," Abigail kidded.

"I'll be glad when the scratches disappear. I'm continually bugged about it. I blame it on the cat."

"I'd say someone with catlike reflexes put their paws on you."

"Okay, stop, or this'll go on for hours."

"I'll let it go for the sake of positive relations with the CMC president."

"Thanks."

"In the spirit of good communication with the press, could I get a few moments of your time and maybe David's for a quick interview?"

"I wouldn't mind. But, if I know David, he'll want to get back to the office."

"It'd only take five minutes."

"We would need to get across town to your studio."

"We could do it here. I have a place just around the corner where we could sit down. It would really mean a lot to me."

"Alright—let me grab David."

"Thanks, Ethan," Abigail gratefully replied. She turned to her producer, Alex, and instructed, "Go around the corner on the right to the men's clothier. It's the second shop down. The owner's name is Mort. Tell him I sent you; and that we need his place to do an interview."

"I'm on it," the young man replied, helping to pack up the camera, tripod, and sound equipment, then leading the cameraman down the street.

Abigail turned towards Ethan as he and David made their way through the dispersing gathering. Ethan discussed the interview as they approached. She could tell, at first, that Ethan was correct; David did not seem amenable to an interview. However, by the time they reached Abigail, David was nodding and smiling.

"Miss Sanders, it's good to see you again. I didn't catch you a month ago when first announcing our intent—shame you couldn't be there," David said.

"Hated to miss it—I was on an assignment in Houston with Darby Adams."

"Quite a shame what happened to Mr. Adams. Near the end, he seemed to have turned a real corner on his personal life with the Kratometric Engine. The machine's rumored to work like a dream."

"I heard the same. It's unfortunate he never got a chance to see the fruits of his work," Abigail added.

"Ethan explained you were hoping to carve out five minutes with us. Where would you like to do the interview?"

"I have a standby studio nearby if you'll come with me."

"Certainly."

Ethan trailed them—beaming about getting his old job back and seeing Abigail. As they turned the corner, Abigail asked, "David, could I ask another favor of you?"

"Go ahead."

"Would you grant me an exclusive for the day? The Worth's issuance and Ethan's reappointment are big."

They reached the shop and Abigail motioned them to the door. David replied, "Actually, Abigail, I wasn't planning on granting anyone an interview today. There are still quite a few things to do this weekend. Ethan convinced me that it would be good for the note's acceptance not to keep people in the dark for any length of time now that our intention to go forward has been announced. If you'd like, I could extend that exclusive for the remainder of the weekend. You've always been fair with the CMC. That, of course, is a lot more than I can say for your friend at the network."

"Frank?" Abigail asked.

"No, the other anchor."

"Daniel. Yes, he has a talent for rubbing people the wrong way. I'll see to it that you never deal with him again."

"Thank you."

"Please step this way," Abigail invited, as she opened the door to the shop.

Ethan joked, "I didn't realize TTN owned a men's clothing line."

"Cute," Abigail replied.

A short, balding, portly man dressed in a black suit smiled—locking eyes with Abigail. He immediately hugged and kissed her on both cheeks.

He exclaimed in a jolly Italian accent, "Abigail, it's been too long since our last visit! Where have you been all this time? Your man tells me you need a spot to do a quick bit. I have them setting up right over there where the lighting is best. Now, tell me the truth, are you staying out of trouble? I saw that interview of yours. A warzone? What were they thinking sending you to such a place? Tell your bosses, if it happens again, then they're going to deal with me." Abigail sweetly smiled. "I'll tell them, but I doubt they'll listen. Mort, thanks for helping. I would like to introduce you to two very important people. This is…"

Mort interrupted, "No introductions are necessary, my dear. This is our intrepid senator who told those Bone-Yard bozos where to take their underhanded deals. Senator Scott, all New Yorkers are proud of you. We hated to see you go; but know you'll do better for us with the CMC. And I especially know you, Mr. Samuel. They've been giving you hell for sometime now I think. Way to hang in there. I hope this stunt of yours works. We need new blood in Washington; and how."

Ethan and David were endeared by Mort's gracious and gregarious demeanor.

Abigail said, "Mort, I hope we don't disrupt business today."

"For you, Abigail, nothing's too good. Let me help your people finish setting up in front of those fabric bolts. It was nice to meet you both," Mort said politely, before quickly moving on to help Alex.

"Why don't you two take a seat? I need to make a few quick calls."

"Certainly," David accepted, as he and Ethan walked over to the chairs Mort had set out. Following David, Ethan looked back over his shoulder at Abigail, his feelings for her welling up inside him. Abigail noticed his glance before he could dart his eyes forward again.

As David and Ethan waited, Abigail tapped her phone screen. David abruptly asked, "By the way, what the heck happened to your face?"

"Haven't heard that one yet—let's just say that I picked the wrong way to break up with my girl."

David chuckled, wondering about the details. "Is there anything you need to tell me? You and I have a checkered past when it comes to your dates."

"Hey, for the record, Anne was…not what she appeared to be. In any case, I learned my lesson about political operatives," Ethan explained with a genuine smile, as his gaze returned to Abigail talking on the phone.

"They are—at Mort's; near the corner of Wall Street and Nassau. Yes, an exclusive for the weekend. We can go live in three minutes. I know; we're running that story all day. That's the point. He's here now; and willing to talk alongside David about it. Lead in after the next break, and be sure to cue us at this end. We'll verify satellite uplink now. I just need the frequency and we're gold.

"What about Frank? He's not in the office. I know what he's like. I'll take the heat for this. Look, assign me a frequency and have the weekend crew ready to run with it. Okay. Yes, I have it. I'll be back in three." Abigail end the call and then said, "Here's the satellite freques. Verify uplink and let me know when we're set. Is the lighting and sound ready?" Abigail pressed Alex, as she forwarded a text message to his phone.

"We can shoot on your go," Alex assured.

"Good work. We're live in two minutes." Abigail's phone rang again. "Hello? Daniel? Frank. I thought it'd be something like that. I know you wanted me to cover the rally only. Because it's news and he's giving us an exclusive until Monday. That should punch up our numbers for the weekend, and give the advertisers something to be happy about. It seems to be the only thing you understand. Brian's already set it up. I'm live in one minute. I don't have time for this conversation. Because it's news. I'm doing it, Frank. Yeah, you've been threatening me with that for a while. Fine, come in on your day off. I'll be back at network in an hour. Frank, I need to go," Abigail said impatiently—hanging up as Frank continued to argue.

Abigail quickstepped into position next to David and Ethan. She looked behind them at Alex and asked, "Where are we?"

Alex intoned, "Live in five, four, three, two—"

"This is Abigail Sanders, TTN, New York. We're talking with David Samuel of the Citizens' Mandamus Council, and Ethan Scott, recently resigned senator for the state of New York.

"Gentlemen, you gave quite an interesting public announcement.

Can you tell our viewers more about it; and what you both hope to accomplish in the days ahead?"

CHAPTER
XVIII
MOB OVERTURE

An hour later, back in the TTN building, Abigail was savoring making a command decision in the field that benefited everyone: the CMC, TTN, and her career. It reminded her of the days when Sandra was in charge. While a ruthless slavedriver, Sandra trusted Abigail to bolster the network's integrity and perception as a news leader.

Abigail went over the interview in her mind; it was running north of twenty minutes instead of the five they agreed to. Once David and Ethan had laid out their current plans, both began to consider other possibilities.

If there'd been a call-in bank prepared to receive viewer questions, it would've been perfect. Frank will be in first thing Monday morning, lecturing on the chain of command and threatening to fire me again—doesn't matter. This was news—right place, right time. I love it—journalism doesn't need an excuse.

A polite bell dinged and the elevator doors opened. Abigail strutted straight to the editing room to begin assembling a segment the network would repeatedly run over the weekend. As she turned the doorknob, Frank caught sight of her as he marched down the hallway.

"Miss Sanders, in my office now!" Frank barked.

Several employees nearby turned around to go in the other direction. Abigail pulled the door shut and headed towards Frank's office; he followed behind in lockstep. Abigail began laughing to herself; realizing this was the first time Frank had ever displayed any kind of grit resembling Sandra.

After they had entered his office, Frank slammed the door shut and demanded, "Miss Sanders, sit down if you please!"

"Frank, there's no need to shout. I'm close enough to hear you. If you're going to continue screaming, you'll need to open the door again so as to rattle the troops within earshot. Your loud and coarse demeanor has no effect on me."

"Miss Sanders, I'll have you call me by my surname."

"And how will you have that, Frank? This has gone on long enough. Your given name works fine. I wouldn't mind calling you Mr. Lambert if you were my superior. You're not. You just happen to be the boss."

"Never in all my years have I been treated with such disrespect. I have a mind to…"

"To what, Frank…fire me? You can't, and you know it. Only Sandra Buchanan or the executive board of TTN can do that. But of course you know this, because you would've already done it otherwise. I'm positive you've thoroughly read the terms of my employment contract. That's all you're concerned with right—business? By itself, it's all well and fine. We do need to make profit. However, this is the news business and not a widget shop."

"What gives you the right to change programming in the middle of the day?"

"Again, Frank, do I need to spell it out? This is a national *news* agency. We report the *news* first and foremost. We have regular programming to boost advertising sales. The programming is subordinate to the *news* and not the other way around. That story I picked up was good work and will boost ratings the remainder of the weekend. This of course translates into higher ad revenue. I'm sure you can get your mind around that. This is what we do."

"Miss Sanders, this is not what we do here now. My predecessor may have possessed a flair for haphazardly managing a successful operation. However, I run a much tighter ship, and expect those in my employ to follow instructions to the letter."

"It's for this reason that you fail. You lack a reasonable grasp of network leadership. You don't belong in news!" she shot back contemptuously.

"That's it. I will no longer sit across from a woman who does not understand her place. You may consider yourself on suspension, pending an investigation into your actions this afternoon. I intend to approach the board about the status of your employment."

At that moment, Xavier and the executive board walked into Frank's office, laughing about a joke Xavier had told. Xavier looked at Frank and said, "Frank, that was fine work on the CMC piece. How did you get an exclusive for the weekend out of 'em anyway? Brian just explained that Abigail did some fancy footwork to broker a quick deal. We were downtown getting lunch—watching our coverage of the CMC's propaganda in front of the Phillips Stock Exchange. Ten minutes later we have an exclusive with David Samuel and Senator Scott. Nice work people, very nice!" Xavier bellowed.

"Thanks," Abigail replied.

"I know I heard some butt-chewin' a minute ago from outside. What'd I miss? Which one of you screwed up?" Xavier poked.

"Xavier, as much as it pains me to make such a request, I think the time has come for Miss Sanders to part ways with TTN," Frank declared with faux regret—attempting to appear composed and unflustered.

"Xavier," Abigail carefully annunciated.

"Yes. You have something to say, Abigail?"

"I'll take the job."

Xavier understood what she meant and curled a smile; a child stealing away their favorite treat. Xavier was utterly thrilled with himself. "About Goddamn time!"

Abigail turned to Frank. "You're fired! Frank, you have five minutes to pack up and make for the front door—clock's already ticking. Get going."

Frank looked at Abigail, then to Xavier and the rest of the stone-faced board members. He then exclaimed with a nervous smile, "This must be a joke. Xavier, what's the humor I'm missing?"

"Don't look at him! Look at me, Frank. You have four and a half minutes left, and then I'm calling security."

"Xavier, why are you doing this?" Frank whined.

"Sorry, Frank. It's gotta be this way. Your time's running out. I'd do what she says."

Frank grabbed his briefcase and quickstepped out of the office, looking as if he were about to cry. Abigail stood up to clasp Xavier's hand. He smirked and shook his head. Xavier and the board turned to leave without a word; everyone looked pleased.

"Wait a moment, boys. All of you hold on a moment. I want an explanation. What were you thinking hiring that bureaucratic pinhead to begin with?"

They chuckled and spun around to face her. Xavier stepped forward.

"We knew it would take someone like him for you to accept the job."

Abigail smiled as they openly laughed about the hell Frank put her through. She was the right person for the job and they were not taking no for an answer.

"Alright, enjoy your little joke. My acceptance is contingent upon something from you, Xavier."

"What's that?"

"Two things actually: I want to stay behind the news desk. I'm not ready to give it up. I also want the seventeen paintings delivered to my apartment this afternoon."

Xavier's smile somewhat diminished, though still held its fervor. He asked, "What are you talking about?"

Abigail coldly locked eyes with him. He wondered why they meant anything at all to her. Xavier looked away for a moment and then back again.

"Fine. They'll be dropped off this evening."

The board filed out of Abigail's new office, exiting as boisterously as they entered. Xavier was last to leave, and stopped at the entry.

He faced Abigail as she sat at her new desk, and said, "The show's yours."

Xavier then turned away and walked out. His footsteps grew faint as the moment caught up with Abigail. *President*, she thought. It thrilled her; then nausea and deep regret registered.

"No," Abigail told herself, switching off her feelings. She picked up the phone, tapped on it, and awaited an answer.

"This is Ethan."

"It's Abbey."

"Abbey, I didn't expect to hear from you so soon. I assumed you'd be working on your trophy piece."

"I'll be getting to that in a moment. Is David nearby?"

"Yes, he's right here. We're back at the office going over what I missed while away."

"Tell David that Sasha has the job. Have her report to me at network first thing Monday morning."

"I'll do that. Abbey…"

"Yes."

"It's good to be back."

"Glad you're here."

Senate Office Building Monday mornings were always off-putting for Hubert; too many inane pleasantries.

"Good morning, Senator," a plain-clothed security guard greeted him, as Hubert hoofed by, lost in fuming over Ethan's precipitous departure. He had invested a great deal of energy positioning Ethan to be leveraged. Now that it was not to be, a vacuum of underserved duties remained.

After reaching the private office and settling down at his desk, Hubert knew what had to be done. He picked up the phone and dialed. "Ken, it's Hubert."

"Yes, Hubert, what can I do for you?" Senator Ken McClintock asked.

"I want you to nominate me as the new president pro tempore. While you're at it, have Christopher Royce second the nomination. Make sure it's brought up in today's session."

"Should we also call for a vote then?"

"That's the idea."

"Not to be insulting, but why you, Hubert? It's not your style."

"Just do it."

"Alright, Hubert, if that's what you want. I'll call Senator Royce right now. Is there anything else?"

"Yes. When the Liberty lilies raise a stink that you both are on the Homeland Security and Government Affairs Committee, and nominating the chairman, you're going to need to be convincing that it's for the good of the Senate. Are you up to it?

"I can handle anything those liberals throw my way. Just get started on your acceptance speech."

"See you in session."

After ending the call, Hubert began to think about how to hold the position without ridicule for the ever-present lack of results— it wasn't a prudent move. Recent polls continued to highlight a plummeting confidence in Congress based upon the worsening wealth divide, growing food costs, and lack of well-paid jobs. This kind of disenchantment with Washington had not been seen since the 1930s.

Hubert stopped obsessing and keyed a familiar phone number. It repeatedly rang and then was picked up. "This is Ethan. Can I help you?"

"Ethan. It's Hal."

"Hubert…I'm surprised to hear from you. Given all that was said in chambers last Friday, I honestly never expected to hear from you again. What is it that you want?"

"Are you still in New York? I saw you on the news all last weekend."

"Yes."

"Will you be making your way back to Washington in the near future?"

"I'll be there Wednesday to pack up my apartment."

"Have time for lunch?"

"I'm afraid not, Hubert. I have a day to move; there's a lot to do in a short amount of time."

"Would you mind if I stopped by to talk?"

A silence stretched for a long moment, then Ethan relented, "I suppose that'd be alright."

"Good. I'll drop by at noon."

"See you then, Hubert."

After setting down his mobile phone, Ethan looked bewildered.

David asked, "What is it?"

"The chairman of the Homeland Security and Government Affairs Committee wants to visit with me on Wednesday."

"Ethan, be careful. I've had dealings with Riley. He doesn't take prisoners. I'm sure everyone in Congress sees you as a traitor. You might consider hiring security while moving your things."

"A little dramatic aren't you, David? He wants something…some sort of horse-trade; simple as that. Still, you're correct—with Hubert, anything's possible. I'll be fine."

By morning's end, Hubert had emerged as the new president pro tempore. He was the last to leave chambers, with Senators McClintock and Royce. Both Ken and Christopher felt Hubert was indebted to them for the nomination; they walked with him as if to boast of their trophy, serving as a reminder that one day they would ask for a favor.

"Hubert, that was some speech in there," Senator Ken McClintock sarcastically gushed.

"You liked it?" Hubert asked.

"No. It was too long," Ken complained.

"Really, Hubert…you need to work on that in the future. Didn't you notice everyone rustling in their seats? That should've been your cue to cut it off right then," Christopher sniped.

"I didn't ask either of you for a critique. Their distress had nothing to do with me; it was Scott's play. That speech created more headaches than this economy. It's getting ugly out there, boys. We're going to need to do something drastic—and soon. Or the trouble coming will be more than the job's worth."

Ethan landed at Reagan National Airport on the six o'clock morning flight. His taxi was pulling to a stop at his old apartment before sunrise. It was a frigid morning: snow flurries whisked along the street. There was a long day ahead—he had to get packed up before the moving truck arrived that evening to load his belongings.

The entry door swinging open seemed to suck Ethan into the darkened home. Within a week, it felt like years had passed. After such a bold and controversial resignation, his presence in Washington felt like ill-fitting shoes. He no longer belonged here and desired a hasty departure.

Before getting to the task at hand, Ethan brewed a pot of coffee. He sat down in the kitchen, sipped the coffee, and read the newspaper. A pleasing coffee aroma drifted through the nippy air. The turning pages sounded a familiar melody as Ethan contentedly leafed through what felt like an old friend.

As he browsed, page after page disparaged the lofty and persistent underclass. One article profiled a man laid off from his job who had returned to shoot everyone at the office later that day; twenty-three people were killed. Another article discussed an importer of Asian goods caught in a cover-up, knowing all along the products sold in one of America's largest retailers caused birth defects in unborn children. On a separate page, another international corporation was moving production to India. By the time Ethan reached the opinion section, he couldn't read anymore and laid the paper down.

He gawked through the kitchen window, contemplating his yearlong journey. It was not a direction he would have ever chosen for himself; and yet he could not imagine doing anything else. Then, the first days of Worth issuance came to mind. He mulled over the past few days, which had seen the first issuance of the Worth note. Praise and protest had swept the country in what felt like equal measure. Many felt they finally had the Federal Government on the run. Still others feared this was a final blow to forever ruin the economy. David and Ethan were branded saints and sinners, with no clear consensus. One thing Ethan saw with his own eyes was certain: People were exchanging dollars for the Worth.

Not wanting to languish in perplexity, Ethan got up and finished the dregs of coffee. He banged his cup on the table, resolving that there was no turning back. Like the new note, it was time for Ethan to clear his head of doubt and get moving.

He opened up the kitchen cabinets and began loading boxes. His apartment was small and so he had managed to pack up everything on the first floor by noon. As Ethan folded clothes upstairs, Hubert rapped the bedroom door, walked in, and announced, "I knocked downstairs but didn't get an answer. Assuming you were busy and couldn't hear me, I let myself in—hope you don't mind."

"Not at all. Please have a seat. I'll get another chair from my office so we can talk comfortably. I'm ready for a break anyway."

As Hubert sat, the dull ache of steel spikes bore into his hips. While Ethan walked the hallway, for a passage of one step, he felt hot coals and open flame at his feet and then the feeling was gone. Both men smelled the brief presence of sulphur in the air.

Ethan returned with a chair, sat down, and toweled off his sweaty forehead. The growl of a wild animal gurgled in both of their heads; both put the experience out of their minds as if embarrassed to entertain some childish latent phobia.

Ethan exhaled and opened, "I understand you were named my successor as president pro tem."

"That's right."

"Congratulations. I can't think of anyone I'd like to see bogged down by the responsibilities of that position more than you. It's poetic justice for the way you put me up for the job," Ethan joked; masking his subtle contempt for being nominated after explaining his busy schedule. "So, Hal…you wanted to talk with me about something."

Understanding Ethan's meaning, Hubert got to the point. "I want the CMC to back off."

"Hubert, what do you mean? Did not the Senate vote this last Friday to reverse its course on the CMC matter? A roll-call vote on national television decided there and then. I've seen a copy of the court documents dismissing the case and court order."

"I'm talking about this shell game you call a currency: the Worth. Ha—it's nothing of the kind! It has no worth!" Hubert stated aggressively.

"It's in good company then; neither does the dollar. It hasn't since shimmying off the gold standard. But you know this already. And, let me beat this dead, rotting horse carcass—the Worth is not currency.

It's a note of value."

"We issue bonds for the dollar, guaranteed by the ability of the government to levy taxes to pay back the bond."

"Collecting taxes for a currency lacking any value; is that what your argument is based upon? We've issued bonds as well. Brazil, Russia, China, Japan, and a multitude of European countries have bought our bonds," Ethan informed Hubert as he smiled to purposely antagonize the man.

"The United States can guarantee the dollar."

"Incredible! Are you attempting to intimidate me with the threat that a liar is vouching for the dollar? America doesn't have the wealth to back its fiat in circulation. If everyone in the world suddenly demanded the United States government make good on the dollar, then we'd be bankrupted. That promise you so proudly wield is nothing more than a prevarication no one's dared confront. You yourself even claimed that the US government was a lie—that our democracy was shallow. At least the Citizens' Mandamus Council doesn't make that kind of promise regarding the Worth."

"Do you and your fanatics want to ruin this country?" Hubert charged.

"Ruin it? Hal, buddy, you and your congressional tribe have done that already. You've left very little for the Citizens' Mandamus Council to do."

"This is getting us nowhere. I'm warning you—end this currency issuance."

"Or what? What can you do to stop us? We're doing nothing illegal. You may have been able to break the law by court order before. But that train's already left the station. People are watching now. The Congress won't easily be able to break its own rules anymore. And again, it's not a currency."

"We'll crush you! There will be nothing left when we're finished. You're dead! Do you hear me? Dead!" Hubert ranted.

Having negotiated for years with paper suppliers threatening to end his newspaper by cutting off any other suppliers if he didn't agree to their price per ton, Ethan reacted in kind. "Hubert, you do realize that most of the Worth's initial printing will be issued from our nine reserves by this Friday. The foreign countries, having purchased our bonds, already received their blocks of Worth last Monday."

"Stop printing any more! Halt issuance immediately and recall all issued notes; to be exchanged for the dollar!" Hubert demanded.

"In return for what?" Ethan probed.

"Anything…if you want back into the Senate, the seat's yours. I'd offer millions of dollars, but it seems your exchange has plenty. What do you want? Name it," Hubert offered, assuming Ethan would be willing to accommodate.

Ethan turned away, as though considering Hubert's offer. He then looked into Hubert's eyes and asked, "Do you remember that conversation we had in my office about power? We never did finish it."

"Power. That's what you want: power? I can provide limitless power; all the power you'd ever need."

"No," Ethan replied—annoyed with the misunderstanding and interruption. "Our early-morning discussion about the nature of power, do you remember it?"

"Vaguely."

"We came to an agreement on the nature of power. You agreed with the definition but would not give in on my interpretation that people maintained the same power that is enjoyed by Congress."

"Yes, now I remember; and my position's the same. People do not hold any discernable power."

"Would you say this is necessarily so now? Look at what's going on. The underclass jobless rate will rise above twenty percent by the end of the year; and those are safe estimates. Citizens are conservatively exchanging the dollar for the Worth; but are doing it immediately nonetheless, for no other reason than to hedge their bet that the US currency will be worthless. Without the dollar's perceived strength and stability, your time in office could be cut short by a government collapse. You still think you have something the people don't, Hubert?"

Frustrated, Hubert demanded, "What do you want?"

"I want every state in the union to hold new elections for both houses of the US Congress; every last representative and senator. If not, then the Worth's issuance continues," Ethan explained emotionlessly.

"Ethan, have you lost your mind? We just had an election of all four hundred thirty five members of the House of Representatives and a third of the Senate."

"The CMC wants new elections for the lot of them; including the Senate two-thirds that did not participate in this year's elections."

Hubert shot up, stomped, and exhorted, "This is treason! The Citizens' Mandamus Council can't snap their fingers and negate election law. It's unconstitutional! No one will stand for it. The elections won't count. This is outrageous!"

"Funny, Hubert, but the Senate didn't find it so contemptible when they denied the CMC their constitutional right to file grievances with its government. No, I don't think anyone will have a problem with Congress being held accountable. Put it to an immediate vote—see if people truly want your brand of leadership, given what's happening to our economy and society. All that's needed is a majority of governors, a super majority in the House and Senate to amend the Constitution."

"By God, this is unpatriotic," Hubert grumbled.

"By unpatriotic, do you mean a people holding their government accountable for selectively enforcing laws favoring politicians and large corporations while stripping the middle class and poor of their wealth? Is that what you consider unpatriotic?"

"Fine—we'll do it!" Hubert yelled, as the veins on his forehead visibly bulged.

"Good. So you'll hold all-new elections?" Ethan confirmed with boyish giddiness.

"Yes. I said yes. We'll hold new elections in a year."

Ethan hopped to his feet and stepped up to Hubert—throwing a book he was holding on the floor; it thudded as it struck the hardwood. His face reddened with anger. "Paper ballots; One month and not a day longer!" he hollered at Hubert.

Ethan returned to his chair to calm down. Hubert also sat and gazed out the window. Both deliberated in silence, considering what had been said.

Hubert finally injected, "Ethan, even if that were possible, the election process itself would take a great deal more time than that just to start up. You need to be reasonable about..."

Ethan interrupted, "Reasonable? It's too late for that. Now listen to every word I'm about to say. The internet provides the only needed platform. Any ordinary citizen can launch a website explaining to the American public why they would be a good senator or representative. No money's needed to participate.

"And before you say 'voting machine,' more than seventy percent of states use automated voting machines. States that don't have them could borrow from states that do. Within a week's time, the process of actually taking up the votes and accounting for them could be accomplished. DC's influence brigade would be completely shut out. A true representation of the people would once again hold office. Now, Hubert, no more delays. Do you want the issuance to stop or not? Make up your mind. With either decision there are consequences."

"And the Electoral College?"

"We'll need new electors too."

Hubert rose slowly, tracking Ethan's eyes all the while as if he hoped Ethan would fall dead. Hubert's blood boiled considering Ethan's leveraged and his foiled future intention for Ethan to take the US presidency—later falling in disgrace; making way for Hubert to assume the high seat of power. Hubert then pivoted and walked out of Ethan's bedroom.

Ethan asked towards the open doorway, "What's it gonna be, Hal?"

Hubert turned around and chaffed, "You have your elections."

Back in New York, personal belongings now returned to his old apartment, Ethan found himself waiting in the cold outside his apartment building. The cab was late—it was a few minutes after five in the morning but the streets already busied with commuters. Aegean hues colored spaces in and through the steely forest.

A stranger loitering on the sidewalk across the street appeared out of place. It wasn't his dress but how he stood. A nervous tension prodded people along this time of day; everyone hoofing it to work. This man was not anxious to get anywhere fast. He just stood there. It was obvious to Ethan, like a pebble poking inside a shoe.

Ethan's taxi arrived and he was on his way. At the airport, he made his way through multiple security checkpoints. While shuffling through the last metal detector, the uneasy feeling returned. On the other side, he stepped forward to pick up his things, but a security guard intercepted him before he could do so.

The officer requested, "Sir, can I ask you to step aside for additional screening?"

Put out with the inconvenience, Ethan nevertheless replied, "Okay." He waited as his shoes were inspected. His briefcase's contents were deposited into a container. The officer stood six foot tall with dark hair and olive skin; a classic Italian appearance. He was twenty-nine years old going on forty and deeply desirous of proving his loyalty and worth to Homeland Security. Ethan looked straight ahead as Anthony ran his hands over the surface of Ethan's clothing, attempting to find anything considered contraband.

"So you are flying to Washington DC this morning? What is the nature of your visit?" Anthony asked.

"The nature of the visit is my own concern, and a private matter. Now please finish your job and let me go before I miss my flight."

"I'm sorry. I cannot do that, sir. Pursuant to the USA Freedom Act, airport security is empowered to ask questions of suspicious-looking foreign nationals and American citizens regarding the nature of their travel. Now, will you please answer my question?"

"No, I won't. I am not traveling out of the country. I may move about the continental United States undisturbed by anyone with a badge, so long as I'm not breaking the law. Now, if I've done something wrong, then point it out; otherwise leave me to my business."

The officer grabbed Ethan by the arm and said, "Sir, please step this way. You will need to wait for my supervisor to arrive before I may release you. Have a seat and he will be with you shortly." Anthony sat Ethan down in a room with no windows, off to the side of the security screening area.

People checking through the line ogled Ethan as if he were dangerous. Anthony closed and locked the door, and returned to his duties, leaving Ethan next to a steel table bolted to the floor. A security camera bore down on him from the ceiling. The dull hum of an overhead florescent light pricked his patience—time wasted in a jail cell fashioned to be a government office.

 After ten minutes, Ethan looked at his watch and realized he was going to miss his plane. *Would it have been that bad to answer the young man's question? Look at this.*

He slapped the table, making a loud whack; then calmed himself. *They can't hold me forever. I'll just be a little late.*

Three hours passed without his being seen. His flight, and the next two, had already departed. He was reminded of an incident from his military days when he had been pushed to the breaking point; but then denied the Platoon Sergeant the satisfaction of doing so.

Ethan leaned back in his chair, put his feet up on the table, and said, "This is nothing."

Moments later a man opened the door and hurried into the office. He stood four inches taller than the security guard. Dark brown hair, streaked in gray, provided an air of regal confidence. He wore a black double-breasted suit tailored to his muscular build. An earthen complexion and a strong Italian accent completed his strong European-immigrant persona.

Graciously, the man extended his hand and said, "Mr. Scott, I am very sorry to have held you up this long. I am Luciano Rossi. We are a government agency and have too many duties to respond as quickly as we would like to non-emergency situations. You understand, don't you?"

Ethan, not bothering to put his feet down, extend a hand, or even open his eyes said, "No, I don't understand."

Luciano swiped at Ethan's shoes with a large left hand, knocking his feet off the table. As Ethan's legs fell to the floor he sat up without emotion. He was familiar with the tough interrogator ploy and maintained composure, understanding now that there was trouble to contend with.

As Ethan straightened up, he noticed two armed guards outside the door. Luciano, seeing Ethan take notice, slammed the door shut with a bang. He then turned to Ethan, smiled, and sat down at the table.

"Now, Mr. Scott, let's start from the beginning. Why are you here?"

Ethan knew the establishment of dominance began the moment his captor occupied the room and swatted his feet. In Ethan's mind, this was where the battle for ground would be fought; because he was not giving up another inch. He smiled, stiffened his posture, and crossed his fingers.

"Mr. Rossi…"

"Call me Luciano."

"Mr. Rossi. State for me the exact law I have broken."

Luciano smiled and his eyes bored into Ethan's as he laced his fingers behind his head. "Maybe you misunderstand me. You are currently in my custody. I can hold you indefinitely, without a single charge filed. If you even smell like a terrorist, then I can lock you away and forget where I put the key."

"So the United States is no longer even keeping the façade that it's a just and law-abiding society?"

"Ah, I see you fancy yourself Doctor Manette, having renounced your power and been taken prisoner to the Bastille; awaiting the blade, eh? Yes, Senator, or rather Mr. President, I am very aware of who and what you are. Make no mistake, the hands of the bloodthirsty now clutch at your neck."

"I certainly wouldn't give you the pleasure of stating that this is the worst of times. However, I've seen better," Ethan said wryly, keeping the worry off his face.

"Are you finished, Ethan?"

"Depends on you."

"You're so right. Your life depends on me right now."

"Mr. Rossi, issue subtle threats as long as you like. It's not getting you any closer to what you want."

"Would you prefer I make direct threats, then?" Luciano asked flippantly.

"Would you? That would help me a bunch. I can be slow sometimes, and am not the best at guessing games."

"Ethan, you like to play dangerously. I like that about you. However, I must withhold anything like that until given permission to do so."

"Permission…what would a man like yourself need permission for?"

"We all have people to answer to. Much like your King David—you must report to him. I have my king to answer to." His mobile phone began to ring. Luciano noted, "As a matter of fact, there is my king calling for me.

"Hello. He is sitting across from me right now. Yes, it's secure. I think so too."

Luciano laughed at a joke from the caller and then replied, "Certainly. Can't I have just a little fun? He's so smug. You know how I enjoy stripping a man of his pride. You are right, of course—always next time. Is there anything you would like me to tell him? Ah, very good. I will do that. Goodbye."

Ethan looked to him, waiting for the catch. Luciano then asked, "Would you consider your detainment an exercise in power of the government over its people?"

Ethan smiled, knowing now who was on the phone. He leaned back in his chair for a moment to make Luciano wait for his answer, and then stood up to stretch out his arms and legs. He paced back and forth from one wall to the opposite three times as Luciano watched with a diminishing smile.

Ethan stopped and focused on Luciano's face—locking eyes with his. He finally said, "No, this morning's delay was not an exercise of power, but a demonstration of unchecked corruption that's been allowed to exist for far too long. I promise you that one day our position and fortune will change."

Luciano exhaled with disappointment that he did not get the opportunity to do to Ethan what he wished. He stood and pursed a mindless grin. He strolled to the door and knocked four times.

"Open up," Luciano demanded. The door opened. "He is free to go."

While passing through the doorway Ethan stated, "I always was."

The guard handed Ethan his property. His shoes were missing their laces. The briefcase's leather exterior was sliced open on both sides. A side pocket had been ripped from the jacket. And his mobile phone had been broken into pieces and placed in a sealed clear plastic bag. The guard smiled at Ethan, raising his eyebrows when Ethan looked back with astonishment.

"What's this?" Ethan demanded.

Luciano silken voice whitewashed, "We had to check to be sure you weren't carrying a bomb. Careful is our business you know."

"Don't you mean careless? You're going to pay for the mending and replacement of these items!" Ethan demanded.

"How does the saying go in our country: Sue me? Oh, Ethan, there is just one more thing."

"What?"

"We at Homeland Security are fair-minded. You have missed your flight on our account. If you would like, we would be happy to fly you in one of our private jets to Washington?"

"I don't think that would help me get where I need to go. Good day, commandant."

As Ethan distanced himself from the security checkpoint, he looked back. Luciano posed like a statue, watching him walk away. Ethan's scalp tingled; certain it would only grow worse from this moment on.

Ethan caught the eleven o'clock morning flight to DC—arriving on schedule. He deplaned, picked up his luggage and caught a taxi without mishap.

Along the way, Ethan finally felt safe enough to relax and take in what had happened. As he passed historical monuments and buildings his mind raced. *How can we ever touch this place? God, it's so much worse than I even knew.*

He pulled up in front of the CMC's DC office. Ethan paid the driver and got out. After the taxi drove off, Ethan noticed the same man who had been across the street in New York that morning now standing on the corner in different clothing, malingering. It spooked him.

Ethan picked up his bags and entered the office, setting them down in the foyer. Charity came out from behind the desk to greet him.

"Ethan, I'm so glad you're back."

"Thank you, Charity."

"We were expecting you earlier today. I tried calling you myself. But it wouldn't connect to your mobile phone."

"Uh, yes, well, my phone was broken this morning. Is Ted still in the office?"

"He is. Go right in. I'll take care of your luggage."

"Much appreciated," Ethan said as he marched off.

Ted was talking on speakerphone when Ethan entered his office. Ted broke off and then continued, "Okay, he's here. Ethan, I know you want to ease back into the job as president, but four hours is what we in our business call late," Ted ribbed.

"Who's on the line?" Ethan asked.

"David."

David asked, "What happened? Was your flight delayed?"

"No, but I was," Ethan replied in an exhausted tone as he sat down in front of Ted's desk.

"Whatever happened, it doesn't look good," Ted commented.

"It's not. I'm angry, tired, and don't want to talk about it right now. I'll explain later. There is a pertinent question to ask. Have either of you been followed the last few days? There's a man hanging about on the corner outside this office, who was standing across the street from my apartment building this morning."

Ted realized, "Now that you mention it, I thought I'd seen the same person more than a few times in different places, but dismissed the notion. David, have you seen anything?"

"I'm afraid so; in front of the Phillips Stock Exchange, and three other times this week. At first, I thought it was my imagination. But it's clear, especially after the deal with Senator Riley was struck, that someone, or many someones are not going along with the program. For now, we should stay on course. If they contravene the agreement, then we'll deal with it at that time."

"David, don't you suppose this line of thinking is foolhardy?" Ethan asked.

"Ethan, our hands are full. We're committed and don't have time to flinch every time a move is made. They have thirty days to finish the election process. Candidates are already posting their websites on the internet."

"David's right. Let's not lose our nerve," Ted agreed.

"I'm not losing my nerve, you two. I just don't like having my hands tied behind my back. I'll do my part. Now, what do we have from our directors; in so far as court actions taken? What are the representatives doing now that a new election has been called? Finally, what does the board think our next move should be?" Ethan asked.

David replied, "All the final numbers were reported this morning. With the rush to get these cases into court, a little over two thirds of the Senate and House of Representatives are under some sort of investigation and have been sued, and compelled by court order to cease some action, take up some neglected responsibility, or address some form of uncovered corruption."

"Two thirds…is that right?" Ethan mused. "I knew we had a full load just before leaving for the Senate. But we were so busy with public outreach speeches that the number of cases underway must have slipped my attention."

"Hey, at least you two only have New York to contend with at the home office. I'm on the front line with this taskforce to revive all shelved files. Either one of you want to switch offices with me?" Ted offered humorously, although there was truth in his words.

"David, Ted's right. Maybe we should temporarily close down our DC office until the new elections are held."

"I don't think so. You don't take your flag down when the shooting begins. Listen to me; both of you. Don't be surprised if things quickly become questionable. Your friend, Senator Riley, isn't the type who's been told what to do since he was a child. With the kind of power the Freedom Act provides, we must be ready for anything.

During the next thirty days I want you to be wary of where you sleep, eat lunch, and any other habitual activities. The only way we can stay ahead of them is to be unpredictable," David cautioned.

"You're right to be concerned, David. But I have something else you may want to consider before becoming too alarmed."

"What's that, Ted?"

"What I'm getting from my DC contacts is that a great many in Congress don't really care if they're reelected. From what's floating around, they're treating this election like a final night of Mardi Gras. Lobbyists have already provided handsomely for their early retirements. Leaving political careers behind is something many of them hoped for. We're merely providing an excuse to be paid off one more time," Ted said.

"Nice work, Ted. You may be correct. Still, not everyone in Washington is happy with the idea; otherwise we wouldn't be stalked. All the same, I want you both to be careful. Now, where are we with the second printing?" David redirected to Ethan.

CHAPTER

XIX

TEMPTING THE TEMPEST

Sasha stared into the camera and opened, "Welcome to Day Topics. I'm Sasha Ericson. For the first time since the United States was made whole after its Revolutionary War, both houses of Congress held elections for every member: four hundred thirty-five representatives and one hundred senators. The stagnant economy and political unrest took on a life of its own after Senator Scott's address to a joint session of Congress. Because of the recent November election cycle in the House of Representatives and a third of the Senate, very few lobby-furnished advertising dollars remained to bombard media channels. The fight for public office was as fair as it was going to get.

"An overwhelming majority of those reelected competed side by side on the internet with everyday citizens seizing the chance to take public office at the federal level. Generally, incumbents were regarded with disdain. Many voted for the untried aspirant, although lacking any familiarity with the candidate's political goals. Anecdotally, the prevailing sentiment around the country purported that, no matter how little the average citizen knew about government, they're a far cry better than a current officeholder.

"It was the fastest congressional election in US history. Pollsters were caught off guard; unable to influence results with unscientific pre-election day prognostications. Citizens were left to make up their own minds, bereft of election brinksmanship. Just ten percent of congressional incumbents survived the second election of this year, inspiring the name 'The Great Reformation.'

"Our citizens and the world have cautiously anticipated how the United States would change policy towards its people—and the rest of the world. America's allies nervously hoped the new government would honor its previous military commitments, as its enemies were already challenging former allegiances. Major trading nations are seeking assurances that America will continue buying their goods and services, while at the same time selling back military arms and giving away the best US-held jobs to people in their own country."

The newly elected senator from California, Dean Walden, had run his campaign with a passionate agenda: technology. He owned a San Francisco-based software company, developing accounting programs, missile guidance software, and tracking systems for military mess halls. He was accustomed to market volatility and the straining pace of continual reinvention. By his late thirties, Dean had become disenchanted by industry efficiencies in driving American productivity to its pinnacle; witnessing the deluge of industry workforce scale-backs to accommodate innovations that he and others like him had incorporated into their business models. Some market segments had disappeared altogether; and Dean played a hand in it.

Dean never took a wife; never made the time. To him, work and life were one. Not an unattractive man, he stood five feet eleven inches with wavy blond hair, blue eyes, and a sun-kissed complexion indicative of one who enjoyed the beach and early-morning swims. Friday following the new elections, Senate and House Representatives assembled in their separate chambers to make necessary appointments and request assignments to committees. In the Senate, the Blue Coats Party maintained a majority presence. Ninety senators were new to politics—no alliances or leveraged positions yet existed. For the sake of expediency and the need for a fully functioning government, Hubert determined that the Senate would offer a one-time opportunity for any new senator to request which committee he or she wished to serve on. The normal committee nomination process would resume thereafter.

Dean was most interested in the Commerce, Science, and

Transportation Committee, as it oversaw America's business and technology policies and every facet of their application. He felt his talent would be best put to use there, and hoped to positively influence technology's application to the economy.

He had also taken a keen interest in the Banking, Housing, and Urban Affairs Committee. The current wealth disparity America suffered was directly tied to the energy sector and its relationship to the major stock exchanges and the banking industry. He wanted to end Oil's stranglehold, and banking's complicity.

Dean also wanted the USA Freedom Act repealed, fearing that, if enough time passed, people would forget the principles the country had been founded on. The Homeland Security and Government Affairs Committee oversaw the authoring and implementation of that bill. When first enacted, the public was largely supportive, having declared war on radicalism. Though it maintained the appearance of propriety, anyone willing to honestly look at its broad scope understood the legislation's threat to American civil liberties.

Committees assembled at different times throughout the day, so that new senators could investigate departments of interest. For the first time since Dean was a child stating the Pledge of Allegiance, he was excited about America and the possibility it held.

Dean first attended the Banking, Housing, and Urban Affairs Committee meeting; he was the last of twenty-one senators to sit down. "Welcome everyone. My name is Ken McClintock, committee chairman and Senate Majority Leader. The Banking, Housing, and Urban Affairs Committee's first priority after the Senate returns to session in January is to address the most pressing issue this committee contends: banking."

Dean straightened up in his chair, listening intently—already incensed by Ken's words. Dean had strong opinions regarding reform.

"The real threat to our financial stability does not exist within our financial institutions, but without. The Citizens' Mandamus Council, in its most recent move to destroy our way of life, issued its own currency. You may have exchanged American dollars for the Worth yourselves. Let me be clear. If you join my team, this will be our first task to address. We must move on legislation; quickly making illegal the very thing the CMC released onto the American financial markets—nearly destroying over two hundred years of financial growth and stability."

"Excuse me, Senator McClintock, I have a question," Dean interrupted, raising his hand.

"Senator Walden, is it?" Ken responded. "This is not a symposium. Please save your questions for another day."

"I must respectfully object to your statements, Senator McClintock. You stated that the CMC's financial move was the greatest threat facing America's financial stability and future. The facts say differently. Was it not large banks, guardians of our country's financial solvency, that continued looking the other way during the run-up to the last recession; making irresponsible loans to people who would not have qualified for them in normal and more prudent times? Was it not the Federal Reserve who continued lowering interest rates for years, thereby enabling this unthinkable malfeasant borrowing cycle? Wasn't it the large investment houses that created the financial vehicles, mortgage-backed securities, promising fast financial returns, thereby promoting continued irresponsible borrowing by consumers and ultimately leading to the near collapse of stock markets and banking institutions round the world? Honestly, Senator McClintock, wasn't it this cumulative fiscal irresponsibility and greed-driven excessive risk-taking that caused the Great Recession? Were not those actions a much greater danger to America than what the Citizens' Mandamus Council has threatened?" Dean grilled.

A hush fell over the room—everyone had stopped fidgeting. Dean had their attention. Ken peered at Dean with an openly annoyed look about his face. Little remained for Ken to offer to rebut Dean's assertions. The newly christened senators' awestruck gaze towards Ken had turned to disdain, and they were reminded why they had been elected to public office—to represent the people of their state in the Senate and not merely go along with career politicians like

Senator McClintock.

"Senator Walden." Ken patronizingly addressed as he looked condescendingly at Dean's nametag. "From a layman's perspective, you would appear to be correct. However, government workings are quite a bit more complicated than they appear on the surface. If you will…"

Dean stood, knowing he could not serve under this man. "You're right, of course, Senator McClintock, governance is much more complicated than it first appears. But it doesn't need to be, wasn't designed to be by our Constitution's authors, and should not continue to be. I hope to do something about that while in Washington. I've seen all I need to see here. You'll be relieved to know that it's not a body I wish to serve on. Good day to you," Dean stated firmly, as he turned his back and walked out of the room, allowing the door to silently close behind him.

Dean waited a half-hour outside the conference room where the Homeland Security and Government Affairs Committee was to be held. Suddenly all of the conference rooms simultaneously opened. Well-dressed women and men busily made their way from one conference room to another. It reminded Dean of high school.

After the other attendees had entered the room, Dean stood to enter as Hubert approached the door. Hubert stopped and gestured for Dean to go in. Dean nodded and walked through.

Hubert closed the door as Dean sat at the table. Hubert moved to the front of the conference table and said, "Thank you all for coming. I am Senator Hubert Riley, one of the ten incumbents having survived The Great Reformation." Hubert stressed a sarcastic tone while uttering the word "Reformation".

A few laughed and quickly quieted. Hubert smiled and continued, "For those of you who do not know me, I've been a senator for some time. I also happen to be the president pro tempore; third in line of succession to the President of the United States. I am also the chairman of Homeland Security and Government Affairs. I'd like to introduce Senator Ken McClintock, Senate Majority Leader."

Senator Jerald Roth, a jewelry-store owner and newly elected senator from New Jersey, politely interjected, "Pardon me for my ignorance. After having read through the special procedures regarding chairing rights and responsibilities of all Senate committees, I understand that all chairman or chairwomen must be nominated. If more than one senator is nominated for the same chair position, then the matter must be voted on by the committee members. Respectfully, how can you be chairman of this committee when the committee is only being considered at this time? The committee body has not even been formed. Are we all not here today to come to a better understanding of what this committee is responsible for and determine if it is the proper fit for us and our limited time?"

Continuing to smile, Hubert placated, "Senator Roth, that's a fine question. I'll not bore you with the details of how or why at this point. Suffice it to say, I am the president pro tempore and chairman of this committee. For the sake of expediency in reassembling a functioning Congress as quickly as possible, it was determined that all incumbent senators holding their seat after this second election would take up the responsibility of leading a committee."

"I see," Jerald replied, attempting to be polite.

"Now, if there are no further questions, I'll be moving on," Hubert stuffed.

"I have a question," Dean obstructed.

"By all means, Senator Walden, please make yourself heard," Hubert invited, attempting to suppress his annoyance.

"Who determined that incumbents would be given preferential treatment in the Senate? We were all democratically elected the same way; the operative word being 'democratically'. So do please explain what law you and the other incumbents descry guiding your decision to assume these positions of power and responsibility?"

"What state are you from, Senator Walden?"

"Please stop deflecting the question, Senator Riley, and tell us the law you and the others utilized to assume power that was not granted by the electoral process and laws of the land?"

Clearing his throat, Hubert bolstered, "As I stated earlier, for the sake of expediency and in benefit to the American people, our incumbents determined that it would be best to quickly facilitate the government processes to…"

Dean stood up, shaking his head from side to side, and chummed, "So no laws provided the right to do so. I'm quickly becoming a student of our previous Congress. As with the last committee visit, I'll not serve a body willing to ignore procedure and the law. I'm hoping the next committee doesn't suffer from senatorial squatters' rights. Good day to you all, gentlemen." Dean turned away from Hubert and walked out of the conference room.

Hubert knew Dean was going to be a problem for him. It had been years since another senator outwardly defied him; especially one so new to politics. Not since Seneca. Hubert would be putting some time in on this surefooted fellow in the near future.

Dean made his way to the next committee conference room and sat on the bench outside. Forty-five minutes passed before every meeting room door swung open and the dance of the bumblebee ensued; senators quickly buzzing their way to another scheduled political pow-wow.

Dean was first to enter the empty room, quietly sitting at an empty table—hoping this committee would fare better than the previous two. Within five minutes, the room had filled and its doors closed. Senator Ken McClintock was the last to enter. When Dean noticed Ken sitting down, he smiled, assuming his last choice was already bought and sold.

Senator Armstrong rose to his feet and said, "I would like to thank all of you for attending this meeting of the Commerce, Science, and Transportation Committee."

Here it comes, Dean thought, expecting Senator Armstrong to justify his incumbent right to life; that out of heartfelt graciousness he had decided to save the Senate from itself by showing the newly minted senators the favor of assuming non-granted power.

"My name is Jeremiah Armstrong from the state of Missouri. Folks call me Jerry. I was a building contractor a month ago and now I'm here in the Senate. I didn't even vote in the last two presidential elections and now I'm a senator. Don't that beat everything?" He reveled in the humor of his own admission. The other senators laughed with him; showing courtesy to the plain-spoken man whose jittery manner showed that he was struggling somewhat with public speaking.

"I was asked by Senator Riley of Alaska to serve as a proctor for this committee. There are just a few duties I must perform and then I'll turn over the floor to whomever wishes to speak next. I need to read to you the charter of responsibilities for this committee. We would next need to nominate a senator as chairperson. Finally, the committee must set forth its goals for the coming year, starting in the January session. Why don't I just go ahead with the tedious part first and then we can move onto the goals? I find them much more entertaining."

Jeremiah began reading committee mandates. Dean intently listened, occasionally glancing in Ken's direction. Ken didn't seem to care what Jeremiah was reading—instead he viciously stared back as if Dean had injured him earlier that day.

After Jeremiah had finished covering the material he joked, "Well, that was a mouthful wasn't it? Now, given all that I've just read, are there any senators here who feel as though this committee could be for you? If so, please print and sign your name on the sheet being passed around. There's a lot to cover in this committee. Are there any suggestions for a starting point?" Jeremiah asked.

"I have one. I think the time has come for America to address the problem of outsourcing jobs to foreign countries for the sole purpose of saving money and negating taxes. Our economy is plodding along—high-paid job creation must be one of our priorities," Dean asserted.

"That's a fabulous idea, Senator," Jeremiah supported.

"I'm sorry, Senator, but that falls under the Appropriations Committee," Ken interjected.

"Appropriations?" Dean burst out in an overtly annoyed tone.

"Yes; specifically the subcommittee on Labor, Health, and Human Services, Education and related Agencies," Ken smugly pointed out.

"I own a software company in California and possess a large measure of experience in how technology affects our economy. What about addressing the issue of the speed with which technology is released onto the open market and made obsolete by the next generation of technology before its stock is depleted? Expedient obsolescence is very detrimental to long-term economic health," Dean claimed.

"This committee does have authority here. However, we share it on this particular topic with the Small Business and Entrepreneurship Committee. I guarantee they're going to want to have great input on any legislation drafted that might encroach on small businesses like your own, Senator Walden," Ken chided.

"How about technology security? A large-scale attack by our enemies won't necessarily come from a bomb. Terrorism, through advanced technology and communications, is likely America's next threat," Dean shot back.

Ken smiled and patronized, "I'm sorry, but your suggestion cuts right into the Homeland Security and Government Affairs Committee. I believe you attended that meeting just before this one, did you not, Senator?"

Jeremiah extolled, "Well, it seems like we've already started off on the right foot. This leads us to the next issue at hand: nominating a leader. It appears we have two here that are ready to hit the ground running."

Ken assured, "I'm afraid I must refuse any nomination. I already chair a Senate committee. In accordance with Senate rules, I may only head one committee at a time. We must strictly adhere to the rule of law. Though I think I know who would accept the post."

At the CMC's New York office, Ethan stood before the executive board. "I think in the immediate present we'll have very little legal business. With only a ten percent congressional incumbent presence, most of our caseload is moot; with the exception of files involving criminal activity. Those cases should be turned over to their states' Attorney General."

"Why not the US Attorney General?" Daphne asked.

"Because that office was investigated earlier this year for corruption—if Ruiz is guilty then there could be linkage to some of the cases we're discussing," David explained.

"Good. Now that this is taken care of, we need to discuss our DC defensive posture." Ethan looked to David and placated, "And I know what you're going to say: 'This not in our mandate.' But we can't stand still—let K Street storm Congress. We have a real chance to move in a positive direction, on fairness and America's betterment."

David smiled. "What? I didn't say anything. You're the commander-in-chief here. If you think the Citizens' Mandamus Council needs a new mandate, then by all means draft and submit it to the board for consideration. It's not as if issuing paper was ever a part of my original plan. While you're working at refining the council, make sure to add bond issuance to our bylaws, will you?"

Ethan ribbed, "Someone stop starching your shirts? This side of you is exciting; and a little disturbing."

"Like I said, Ethan, you're in charge. Lead us the best way you know how."

Ethan grinned, warmed by David's support, and then expressed, "As I alluded, one of my biggest fears is that our clean slate won't stay that way. How do we eliminate the lobbyist threat?"

Emily suggested, "How about approaching one of the newly elected congressmen to sponsor a bill outlawing lobbying?"

Ethan bolstered, "It's a good idea; and a long-term solution. However, in the immediate present, with a looming and long-anticipated stock market correction, there are more pressing needs for Congress to address. Legislation, of the kind you're suggesting, belongs at the bottom of our urgent list. We should act on it soon, though. I'll talk with Ted about pitching someone from the House to put a bill in the hopper. It won't help us today; but that's okay. Crops take a season to grow…and we have a great deal of tending to do."

Ted added, "I'm thinking of something a little more aggressive. We need immediate and positive change. To stop a dripping faucet, a plumber would go to the leak's origin; it seems obvious that large corporations are the source. If the money supply's cut off, then the threat's eliminated."

"That's good, Ted. But how do we keep corporate out of it? We currently have laws making certain lobbying activities illegal. They just work around the statutes, or ignore them altogether. How about you, Betsy, you've been quiet today; any ideas?" Ethan pivoted.

"You know, Ethan, I'd wager that our founding fathers asked themselves the same questions before finally standing up to King George. I don't imagine it was an easy decision. They knew then, as we know now, that eventually tyranny must be confronted. It's a horrible lot. But when the short straw's drawn, the holder accepts their fate. I think everyone here realizes what this means," Betsy issued.

"What are you getting at, Betsy? You want the Citizens' Mandamus Council to declare war on the boardroom?" Emily asked, sounding amused.

"Well, isn't that what we were talking about, in not so many words?"

"No, we were talking about stopping the flow of money between big business and lobbyists," Ethan clarified.

"Ethan, that's true. But if you review your history, you'll also see that this is exactly what the American colonists were doing too. The Boston Tea Party was nothing more than a political message sent to George the Third that our colonists were not going to pay his egregious taxes and needed self-rule. George wouldn't have it and sent troops to enforce his justice, just like corporations have done; now using lobbyists and Congress as foot-soldiers to enforce their will over that of the American people. Tell me how either one of these are different?" Betsy challenged.

"Well…certainly have touched a nerve, haven't we?" David joked.

Ethan bolstered, "David's right. This is a sensitive subject. Let's try not to go at one another while looking for solutions. Betsy's also right, though; our focus will need to change after we've shored up DC's lobby juggernaut. In the coming year, we'll sight up on our corporate lost sheep; especially those generating revenues far exceeding many American states. Banks, defense contractors, internet service providers, web-based directory services, large retailers, manufacturers, pharmaceutical companies, and importers are some of the country's most coercive threats to its sovereignty."

The conversation waxed hopeful after that. It was a warm moment; those had been all too uncommon of late. After the meeting had dispersed, Ethan and David took a walk. As they meandered through the steel and concrete forest, Ethan asked, "Still glad you asked me back?"

"Don't look at me. The board tendered your invitation. I was outvoted," David replied.

"Thought as much; you didn't have me convinced on stage. But you're accustomed to it—on stage that is." Ethan was taking a good-spirited jab at David's oratory.

"Okay, now; no need to make it personal. I've been speaking for years. You've only been doing this a little while. I'm bound to be better," David returned, attempting to gloss serious his escaping smile.

"Sure you didn't fall off the stage last weekend? I remember setting a CMC record for the most donations earned in a night."

"Yes, Ethan, but I gave you all the easy markets."

"I see; out of pity, then?"

"That's right. I didn't want to say anything to you but..." David's smile ever-widening.

After a brief silence, Ethan's grin disappeared. "You know, David, Betsy's right. I didn't want to say anything in front of the others—it sounds so radical. But, we've reached a point where the laws only apply to Joe-on-the-street. How do we force a company to follow legislation when doing so prevents them from making more profit? How do we reason with a legal entity more solvent than the United States Government? War cries sound like the declaration of a fanatic. And yet, I'm finding it hard to locate another sentiment better capturing what may come to pass if we're truly going to save America from itself," Ethan lamented, shocked by his own words.

"Ethan, I know how you feel. Difficult times tend to prod the imagination, magnifying a problem's desperation. Events are dire. But I don't think things will continue to—"

Rubber tires screamed from the street, adjacent the sidewalk. A gray van skidded to a halt five feet away. Ethan and David turned towards the noise.

Four men clothed and masked in black emerged from the side door; rushing towards Ethan and David; punching both again and again. Before either could react, both were laid out, backs to the concrete; their hands and feet bound. As their assailants dragged them into the van, bystanders recoiled in shock and then ran.

The door slammed shut as a man yelled at the driver, "Drive, you fool!"

David and Ethan had been thrown in back and seated on the floor. The van sped off; occupants thrown about inside as sharp turns finished the getaway. Cloaked strangers aggressively punched each other and kicked at David and Ethan. Both remained still, trying to grasp what was happening.

The van exited onto a highway—ending their tussle. The tallest captor moved close to Ethan while the others kept watch from windowed perches to ensure police were not following. The man landed a playful slap on Ethan's face and assured with a strong Italian accent, "I know what you're thinking, Ethan."

"You know my name," Ethan replied, his eyes widening.

"You're thinking that a way should be found to escape as soon as possible, aren't you? You're a good little soldier boy, aren't you? Isn't that what a good little 101st Airborne soldier would do?"

"How do you know that?" Ethan asked. His skin flashed hot, but icy razor blades pulsed through his heart, and his brow clenched as he forced himself to remain calm. *I gotta get outta here.*

The man pulled off his black head covering. It was Luciano from the airport. Ethan's face contorted in shock.

"That's right, Ethan. Take it in. I wasn't going to provide the satisfaction of allowing you to know. But, I just couldn't resist," Luciano boasted.

One of the other men grabbed Luciano and yelled in a strong Italian accent, "Have you lost your mind? He knows who we are. He can finger us. We'll need to kill them both for sure now."

Luciano seized the man's index finger and bent it backwards, as it was poked into his chest. He then twisted the attacker's arm, kicked behind his knees and violently slammed his face into the floor. Luciano said, "Do not forget your place and never touch me again, or you will find yourself bound and seated next to them. Is that understood?"

The hooded man rolled over clutching his hand—trying to catch his breath and not scream. He nodded and moved near the front of the van to cradle his broken digit.

Luciano turned back towards Ethan and David. He smiled and said, "As you both know, good help is always in such short supply." He drew close to Ethan, and then looked back at the man holding his hand and joked, "He can't finger us. He can't even finger me. And, if there is any killing to be done, then it will be my pleasure to do so. But let's not get ahead of ourselves just yet."

Attempting to show courage, David looked over at Ethan and said, "So you weren't kidding about the Italian guy at the airport?"

Gaining an emotional footing, Ethan confirmed, "Yeah, he's the one; though much more scary the other day. It's always that way."

"What's that?" David went on, pretending to ignore Luciano.

"After one sees an opera the first time, it's never the same the second time," Ethan explained.

Luciano clapped. "Bravo. Bravo to you both. You know we had a bet that at least one of you would be crying and begging for your life by now. I was convinced that David would fall to itty-bitty pieces. He never had the courage to sign on the dotted line. Ethan, I was certain you wouldn't break in the beginning. The infantry would have kicked you out for being weak."

"Is that so, Ethan?" David broke in. "About the dotted line; did it take courage?"

"Yes, Ethan, tell us," Luciano pleaded.

"Nah, I was drunk when I signed up—woke up the next morning to a sergeant screaming in my ear that I was in the army," Ethan narrated, attempting to mock Luciano.

Luciano momentarily laughed along with the mockery and then struck Ethan with a closed fist, knocking him over. "Oh, Ethan, I must thank you in advance. I haven't been allowed to indulge myself in some time…and this weekend should prove to be most amusing." Again Luciano punched Ethan's face, knocking him down before setting him up to be clocked again. With each delivered blow, Luciano made exultant moans of pleasure. His scalp tingled as endorphins and adrenaline charged his blood. His mind filled with the psychopathic satisfaction of feeding his ravenous rage against a helpless victim. Ethan groaned and gasped for air. On and on it went this way for ten minutes. Finally, Ethan watched Luciano's fist hurl towards his face in slow motion; turning the world black.

During Ethan's beating, David attempted to show no fear; knowing his turn was next. After Ethan slumped over for the last time, David held forward his face to be struck. Luciano burst into hearty laughter. "Oh my goodness, such bravery to offer me your chin, but I have something different for you. I want you to feel loved, knowing some thought was put into your tender touches," Luciano assured and then kicked David's groin.

David screamed and fell onto Ethan. Luciano dragged David away and laid him on his back. Luciano had the others hold him down at the shoulders and knees as he punched David's ribs and stomach with alternate repetition. David vomited and gasped for air as Luciano hummed a ballad from The Beggars Corner Opus—beating him with passionate exaltation. After fifteen minutes David's bellowing ceased and his head fell to the side, facing Luciano.

Sweat rolled down Luciano's face. "There, now. Isn't that better, David? I didn't want you to feel neglected. Now we can have a quiet ride in the country."

Luciano looked forward out over the hood of the van, still humming in merriment. The windshield swallowed the New Jersey country road as if it were devouring everything in its path. While attempting to gain control of the pain, David passed out to Luciano's happy sounds.

David awoke as the men in black hauled him into an old farmhouse. Late November jagged frozen mud ruts grated his back and head as his offloaded carcass traversed the ground, dragged by the feet.

A wooden door creaked open—faded, peeling lime paint cracked and curled outward. David lifted his head after it struck the first rotted step leading to the cellar. At the bottom of the stairs he landed hard on a stale dirt floor. Moldy dust mushroomed upward, filling his nose and eyes with earth gone undisturbed for years. One of the men retrieved a pocketknife and cut David's leg bindings. As blood circulated through his feet, a warm painful tingling sensation throbbed. Relief was blunted by a rope binding his ankles together. David legs were hoisted upward. He heard Ethan being dragged down the stairs in the same manner. The only visible light spilled through the doorway leading to the entrance. With the sound of two men grunting in the dark, straining against a heavy weight, David's body lifted aloft; hanging upside down, hands still tied. Ethan was suspended in identical fashion. After Ethan was secured, one man grabbed David's jaw and ordered, "No talking!"

A single light bulb dangling by a ceiling wire leading to the floor above was lit by a yank of its chain. The last man left the basement and the door closed.

David whispered, "Ethan…you awake?"

"Yes," Ethan replied.

"Can you get your hands loose?"

"No. They're tied off. How about you?"

"I can't feel my hands anymore. How long have you been awake?"

"Since my head hit the floor. Where are we?"

"I don't know. I came to when we arrived. We're in the middle of nowhere. I think I saw harvested frozen fields; can't be sure. I was thrown around a bit after they pulled me out of the van."

The cellar door flew open, slamming against the wall. Luciano sauntered down its stairs, to anticipate the moment. When the bottom step was reached he said, "Gentlemen, maybe you misunderstood my associate. His English is not so good. He said there was to be no talking. Now look what you're making me do. I'm going to have to train you to follow orders."

"No instruction is necessary. We understand," Ethan desperately assured.

"Oh, but I cannot fail you. It is my duty to ensure you understand that in every learning environment there can only be one master. You see what I mean? When you are ready to accept my teaching, then the message is made most clear. I want my wisdom to be meaningful."

"As I said, that won't be necessary. We'll follow your instructions to the letter."

"Tsk, tsk, tsk. See, there you go again; talking in school. I must teach you both this lesson on following the rules."

Luciano started chuckling to himself as he glided to the far wall—picking up and putting down objects out of Ethan and David's sight. Luciano returned to Ethan with a rod made of numerous thin bamboo sticks bundled by thin leather straps. A hatchet blade gleamed at the end. He bent it to demonstrate its strength and pliability. Their eyes widened.

"Ha, ha! Oh, friends, you do tickle my funny-bone. The steel is not for you. No…this fasces has but one purpose today. From Paul to Lincoln, its meaning has been apparent. The state's prerogative is absolute—to injure or kill; depending upon which end is plied.

"Ethan, the other day, at the airport, you said so many charming things. My favorite, of course, was that the next time you and I met things would turn out different. I must admit, you were right all along. So do you like the direction we have taken this time?" Luciano asked, as he struck Ethan's back with all his might.

Ethan let out a yell as the stick broadcast a slashing sound. Luciano took two more swipes. Ethan wailed in anguish.

"Leave him alone, you bastard!" David shouted angrily.

"Ah, I see you are still participating, David. Good. I would hate to think you were going to miss this lesson," Luciano assured as he hit David with the stick.

The bamboo curled around David's chest in a whipping action, causing more pain. Like Ethan, David yelled out.

Luciano stepped back for a moment to catch his breath and to see both together. He sighed; pleased with himself. He realized his captives were both quiet and felt that more screaming was called for in an exquisite moment such as this. He went on, "Now, gentlemen. Do we understand each other? When you are given an instruction, then you will follow it, yes?"

Both vehemently exclaimed, "Yes!"

"Good. Now just to be certain the lesson holds, I'm going to thrash you a little more. It's for your own good. Don't take it personally. I just want to make doubly sure you never make this mistake again."

"No!" David screamed.

"Ah, a volunteer; so cavalier of you, David. Again, I would have never guessed you possessed such valor," Luciano gushed, and then continued bludgeoning David and then Ethan for the next hour. With each delivered blow, Luciano's blood pressure rose in delight and beckoned for another shot against their bodies. He was rewarded with an ever-deepening wave of dark pleasure, ecstasy with every helpless agonizing cry—a vicious hunger satiated for just a moment. Luciano wanted more, and more—striking harder, faster and with greater wickedness. As it went on, his body gorged a barbaric high approaching emotional orgasm. Unrelenting screams harmonized from both men. Once again, Ethan and David fell silent in exhaustion as Luciano experienced his release. Near the end, the sound of a rod striking their battered shells and Luciano's forceful exhale sounded; their voices singing in unison.

"My goodness, David, look what I have done. My manners...I dripped sweat on you. This will not do. For this I must be punished." Luciano stepped away and struck his legs with the fasces—letting out a bloodthirsty, "Yes!" He fell to his knees—hands shaking after dropping the tool. In a rush, Luciano reached into his pocket to retrieve a clear plastic bag. It was opened, pulled over his own head and cinched closed by a drawstring.

The head covering fogged as it pulled in and out. His breathing began to accelerate. Luciano reached for the strapped cane and began striking his back—each over-the-shoulder blow slapping harder than the last. Every impact was accompanied by a shriek of agony and moan of pleasure.

Faster and faster it went. As the action hurried to a spasmodic conclusion, Luciano released the weapon and fell prostrate to the dirt below. His pelvis gyrated as a trembling hand reached up to loosen the hood's cord.

He inhaled, deep and hard, for minutes, and then his gasping calmed. Luciano got to his feet—euphoric and relieved. His twitching fingers clutched at and lifted the shroud, dropping it to the floor. He stared in silence at the unconscious pair. *How strange that I cannot share this with them. There my beloveds hover aloft. How peaceful they are.*

After allowing his mind to clear, Luciano reached for a pocket-blade and began sawing at the ropes; first David and then Ethan fell to the ground. One at a time, he bound their arms and legs to wooden chairs. Endeared by their vulnerability, he waited in silence for them to wake.

A vast horizon of fire-blackened landscape stretched out in every direction. Rolling hills and towering mountains stared down on Ethan. Everywhere there were embers, fire and soot. Death's wretched smell overpowered his nose. Without warning, an armor-clad dark prince appeared before him; clutching Ethan's neck with a steel-plate encrusted glove, sharp metal edges cutting the throat's skin. *Can't breathe.*

Ethan had wet himself after Luciano's last attack. A line of urine ran down his leg, spilling onto his shoes and the floor. Soon, both he and David began to rouse.

"Yes…the stench. It's the ammonia. It does help in regaining consciousness. Please take your time. Whenever you're ready, then we can begin," Luciano nurtured.

As Ethan fully woke, his brief nightmare faded away as the potent laughed the laugh of an evil which ultimately devours itself. "What is it you want from us?" Ethan asked, wearied and demoralized.

"Very good, Ethan. I like your style: right to the point. Now that your attention, I would imagine, has been captured by this modest display of what you called 'corruption' in the airport, I think we can understand each other."

"What do you want?"

"Mind you, this is not what I want. If I were allowed to have my way, then there would have been cutting. No, it's what they want. They want you to put a stop to that currency of yours. They want all, or most of, the paper money you issued off the streets like you promised. They also want the Bitworth converted to digital dollars."

"Retrieving notes has proven to be more difficult than we anticipated. So far, people are not exchanging the Worth back to American dollars. I'm not sure how…" Ethan said.

"Ethan, Ethan, this is of no concern to me. I am just a messenger. You owe me no explanation. As I said before, you have your king and I have mine.

"Now, it seems you have some work to finish, and soon. My king is impatient. I was asked to make my message clear. I have accomplished that today, wouldn't you both say?" A quiet moment passed. Luciano stomped his foot and raged, red-faced and spitting, "Wouldn't you both say so!"

"Yes, you have made yourself plainly understood," Ethan responded with haste.

"I don't think I like that word, 'plainly'. I could make my message less plain if you like?"

"That's unnecessary. We understand."

"Good. Then we can be friends. Well, I have other work to do. So I will leave you here for the weekend to think over what we have talked about. I'll be back Sunday morning to collect you," Luciano explained.

He began climbing the stairs and then stopped to say, "Gentlemen, do let me be plain on this point. If you attempt to escape while I'm away, then we will do this all over again; only the next time I will be mean. Ciao." Luciano then looked towards his jacket lapel and retrieved an adorning orange poppy, tossing it into the air. It landed at their feet as he continued hiking up the stairs. "For you," Luciano bestowed.

The door latched shut with a loud metallic click. Footsteps plodded across the floor overhead, followed by a door slam, and the still fainter clicking of another latch. The van's engine outside quickly grew faint and then disappeared.

David and Ethan froze, anticipating sounds from above. After minutes passed that felt like hours, both immediately began wiggling arms and legs at their bindings. They attempted to escape for the remainder of the night. By early Saturday morning both had given way to fatigue; sleeping well into the afternoon. Ethan woke first and then David. David immediately discovered after he and Ethan began to open their eyes that the ropes had loosened while they were passed out, creating a small amount of slack in his bindings. It was enough to work with. That evening, David freed one hand and rocked his chair back and forth until it tipped backwards. He flailed on the floor for an hour until breaking a chair leg and disintegrating what remained, finally freeing himself and Ethan.

As they looked at each other's bloodied bodies, Ethan said, "You couldn't move any faster…pitiful."

"I didn't see you do any better, G.I.," David shot back, his smile making a cut on his lip bleed.

"Can you stand?"

"I think so. You know, Ethan, I think we need to have a meeting with the board regarding strategy for aggressive confrontations like this. I'm not sure taunting our captors is the way to go."

"You misunderstood what was happening. In tough negotiations, it's always important to size up your adversary. I was just trying to see how far he'd go."

"I think we found out."

"No, that was round one. We're still here. We won't know how far he'll take this until his return."

"So you want to wait here for round two?"

Ethan chuckled and offered, "I think it's best we throw in the towel and get out of the ring. What do you say?"

"Agreed; we should depart his hospitality."

Ethan kicked dirt over the flower petals. The dust settled as he picked up pieces of broken chair. The two of them ascended the stairs to the locked door. David attempted to pry open the door from a position just under the knob. Ethan watched David's efforts with his left eye; his right eyelid was swollen shut and trembling. With only room for one to work on the door at a time, Ethan waited for a turn. After ten minutes of trying to gain side-leverage, he gave up and attempted to force up the door from the bottom. The entrance was perfectly sealed on all four sides.

Two broken arm rests and an hour later, David sat down on the top step. "They don't make doors like that anymore. It won't be wedged open. Any ideas?"

Ethan looked around the basement to ensure he hadn't missed seeing even a small window. There were none. He turned back towards David and replied, "Give me a minute on this one." After a few silent moments, Ethan said, "Boy, he sure did like working us over, didn't he?"

"The man lives for his work."

"Do you suppose he gets paid overtime?" Ethan quipped.

They broke into hearty laughter. While it felt good to laugh, the pain reminded them of their torture and the levity ended abruptly. Both became quiet as their mortality and the helpless way they had endured the beatings rushed into their minds.

The hush was more than Ethan could bear without talking about it. Not wishing to lose control in front of David, he diverted from his anguish by asking, "Why does he do it?"

"You mean Captain Homeland Security?"

"Who else?"

"I think because he loves it."

"No, more than sadistic pleasure; why is he the way he is? How did he become so distorted? Why do people allow it?"

"Fear, Ethan; the Washington fools are no different. Oh, their reasons in DC are as varied as can be. But at the core of those rationalizations is fear."

"They were all this way long before my short stint in politics. How do you see fear as the cause?"

"It's not fear of you, Ethan; it is of not-enough. Fear of lack is gluttony, greed, and jealousy's common link. People like this only know they'll never be satisfied with what they have, and, like any drug addict, will continue to feed their addiction; even in the face of their own self-destruction. They can't help themselves. Even deeper still is a self-hatred; and that's a true human tragedy when one considers the potential of just one person to act, create and build great things. This man, like DC, is corrupt—scared the food will be snatched from his very mouth."

"Well, I hope you forgive my lacking empathy for them."

"Don't worry about me, Ethan. There's no bleeding left in this heart for their kind."

"Okay, enough of that. Why don't you let me take a swing at her for a while?"

"You have an idea?"

"I wanna crack that door. It's made of wood. It oughta break if we beat against it long enough."

"Go ahead; give it your best."

Ethan began striking the door with a chair back. A few dents and scratches adorned the wood's surface, but added no significant damage. David switched with Ethan, trying his hand at breaking the middle panel. Back and forth, they spent the remainder of the night attempting to leave the cellar without progress.

The van's arrival sounded outside before sunrise, announcing Luciano's return. The unlatching front door alarmed Ethan and David; they retreated into the cellar below, seizing chair remnants to use as weapons.

The door slowly creaked open; down rushed four pistol-wielding men dressed in black, as before with covered heads. Ethan and David dropped the clubs and lifted their hands. Two men holstered their weapons, rounded behind Ethan and David, and kicked their legs out from under them.

One man, pointing his pistol at Ethan, hollered, "Clear."

Luciano glided downstairs and charmed, "Ah, once again, a bet has been lost. We wagered whether you would wait for us to return or attempt an escape. I won! I knew the soldier in you would be too irresistible to ignore.

"Well, we are in a hurry, so let us be off. We have a drive to make back to New York. I want you both to trust me now. Don't fight. I'm not going to kill you. I could have done so days ago. I only say this because I have other things to attend to today and need you to come with me. Also, if I were in your position, and were not bound, my first thought would be to get a gun and shoot all of us. I know you are thinking the same thing, Ethan. So, we can do as before or you can walk out like men. How would you prefer to go?"

David got up and said, "Mr. President, on your feet. We're walking out of here."

Ethan stood and smiled at David, not knowing if he was about to be shot or allowed to go free. In any case, he could smile at a friend for doing what a man of dignity would do.

"Fine, then; let's go," Luciano ordered.

Two men followed behind Luciano. The two with guns silently waved for Ethan and David to move. As they emerged from the cellar, an open front door invited them to the van outside, which was still running, exhaust spewing from its tailpipe.

The crisp late-fall morning air reminded Ethan of so many recent days when he drove into work early as a senator. He wondered if it would have been better for everyone that he had remained in the Senate. As he stepped into the van, looking into Luciano's eyes and sadistic smile, he knew the right choice had been made.

The ride back into the city was slow and quiet. David thought every minute along the way would be his last. Nothing these men promised had value. They wielded immediate power of life and death over him; there could never be trust that his life would be his as long as this was so.

Then, they passed over a long bridge. Ethan and David could not see the river from their vantage point on the floor. They did, however, recognize familiar office buildings illuminated from within—now feeling their lives were more secure.

The van began making sudden turns through side streets and then dashing back into main street traffic. It came to a screeching halt.

Luciano made his way though his crew to the back of the van.

"Gentlemen, we're right where we started a few days ago. I'm positive we understand each other. I would say we should do this again sometime, but I imagine you would decline the offer. Ethan, do remember to keep your word. You ask nothing less of your government," Luciano humored. The back doors flew open. Ethan and David were shoved out, falling to the concrete below.

As the van drove off, Luciano smiled and saluted them in earnest. The doors closed and the van took an abrupt right turn to disappear into an alleyway. Ethan and David crawled to the sidewalk and sat up, staring upward into the shadowed city morning.

There were no words worth uttering to express what they had experienced. The world's cruel and cold savagery had never been clearer to either one—iniquity swallowing life's light.

No amount of joy could ever remove this weekend from their minds.

CHAPTER

XX

WE KINGS, THE LOWLIEST OF SERVANTS

Anne found herself out in the city with Hubert on a warmer than usual New York City December day. Breaking through the typical metropolitan disquiet, Hubert caught the sound of an axe blade dragging across the concrete sidewalk, accompanied by a low growl. Hubert had, by now, made a habit of not acknowledging the other place in his mind.

Anne interrupted his distraction, "What was that?"

Not knowing what Anne had experienced, Hubert replied, "Must be a crane working a nearby building."

"So why are we slinking along like two clandestine lovers?" Anne mischievously prodded. "Not an invitation by the way."

"Trust me, I've no wish to be a chalk outline. We're out and about because I wanted to get some air after being cooped up in an airplane. I also trust no one. It makes more sense to walk outside where I can see my enemy coming."

"Paranoia or caution?"

"A little of both is healthy these days."

"If you say so…You wanted to talk. What do you need?" Anne sweetly intoned, as if asking her husband what he wanted for dessert.

"You dropped the ball with Ethan Scott."

"Is that what this is about? You want to whine about not getting your way. Is that fault at my feet?"

"Hold up. I'm just stating a fact. I wanted to offer you some additional work."

"Hubert, before saying anything more, there's something you need to know."

"Did you find religion and are forsaking debauchery for the way?"

"Hardly—nice touch—no, things are changing in Washington."

"You don't say." Hubert sarcastically retorted.

"I'm starting a lobbyist concern based in Washington."

"What—like a union?"

"Something like that. Congress is filled with new faces. Old K Street alliances are dead. A consolidation of those who will be guiding the club is necessary. DC's brimming with all the usual PAC faces attempting to regain lost territory. Someone needs to be the go-between. It just makes financial sense. Clients like George Weatherby simply don't come along often enough. I can't afford to wait, and so will be taking charge of the Bone Yard."

"On whose authority?" Hubert demanded.

"Why, on my own, Hubert. Do I need any other? I'm no different than you. I'm deciding what I want and taking it."

"Don't like the sound of that."

"Stop worrying your little head. I'm sure a discount can be arranged."

"Speaking of George, have you met the replacement?"

"His nephew, Sean—yes, I recently visited with him. Sean's got a chip on his shoulder—believing he can do it himself. I thought, for a moment, to help the sapling see the light. But as is typical of the young, they want to have it their way or not at all. Better to let him learn by losing some of his hard-earned recently inherited billions. He'll eventually call on me."

"You sound so certain."

"Why, of course. Hubert, I have you to thank. So long as you're around, I'll always have work."

"Alright…enough of the useless needling. When do you plan to start your little enterprise?"

"Oh, it's already open for business. I have a little work to do this week in Washington. The emergency congressional meetings to organize and ready our newly elected brown-nosers to assume their posts in January finish tomorrow. Then there's Christmas next week, of course. Nothing worthwhile is accomplished until after New Year's Day. What a waste of time!"

"If the gossip's true, you'll be spending the holiday alone," Hubert slid in; getting one last jab after calling a truce.

Anne smiled. "Well informed, aren't you? No, my dearest darling will be among friends, family, or whomever; but not with me."

"I also understand you left him with quite a shiner," Hubert deviously added.

"I hear you did the same. I read about Ethan and David Samuel's recent abduction. He actually claimed someone from Homeland Security did it. I assume no one from the American government would have anything to do with kidnapping a citizen," Anne stated with a vicious smile.

"I saw that article too—don't know anything about it. The man he cited doesn't work for Homeland Security."

"Those are the best people to have around."

"Such a sudden agreeable mood."

"Been this way all day—so you've never heard of the man? If ever I needed to make use of such a talented individual, then you wouldn't know where to find him, would you?"

"Can't say I do. However, if I were looking, a good place to start might be Rome."

Anne looked pleased; understanding his meaning. "You don't say. I never knew Uncle Sam's squad was so devious. I'm feeling more patriotic all the time. Thank you, Hubert. I'll keep that in mind. Now, tell me, how can I be of assistance?"

"I'll think on it and get back with you after the first of the year."

"Whatever suits you—I'm available when needed."

"Now that shop-talk is out of the way, are you interested catching up with old friends?"

"As a rule I leave them in the past where they belong. What's on your mind?"

"I need to drop by to discuss a little business with Ethan. I thought you might enjoy coming along for the sake of amusement."

"Pass. We've seen the last of each other. I'll admit that he was a loss. I haven't had many men with his grit. But all things come to an end. You go on ahead; enjoy yourself. I'm sure he'll be happy to sit down and talk. Does he know it was you?"

"What you are talking about?" Hubert stalled for a moment, then admitted, "I'm sure he suspects."

"You're a peach, Hubert. Don't let anyone say otherwise. This is where we part. I understand why you wanted to walk in this area of the city. The CMC's office is two blocks ahead. See you in the Bone Yard next year, Senator," Anne trilled as she stopped walking, stepped to the curb, and waved for a taxi.

"Goodbye, then. Will you be breaking any other men this festive season?"

"Anything's possible," Anne suggested with a wicked grin, stepping into the waiting taxi.

The cab jutted into traffic, disappearing into the colorful street collage. Hubert moved on towards his destination, dismissive of all who surrounded him.

At last, Hubert reached for the entrance door, pulled it open, and lurked into the foyer. David, perched at the front desk, recoiled at the sight. Rage filled his face as he got to his feet and closed on Hubert, a few inches too close to be appropriate. "What do you want?"

"Why, David, there's no reason to be rude. I'm here on business. I need to speak with Ethan right away."

Ignoring Hubert's request, David circled around behind the desk and pushed a button, entreating sarcastically, "Ethan, can you come up front? We have an honored guest here to see you."

"Right away," Ethan replied from the speaker of the phone.

David was struggling to continue standing, and so eased himself into the chair.

"David, I hope you're not ill? Oh, you should take care of yourself. You know it's the only body you'll ever have."

Once again ignoring Hubert's nonsense, David looked past him, awaiting Ethan's arrival.

Gated steps scraped the floor, making their way from the back hallway until Ethan came into view. Shocked to see Hubert, Ethan shuffled a few steps farther and then stopped. "Senator Riley, why don't you join me in my office? I'm a bit under the weather, as you can see."

Without any more regard for Hubert, Ethan turned and hobbled back to his office. Hubert followed. Ethan lowered himself into a chair—groaning on the way down.

"Shut the door behind you, Senator. We should observe our privacy."

"I was thinking that very thing, Ethan," Hubert agreed, closing the door.

After Hubert sat, they both stared across the desk, appraising each other in silence. Both smiled to mask mutual reproach. The friendly appearances faded into frowns, and then scowls.

"Ethan, I read about your abduction last weekend. It must have been awful. Your face is still so swollen and disfigured," Hubert consoled.

"It certainly was a telling experience. I must say the assailant and his associates were quite well trained and efficient. It resembled a military-style operation," Ethan suggested, describing the ordeal as if reading a report.

"If I remember correctly, you told the police that one assailant posed as a Homeland Security Officer?"

"Yes, he did. They fall under your jurisdiction, do they not?"

"Of course; you know my committee oversees their budget and implementation. But really, anyone could have made those claims."

"Yet only your personnel have complete access to security and holding rooms at JFK International Airport."

"Rest assured, we are doing everything to ensure this kind of thing doesn't happen again. We simply experienced a glitch in protocol. None of our security cameras recorded the man you described being at the airport the day you claimed to be detained at JFK International."

"Of course not," Ethan patronized.

Hubert suddenly blurted out, "You promised to ditch the second printing! I gave you Congress! Now keep your end of the bargain! You're killing your country!"

Ethan ignored the explosive behavior. Black and blue bruising from Luciano's tender mercies translated his ambivalence for Hubert's words. He clarified without emotion, "You didn't give me the Congress. It was never yours to hand over. It belongs to me and every private citizen. I might just be killing this economy; you may be right. But don't you think it was going die on its own anyway? Really, Hubert, look at it. This is a crooked man's paradise. Only the extremely wealthy and the poor exist now. The middle class is extinct. It was the plan all along. Only you, and the other architects of this financial deconstruction, have forgotten that without the lower classes, none of this can exist—the middle class, you know, the ones you continue to strip every last bit of wealth from to force them to acknowledge your right to rule; or even the currency value you stuff down our throats. You'll have a breath of time more after the last of us has been squeezed dry of our life's blood."

"Is that so?" Hubert's voice was chilled.

"Yes, Hubert, that's so. What's more, it takes being beaten and tortured to make people realize that they never really needed you to begin with. You're obsolete, Hubert. You just haven't come to terms with it yet."

"Fine speech, Ethan, but I'm not buying and—"

"We're done here, Hubert. You must understand I'm quite tired from captivity. You understand, don't you?"

Hubert rose up and slammed his palms onto the desk, barking into Ethan's face, "Stop printing and return the money!"

Ethan reached across the desk and grabbed Hubert by the jacket lapels, pulled him close and taunted in a vile tone, "Return the money. Now, why would I do that?" And then he shoved Hubert backward, causing him to fall into his chair.

Ethan tottered around to the front of the desk and stood before Hubert as if he were about to attack; instead he sat on the desk, shook his head, and started laughing. "Oh my goodness, Senator… return the money? You want the CMC to return the money?" Ethan then slapped a knee and continued, "We can't. People, for the most part, don't want it back. We've tried, and have only exchanged eight percent."

Ethan then let out a hearty laugh that withered, and then quieted. "We had no idea how hungry the American people were for different leadership. As far as I can tell, there's still rule of law. Hope's alive that America can be turned around. But it can't be done by the likes of you. Return the money? For the love of…This makes me jubilant in a way that causes my side to hurt. Really…Hubert."

The room grew silent as both stared away. Ethan then broke the troubled stillness. "Hubert, I'm going to share a little secret. Are you ready? It's gonna blow your hair back. It does mine…still. Okay, here it is. The CMC had no idea this would happen."

"You didn't know what would happen?" Hubert repeated—confused but intrigued.

"This…all this; this outcome was completely unexpected. We had no intention to cause the market exchanges to shed now going on forty percent of their value. David only wanted to force the government to work on behalf of its people. That's it. When the Congress dragged its feet, the CMC made good on its threat. Here we are."

"But we can still do something about turning this economy around if you will just stop printing more money. Convince people to discontinue using the Worth, and get them to exchange it for the United States dollar," Hubert pleaded, as if he truly cared about what was happening to his people.

Ethan stood and returned behind the desk to sit down—groaning as he settled. "No. This second printing run is nearly finished. It's a day away from being trimmed, packed and shipped. This run will remain in safekeeping at our reserves throughout the country; to hold this fledgling Congress in check. America can never again allow a willingness of wishful thinking to obstruct our view of human nature: the proclivity to gravitate towards that which most quickly and efficiently corrupts. In so far as the exchange is concerned, I can't give you that. The American people don't trust you anymore, Senator. And this time, there will be no earning it back. Congress should never have had the trust of the American people anyway. Congress will never again bask in the warmth of blind faith. That period in American life has passed away; and good riddance. My best offer is to speak with people about exchanging the Worth for the US dollar at the current exchange rate of sixty percent of the Worth to the dollar rate as of the closing markets today," Ethan offered.

"Sixty percent! You issued the Worth at an even one-to-one

exchange," Hubert fumed.

"Hubert, that's correct. At the time of issuance, it was worth that exchange rate. Since then, the value of the United States dollar has precipitously plummeted against all other world's currencies, including the Worth. We have issued bonds for our Worth. Its value is based on the market; free of manipulation. Take it or leave it, Hubert. It's the best I can do anyway."

"It's going to be difficult moving forward, Ethan, without some measure of trust between us."

"Trust…trust?" Ethan angrily exclaimed. After a moment, he calmed himself and asked, "Have you seen the Worth yet?"

"Yes."

"What do you think?"

"About the note, or the fact that you and yours are taking our country down for good?"

"The inscription at the top center," Ethan pointed out—tossing a fifty denomination across his desk to rest before Hubert.

Hubert picked it up and read aloud, "'Value is truth.' Catchy." He threw it back at Ethan. "Keep it."

"That's alright—I got plenty. You keep it. Never know when a thing of value may come in handy."

Hubert snatched it back, smiled at Ethan's last comment, and offered, "You're right. I may be in a public restroom that's out of toilet paper."

"I don't know, Hubert. You may just want to hold on to it and use what's in your wallet. There's at least a forty percent chance I'm right," Ethan cautioned with a dead serious facial expression.

"What about the printing? You told me you wouldn't produce any more."

"I did say that. However, there was no way to know that people would put so much faith in the CMC while disregarding the dollar. At this point, Hubert, I think you and the few who survived the Great Reformation are going to have to accept that the Worth may be here to stay. As I said, the second printing is only going forward to serve as a check to balance the Congress's power. We won't negotiate that away. However, at this time the CMC has no intention of printing any more—don't need to."

"Ethan, this won't do. It's not what we discussed," Hubert charged, expecting nothing could be done about the damage leveled. He simply wanted to end the conversation having some leverage over Ethan.

"You're right, Hubert. This is not what we discussed. Tell me something, was last weekend part of what we discussed?"

"This is Big Tawk Show in the heart of New York City. We've been talking this morning about the growing American suicides related to our Flash Recession. With us today are two beacons on the front lines to provide words of hope on this Christmas Eve. We have former Senator Ethan Scott and David Samuel, both of the Citizens' Mandamus Council. Good morning, gentlemen," the DJ, Thomas Radcliff, opened.

David said, "Thank you, Thomas. I wasn't told we would be speaking about hope this morning. Ethan and I'll have to wing it."

Ethan interjected, "I think what David meant to say is that we know many across the country are worried about their lives and wondering if they'll continue to have one in America. The constitutional promise our country makes with its citizens to life, liberty, and the pursuit of happiness has been under attack from an enemy within our own borders; an aggressor controlling America's armed forces and economic markets. It is our government that has become America's greatest foe. We've turned the tide; forcing Congress to hold honest elections. It surprised no one that, lacking time and resources to bombard the public with propaganda, people actually voted into office citizens who simply want to make a difference. It's been a rocky start the last few weeks, to say the least. But we now have reason for hope; that our country's resources will be used for purposes intended by its electorate."

"That's something worth having hope for," Thomas commented.

"Tell us then, David, what did you come here to talk to our listeners about?"

David replied, "There seems to be confusion about the Worth. We will exchange the currency you are holding at the current market exchange rate of fifty-eight percent of its original issue. The United States dollar is continuing to fall in perceived value based on the recession we are experiencing. As we all know, the US dollar is tethered to the cost of oil. With benchmark crude projected to reach one hundred sixty-five dollars a barrel this next calendar year, the value of the dollar and its inverse relationship to oil will only continue to drive down the Worth to dollar exchange rate. My message to the American people is that if you wish to exchange your Worth currency for the dollar, then now is the time."

Ethan added, "We've halted any further Worth issuance. If the new Congress sells their votes to corporate giants, the Worth will again stand its post as vanguard to future US government corruption."

"That doesn't sound so hopeful, Ethan," Thomas whispered into the microphone.

Ethan riposted, "Thomas, I disagree. It's true; a lot of work is necessary to rebuild our economy. But that we will is a reason for joy. Hope is the promise that good things can prevail if we're steadfast and willing to work. It'll come at a price. But, hasn't that always been the case anyway? When did drawing breath on this planet not cost something? America really hasn't fallen. It's just awakened from a stupor. Our future is still so very bright."

"Well, there you have it from the CMC. A bright future awaits if we fight for it," Thomas summed up. As they all stood and stepped away from the camera and lighting, Thomas assured, "Hey guys, thanks for the spot. It's good stuff. I'll have it uploaded to all our internet channels in about an hour. Let's do this again."

A half-hour later, Ethan and David found themselves closing on the Financial District. Dry snow compacted underfoot, sounding out as they walked. Sidewalks were largely deserted compared to an average workday, when every inch of pedestrian space would be clogged with bankers, investors, and international finance professionals making their way to offices and meetings. The holiday ushered these concrete settlers off to leisure activities elsewhere. A dusting of flakes began to fall again, whisking and dancing aloft a hinted breeze.

"How are your injuries healing?" Ethan asked.

"Fine—I can sit down now without feeling sick. How about you? Your facial swelling is finally gone."

"I'm not walking with a gate anymore. The crack in my jaw aches in this cold, though. The doctor set my nose straight. It's straight, isn't it"?

"Hmm…so long as you're looking into the mirror at an angle," David joked. "You know, Ethan, I was terrified for a while. I didn't think we were going to live past that first day. I'm not like you. I wasn't a soldier."

"Don't think for a second I wasn't scared. However, once the beating began it reminded me of a platoon sergeant I knew in the army. The man didn't like me—he hated that I wasn't making the army a career. He despised that I would be attending college and went out of his way to hurt me when he could.

"There was an important moment once when he was working me over in front of the rest of the platoon. The men surrounded us and quietly watched, all the while knowing he was taking things too far but afraid to say anything. I remember being on my back laying in the dirt as he stood above me and asked if I was hurting yet. I simply replied, 'You can't hurt me.'

"I realized in that moment, no matter what he did to my body, at worst he could kill me, and only once; and that granted a peculiar peace. What he wanted was to torture me without end. If I lost my life, then he would lose the ability to inflict pain on me. That also provided peace, for I would deny my enemy his only pleasure in my passing," Ethan explained.

"You're a strange and interesting person, Ethan."

Ethan smiled as he removed a small gift-wrapped package out of his bag. He blurted out, "Merry Christmas, David!"

Touched by the sentiment, David said, "Ethan, thank you for the present. But I didn't get you anything."

"You didn't need to. I think we'll both make use of it," Ethan eluded, with a boyish grin.

As they continued into the heart of the world's wealthiest financial institutions, the sky was consumed by prominence and close proximity to surrounding structures. Coming upon one particular building, Ethan stopped and stared at its gothic architecture.

The main entrance climbed three stories, comprised of spotted gray and white granite. Gargoyles stretched out from its corners every ten stories. Above the archway was the name: International Monetory Consortium American Branch—the building itself seemed a ravenous predator with cruel, insatiable hunger.

Ethan continued gazing at the intimidating edifice. David relented, "Alright. I give up. Why are we here? If you're going to open an investment account, I think you'll need to wait until after the holidays."

Suddenly, a purposeful facial expression fell upon Ethan as he turned to David and instructed, "Come with me."

Ethan marched down the sidewalk. Just as David caught up, Ethan rounded the corner into a side street. He walked about twenty paces and then stopped to face the International Monetory Consortium building. Again, he stood, staring at the building.

"Ethan, you're losing me. Why are we standing in an alley?"

"It's time for you to open that present."

"Okay," David acquiesced, understanding that there was some hidden meaning to his gift.

David pulled the silver bow. It unraveled and fell to the ground. The bright red wrapping paper perfectly fitted to the box. David thought he would delicately unwrap the box, but then ripped it open as a child might on Christmas morning.

He made his way through the paper and pulled off the lid. A wicked smile beamed from his face as he glanced at Ethan. Ethan's face scrunched mischief.

"You don't really mean to do this, do you?"

"Of course; we met this way. It's only fitting that we commemorate the moment. We're moving into new American territory—an exciting and chilling thought. If we fail at our task, then the United States will find itself back in the same place we just left behind," Ethan cautioned.

"Yes, but—"

"But what?"

"I always did this alone. It's been a great source of pride and shame."

"Well, David, it's us now. You're not alone anymore. So what do you say we get this show on the road?"

David smiled the smile of a child breaking the rules. He reached into the box, retrieving two cans of bright crimson spray paint. After handing one to Ethan, he started rattling his own, ensuring a good mixture, and removed its cap, dropping it onto the concrete. The hard plastic top popped as it struck the silent street as if to inaugurate their act.

David stepped forward to a pristine granite wall and painted a three-foot high letter V; and then the phrase "Wide is the path" next to it. Ethan continued eyeing both ends of the alley, ensuring no one approached. It was an exhilarating moment for David. He felt young again.

"I think you missed something," Ethan offered, then sprayed a circle above the letter V; finally dotting the circle center. "That's better: A new purpose needs a new symbol."

"What's this about?" David asked.

"The dotted circle is an ancient symbol for power. To some it represents the ultimate source regarding the origins of power, or the absolute beginning of all things. Its use dates back to early Christianity, Ancient Egypt and Pythagoras in Greece. It really doesn't change the meaning you originally intended, David. This clarifies it. Wide is the path; you were right to choose that battlecry. It's the truth that the wealthy and corrupt have attempted to keep from the disenfranchised through most of human existence. We all have access to a power to achieve whatever we set our minds to doing. People don't need these charlatans proclaiming their leadership to the world, forcing it down our gullets before we have time to refuse."

David listened in silence to Ethan's words of life, words of truth—replete with gladness. David warned him, "This direction we're taking now; you know we can't go back."

"I know. But isn't that true of each day? There's never a turning back. Those who try living in the past only succeed in killing the life they possess in the present."

"Let's get out of here. Getting away with this little act of vandalism is also part of the activity," David reminded, as he started out towards the main street.

"Yes, I remember that about you during our first encounter," Ethan added as he tossed the spray cans in the box and joined David on the sidewalk. They began to make their way towards the CMC office, out of hostile territory.

Black jagged edges of what looked to be a king's crown adorned the blackened, blurry, shadowy-figured man. He shouted down to Ethan; pointing first at Ethan and then to a hilltop off in the distance where a narrow sunbeam spotlighted a single healthy green tree. A grassy plateau at the hill's crest pushed back the storm-clouded skies and burned-out valley below that separated them, where a prairie fire closed on the last of the living there. It was an eerie sight.

"Pardasa ongirta!" it roared and then stamped its armored foot to the ground. Fresh earth shot upward through the grass, knocking Ethan onto his back and forcing peat into his nostrils; shock and fear seized his mind.

"I don't understand," Ethan replied, feigning strength.

Unintelligibly shouting again, the figure pinned Ethan to the ground with his foot, a cold steel boot-tip cutting into Ethan's chest. Ethan grasped the metal-clad appendage, attempting to fight off the crushing weight and searing of his flesh. His bones compressing to the breaking point, all remaining air was forced out.

Can't breathe…help…no air… pain. The darkest night and desolate despair occupied every mindful space. And then, abruptly, flickering snowflakes tickled his retinas; rescuing his wits. What had been witnessed malingered a moment longer, ignoring the city traffic passing outside as he grappled with awareness. *What was that? It was so real. I want to die; I think. This was my fault! Oh my God, what've I done?*

Suddenly uncertain of reality, Ethan's revelation left his waking mind. Next, his present was clear, the message stealing away without a trace; save a suspicion that something monumental was lost. Ethan fought to hold onto the thought as it vanished.

New Year's Eve morning, Abigail sat across the booth—her face a rose garden's shade, having just come in from the cold. Silverware clinked against plates of half-eaten breakfast food. A symphony of inaudible conversation filled the space left by intermittent traffic noise. Snowflakes listlessly descended outside the diner window. Deep snow blanketed Manhattan from the previous night's storm—a magical landscape welling in Abigail optimistic presumption. It also rejuvenated Ethan with the notion that everything would be as it should. But it couldn't last; such moments linger only a short while, and so must be devoured of every taste, touch and smell.

Startling his deep thoughts, Abigail reached across the table to interlace fingers. The touch felt right and natural. It was the first time they had held hands in a year of many firsts and lasts.

From their coffee cups, a mystic boundary of steam rose. For him, the aroma created a dizzying feeling of unlimited potential and the promise that something magnificent would be built out of the day's happenings.

"You've been quiet since we left my apartment. What has you so entranced with the street outside?" Abigail asked.

"Lots of things…there's so much to do."

"Can't help yourself, can you? Always busy with something."

"Look who's talking, Madam President."

"Back at you, Mr. President," Abigail volleyed. "What's bothering you? Staring out the window just now, your face was first hopeful and then sad."

"The US is marching into uncharted territory. I can't help but be excited for the possibilities. But, there's so much suffering right now. It's going to get worse; and the fight's just begun. We have a handle on Washington for the moment. It's fragile and must be protected. The real threat has always been the corporations. Things are going to become more dangerous for the CMC as we take on this country's deepest-rooted problem."

"Ethan, all greed isn't bad. Can you say your success with the *Kansas City Banner* was not driven by greed? Profit isn't the enemy. At one point, it provided you the luxury of whatever life you chose."

"It's not greed I take issue with. It is the infatuation with greed I'm fighting. Money, in and of itself, isn't evil. I consider its existence to be quite honorable. Money stands alone, devoid of human intervention as value. Its unmolested treasure stands on any given day to represent an agreed upon worth by governments, markets, and people. There's no deception. It is what it is: an honest measure of exchange. If it weren't for people, money might be considered holy for its pure intent. It's one of the greatest human struggles; taking a fine thing and destroying it with our lust to have control. Like sand falling through a person's fingers, the more we seize a thing instead of letting it be what it is, the more it slips away."

"You're so dark. Enough abstraction—what is it?"

Ethan's introspective face turned stark. "Something's coming with big business. I don't know what yet; but it'll be bad. Legal entities, such as they are now, were never meant to be—cruel, insatiable, and lacking commitment to anything other than their own preservation. When an animal is cornered, everyone is hurt before the day is finished. The Citizens' Mandamus Council has already turned its focus towards dealing with this mammoth threat. They're into everything. No matter which direction we turn, their influence and money are there. I'm concerned with the coming."

"Whatever happens, I'm sure you'll handle it. What's your plan?"

Ethan raised his eyebrows, smiled and said, "What, tell you? You're the media. Know how best to keep a secret?"

"How?"

Ethan pursed his lips together.

"Fine, I don't want to tell on my boyfriend anyway." Abigail's face blushed—words having escaped before she could contain them. Still swimming in his eyes, another impulse seized her otherwise controlled mind and she leaned in to kiss him.

They were visible to the coat-clad passersby traveling along the sidewalk. Humidity frosted their picture window's periphery, framing two nuzzling souls, content and complete—one beautiful possibility among the infinite.

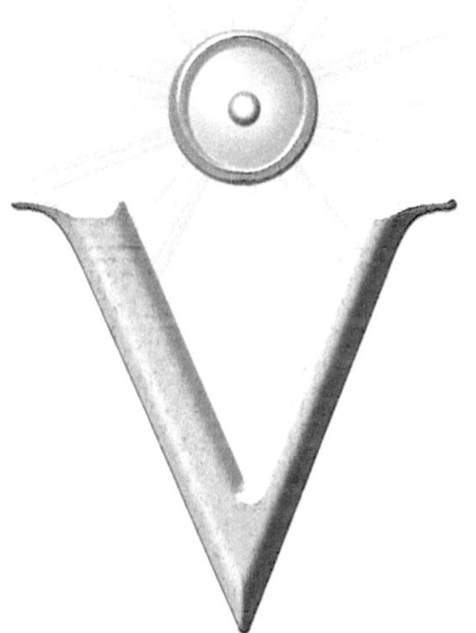